To!

Thanks for the support

June 25, 2018

 Ray the 'Rat'

A FUTURE PASTIME

A COMPLICATED BASEBALL STORY

Raymond F. Boudreau

A Future Pastime – A Complicated Baseball Story
Copyright © 2018 by Raymond F. Boudreau

This book is a work of fiction. The characters, names, businesses, incidents and events in this book are either the products of the author's imagination or used in a fictitious manner. Any resemblance to actual persons, living or dead, or actual events is purely coincidental.

No part of this publication may be reproduced, distributed, or transmitted in any form or by any means, including photocopying, recording, or other electronic or mechanical methods, without the prior written permission of the author, except in the case of brief quotations embodied in critical reviews and certain other non-commercial uses permitted by copyright law.

Tellwell Talent
www.tellwell.ca

ISBN
978-1-77370-630-6 (Hardcover)
978-1-77370-629-0 (Paperback)
978-1-77370-631-3 (eBook)

TABLE OF CONTENTS

**RULES OF ALLIANCE
MAJOR LEAGUE BASEBALL** .... **V**

"A FUTURE PASTIME" .... **XXXI**
    Prologue

CHAPTER ONE **1**
    Boys Will Be Boys

CHAPTER TWO **33**
    A Killing Loneliness

CHAPTER THREE **59**
    Learning Quickly to Lie but not Die!

CHAPTER FOUR **77**
    Being the Grunt of Them All

CHAPTER FIVE. **95**
    A Familiar Meeting with a Bad Ending

CHAPTER SIX **109**
    A Climbing Rage

CHAPTER SEVEN **137**
    Leading Up to a Serious Meeting

CHAPTER EIGHT.................................**149**
Making a Plan and a Play

CHAPTER NINE **159**
Crooked Politics

CHAPTER TEN....................................**169**
Game On!

CHAPTER ELEVEN **193**
The Long Road Back to the Top

CHAPTER TWELVE................................**209**
The Last Supper

CHAPTER THIRTEEN.............................**225**
'All Over' Accusations

CHAPTER FOURTEEN **233**
Games Leading to the Great Game

CHAPTER FIFTEEN...............................**245**
The Final Game

CHAPTER SIXTEEN...............................**303**
Game-Ending Revelation

Epilogue 325

RULES OF ALLIANCE MAJOR LEAGUE BASEBALL

GAME STATEMENT

The heart of this futuristic game of Alliance World Major League Baseball is the same as the Great American Pastime played today. That is, score runs and stop the opposition from scoring in a game. However, in this new, futuristic version of baseball, you may kill your opponent(s) on the field of play.

Just about every rule from the old game, both on and off the field, has been altered to accommodate this new version of an old game.

THE NEW GAME

A starting team shall consist of nine regular starting players that start at the regular designated positions. This is the same as the old game, except that two 'minor' infielder starters will be added to the starting lineup. These minor infielders will play ninety degrees to the right of first base and ninety degrees to the left of third base, respectively, in the foul zones. These minor infielders can only field the ball, legally, from areas behind the catcher, parallel, and along the first and third baselines one hundred and eighty feet past each base into the outfield, again in the foul area only. Never can they enter the active, fair, field of play areas. These two minor players are in their respective positions to only field the ball if it goes by their base defensive player at first, third, or home plate, or if the ball enters their playing area(s) on the first and third foul areas between home plate. The minor infielders can only go past the first or third bases by one hundred and eighty feet past these respective bases they are playing near to the outfield, and again only back to behind the catcher also. Though subject to the rules of Alliance Baseball, they shall be included only in the plays mentioned below.

Minor infielders are only there, in the foul areas, to field the ball and get it back into play to their regular starting team players because of today's larger size of field. Minor infielders are not allowed to throw the ball intentionally at offensive runners. They are only allowed to throw the ball back to their respective team players, thus the designation 'minor infielders'. If they get too close to the opposing players or to the action on the field in their foul areas of play, then they shall be considered neutral, as part of the play, just like seats, a fence, or a foul pole. If they intentionally get in the way of play or of players, or if they intentionally alter a play, then they shall be ejected from the game and the offensive (offended) team shall be awarded a run. Also, the minor infielder's position of the offending team shall remain unoccupied until the end of the inning in which the infraction took place. That means that a penalty of one inning shall be assessed to the offending team so that minor infielders will not be present when the defensive team goes out onto the field of play in the upcoming inning. The position of minor infielder will be filled once the play for the defensive team resumes in the next inning. That particular base umpire (first or third) will rule on any actions of the minor infield players on the field of play, in their respective playing areas, and the home plate umpire shall oversee their particular calls in the home plate areas. If these minor players are injured during play, then it is up to the coaches and field umpires to decide their fate of being replaced. Minor infielders getting too close to regular play on the field run the risk of being killed by the regular offensive players of the opposing team. Having these minor players field errant balls eliminates the 'pass ball' rule at first, third, and home plate, but does allow a runner extra base(s) if the ball goes by the defensive base players and is not caught by the respective minor infield players at these bases when it is thrown to them by their teammates from the infield.

The new game of Alliance Baseball has opposing players now trying to eliminate (kill or maim) each other on the field of play through innovative ways of putting out offensive runners by defensive players during the same plays on the playing field. An offensive base runner must physically be 'hit' by the ball by a defensive player to account for an out, or a 'bean', in the game. A defensive player cannot tag/touch an offensive runner with either the ball in his glove or the ball in his bare hand. This action does not count as an out. The ball must be **'thrown'** at the offensive player/runner by the defensive player fielding the ball. The field umpires call a hit or a 'bean' on the runner's body by this action of defensive players throwing the ball at runner(s) attempting to get on or going to another base. The proximity between offensive and defensive players does not matter, so long as a thrown ball 'bean' is recorded for the out by the umpires. If the ball misses the runner, then an error shall be charged to the defensive player who threw the ball and the runner shall be deemed safe if they reach base.

Outs in the game: Outs in an Alliance Baseball game now consist of defensive players trying to 'bean' offensive runners with the ball. One bean or two 'beans' (hits) by a defensive fielder on an offensive runner is considered an out in the game. There are no more rules of runners tagged, thrown out at base, forced out, or allowed to run from home plate on a third strike swing to first base, even if the catcher drops the ball. No more fly outs for outs on the field of play. These rules are redundant. One and two bean rules apply to **outs** as follows:

One bean rule: A batter comes to the plate, hits the ball, and runs for first base. The ball is fielded by any infielder or outfielder on the opposing team and is thrown at the runner going to first. If the ball hits the runner, say in the neck, thereby rendering him unconscious, dead, or crippled, and unable to continue, then the runner that goes down (beaned) on the first hit and cannot continue is considered an 'out' in the field of play actions in one inning. A raised, red, holographic light shall surround the downed runner so that no further actions can be made against the downed 'beaned' runner. Then the beaned, downed runner shall be removed physically from the playing field. This applies to multiple runners on the bases if they make it from batting to running due to hitting for extra bases, are walked, or are put in as pinch runners relieving other runners on the bases. If these runners are beaned (hit) once and cannot continue physically on the bases, they are considered an out in the inning of play. A red raised light will be holo graphically raised around the downed/injured runner(s) by the umpire, so that the beaned runner is no longer considered eligible as part of the infield play. This means that he cannot be hit anymore with the ball. But other runners on his team, on the bases, can now go by this downed player, who is now considered out, to reach the open base that he was going for. This 'one bean' rule will be applied to the runner(s) who will be deemed incapacitated (unable) to run by the on-field umpires. This runner will be called out during regular actions of play during a regular baseball game.

Two bean rule: If the runner is conscious after one bean, that is, floundering, writhing, moving in positively towards a base in any way, or can continue physically after being hit once (he is not considered out), then the two 'bean' rule will apply in that any infielder or outfielder from the opposing defensive team can now pick up the ball again and bean the runner a second time with any amount of force they wish. After a second hit, they are now officially 'out'. A raised, red, holographic light will surround the offensive player deemed out on the second bean and no more actions will be taken against him, even if he is still able to move on his own power. This 'two hit' rule also applies to multiple runners that are trying to make it to a base or as pinch runners relieving other runners on the bases. A batter/runner cannot be hit more than two times on one play in an inning with a hard baseball. A runner/batter can be hit again on subsequent plays in the same inning. If that runner is not taken out on the one bean rule, then that runner who has survived the beans (hits) on his body may continue to play until he has either reached home plate or his team has three single/double beans (outs) against it in the same inning against the at bat team.

Strike out and walks: A batter can also strike out at bat. That is counted as an out in the game, and a raised, red, holographic light will surround that batter who has struck out. This holographic light will follow the struck-out batter to his team's dugout. Also, if the batter can attain a 'walk' on a four-ball count, then a yellow raised holographic light shall signify this and the batter will proceed safely without being interfered with by defensive players until he reaches first base, at which point the yellow light is turned off. He now becomes part of regular play. Also, any players base that are forced to walk from the issued walk of the batter shall have a yellow holographic light over them so that they can safely proceed to the next base they are granted due to the walk at home plate. Intentional walks are no longer allowed in the game of baseball. Team pitchers must try to intentionally strike out batters. The pitcher cannot intentionally throw the ball at a batter at any time in the game, due to the 'bean' rules. Penalties will be explained later for this infraction as well as the 'yellow light' rule.

The game will consist of nine innings with three 'outs' per inning per team. Four outs special will be allowed in any inning when the bases are loaded. This includes the batter, if the defensive team can bean (hit) all four players incapacitating them before they reach the base(s) they are going for. There are no more shortened seven game innings due to weather conditions that warrant the game to stop, because all playing stadiums are domed and thereby protected from the weather. Nine innings are completed for the amusement of the fans. Two exceptions to the rule are made here for special circumstances: Games can be 'officially' determined complete after seven innings if a 'sand tornado' strikes with great force to structurally damage the stadium, or the 'sand lizards' from the global deserts interfere with regular game playing conditions.

Safe after one bean: If a runner/batter reaches the base he is going for, even after he has been hit by one bean, then he is considered safe on the base he has acquired. If the ball is being thrown a second time at the runner who reaches his intended base safely, then the ball will instantly turn marshmallow soft, so as not to cause injury to the safe runner. The playing color of the field will remain green. The electronic field umpire will monitor the positions of runners on the bases and will make the ball go soft in situations where the runner will be made safe by electronic sensors on the bases that the offensive runners touch. If a runner can outrun the play and reach the base(s) he's going for without being beaned (once or twice) by the ball thrown at him, again the ball will go soft so as not to cause injury if he makes it to a base safely just before the ball hits him. Overrunning a first base is not allowed. If a runner overruns a base, he is fair game to the 'out/bean' rules stated above, even at any base. First base can normally be overrun, but at the runner's peril. The beans are discounted between plays. That is if a runner is hit once on one play in an inning and he makes it safely to another base, then that runner will have the beans on him discounted and the one hit, two hit rules will re-apply only on the next time play is started when the runners are ready to advance to other bases before them on the field of play.

Field of play: The size of an Alliance Baseball Field will be three times the size of the 'old' playing fields. That is, the ball park fence will be over eleven hundred feet from home plate. Bases will be two hundred and seventy feet apart and the bases will be twice the size as 'old bases'. Home plate will be kept the same size as the 'old field' home plate.

The pitcher's mound will be two hundred feet from home plate and will be raised three feet above the elevation of the playing field.

The playing field will consist of holistic-colored turf that will change colors to designate game play situations. On field, the levitated home plate umpire will change the turf colors as field play progresses. The four colors of white, green, yellow, and red will be primarily used. These colors will indicate the status of offensive runners, batters, and defensive players on the field of play, what play(s) can proceed during an active inning, and when play can start or stop. White turf will indicate that the game is about to start or that the game is over.

COLORED TURF AND THE RULES OF PLAY OF ALLIANCE BASEBALL WITH 'ON FIELD PLAY COLOR RULES'

Green rules of play: Green turf means go! Play can start and the pitcher can start pitching. Also, when a ball is pitched and hit, the batter and/or runners on the bases can advance and the field will remain green in color for play to go on. If only the batter is hitting and there are no base runners, then the batter, when he hits the ball, must run to acquire first base and touch it without getting beaned in order to be called safe. The turf will remain green while the one hit or two hit rules (beans) are applied to the runner. The runner, if he can, may take out the first baseman with his razor gloves or shoes to stop the first baseman, if he is in possession of the ball, from beaning the runner once or twice with the played ball. This action may only take place in the designated running corridors of the runner. An offensive runner cannot go out of his base running lane to take a defensive player out. The same holds true for a runner trying to take out the second baseman, the third baseman, or the shortstop. If the defensive players in possession of the ball are in the runner's running baseline, on green turf, then the runner has the right to take that defensive infielder out with the razor insets in his gloves and running cleats. If the ball is hit to the outfield, then it is up to the outfielders to send the ball in as quickly as possible to the infielders, to either make a play to bean the advancing runner(s), or to stop the play in progress. This will cause the field to turn from green to red if all offensive players are on the bases and they wish not to continue running to other bases. If there are multiple runners on the bases, then the field remains green until all plays are done where no offensive runner(s) are advancing and they are staying on their respective bases. Then the turf shall be changed from green to red to temporarily stop play. If he wishes, when acquiring the ball either by catching it or fielding it, the outfielder can try to bean the runner(s) from the outfield when the runner(s) are advancing on the bases. If the outfielder is successful at beaning the runner, then the one or two bean rules will also apply. If the ball is hit to the infield and fielded, then the infielder who acquires the ball shall have the right to throw the ball at any of the runner(s) trying to get to first base or to any other base. The infielder may try to bean the runner(s) before they make first base or any other base on the infield. If a defensive player is successful at beaning a base runner once and slowing him down enough so that the offensive base runner has trouble getting to first base, or any other base, then any other infielder, outfielder, or the same infielder can and shall pick up the ball and put the second bean on the advancing runner trying to get to first base for the out or at any other base. If the runner does not reach first base and is beaned once but can continue, then a second bean must be performed by the defensive team to make that runner 'out' before he touches first base safely. This applies to runners running the other bases as well. All the while the playing turf will remain green. When all possible plays are made on the field of play, play will be stopped by the field umpires who will turn the playing turf from green to red to signify play has stopped. The ball in play will go marshmallow soft and be returned to the pitcher. Only the home plate umpire will electronically reset the ball to its hard state.

Red rules of play: Red turf means stop! No matter what plays have taken place, when all possible plays are made on the field and runners are not advancing, the surface running turf is changed from green to red by the field umpires or home plate umpire. This signifies that no further play actions by players may be made against each other, advancement on the bases by runners has ceased, and all play is to stop. No beaning or aggressive play may be carried out. This red color shall also only be used in an inning in an emergency situation such as a field umpire getting hurt, a fight on the playing field between opposing teams, damaging weather conditions, or an imminent sand lizard attack.

Players must hold their positions until 'play ball' is called by the home plate umpire to resume play. All injured/incapacitated players shall be removed from the playing field during red turf designation by clayon medics, and replacement runners and defensive players shall be installed where applicable. The ball that is in play will also go marshmallow soft on red turf so that players cannot arbitrarily hurt each other with the ball should a fight break out on the playing field during a red turf situation. The ball will be returned to the pitcher as stated above and made hard before play is resumed.

When the home plate umpire calls out 'play ball', the field turf will be turned green by him, the ball will be returned to its hard state, and play shall resume by the pitcher pitching to the next batter.

An infraction of the red rules could mean a game ejection. An ejection from a league game shall be investigated by league officials and penalties will be applied according to the seriousness of the infraction.

Two infractions of red stop rules in one game by any player on either team will mean an ejection from the game. An automatic two-game suspension will be applied to the offending player, and the coach and the team will be fined credits accordingly.

Infractions when a red turf is on: No runner shall advance on the bases. No defensive player shall throw the ball at an offensive runner when the red turf is on. No offensive player shall attempt to injure a defensive player on red turf or when illuminated by a red holographic light. No player on any team shall incite or start a fight on the field of play or from their dugouts, no matter the turf color. Fighting on any turf color is an automatic red infraction and an ejection from the game. Scoring from third base on red turf is not allowed. If the runner is advancing on red turf, then he must return back to the base he was advancing from.

Raised red circles around a player on green turf: A raised, red, holographic circle indicates that an offensive, downed, injured player is considered 'out' on the field of play, even if the rest of the playing turf is green and play is continuing. This means that the ball cannot be thrown at the injured offensive player who is indicated 'out' on the field of play by an umpire. This usually occurs when a runner has been beaned once and cannot continue due to unconsciousness, incapacitation, or death. This rule also helps to protect players that are unconscious or incapacitated so that they may have a chance to recover and revive and possibly play in the ongoing game or future game(s). This is called 'the mercy rule'. If a defensive player is taken out by an offensive player and cannot continue to play due to incapacitation, unconsciousness, or death, then a raised, red, holographic light shall protect from further injury by an offensive player. **The field turf will remain green, even when a defensive player is incapacitated, and play will continue.**

Home runs and green/red striped turf: When a batter clearly hits a home run over the stadium walls, the umpire(s) will signify a home run and the playing turf will be turned from green to green and red stripes. A raised, yellow, holographic light will illuminate the runner(s) to signify that the runner(s) can safely advance, because of the home run hit, on the bases to home plate without fear of injury.

Yellow rules: Raised yellow lights are a protection rule that allows a player(s) to proceed safely on the field, usually between the bases. When a batter is walked and there are other runners on the bases, the runners and the batter/runners will have raised, yellow, holographic lights surrounding them to indicate that they are to proceed to the next base safely without having the ball thrown at them by defensive players. Once all players reach their bases safely, then the yellow holographic safety light(s) will go off and regular play will resume. Runners and the batter will be given a raised, yellow, holographic light to proceed on the bases to home plate when a home run has clearly been hit and designated by the field umpires. The turf will remain striped green and red during the yellow light rule and also during a home run.

White rules: White turf simply means that a game is about to start, the game is over, or a team has won the game. Also, a defaulted game, even by a winning team, will cause the playing turf to be changed to white and the game results shall be posted on the jumbo tron for fans to see.

Change of direction on the field of play: This is called the 'sacrifice play'. When a runner is on third base and a batter at home plate hits (or bunts) the ball anywhere onto the playing field, then the runner from third going home can be protected by the batter running for first base (who has hit the ball) by changing his direction of running from first back to home. The turf will remain green during the sacrifice play. The batter will take at least three steps towards first base after he hits the ball, and then he may change his direction of running so that he can put himself in front of the runner coming from third to home plate to protect (shield) him from the ball. The batter may take one or two hits by the ball to allow the runner from third to score a run at home plate without getting hit or incapacitated by the ball. The batter may not interfere with defensive players physically on this particular play; he may only put his body in the way of the ball. However, the runner coming in from third may injure or kill a defensive player. He, the runner from third, can take out any defensive player on his way to home plate if they are in his running lane and in possession of the ball. The runner coming in from third base must score at home plate before the one bean (incapacitating the batter returning) or two bean rule is applied, or else the run will not count. If the batter is only hit once but can physically function, he can continue to run to shield the runner from third base so that the runner from third can score at home plate safely. The batter, if he is able to continue, may try to get to first base before the second 'bean' is applied to him making him 'out'. In his bid to get to first base after the 'sacrifice play' has been performed, the batter may take out offensive players who are trying to stop him from getting to first base if they are in his running lane or behind him fielding the ball. It is a very rare occasion where a batter can get the run in from third by shielding the runner from third. In this case he may get to first base safely by getting himself out of the sacrifice play without being killed. Other runners on the bases may advance as the sacrifice play is being carried out. This is the only time a player can change his direction of running on the field of play. Nowhere else on the bases is this change of direction allowed during regulation play. A runner caught between bases in a run-down may change his direction of running to try and get safely back to a base while avoiding beans by defensive players, but no other runner on the bases may change his direction to come to his assistance. The one or two bean rule applies on the sacrifice play to the batter that changes his direction of running. That is if the batter changes his direction, gets 'beaned' once, and the runner from third scores, then the batter can continue, if he is not considered an 'out' on that particular play to go for first base. Then the second or 'two bean' rule shall be carried out by the defensive team if they can bean the runner before he reaches first base safely. If the sacrifice play is the third out of the inning, then the advancing runner from third base must touch home plate before the sacrificing batter is called out. That is, if the batter that changes direction during the sacrifice play cannot get up or move in any way to try and get to first base, he is called 'out'. The run advancing from third base will not count if the scoring runner doesn't touch home plate before the out is called. Also, if the sacrificed runner is not the third out, then the runner from third base trying to score is open to being beaned (one or two times). The sacrifice play will be monitored by the third base and home plate umpires. The sacrifice play may be challenged by team coaches.

Defensive players on the playing field: These players shall wear a team uniform and all the mandatory technological equipment. They shall also wear a single digital tracking device over the eye of their choosing, to monitor where the ball is on the field during play. One eye shall remain open and not be covered by any device. The digital eye devices will also gauge ball speed for defensive players fielding or receiving the hit ball. A defensive player may only bean an offensive runner once or twice on a single play in an inning. If a defensive player hits an offensive player more than twice with a hard ball that the field umpire hasn't changed to a soft state on one play or while a protective red, raised, holographic light is on a downed or designated out runner, then he, the offending defensive player, shall be ejected from the game. A defensive player shall not make any plays against an offensive runner that has a red or yellow raised holographic light around that offensive player(s) or when the field of play, the turf, is all red in color. Defensive players may not intentionally impede a runner's progress physically with their bodies. A defensive player may not intentionally knock a runner's helmet off with any part of his body. He may only use the ball to carry out this action. Also, enhanced running and throwing robotic gear will be worn by defensive players to allow them to cover larger distances in the infield/outfield, field the ball, and throw farther and faster with more accuracy on the larger playing field. The robotic running gear will give the defensive players fifty percent more running speed than their natural top running speed on the field of play. A fielding glove worn by defensive players on the field of play will be illuminated (glow) when the ball is fielded into it to indicate to the umpires and fans where the ball is during active play. The only way a defensive player can impede the progress of a runner is with the ball. A defensive player, if injured, may only come out of the game if he is physically unable to continue. This will be judged by the on-field umpires, on his coach's say so, and if the coach wants to replace him; otherwise, he has to continue to stay and play with the injury(ies) sustained.

A downed defensive player with the ball in his possession who has a raised red holographic light around him shall be considered 'out of play' and can only be touched by another defensive player on his team to retrieve the ball from that designated downed player. The defensive player who has/retrieves the ball from his downed teammate will continue play on the field so long as the turf is still green. Offensive runners may not touch the downed defensive player that has the protective red holographic light around them while they are running the bases. If a downed deemed incapacitated defensive player in possession of the ball makes an action towards an offensive player, even with a red holographic light surrounding him, the offending player and team will be assessed a run against them. This illegal action opens up unsafe and unwarranted injurious conditions to offensive runners not giving their attention to the downed defensive player.

Catchers: The catcher shall be the most physically protected player on the field of play due to his position and vulnerability at home plate from incoming offensive runners. The catcher will wear a catcher's glove that will become illuminated when the ball has been caught so that umpires and fans will know the position of the ball during play on the field at all times. The catcher shall wear a single digital tracking eye wear device over the eye he chooses to allow him to gauge the speed of the incoming ball from the pitcher or from any fielder on his team. This device will allow him to gauge the running speeds of offensive runners on the bases, and it will also be helpful when he wants to throw the ball at an offensive runner trying to steal bases, for 'bean(s)', or for a runner coming in to score at home plate. The catcher shall wear enhanced robotic throwing gear that will give him eighty percent more speed in his throws at base runners, to his teammates, and back to the pitcher. The catcher will also wear robotic running gear comparable that of his field playing teammates. The catcher's protective armor shall cover the whole front of his body. The back/behind section of the catcher's body, from the ears, neck, and back, shall not have protection armor on it anywhere. The catcher's mask is subject to the same rules as the helmet of the offensive runner. If the mask comes off during any play in an inning on the field of play while the turf is green, the mask shall stay off and the catcher's face, neck, and entire head area will become a target for offensive runners during plays. An exception here is that if a catcher can get his mask back on before play ends on green turf, then he will be protected again by his mask from offensive runners' actions against him. An offensive runner can intentionally knock off a catcher's mask only with his body, arms, or legs trying to score at home plate and not with the ball. This action is allowed so that runners wishing to score after an offensive runner has made contact with the defensive catcher can have the advantage of taking out the catcher not wearing his mask on subsequent plays occurring before play on the field is stopped. Offensive players are strictly prohibited from touching the baseball in play. Only a runner trying to score from third base may knock the mask off of the catcher if the catcher is in possession of the ball. No other offensive player may knock the catcher's mask off. The catcher is the only player on the field of play that may impede a runner's running lane path by blocking home plate, but only if he is in possession of the ball. A catcher has to hit a runner once or twice (bean) with the ball for an 'out' if he has possession and control of the ball. A dropped or missed ball on strike three by a catcher is only a dead ball in the game of Alliance Baseball, and so the batter is called 'out' on strikes. Batters do not have the option of trying to run for first base on a dropped or passed ball on a third strike call; instead, they are automatically out.

Pitchers: Pitchers shall be fitted with the same robotic gear as defensive players except that pitchers will be fitted with special robotic throwing-arm gear that will allow them to throw the ball ninety percent faster than the pitcher can naturally throw. This will get the ball to home plate over the longer distance from the pitcher's mound to home plate more accurately and with much more speed than 'old game' pitching. This speed will also assist in beans while runners are leading off bases or are off the bases in the infield during play. For example, if a pitcher can throw a ball ninety-one miles-per-hour naturally, then the robotic throwing gear he's wearing will give that pitcher's throw approximately another eighty-six miles-per-hour boost to his pitch going to home plate to one hundred and seventy-seven miles-per-hour or at this speed to his defensive team players.

A pitcher may not intentionally throw a ball at a batter at the plate because of the 'bean' rules now incorporated into the game. If it is proven by video replay judges and field umpires that the pitcher has intentionally hit a batter, he, the pitcher shall serve a one-month jail term from the day of his conviction as a suspension from Alliance Baseball with no pay from his team. If a batter intentionally puts himself in front of or into a ball, then the pitcher shall be cleared of wrongdoings and the batter shall have a 'one bean', one-strike rule applied to him during his at bat. If this action occurs twice during the same at bat, then the batter shall be called 'out' according to the 'two bean rule'. If a batter puts himself in front of a ball intentionally, gets hit, and cannot continue to play, then that batter shall be deemed out.

A pitcher may throw the ball at an offensive runner leading off of any base to try and bean them for a one hit out or incapacitate them and invoke the two bean rule if one bean stops the runner from returning to his base he was leading off of. That is, the pitcher may hit the incapacitated runner for a second time, thereby stopping him from tagging up the respective base he was leading off from. If the base runner can return to his respective base before the ball hits him, then the ball will go instantly soft

A FUTURE PASTIME – A COMPLICATED BASEBALL STORY

so as not to cause injury to the 'safe' base runner. If a pitcher misses a leading base runner with the ball, then the base runner has the option to stay safely at the base he's on or run to the base he intends to go for. If the runner goes for the steal, then the minor infielder can retrieve the pass ball by the pitcher and put it into play to a regular player to still try and get the base runner stealing the bases.

A pitcher may not alter the ball or add any substance to it to enhance the movement or surface of the ball. A monitoring device shall be put into the ball to monitor the pitcher's actions in this regard. Thus, chemical solutions or illegal abrasions cannot be applied to the baseball to alter its surface. The ball must be pitched within the prescribed pitching lane going to home plate. If the ball goes outside the three-foot pitching lane area before it crosses home plate, as monitored by the electronic field umpire, then the home plate umpire automatically calls the pitched ball a 'ball'. The home plate umpire will be notified immediately after the wild pitch is thrown that the pitch has gone outside of the respective throwing lane by the electronic field umpire. This rule stops pitchers from throwing real far out curves or high up manipulated balls dropping down towards the hapless batters. In this way, pitchers are made better controllers of their pitching and speeds on the ball.

The Ball in Alliance Baseball: The ball will be slightly larger than the 'old style' hard ball. It will consist of the regular leather, cork, and rubber materials of the old balls, but twelve half-inch spikes shall be incorporated into the ball that shall come out when the ball is thrown at a base runner, not when it is hit by the bat. The electronic field umpire will be in control of this action. If the ball hits or misses a runner after being thrown, then the spikes shall retract automatically and will only come out again when the ball is retrieved and thrown again at a base runner. The spikes will remain retracted during pitching and hitting so as not to detract from the throwing, fielding, or hitting actions of players on the field of play. Only defensive players can throw a ball at offensive runners. Offensive runners will not touch the ball intentionally or throw it at defensive players. If offensive runners touch the ball intentionally, then the field umpire shall automatically call out the offending runners. If the ball accidentally hits a runner after it has been batted, then he shall not be called out if it is seen that the runner has made an effort to avoid the ball. The old rule of a player being called out when the ball hits him is redundant.

OFFENSIVE PLAYERS ON THE FIELD OF PLAY

Batter(s) and runner(s): Batters and runners shall wear a team uniform, the required running gear, and all relevant required body armor. Batters and runners shall wear a form-fitting helmet without a restraining strap to start batting and while running. If the helmet accidentally comes off of the runner's head during a running play, then the helmet will stay off for the rest of the inning being played. While that runner is actively on the bases, his head shall become a vulnerable target for a bean(s). If the helmet accidentally comes off while batting, then the batter shall be allowed to put it on again and resume his at bat. The batter shall wear digital eye wear on the eye of his choosing to gauge the speed and position of the ball being pitched at him. A batter can use a straight single piece bat or a jointed, articulated bat. The jointed bat shall consist of between three and five joints and it (the bat) will be allowed to wrap itself around a batter's body while he is at bat at home plate. The jointed bat's joints shall be controlled by the pressure of the batter's hands that will straighten out the joints on the bat for the bat to connect with the ball in a regular hitting fashion. The catcher will not interfere with the bat with his glove. The batter shall not make any overly excessive showmanship (extra movements) with a jointed bat for the purpose of distracting the home plate umpire, the pitcher, or the catcher of the defensive team. That means he shall not wiggle the jointed bat around nor shall he show off with the jointed bat in a showman-type style. If called for, this action of distraction by the batter will be assessed as a strike; if it is a third strike, then the batter will be called out by the home plate umpire.

The batter/runner shall wear limited armor while at bat and running the bases. This armor shall consist of four inches of hardened carbon nano-tube materials above and below the elbow and knees, including the body joints mentioned. A four-inch long and two-inch wide armor plate shall be worn between his shoulder blades over the spine in that area, and he shall wear a helmet on his head. All armor shall be worn on the outside of the uniform and be visible at all times to the field umpires to prevent any cheating in this regard. With the exception of the feet which will be protected by armored shoes made of the same materials, no other body areas of a runner shall be protected with armor. All body areas of the runner are open to being hit with the ball.

The running cleats and batting gloves of a batter/runner shall be armored with built in retractable four-inch razor blades to allow for offensive runners to make offensive plays against defensive players on the field as well as to the catcher, pitcher, outfielders, or minor fielders who may become involved in on field plays. This use of blades in the cleats and gloves gives the offensive runner a chance to take out (kill or injure) defensive players who are trying to put a 'bean' on them or other runners on the bases. A base runner or batter may only intentionally attempt to injure, incapacitate, or kill a defensive player when that defensive player is in their running areas (lanes) between or on the baseline of the offensive runner and that defensive player is in possession of the ball. An offensive base runner may take out two defensive players at one time, if one of them has possession of the ball, they are both beside each other simultaneously, and they are in that runner's running lane or on the baseline of the runner. If an offensive runner goes off his running lanes to injure a defensive player, then that runner shall be called out and ejected from the game and penalties will be applied to that offensive runner for the severity of his actions on the field by league officials. It has been emphasized to all players that the game is to be played as a precision game and not a free-for-all killing-fest. Also, offensive runners cannot use their blades in their gloves or cleats to injure or take out a defensive base player or any other defensive player unless that defensive player is in possession of the baseball, is going to throw the ball at them, and is in their baseline. Now, if the said offensive runner can time his knife-like blades to injure the defensive player just as he gets possession of the ball, then it is legal for the offensive player to use his blades on the defensive player to injure or kill the defensive player. This action prevents a 'bean' on the offensive runner by the defensive player.

If the offensive runner uses his blades to injure the defensive player before the said defensive player has possession of the ball and is not in the runner's baseline, then the offending offensive player will be called out and the defensive team will be given or assessed a run because of the offensive runner's actions. If a defensive player is killed by the offending base runner in the same aforementioned rules, then the offending offensive base runner will be ejected from the game and given a one-month jail term suspension with no pay from his team. The defensive team will be given two runs for the fatal infraction of the offensive team to the defensive team for this illegal action.

Enhanced running robotic gear will be worn by batters/runners to help them run faster over the longer distances between the bases. This robotic running gear will give base runners fifty percent faster running speeds than their regular natural top running speeds. To give an example of enhanced running speeds, a runner who normally runs a top speed of eighteen miles-per-hour will get a fifty percent lift from his robotic running gear to elevate him to twenty-seven miles-per-hour on the bases. If the runner has an adrenaline rush from the threat of being killed and runs twenty miles-per-hour, then he could possibly get a boost of ten miles-per-hour more to raise his speed to thirty miles-per-hour to avoid injury.

Pinch runners who come in to replace a runner on the bases shall wear all of the above-mentioned articles including helmet, body armor, digital eye wear, armored gloves/cleats with blades, and robotic running gear. If a runner on the bases who is being replaced by a pinch runner has lost his helmet during a play, then that pinch runner will continue to play in that inning without a helmet on to the end of his playing time in that inning (or injury or death) or to the end of the inning, whichever comes first. All of the rules of Alliance Baseball will apply to these pinch runners also.

Team numbers, requirements, and defaults for an official Alliance Baseball game to be played: The number of players that must be present on a team roster before a game is nine (9) starting players, two (2) minor infielders to start the game, forty (40) spare players including other minor infielders, ten (10) designated back up relieving pitchers (who can be put anywhere in the game) in the bullpen, one (1) head coach, and four (4) other designated team sub-coaches (can be players if necessary). A total of sixty-one (61) players and five (5) coaches must be placed on a roster for a regular season or play-off game.

Defaulting a game: If a team loses all of its spare players due to play actions in a game, a minimum of seven regular players and two minor infielders must be on the field at all times to finish a regular or playoff game. If at any time after that the roster falls below the required seven regular players, then the game shall be defaulted, even if the defaulting team is winning the game. The playing turf shall be made white in color to indicate the end of the game and the default will be indicated on the stadium's jumbo trons.

Umpire calls on the field of play: Umpires will not go down onto the field of play unless summoned by the home plate umpire to do so. Home and base umpires will be levitated fifteen feet above the playing field at all times during regular play. All umpires will have a stun gun in their possession to help them stop or break up fights on the playing field. Umpire calls on the field are final and shall only be disputed by video replay as requested by coaches. Coaches get only two video requests per game. There will be three base umpires. One home plate umpire will make calls on the field of play with an electronic recording device on his digitized protective face covering. A full field electronic umpire will be used to monitor where the base runners are, and where beans and outs are recorded. The full field umpire is an electronic sensing system that helps the umpires know when plays like beans have occurred or whether runners have touched bases safely or not. The home plate umpire will call strikes, balls, and plays at home plate with the use of an electronic monitoring device covering the strike zone and home plate. He will also oversee calls on the field. The base umpires will make turf color changing calls on players, calls of 'outs' on the infield according to the 'beans' made, and calls to the outfield also. The electronic umpire will oversee the positions of the runners on and between the bases and will designate them safe or out when the field umpires have made their calls. The electronic umpire will cause the ball to go automatically soft when required during the game.

CALLS ARE AS FOLLOWS:

An offensive batter/runner who fakes an injury to try and stop play (by not continuing running the bases) due to a single 'bean' from the ball shall be designated as eligible for the second 'bean' for the out on the field of play by the umpires above the field of play. No raised red holographic light will be raised around that offensive player feigning injury, and unless the faking runner is not on a base, he is open to being hit a second time with the ball by any defensive regular player for an 'out'.

A defensive player who fakes an injury to try and stop play by showing that he cannot play will not have a raised red holographic light put around him and the turf will remain green. This call will be made by the on-field umpires. The defensive player is then eligible to be injured or killed by an offensive runner if that feigning defensive player is in the offensive running lanes or on a base wanted by an offensive runner.

A batter who wishes to try for an infield home run on a ball that has not gone over the outfield wall will have the turf kept green in color by the umpires and all advancing runners ahead of him will be open to the rules of play on green turf.

When an umpire makes a call that a defensive player is incapacitated, a raised red holographic light shall surround that downed defensive player on green turf. Offensive base runners can, without touching the defensive player in any way, run by that incapacitated defensive player to the intended bases they are running for and not cause further injury to that said injured defensive player. This can happen to multiple incapacitated defensive players on the playing field. When a defensive player who is injured but not given the red holographic light can still play, then that defensive player is open to injury from offensive runners if the injured defensive player is in the offensive running lanes.

When an offensive runner is incapacitated and designated as an out by the field umpire, a raised red holographic light will surround that downed offensive player and his offensive running teammates that are behind him may run past their incapacitated teammate(s) to the bases they intend to try and get to. This rule can apply to multiple incapacitated, deemed out, offensive runners.

One hit and two hit 'beans' will be called by the base umpires unless the 'beans' occur at home plate, in which case the home plate umpire will call these 'beans' (or outs) accordingly.

Plays at the plate will be called by the levitated home plate umpire who can get as close to the play as he deems safe for himself to make those calls. This means he can levitate himself to only inches from the plays at home plate and make his calls.

Minor Infielders: With the size of the playing field in Alliance Baseball now three times larger than the playing fields of the 'old' game, minor infielders are required in the first and third base foul areas to go after the ball if the ball goes by the first or third baseman when the ball is thrown at an offensive runner trying to get to these bases. Also, if the ball gets by the catcher on a pass ball or wild pitch, then the minor infielders may go after the ball and assist the catcher in getting the ball back to the catcher. If the ball also misses the offensive runner going to first or third bases, then the minor infielders will go after the passed ball to retrieve it and get the ball to his teammates effectively. This will put the ball back into play quickly, as play will not stop on a pass ball and will possibly stop an offensive runner from advancing to another base. If the ball hits a runner going to first or third and goes into the foul area, then the minor infielder will go after the ball to put it back into play so his teammates can apply a second bean to that runner if he, the runner, is not incapacitated or not safely on a base. Minor infielders can only go one hundred and eighty feet past first or third base to retrieve a passed ball. They may not go into the outfield. There are markings on the field for the boundaries of the minor infielders. There will be no second base minor infielder, as the regular center fielder, with his enhanced running speed and throwing abilities, will cover the area behind second base. Minor infielders are not allowed on the regular field of play, so having one (a minor infielder) there (at second base) is against the rules.

The minor infielder's areas of play shall be from behind home plate to one hundred and eighty feet past the first and third bases into the outfield areas. The minor infielders may cross into each others areas by going around and behind home plate to help each other field the ball when a ball enters the aforementioned areas. A minor fielder must never enter the regular field of play under any circumstances, or they will be ejected from the game. If a minor infielder interferes with a regular offensive runner in the regular playing area from the opposite team in any way, he (the minor infielder) will be ejected from the game. The opposing team that was interfered with will be given a run if it's at third base and an extra base to the runner interfered with if it's at first base. Then the ejected minor infielder's position shall remain vacant for the rest of the inning and will only be filled in the next upcoming inning of the offending team. If a regular player intentionally or accidentally interferes with or runs into a minor infielder, then the minor infielder shall only be considered part of the play like the same as a seat, a foul pole, or a wall in the game of play. If a minor infielder is in possession of the ball near an opposing runner in his field of play, then he (the minor infielder) is fair game to be injured or incapacitated by that opposing runner, provided the runner does not go out of his lane of running into the foul area to get the minor infielder who is trying to get the ball. A minor infielder will go after the ball behind home plate if it (the ball) gets past the catcher and get the ball back to the catcher or whoever is at home plate to get it back into regular play. Red and green turf holographic light rules apply to minor fielders as well.

Scoring in Alliance Baseball: The rule is simple for scoring runs. Get as many runs across the plate before the third out is called against your team, even on the sacrifice plays or bases loaded situations.

Coaches: Coaches have many variables they can apply in Alliance Baseball. They can alter their batting lineups from inning to inning or even during an inning. That is, they can put up to bat whomever they want, when they want, at any time during the game. They cannot put a player up twice in a row, but they can put a player up twice in an inning sooner than the rotation calls for by altering his line up. The batting order must be followed in each inning but may be changed from inning to inning or at any time. For example, a batter can go up to bat, get a base hit, and be relieved of running, but this batter can only go back up that inning if the first three in the batting order has all batted. If the batting team goes down in three consecutive outs, the coach may then put the batter that was up in the previous inning up to bat in the next following inning ahead of anyone else in the batting order. Coaches have the option of leaving injured defensive players out on the field if they agree with the home plate umpire that their injured defensive player can continue to play.

Batters who make it to base can be relieved of their running duties by coaches inserting pinch runners for the preferred batter, thereby making them safe to play in the following innings. Coaches are allowed two 'play reviews' on questionable plays per game when they want a play reviewed when they do not agree with on calls made by the field umpires. Coaches are allowed four time-outs in a regular game and two more time-outs in overtime innings to change players or to confer with umpires.

Game ending rules: When a game has ended after nine innings with three outs, then the ball will immediately go soft. When a game is tied in the final inning or is being played in overtime, then the ball will immediately go soft when the scoring run is made by the winning team so long as there are no more than two recorded outs at game's end. This is so that any runners or batters on the winning team are not subject to an illegal bean when the game has ended by the losing team.

Rule queries: For a complete explanation of the Alliance Rules of Baseball or answers to questions about Alliance Baseball, email your questions to rayboudreau@hotmailcom or write to Ray Boudreau "Themondo 13", 316 Regional Road #3, Whitefish, Ontario, Canada, P0M 3E0. I'll try to promptly answer your queries.

"A FUTURE PASTIME"
PROLOGUE

THIS IS A STORY SET WELL INTO MAN'S POSSIBLE FUTURE, SEEING how the human race is progressing today. This could be our fortune, be it anywhere on the futuristic new Earth where the advanced game of Alliance Baseball is played.

Sports and politics play a big part of our everyday lives, in present-day society, for a lot of my personal friends and for many members of the Earth's population. In this story, sports and politics exist in the lives of almost everyone on Earth; that is, when they are not prepping star ship spacecrafts or rocket freighters from local or galactic space at Earth's great space receiving/repair docks at either pole.

The Alliance Major Baseball League, a futuristic way to play present-day baseball, is intertwined with Earth Alliance politics. Each regional government struggles for dominance of the people's attention in their respective domains. Politics and baseball cross over into each others realms when the villains and good guys of each domain want certain people removed from their lives. Honest people of Earth try to control the out of control, in politics, of the Earth Alliance Council, and our story unfolds as such.

Earth has become super warm, and because of this, there is no natural ice to be found anywhere on its surface at any time. The ice at the North and South poles, Greenland, and all continental glaciers have melted. The areas between the tropics of Capricorn and Cancer and anything living there have literally turned to dust and desert because of the rise in global temperatures. Temperatures often reach one hundred and fifty degrees Fahrenheit or higher in these equatorial tropical zones. There are no clouds over the desert areas to bring much-needed shade and moisture. Tornado-like dust storms in the giant, global desert annihilate everything in their paths. If it isn't killed, it is buried or else shredded by the monstrous, whirling clouds of dust. Sand covers the Mediterranean Sea, Central America/Upper South America, the Amazon rainforests of Old South America, the upper half of the African continent, India, Southern Asia, and most of the lower continental United States. All equatorial islands including Indonesia, The Philippines, and even Hawaii have gone to dust. Sand blows far out into the oceans also, covering the ocean floor, and annihilating millions of square miles of life-giving aquatic animal habitat. The ever-blowing sand has caused continental land masses to form misshapen extensions of sand far out into the once bountiful waters of Earth. The continents of Old South America and Africa are now only four hundred miles apart because of sand deposited into the Atlantic Ocean.

With these catastrophic environmental changes, man has had to move its populations from the equatorial/tropical regions to the cooler northern and southern regions of Earth to survive. With this moving of people, cultures have had to mingle and merge. Instead of countries being reformed, radically different entities, or 'Alliances', have been formed out of the people joined together by the global circumstances presented to them.

There are now six Alliances on Earth, comprised from the over one hundred eighty-five 'old countries'. The North Am-Alliance consists of Canada, USA, Mexico, the Central American states, and Greenland; the Euro-Russo-Alliance consists of the old 'Russian' Empire, Europe, and China. The South-Am Alliance is made up of all countries from the old South American continent, including the Antarctic and islands near there. The Austro-Asian Alliance is made up of Australia and the Far East Asian states including Malaysia, Indonesia, The Philippines, and Japan. The Africany Alliance is made up of Africa and the Baltic and Western Arab states. Finally, the Pak-Indo-Stan Alliance is made up of India and its satellite countries.

With the mergers of the old countries, ideas, people, cultures, and economies were forcibly united into newer, stronger cultures. Man, in each region, pooled their resources and became a much better society based upon significant co-operation. The human race has now reached the stars, importing all manners of goods, minerals, and biological life. New inventions abound in medicine and space transportation that have the Alliance politicians vying for strategic ruling power of what is supposed to be a democratic world.

With the expansion of the Earth's desert areas, a huge 'sand lizard' species was brought from another world into our to control and stop the desert edges from expanding further into fertile livable areas. The super fertile dung from these huge reptiles causes dry sand on the edges of the desert to become large, twisted, matted trees that grow to over seventeen hundred feet tall. These trees have helped to contain the hot, windblown, sands of the global desert. The three-mile-wide ring of forest encircles the entire globe near the northern and southern tropics.

Man has had to deploy a military force of millions of clayonic robots to guard the outer forest edges. Large and high electrified stainless-steel chain fences have been erected to keep the sand lizards in check so they can only wander in the desert and not into man's urbanized new world. Yet sometimes the desert sandstorms overwhelm the forest's edge. At these times the sand lizards travel over the sand covering the protecting forests to wreak havoc in populated areas. No Alliance area is safe from the sand lizards or the sand-like tornadoes, for all Alliances touch the desert's edges. Great resources from other planets have been brought in to help eradicate the global deserts, but to no avail.

Futuristic baseball has become the major sport and central pastime of this new world of Alliances. All other sports have taken a back seat to the new baseball, a technology digitized blood sport for all of the combined races to hate or enjoy, whichever way you want to look at it. As in any pastime, man has had to try and keep the interests of the people focused on this sport. Future baseball has become a savage game to replace the ravages of war. Ninety percent of the 'old rules' of baseball have become redundant. New rules have been established. Now people die for the game of baseball, much to the delight of the bloodthirsty fans around the new world who flock to games in droves by the hundreds of thousands. They come to watch this game of Alliance baseball being played by the youth who wager their lives to play it, just like in real war. They play for the riches — if they survive. No wars are fought on Earth any longer, as this futuristic baseball replaces the act of war with the gore of the game. Thus, people of all Alliances may watch their country's team succumb to the horrors of brutal baseball, yet without the detrimental effects of real war.

This story centers on four young boys born with an articulated bat, a spiked ball, and a glowing glove in their hands. These boys have been raised to play the game. The boys' parents, who have lovingly nurtured them since babyhood, have wanted their sons to become baseball stars from a young and tender age. Their parents are motivated by the knowledge that if their boys become monetarily well-off, then as proud parents they can ride out the rest of their lives on the coattails of their son's abilities and earnings from Alliance Baseball. While their sons do eventually play in the Alliance Major Baseball Leagues, the boys are split up due to the 'Alliance Draft'. They could ultimately play against each other in the 'World Alliance Baseball League', as professionals in this fictional tale. When in the minor baseball leagues, the boys were protected by the 'soft rules' of Alliance Baseball where players do not die, nor do they inflict crippling injuries upon each other. The rationale for these 'soft rules' is that they must have opportunity to reach their full skill/athletic maturity and advance to the major leagues on these trained abilities. In the professional leagues, however, they must play according to the 'hard rules'. They must try to hurt or kill each other according to the rules set out in the Major Alliance Leagues.

This story centers on their friendships, their will to succeed in the game, and their efforts to try and not kill each other. Their shared goal, even though they play for opposing teams, is to try and get each other to retirement. You see, if an Alliance League Baseball player can last five years in the brutal major leagues, then he can retire from the game with a full pension. This pension is thousands of times greater than the regular salary of their parents. When they retire, they will never have to play again, or worry about dying, until old age. Of course, their goal of reaching retirement unscathed is the same goal of every player.

An early fatal twist of fate transforms the lives of these four young players in the 'off season', when their fun get-together turns deadly. A misguided joke and sudden environmental changes shift the structure of their friendships. Legally, one cannot intentionally kill another in an open society. In the game of Alliance Baseball, though, one is given the right to supersede the law and kill for all to see on the baseball field of play. Even though they are all near retirement at this point, that doesn't matter. They just want to kill each other for vengeance.

The climax occurs when the season's final game of the 'World Series of Alliance Baseball' is played with these lifelong friends pitted against each other in a deadly dance.

Diamainium Nova: A Futuristic Pastime has all the hallmarks of a sci-fi story that will keep you entertained whether you are a sports fan, a person who values friendships, politically savvy, or a sci-fi aficionado.

Author Ray Boudreau, a professional miner/supervisor for most of his working life, has always liked writing various kinds of stories. Ray lives in Canada in the province of Ontario. His home is nestled just outside of the Greater City of Sudbury, in a small rural town called Whitefish. Sci-fi reading, his favorite mode of causal enjoyment, has now enabled him to find a niche for himself by writing his own sci-fi stories. The 'Diamainium Nova' series, an invention of Ray's imaginative skills, is presented as a trilogy — and beyond — of interconnected stories in which the central characters live on, finding or causing new adventures.

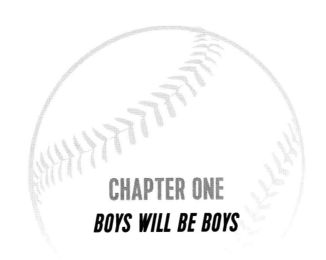

CHAPTER ONE
BOYS WILL BE BOYS

THEY HAD GROWN UP TOGETHER, EACH WITH A SHINY chain-alloyed, metal-articulated bat made especially for hitting an Alliance baseball complete with compressed hydraulic spikes. These four, ambitious young boys wore glowing, mag-holographic, 'Authentic Alliance' synthetic leather gloves, along with various advanced, metal-enhanced, technological devices strapped to their bodies for increased locomotion to play the futuristic game of Alliance Baseball.

The second oldest boy, Dean Luthbert, was a half-black half-North-Am Native Indian from the North-Am Alliance. Boisey Wallers, the youngest, was a black Africany boy adopted into Dean's family from the Africany Alliance region of Earth. His family kept his last name his (Wallers not Luthbert) so if he ever wanted to make the decision to go into his previous family's history he could do so on his own reckoning. Ray Aloyisius Tenner, the third oldest, nicknamed 'The Rat' for his 'moniker' initials, was from the North-Am Alliance region. The oldest, Lenny Peecheh (sounds like peesh-shay) was also from North-Am Alliance. They were the best of friends in their younger years. Ray and Lenny met the Luthbert boys when they moved next door to them. With their parents' enthusiastic support, these four boys had a passion for the futuristic game of

'Alliance Baseball'. The boys wanted the world to see that 'poor boys' could endure, for their family's sake, and to prove that anyone from any background could get to the top of baseball's elite if they kept their passions alive, no matter what.

Technology of the day had made their game much more advanced and more technically exciting than the original game of baseball. This new game had brought the freedoms of hitting, running, and throwing to a much higher-level plane of play. Hitting and throwing were at the center of the game with great running as the backdrop to instill excitement in the fans.

Living enhancements had made lives a lot easier. For example, the social 3-D synthetic plan printing, initiated by the Regional Governments, allowed anyone to cheaply reproduce almost anything they wanted with the right type of chemically supplied products. Virtually anything could be reproduced: buildings, planes, paintings, any toy a kid ever wanted, a luxury vehicle a regular adult could never have afforded in the 'old days', or clothes that even the best designer could never match. It would take all day to tell you what was legally available, so use your imagination. Only food wasn't printable.

Printability had become a new 'build word' years ago, and everyone on Earth used it to their own savings advantage. This allowed 'Print Distributors' the rights to everything and anything, much to the Earth Alliance Government's delight, as they owned the rights to anything sold by the Print Distributors. That is, they owned the rights to anything that could be reproduced by the general population. The Regional Alliance Government made it very cheap for regional people to set up shop wherever they wanted, as long as it wasn't in trailer parks or slum situations. All Print Distributors had to do was connect to printed sewer systems and arrange for garbage pick-up in the printable neighborhoods that would spring up wherever there was space for a family to put down roots and get a job at a spaceport or repair facility

— obviously not in the global desert areas. Printing technology had made life easy for the first time in Earth's history.

Between playing Junior Alliance Baseball in their neighborhoods (street Alliance Baseball) and in their local school leagues, Alliance Baseball was the central passion of each boy (and of every Regional Alliance family). Their parents supported this passion by putting any and all of their credit resources into their sons' playing of Alliance Baseball. With any luck, they could extract a solid gold retirement payout if their sons managed to play five years in the Professional Alliance Major Baseball Leagues of Earth without getting killed. They, the sponsoring parents, would greatly benefit from the great out-paying of credits from their retiring sons' five-year play pension. In fact, they would get the same payout as if they would've worked one hundred and fifty years in service to the Earth's Alliance Government's social program that each individual had to commit to if they wanted a job anywhere with the new "Anyone on Earth Gets a Job Program".

That meant that parents of Junior Alliance Baseball players would put whatever they possessed in credits they had earned by working for the Earth Alliance Government into their sons' playing of Alliance Baseball. In times of old any parent could get their son into Major League Baseball by helping their sons get record playing contracts for tens of millions of dollars based on how their son had played in the minor leagues. Only that didn't happen any longer in the wake of today's futuristic game of baseball and Earth's catastrophic environmental troubles. Earth Alliance Regional Governments had seen to that. The great credit payouts by previous ancient leagues had been eradicated by Alliance Regional Governments invoking a no large payout credits law to restrict the flow of credits to individuals playing Earth Alliance Baseball. According to the Earth Alliance Government, "The great up-and-coming players are not to be paid ludicrous salaries when all of Earth and its people suffer from the environmental maladies." Thus, large salaries would not be paid to the players of Alliance Baseball. They had to earn their keep by their play out on the baseball field. Prospective Earth Alliance Baseball players were taken care of. The cost of supporting all of their needs was paid for by the Alliance League Group Plan; however, there was no great payout of credits deemed for great or regular baseball players to allure them to winning teams. These valuable credits were used to protect the Earth's environmental problems and were not to be paid out to unconcerned professional sports players' wants. The Earth's environmental needs were paramount.

That being said, all baseball owners of Regional Earth Alliance teams supported the needs of Alliance Baseball players. Specifically, only the players' entertainment, food, travel, communications, health, and personal grooming expenses were paid for by the owners' association monetary pool. Credits could not go to the heads of the players receiving them. That meant that if a player was good, he would not necessarily get the monetary recognition he wanted. But if he was a great player, he would always get recognition, no matter where he went on Earth, because his picture would be posted everywhere. Most players who made it to five years and retirement were given millions of credits — more than they could ever use in their lifetimes. They usually gave their excesses to the less fortunate after taking care of their own and their family's needs.

When the boys were very young, the Luthberts had moved into the neighborhood between the Peechehs' and the Tenners' homes in a town called Hyder, in the upper regions of North-Am in the old Alaska region of North America. This was twelve years before they began to play professional baseball. The 3D engineers were there on the empty lot, laser measuring the Luthberts' area between Ray's and Lenny's place. The Luthberts wanted to build a new 'printed' house. The 3D Print Distributor's house printer assembly rolled in on a big mag-drive float on the Luthberts' lot. The huge 3D printer was set up on top of the four corners of the Luthberts' intended house, marked with steel pegs. Then the printer was set in motion so it would print the Luthberts' house to the exact specifications they wanted with flower boxes and shrubs to boot. Once the codes were put into the huge house printer's programming unit, and the trucks, with the cubes of proper building materials, were hooked up to the house printer, then the sequencing for printing the Luthberts' home was set in motion. This consisted of four 'foundation' lasers cutting out a six-foot-deep base for the house into the solid rock base of the lot the house was to be printed on. Once the base was established, the printing units took over, and the house began to materialize from the ground up. No more hammer and nails. With the right chemicals and metals in the right place at the right altitude and proper positioning, a house could be printed in about two days. This house would soon be complete and ready to go with all the working amenities.

All the Luthberts had to do was supply printouts of the furniture they wanted at another location and then they would move into their fully functional new home. Closets, stairs, stairwells, windows, walls, and anything else that was required were put into the printer's plan card. No construction workers were needed to build this house. Only two 3D engineers were needed to set things up, and then they would leave and allow the robotic process to do its thing and make the house. If an error occurred, then the house printer would shut down. One of the 3D engineers would come, erase the error, have the printer correct the error, and then put the house printer back into building mode. It was as simple as that. Technology could print just about whatever you wanted. Put a plan to the local authorities, pay the fees, and watch your ideas come to life right before your eyes. Things like children's playgrounds were custom-made to the local populace's liking. Swimming pools were made in a same day; shopping malls were put up over a fortnight. Bridges were installed in a day or two, and roads were printed (not paved) to the tune of ten miles a day. These roads would last hundreds of years, even in the cold Arctic regions, paved right from scratch over soft tundra. All that was needed was a planning card. The printers, of whatever design was called for, were set up, and voila! It was made.

Once the house had been printed, the Luthberts came and inspected it. It was to their liking, and so they signed off on their contract to accept the house from the 3D engineers. They all beamed excitedly at getting to move into a brand-new house. Next, it was time for them to move their furniture and personal belongings into their newly minted home.

The Luthberts wanted to fit into the neighborhood and meet their neighbors as soon as possible. That would happen sooner rather than later, for it was the boys who met first. Ray was over visiting Lenny at his house early around ten am. Pacific local time. The summers of the northern sub-arctic regions were quite pleasant, which allowed the boys the summer freedoms they deserved. To the south was a different story, for the Eco-systems and weather had collapsed drastically. Heat and blowing sandstorms were the only things allowed to exist in the South.

Lenny had let his dog out in the yard. Two Wheel was happy to jump back and forth, lunging at the ball, as Ray and Lenny played catch. Lenny's dog had got his name because he had two powered wheels for back legs from an unfortunate accident. Billie-By-Law, Hyder's local by-law enforcement officer, had run over Lenny's dog's back legs on purpose (at least Lenny thought so). Two Wheel had to have his back legs amputated and the vet said that 'Poochie', that was his dog's name at the time, wouldn't survive the rehab and surgeries that were needed to keep him alive. Lenny loved his dog. He used all of his credits working at the North Arctic Launch Tower with his dad to save his beloved pet. Lenny had designed a printing card that would make a two-wheeled prosthesis that could attach to Two Wheel's spinal stump. Nerve endings were reconnected and a battery was installed to power Two Wheel's back wheels so that Two Wheel could exact power to his back legs, or wheels, to allow him locomotion. To Lenny's joy, Two Wheel recovered. He was able to once again play enthusiastically with his grateful master Lenny. Dog and boy loved motoring and running at the same time. Thus, Lenny re-named his dog Two Wheel to forget the unfortunate past of Poochie.

While Ray and Lenny played catch, they watched the Luthberts, their new neighbors, move into the formerly empty lot between their homes. The boys were especially intrigued by the two young gents helping their parents move items on grav-floats into their new home. Ray and Lenny could see that some of the objects being moved were sports-related paraphernalia including gloves, cleats, articulated baseball bats, and hardware to run the bases. Ray and Lenny watched intently, hoping that these new boys were baseball players like themselves and that some future adventures were in the offing for them.

As Ray and Lenny watched the Luthbert boys help their parents, Dean and Boisey surreptitiously watched Ray and Lenny throw the ball back and forth. They felt whimsical, as Ray and Lenny looked like they were having fun. Dean and Boisey dutifully helped their parents, as brothers do, while watching Lenny and Ray enact their obsession. Dean and Boisey were missing all the fun.

"What's he snickering at?" Lenny asked Ray, looking over at their neighbors' place. "Ain't he ever seen anybody throw a ball before?" asked Lenny. Lenny saw Dean peering comically and pointing at them through his living room window across the yard from Ray's place.

"I think they're a bit envious of us, Len. They have to work, and we don't, so they are jealous," surmised Ray, while continuing to toss the baseball back and forth. Two Wheel, running after the ball, barked in agreement.

"Yeah, maybe we should start laughing while we watch them, and see how they like it," said Lenny in a selfish way. He immediately started laughing as soon as Dean and Boisey came out of their house to help with another anti-grav float.

Now it was Dean's and Boisey's turn to wonder why they were being laughed at by their neighbors-to-be. Dean and Boisey had laughed because they were happy to have neighbors that coincidentally shared their same interests, and the two Luthbert boys had laughed because they had neighbors who, like them, were sportsmen.

Dean looked at his inexperienced brother and said, "Don't worry, Boisey; we'll be the talk of the town soon enough once we get Mom and Dad to show us around." With that being said, Dean felt he was the best up-and-coming player in the Major Alliance Baseball Minor League of the North-Am Region.

Soon, all of the moving of essentials into the Luthberts' home had been completed, and Dean and Boisey were no longer needed. Dean and Boisey returned to watching their neighbors. With no one to snicker at, Ray and Lenny had set up the virtual batting cage on Lenny's artificial lawn. They practiced hitting virtual balls holistically thrown at them by the virtual thrower, each seeing who could hit the virtual ball the farthest. Dean and Boisey watched from their living room window, and then turned to their parents. They asked if they could get a virtual batting cage like their neighbors. Dean's father quickly put them back to work sorting out things for their mother by saying, "Idle hands mean idle minds; you boys get back to work and never mind our neighbors. You'll get to meet them soon enough once we're settled in. As for the virtual batting cage, you boys will have to earn it by your positive actions towards your neighbors and towards us, your parents. Agreed?" said Darth Luthbert. Dean and Boisey each nodded in positive affirmation to their father.

By around three pm. the Luthberts had completed their work for the day. The brothers ventured out of their new house and went out to see the new world around them. While Dean rested momentarily on their new porch, six-year-old Boisey Wallers went to inspect the back yard of his new home. He particularly admired the lush view of his new play area. He was not used to such colorful surroundings, because he was from the Africany Region of Earth. Before he was brought to North-Am by his parents through an adoption agency, from what he could remember, Old Africa had been filled with quite drab beige and brown colors.

Ray, who was seven, and Lenny, who was eight, watched intently as Boisey wandered around his yard. After a few minutes, Boisey approached the electronic force field fence surrounding their respective yards. He stood and looked at Ray, Lenny, and Two Wheel through the lightly glowing, translucent blue electronic force field fence separating their yards. Boisey had an official glowing synthetic leather baseball glove on one hand and an official Alliance brand-new Big-League baseball in his other hand. His father had caught this baseball from a foul ball at an Alliance Baseball game at the Hyder Alliance baseball dome in their town. At that exact moment, Ray and Lenny knew they wanted that shiny new baseball in Boisey's hand. They didn't have one of their own, a brand new one that is, and so they eyed it jealously through the fence. They coveted that ball in Boisey's hand.

Ray and Lenny just stared back at Boisey as he watched them, but being the extroverted type, Boisey wasn't one to be stared down. He said, "You gots a funny looking dog. My name is Boisey Wallers and my brother Dean is the best third baseman in the whole Hyder League. He can throw a ball better than anyone else I know." As Boisey bragged, he maintained a defensive stance by the force field fence, openly squeezing his Alliance baseball.

Lenny, being older, would not be intimidated by a young pup like Boisey, and he said, "Oh he can, can he?" Lenny sneered at Boisey.

"He sure can! Bet he could throw this ball over this fence and you can't," said the young fledgling Boisey defiantly. Smirking, he waved his authentic Big-League baseball at Lenny and Ray.

"Well, I bet you can't throw it over the fence like your big brother could," said Lenny to Boisey, egging him on.

"I can so! I'm almost as good as my brother Dean at throwing; just watch me," said Boisey. And with that said, young Boisey took a few steps back from the electronic fence, drew his arm back, and gave the ball he was holding a mighty heave. The ball sailed easily over the electronic fence between the yards and then landed right in front of the not surprised but chuckling Ray Tenner and Lenny Peecheh.

"Nice shot, Bozo," said Lenny. The slightly rolling ball slid into his awaiting mitt, and he grinned a wolfishly wide smile. "Hey Ray, look what I've got: a nice original Alliance baseball, compliments of our next door neighbor, Bozo."

Boisey suddenly realized what he had done and began a tirade of words at his next-door neighbor antagonists. "My name is not Bozo! It's Boisey! And gimme my ball back!" Boisey howled. "Give it back to me right now, it's not yours!" His voice grew louder as he went on and oceanic tears began to well out of Boisey's eyes as he realized his mistake of throwing his coveted ball over the electronic fence to Lenny.

"I'd say you gave me the ball, Bozo, by throwing over the fence," taunted Lenny, wanting to get more of a rise out of Boisey's out-of-control feelings.

"Maybe you'd better give it back, Lenny," said Ray. "He's getting real upset, and if my dad finds out what we've done, my hide will get tanned. That will mean I can't play baseball with you in the upcoming game," said Ray to Lenny.

But Lenny, being the daredevil type, said, "Naw, I'm gonna keep it 'cause it's mine now! Bozo gave it to me, didn't you Bozo?" This made Boisey howl and cry with more intensity. Lenny seemed to enjoy taunting the ever-sobbing Boisey while turning over the authentic baseball in his right hand.

At that moment, Boisey's brother, Dean, came off the porch to see what the ruckus was about. "What's going on, Boisey? What's wrong, bro? Why are you crying?" asked Dean, putting his arm around Boisey's shoulder. Dean was looking straight at Ray and Lenny. Lenny was still holding the Alliance baseball, flipping it out of his hand repeatedly for all to see.

"He's got my ball and he won't give it back!" stated Boisey, snivelling. The tears poured from his eyes and his nose ran as he tried to get his point across to his older brother. "I said you were the best throwing third baseman in the whole Hyder League, and he said I couldn't throw. I threw the ball and now he's got it. I want my ball back!" said Boisey in frustration, and he started to cry uncontrollably once again, leaning into Dean's chest for respite.

Dean stood up straight, squaring his shoulders before Boisey's tormentors, and he spoke as clearly as he could. "I want you to give my brother back his ball. He made a mistake by throwing it to you, but it's still is his ball, not yours. It belongs to him!" said Dean politely but firmly.

"Yeah, well, he's going to have to give me something in return if he wants it back!" said Lenny defiantly to Dean, not wanting to back down.

"Boisey doesn't have to give you anything," said Dean coldly. "But I will give you a punch in the head as soon as I have the chance if you don't give his ball back. We're neighbors now, and we'll get close to each other some time, someday. And what I said will happen sooner than later," said Dean in a meaningful tone. Dean, at seven years old, though younger than Lenny, was the same size and build.

Lenny condescendingly threw the ball back over the electronic fence and said, "Ah, what the heck, it was used anyway. I'd like a brand-new one." Lenny knew better than to challenge the future.

And that is how our four young boys met and became close friends. Their parents became close friends also, as they shared much in common. The three families all had their sons playing on the same Junior Alliance Baseball team in the Hyder town's minor leagues of North-Am.

The town of Hyder, population six hundred thousand, was located in the North-Am Alliance mountainous area of the old state of Alaska, now a province of North-Am. The province of Alaska, in North-Am, had become a lush resort-like area with warm oceans to swim in, unbelievable mountainous scenery, and some of the globe's best aquatic food. All of the glaciers had melted away many years before, and the aquatic life from the south seas had moved up to the Hyder oceanic area where they thrived prolifically. Hyder was the center of culinary cuisine, just like the now barren city of Paris (France) had once been, hundreds of years before the global deserts erased it away.

The people of Hyder worked mainly for the intergalactic military installations and repair shops of the North-Am Alliance Government. Some worked in the fisheries, and some worked in the geological enhanced explorations five hundred miles deep into the Earth's crust for super enriched metalized magma veins and for the thermal heat to run industries. Some worked in the North-Am forests that thrived in the more temperate areas along the west coast. But most people in Hyder worked for the Earth's Alliance Council at the North-Am Launch Tower where they serviced the incoming and outgoing military spacecraft, at the

North Pole. This launch tower's purpose was to protect Earth from alien attack and to service ships that went on missions to help the Alliances of Earth get the resources they wanted from other star systems.

The four boys' parents worked for the military, because it was their genealogical duty to do so. Jobs were available to the descendants who continued to live in the area. This arrangement had been established by the Earth Alliance so that there would be no unemployment in North-Am. All would have work, no matter where they lived in North-Am. The North-Am Military Tower was a six-hundred-mile-high, two-thousand-mile diameter launch behemoth anchored two hundred miles deep into the Earth's crust. Built to handle millions of ships twenty-four/seven, it had to appease the Earth Alliance Council's constant desiring of control and power, as well as the powerful military hierarchy that supported the Council.

Now Hyder had been famous for two things over the ages. First it had a two alcoholic drink policy for newcomers. This was a kind of perfunctory event practiced by the locals as a means of accepting newcomers into the community at the local establishments. It went as follows: If you wanted to be accepted by the locals and to become a local at the bar, you had to imbibe a drink of your choice from the menu of the bar you were patronizing. Your first drink you had to pay for, and the second one was free. If you could down the first one and remain standing, without puking, for an hour, then you were reimbursed the cost of your first drink. The first drink was made up of twenty ounces of whatever liquor you had chosen, over ice if you liked, and diluted with a mix. You had to down it within a half-hour, and you had to be standing and not puking before the hour was out. If you didn't puke and you were still upright, then you got the second drink free, equal to the first. This survival of the one/two-drink policy made you 'Hyderized' and accepted by local folk. You would be accepted because you'd be so docilely drunk after your second drink that you wouldn't be able to bother anyone, anywhere, any way, and you'd have a hangover so bad the next day that you'll want to leave town, not come back, and never encounter Hyder again in your travels.

The second thing that Hyder was famous for was its Minor Alliance Baseball leagues which turned out some of the best and most famous professional Alliance Baseball Major League players in the world and in the history of Alliance Major League Baseball. The roster included guys like Mike Russell 'Sliver' Lecourd, a short but very quick man on his feet. He could outmaneuver a baseball thrown at him with dynamic moves while avoiding getting beaned. It would take a computer the size of a huge rocket to figure out how he did it. Most players in the Major League agreed that Sliver was a very hard man to hit and to put out while playing the game. Little Sliver finally retired after his sixth year playing in the Alliance Major League following a nasty lower leg amputation after a play he wasn't quite fast enough on. Doctors put his lower leg back on, but he was never the same runner after that. He was also reported to be Hyder's two-drink champion, in his retirement, in his own constabulary bar called the 'Bull-Mur Tavern'.

Another famous alumnus of Hyder was Jerry 'The Ape Man' Lonchteeay, also a Hyder inductee. He was another dodge the baller with a mean streak for taking out (killing) ball throwers that beaned him if they were on his baseline and in fair play. On almost every play that he was involved in, he would run at and try to kill the ball thrower. He could absorb a bean to almost anywhere on his muscular body. With his ape-like moves, if he was close enough to the thrower before getting beaned a second time, he would brutally try to take that thrower out of the game. He absorbed a lot of punishment, taking out defensive players quite easily before ever being called out in an inning. Jerry Lonchteeay made it to four-and-a-half years in the Major Leagues of Alliance Baseball before being killed on a famously re-run triple play. All three runners on base were killed on a triple play in the same inning. Jerry lost his helmet going for third base and was hit squarely in the face with a mighty heave of the ball. He didn't see it coming. Many players were quite happy when Jerry's demise came about, for he had been hated by players in all leagues. Beloved by coaches and fans for his gruesome style of play, he had definitely been a draw for fans of the game and a great money maker for owners, for himself, and for ticket scalpers of the Alliance teams around the world when he came to town to play (or to kill, as one would say). Jerry played on three different Alliance Regional teams around the world during his tenure in the Alliance Baseball League.

These two awesome former players were prominently featured in the Alliance Baseball Hall of Fame situated in the city of Hyder.

The short version of Rules of Alliance Major Baseball were as follows: Almost all of the regular old-type baseball rules had been thrown out, made redundant, and changed to suit the now savage style of play in major Alliance Major League Baseball. The players wore technological appliances to help them hit, run, and throw better, which added to the speed and drama of the game. The only main rules not changed were the strike one, two, three for an out, and ball one to four counts for a walk. Foul balls were not counted as an out, if caught. Hits to get on base were also left in, as this was some of what the baseball crowds came to see along with the gruesome style of play. These rules remained at the heart of the game so that fans could appreciate some of the old style of play.

A batter still came to bat at home plate, but that batter now wore strategically placed, lightweight body armor along with enhanced running gear. The armor covered the knee areas, and his elbows were similarly protected. The spine area had four-inch wide protective plates, as did the lower neck, the back, and the front crotch area. Armored shoes, gloves, and robotic enhanced running gear instilled extra abilities for the batter once he was in motion to get quickly to a base after acquiring a hit. A mandatory helmet was worn when playing, although with no strap to hold it on. If the helmet fell off when batting, the player would put it back on. If the helmet came off while the player was running the bases, then the helmet would then remain off for the whole of the inning or while that runner was on base. The head was an exposed target for an out. All other areas on the body of a batter not protected by armor were subject to being injured on any play, by the ball being thrown at them, while offensive players were running the bases.

Good baseball players were not paid a salary, nor were they lured by big paychecks, unlike in baseball practices of old. You were paid by your performance on the field. The better you played, the more credits you earned. So, a great player could make great money for himself, his team, and his coaches every game by gruesome play on the field. Killing a lot of players, winning the game, and scoring runs would earn you lots of Alliance credits. You could win by killing players, scoring, and winning the game. You could lose by not killing or scoring runs, and then you would only gain a pittance of credits just for playing the game. So, incentives were there for a player to make a name for himself while earning lots of credits.

The pitcher: The pitcher was never allowed to intentionally hit or throw at a batter while a hitter was up at bat because of the beaning rules. Breaking this rule would result in a one-year jail term for the pitcher if it was deemed that he had done so on purpose. So, a pitcher would be subject to harsh penalties (if he didn't play by the rules). Pitchers were an integral part of the game as they could initiate the beaning process of the game with savage vigor! The Earned Bean Average, or EBA, was the number of players the pitcher had stopped from stealing bases during the game. Also, since the balk rule didn't apply anymore, the pitcher could fake a move to home plate in order to lure the base runner into trying to steal a base. Then, if a runner tried to steal a base, the pitcher had the right to take out the base runner by beaning him before he got to the base he was going for. If the runner was hit by the first bean from the pitcher and he didn't go down on the first bean (not incapacitated), then the rest of the players nearest the ball in the infield would share in applying the second bean rule in the case when the base runner could still function. The pitcher only had to pitch with no worries about any other rules in Alliance Baseball, because there were none.

The batters: The batters used an articulating bat that could have three to five moveable joints that kind of looked like large chain-like joints. The bat would usually wrap itself around the batter's body when being held at home plate, because the ball came in at much greater speeds than in the old game. A batter had to be steady as a rock when the speeding ball went over home plate. When a batter swung his articulated bat, these 'articulating' joints would straighten out the bat with the force of the batter's hands and swing with much more force than an 'old' metal or wooden bat used in the 'old Little Leagues' of baseball. If a batter hit the ball, then he had to endeavor to make it to first base without getting hit twice by the baseball thrown at him by defensive players on the opposing team. This is how an out was produced in the newer game of Alliance Baseball. If he was hit once and made it to first without getting hit a second time, even if he was injured, then the runner was deemed safe by the field electronic umpire. He would be deemed safe even if the ball was in the process of being thrown or was flying at the runner a second time. If a runner was beaned once by the ball and was incapacitated so that he could not continue due to a traumatic physical infliction, unconsciousness, or death, then that player who was beaned once would be called out on the one bean rule by the levitated umpires on the field of play. Also, the electronic AI field umpire would turn the ball marshmallow soft before it hit the runner a second time if he was down and called out or if he was deemed safe by getting onto a base on the field of play.

Now if a batter who hit the ball and got hit by the ball once while running to a base was injured or slowed by getting hit by the ball could continue, then that runner must continue to the base he was trying for. Only then may any opposing defensive team player pick up the ball and have the right to bean the runner a second time with any force he deemed necessary to hit the runner anywhere on that runner's body, thereby making that runner 'out'. So, the opposing defensive player(s) could inflict quite serious harm to the runner up to and including killing the batter/runner or any other base runner(s) on the field of play. A double and triple play could be made with the same rules of running and beaning for outs when a ball was hit in an inning, while players were running between bases. There were no fly outs, tag outs, or force outs in the new game; only beaning caused outs.

So, you see a team could lose up to three players per inning due to injury or death in outs to the team that was up to bat and even possibly four players if the bases were loaded due to a special rule referred to in the Alliance Rules of Baseball which declared that all players running the bases were subject to being hit with the ball. So, if the bases were loaded and the batter hit the ball, then all four players running in the infield were potential targets for beaning. Now possibly twenty-seven to thirty-six players in a game could be incapacitated or die if a game turned quite savage, and even more if the game ran into extra innings due to a tie after nine innings of play. Players running bases could also take out the infielders with knife-like gloves and knife-spiked shoes with blades that came out four inches long when a runner slid or ran into a base that a defensive player occupied or blocked. So, on a single play, base players as well as base runners could be injured simultaneously.

A runner could not change his direction of running to save another injured player or get him safely to the base he was running for. The changing of direction could only happen when a runner was coming in, say, from third base to home plate to score who could be assisted by a runner going to first base. This batter who was going to first base could change direction by going back towards home plate. But this runner who changed direction also ran the risk of being beaned out or injured until he could get to the base he was supposed to be running to (which was first base) without getting hit twice by the ball. This usually happened at home plate where the batter running for first could change his direction and take the 'bean' for the runner coming in from third base to try and get the runner in from third to score at home plate. This was literally called the 'sacrifice play'. The batter running to first base would sacrifice his body or life to get his buddy in from third base and score a run for his team.

Many other rules applied, as brought forth in this story.

Stadium fields were three times as large as the 'old league' fields. The new style stadiums were made to hold over eight hundred thousand people, well up from the paltry forty to fifty-five thousand people that the smaller ballparks of old used to hold. There were ten jumbo tron viewing screens positioned around these big stadiums for the far-away fans to actually see the game in detail. Private box seats had their own screens where fans could watch the play-by-play, in gruesome high definition 3D display delivered in full ionic color.

Due to the faster style of play, the fields were three times larger than the old fields. All players on the field wore enhanced robotic running and throwing gear with technologically advanced digitized robotic eye wear. The fielders, base players, or base runners could use this eye wear to gauge a runner's speed and distance on the bases from the outfield, even at five hundred feet away from the runner. Many a great throw and bean had been made by super throws from the outfielders. The bases were three times as far apart, or one hundred and eighty feet, and the pitcher's mound was also positioned farther from home plate and three feet higher on the playing field. Enhanced pitching robotics were given to the pitcher, for his mound was now one hundred and seventy-one feet from home plate. The best pitchers could throw a ball at speeds of over one hundred and eighty miles per hour with their enhanced robotic gear. The ball had to stay within an electronically monitored area going towards the batter at home plate. If the whole ball went outside this monitored area without touching the electronic sensing field going to home plate, then it was automatically deemed a ball even if it crossed over the plate in the strike zone after being thrown. This stopped the huge twenty-foot curve balls, extra highly lobbed pitches, or constant ground low, slow, rising sliders over two hundred feet long from ruining any hits the batters may get. This also stopped the batters from being at a disadvantage due to the higher ball speeds and overly exaggerated ball movements. The strike zone area at home plate was the same as old baseball, but the delivery zone was a bulged out circular oval extending outwards from the pitcher reaching a width of ten feet halfway to home plate and then shrinking down to the strike zone at home plate.

Umpires did not stand on the field of play, but were instead magnetically levitated fifteen feet above the field of play so that they could telescopically make calls on the field. Umpires also wore advanced technological devices for calling plays on the field of play because of the far distance from the umpires to the play on the field. They used computer-assisted drone robotics to make calls on the field when they are not sure of the plays that had taken place because of the longer distances on the playing field. Also, video replay was used for disputed calls and for the benefit of the fans who especially appreciated the gruesomeness of close up carnage. The fans loved watching players doing each other in on the field of play.

Alliance playing field distances were eleven hundred feet to center field, left field, and right field. The fields were almost four times wider, in acreage, than the 'old fields'. Great batters could hit home runs, but home runs were rare due to the preferred savagery of infield plays and faster ball speeds. Umpires were also equipped with stun guns to prevent fighting and unwanted injuries on the field of play. Stun guns were employed to stop players from breaching rules after plays had been made and actions on the field were called dead. Emotions ran high when deadly plays were enacted, but professionalism had to be maintained to keep fan integrity. No player was allowed to bean a runner a third time (this was a big no-no in Alliance Baseball), and an offensive runner was not allowed to injure a defensive baseman or fielder after calls had been made on plays and the play had been rendered stopped or dead on the field, even when either team had caused catastrophic injuries to players during the 'live action' such as killing a live player when only a simple 'beaning' would have sufficed. Also, the defensive players knife-like projections from their gloves and cleats could not be used for non-play, lethal action vendettas when the play had been called dead or a defensive player(s) using the spiked ball to kill runners after the play on the field had been ruled dead or stopped by officials.

Players were shuttled to and from the batter's box by a flat servo gravity disc platform robot that ferried them on a magnetically levitated large round plate. This gravity-assisted platform carried all the amenities for batters such as rosin, liquids, articulated bats, hand cleaners, and even candy and soft drinks. Coaches were not allowed on these anti-grav servo plates, or they would face immediate ejection from the game, for obvious reasons. The distance from the players' dugout to the batter's box was about a quarter of a mile; hence, coaches were only rarely thrown out of the game because the distance to be covered, on foot, just to argue with umpires, was quite far. The last time a coach was thrown out of a game had been over ten years prior when an incensed coach, from the Africany Alliance League, ran a quarter mile to argue the call with the home plate umpire; he kicked dust and spit on the umpire's boots to make his point. His point was to no avail. After he was ejected from the game, he had to walk back to the dugout while the crowd booed him incessantly. No coach ejections for over ten years is indeed a great baseball record!

Alliance games were a big occasion in this new Earth era of Alliance Major League Baseball. When a game was on, almost everything stopped until the game was over. This was kind of like siesta-time in the old country of Mexico. The midday heat predicated a rest, so that late afternoons and nights could continue at a bustling pace. In the same way, nothing happened in an Alliance city while it was hosting an Alliance Baseball Game until the game was over. Everything else paused so that the fans could be at leisure to watch every detail of every savage play the game had to offer. Work was suspended when a game came to town. You see, there were no more military wars on Earth, and there hadn't been any ever since the global encircling deserts had appeared that cost so many countries their land, their people, and their livelihood. The violence and hardships of war suffered by previous generations were gone and replaced by the savagery of futuristic baseball for all to see. A new game was brought about to allay aggression of any elitist groups and to put the regular population at ease while watching gruesome Alliance Baseball. As the blood and guts of the game were witnessed, the wanting for war had subsided. In short, man's savageness was now satiated by Alliance Baseball. This sports war was played out on the baseball fields between combating Alliance regions of Earth, and not between its people. So, with gruesome reality, a lot less people died in Alliance Baseball than they had in wars of old.

Most games are played north or south of the Earth's tropic lines, as these areas above the tropics had the most pleasant and tranquil, but very warm, weather for playing conditions that wouldn't affect the fans from coming to see games. The games are also played near the globe circling deserts that existed between the Tropics of Capricorn and Cancer.

You see, Earth had become super warm due to increased levels of CO_2, methane, sulfur, ethane, and other greenhouse gases caused by man's relentless past consumption of fossil fuels. Hydraulic fracking of the Earth's surface was the final straw that broke the environmental camel's back and caused the global deserts to appear. Rocket-type planes now carried baseball teams across the deserts between Alliance regions. Teams traveled north, south, east, or west over the desert zones to play their games. Sand from the deserts could blow as high as forty miles into the upper atmospheres, with tornado-like force. Such sand could be very dangerous to the old conventional jet engines that were hardly used anymore, similar to how volcanic eruptions used to cause havoc to flights. Now, the global deserts caused dust to rise high into the atmosphere all of the time.

New breakthroughs in weak gravity magnetic control had man now levitating things up to six thousand miles above the ground. The might of the Earth's core heat was used to run tremendously strong generators to control objects magnetically. Lofty ground-to-space elevators had improved on the 'old' models over the years with three-hundred-mile carbon nano-tube technology giving way to over sixteen-thousand-mile elevator cables going above the Earth's surface without the use of old school heavy lift rockets. The Earth's rotational inertia was now used to keep the space elevators taut. These elevators had been made to increase commerce of the regional areas by using a unique kinetic energy lifting positional system. This system kept dozens of elevating ribbons in place by using outward rotating weights. These weights were aligned in a track that connected to the elevating ribbons in space, so that the outward rotating weights stretched the elevating ribbons outward and away from the Earth's surface. By this method, materials, in great weights, could be elevated to the outer realms of space away from Earth's gravity for the ease of transport to space-faring vehicles with gravity assist for the first six thousand miles up. The Moon had even longer space elevators for assisting exchanges between Earth flights to the Moon or to other planetary systems of people and materials.

These advances took many years of toil by astronauts manning aggressively rocketed weighted ships headed opposite one hundred and eighty degrees to the Earth's surface. The elevating ribbons had to be kept in place while the rotating weights and their tracks could be placed to hold the elevating ribbons in a permanent Geo-synchronous position.

The human race had even gone to the stars by pooling its people's technological ingenuity and resources. The Mag-Hydro-Ion

Drive Engine could go up to eighty-five percent 'c' speeds inside an antimatter cloud. The Mag-Hydro-Ion Drive Engines were an advancement of the Alcubierre Drive proposals theorized back in the twentieth century. Ships of a galactic class could now cross half of the Milky Way Galaxy in three to four weeks using an antimatter envelope as a slipstream medium. Antimatter slip streaming was first discovered when it was found that curved space could be 'straightened' by the use of an antimatter projected field in front of and behind space-faring ships. The antimatter enveloping ships allowed them to go straight through space without magnetic wave or curved graviton space interference. Thus, travel times were dramatically reduced through normal space by as much as one hundred thousand percent. Faster than light speeds had never been officially breached in normal space. Antimatter slip streaming had allowed anyone having the use of it to circumvent the impenetrable barrier of light speed by using antimatter to get by the regular physics of past years and speed into the galactic interval without the constraint of regular physics on people and ships. This new kind of space travel has been compared to the old Russian style torpedo invented in the 1990\s of enveloping a gas atmosphere around the torpedo that would not let the water touch the physical part of the weapon and allow the torpedo to travel by rocketry as if it was flying through air through the water at phenomenal underwater speeds of thousand of miles per hour.

For interstellar travel, double magnetic lensing made use of distant objects and overall celestial body attraction densities coupled with near objects kinetics to enhance straight line linear drive travel without frictional implications. Antimatter was used as the slipstream device to obtain the velocities claimed. One had to have charted area references to be able to do this type of galactic travel. Many a ship with persons and cargo had been lost to trial and error before real travel lanes could be established so that galactic travel to other star systems could be achieved without fatalities. Magnetic lensing had been discovered by astrophysicists of long ago who found that every large stellar object has a magnetic Lagrange point: a gravitational neutral area where ships could enter and begin to slipstream through sub-space at great FTL speeds to other areas of the great Milky Way Galaxy in just a few days or weeks. A system of Magnetic Lensing Lane ways was created for ships from Earth and the Earth Alliance Association of Planets was established because of FTL speeds.

A great project had been started by the Alliance Council of Earth to regenerate the desert areas. They wanted to bring the global deserts back to a livable state and allow man to expand again on the Earth's surface, just as he had before the environmental catastrophe. Galactic ships had been sent out to bring materials and technology back to Earth to help revitalize its parched areas. But messing with the Earth's natural forces was not man's forte. Every time something new was tried to try and quell the desert areas, the sands of the super desert would blow even harder into the faces of the Alliance Government. Great wars had been caused by man's incessant wanting of resources from other races in other star systems in the Milky Way Galaxy. So, the project to revitalize Earth had slowed as a result of the interstellar wars, which ironically used up the remaining precious resources that were needed to help Earth. The Earth Alliance politicians had seen to that. Alliance Baseball was the only normal, consistently predictable thing for the people of Earth. The game would always be played hard and with gruesome effects on the players.

The parents of our four young boys in this story worked in the space industry for the Earth Alliance Military as regular techno laborers. They serviced and repaired the star ships that ventured out across the Milky Way Galaxy on their quest to gather precious money-making materials. The Luthberts, Tenners, and Peechehs had come from a long line of ancestral spaceport laborers. They, the boys' parents, wanted to try and break their cycle of servitude to the Earth Alliance Council's ever-demanding schedules of getting ships out of repair bays, refueling them, and sending them back out into space to get more resources for the Alliance Council. They felt that Alliance Baseball was their ticket out of the required eighty years of service. By putting in untold hours of overtime working for their governments to get an early pension, they would only get enough pension to live meagerly in their golden years of retirement. People on Earth now lived healthily, more than one hundred and twenty years, which made for longer servitude in the work force. The three families' parents knew their boys were gifted athletes, and they wanted out of this long working life ahead of them. Though the parents dearly loved their sons, they would gamble with their lives. The boys would play Major League Alliance Baseball so that their parents could retire on their sons' 'solid gold' baseball pension. Every penny the parents made for their pensions was a gamble spent on getting the boys to love and want to play the futuristic game of Alliance Major League Baseball. If they could get their sons to play five years in the Major Leagues without dying or getting crippled, then their sons could retire with enough credits to easily support all of their parents needs before their eighty years of servitude to the Earth Alliance Council were done. They, the boys, would receive a high paying pension for the rest of their lives, an amount which was a thousand times greater than their parents' meager space laborer's salary. This was what the parents wanted for themselves and their boys. The risk to their boys' lives was a gamble they were willing to take to get themselves out of 'Alliance' labor servitude and a meager pensioned life. Many working parents of Earth, as much as ninety-five percent of them, had this very reason for allowing or forcing their sons to play futuristic baseball in the Major Leagues. Yet because of its dangers, only a fraction of players ever made to retirement for full pension benefits from Alliance Baseball. Most injured players only got double a spaceport laborer's pension if they were injured or crippled in the game. Usually the player's injuries would use up the money from their disability pension, and so their parents would not gain anything and would have to keep on working.

Actually receiving a pension after playing five years in the Major Alliance Baseball Leagues was a rarity indeed!

Now the four boys in this story just happened to love the game of Alliance Baseball. This made their parents happy and joyful, knowing that they had just as good a shot at the golden retirement offered by baseball as other hopeful parents and players of the game.

The Minor Leagues of this savage game played a soft version of the Major League's hard rules. The ball was much softer than the ball of the Major Leagues so that up-and-coming young players wouldn't get seriously injured. Instead, they would only be bruised by the ball as they practiced their skills. Light armor as well as a helmet were worn, and but the knife-like gloves and spikes were not allowed in the Minor Leagues. Only ink-spitting gloves and cleats replaced the real knives of the professional leagues. Players could mature and advance into higher leagues of play without fear of receiving crippling or fatal injuries suffered in the majors from razor gloves and cleats. The razor gloves and cleats used in the Minor Leagues were substituted with a washable ink that spewed out six inches in distance. This ink marked a defender as crippled or dead, depending on where the ink hit on infield plays. If a Minor League player was touched with ink from the gloves or cleats of a junior player, then the amount of ink splattered on the area of the defending player determined the severity of the 'possible' injuries he/she would incur by computerized charts that officials of the game always had on hand. This determined if a defending player could still play in a game or be told to sit out because they were fictionally deemed crippled or dead by an offensive player. These same rules applied to the defensive plays on a runner or batter. Minor Leaguers were already play-killing before they entered the Major Leagues, where the real killing occurred.

For their first eleven years, the four boys played on the same minor teams. They were called the Hyder Rocket Barmen and they move up in age categories accordingly. As they aged, they won the North-Am Minor League Championship five times and the World Alliance Junior Baseball Championship once. This was a great record for any boy or parent to be proud of. Scouts from the big leagues watched these four boys closely.

Lenny was now eighteen and ready to be drafted. Ray and Dean were seventeen, and Boisey was sixteen. Each boy had a skill that made him a good candidate for Major League play. The World Alliance Baseball scouts had been watching Dean, Boisey, Ray, and Lenny since their young boyhood days as they played minor tournaments around the world. Each of the six Earth Alliance Leagues were hungry for them because of their skills. Their parents, eager to finally get them into Major League Baseball, praised their boys on.

Lenny was first to be drafted because he was the oldest. A great hitter, Lenny had played first base in the minors and set the North-Am Minor League hitting record twice in ten years as a junior player. Lenny had been MVP many times in many tournaments over the years. When he was drafted, Lenny was sent to a farm team in the Austro-Asian Minor League for a year to be hardened up for major league play. Dean and Ray spent another year in the junior leagues in North-Am to "better their play", according to the scouts. Boisey still had two years to go before being drafted. The scouts told the parents to really encourage their sons to play well, for it seemed inevitable that they would make it to the Big Leagues. First, they would go to the minor farm team leagues of the Major World Alliance League just as Lenny had.

Lenny's mother and father were elated that their son had been chosen eleventh in the first round of the draft, but when Lenny's mother realized that her hopes were finally coming true, she suddenly broke down in a fit of hysterical weeping. She felt as if she had consented to send her son off to be slaughtered at war. She knew that Lenny's chances for survival were next to nil, and all the credits in the world would not buy back her son's life if he were killed playing baseball. She fought with her husband bitterly after Lenny was drafted, kicking and screaming all the way back to their meager home, saying that she had changed her mind about letting Lenny play Major League Alliance Baseball. Lenny's life wasn't worth the golden pension she craved. It was her son she wanted. But she had willingly committed him to professional baseball. Now, there was nothing she could do about it but regret her and her husband's decision to let Lenny go. "Lenny!" his mom called out to him. "Please don't go! You can get a high paying job at the North-Am Tower, just like your dad and me; I'll see to that. That way you won't have any chance of getting hurt or killed, son!" She sobbed and pleaded as Lenny was led off from the media stage after being drafted to his new home in the Austro-Asian Minor League. Lenny cried like a little boy as he left, but he had no regrets. This was his chance to become a man in an uncertain world, and he wanted to make his parents proud of him.

The next year Dean was drafted. He excelled as a better than average fielding third baseman, and he had a great throwing arm for taking out base runners. His body size and stature had greatly increased from a skinny, four-foot six-year-old, to a sturdy six foot six, two-hundred-and-thirty-pound throwing marvel eleven years later. He had the Alliance Junior League record for the most 'beans' for outs in a single regular season game (11) and in tournament style play (12). Dean was a good player with heart for the game. He would always give everything of himself to the team he played for, and he expected nothing in return except a pat on the back for his abilities as a steady overall starting player. Dean was sent to the Euro-Russo League far from home. He would begin major league play almost immediately for his new team because of his exceptional play on the fields of the farm team minors. Dean's parents kept a stiff upper lip and showed no negative emotions, for they knew Dean's chances for survival, due to his physical stature, were better than most who initially entered the professional leagues of Alliance Baseball. But in the backs of their minds they knew they had willingly allowed him to be accepted into a meat shredder. After Dean was taken away, they prayed fervently for Dean and grimly went back home.

Dean's dad offered these words of encouragement before Dean left, "Know where you come from, Dean; your mother and I have brought you up properly and we know you will be a great baseball player someday soon. Don't let the world close in on you, and call us whenever you can." Dean hugged his parents and Boisey closely, turned, and didn't look back. As he left for his new place in the world of Alliance Major League Baseball, the tears flowed down his face. He made sure to hide his face from the cameras.

Ray was next to be drafted. Ray, a great runner on the bases, had also grown into a bigger than average player, though he was not as big as Dean. Ray had set the Alliance Junior Baseball record for the most steals, the most runs scored, and the least number of 'beaned' outs on himself for regular season and tournament play. Ray had also established himself as a utility player who could play anywhere in the infield except pitch. His prized running skills made him the number one draft-pick of the year in the Alliance Major League drafts as soon as he was eligible. In fact, Ray was the highest draft pick that had ever come out of Hyder. Ray's mom had the same emotional reaction as Lenny's mom, and Lenny's mom had to come and console her as Ray left to play across the world. Ray was drafted to the Africany League's minor team called the 'Bafana Chiefs', located high on the east coast of an island that used to be called Sri Lanka, ten thousand miles away.

"My son!" she yelled in her grief, holding on to her husband. "My son!" As Ray left the media stage for his new home, he felt pangs of guilt at his mother's sorrow. However, he was determined to become a professional player. He held a solemn face until the cameras weren't on him, and then Ray, like Lenny, wept for his parents and vowed not to disappoint them.

One year later, Boisey, the last to be drafted, was nevertheless recognized for his 'tiger-like' out fielding playing abilities. When Boisey played on the field, he was the most focused player the scouts had ever seen. Rarely did he miss a fly ball catch, and he made record outs for his team when games seemed lost. He was sent to play for the 'Michigan River Men' farm team in central North-Am. It was an emotional day for his parents, for they felt they were letting go of their baby, their second son, and now they too had an empty nest like the Tenners and the Peechehs.

Boisey, who was a bit slow socially, was the butt of many jokes played on him by his teammates and brother in the minors. In terms of his thinking, he was 'ninety-nine cents short of a buck', they would say. But when it came to playing in the outfield, Boisey was one of the best at getting the ball into the infield. He had a record of sorts in the junior leagues which had been set in the last year he played. At the World Minor League Finals, he had made the longest bean ever to hit a running player from the outfield. Boisey usually played right field. In the finals of the World Junior Alliance League World Series Boisey took out a runner who got a triple by getting the ball past him. The ball sailed towards the wall of the indoor playing field, but the runner gambled and tried for an infield home run. Boisey got to the ball very quickly and then beaned the runner by throwing the ball eleven hundred feet. The runner, who was rounding third base heading for home plate, was hit from far-right field with a head shot knocking her down. Then the third baseman, Boisey's brother Dean, beaned the shocked runner a second time for the out. This stopped her from scoring an infield home run for the win. That kind of throwing ability got Boisey the recognition he needed to get into the big leagues. Boisey was the luckiest of the four boys, for he got to stay in the North-Am Major League near home. It pleased his parents immensely that their baby could visit occasionally. Boisey was to be hardened up for many months before he could play steadily in the majors. He was usually put in as a relief player here and there, and rarely got to start a game or even bat. Eventually, Boisey would hone his skills so that every runner who played against him would definitely keep their armor pointed at him and their heads up. He had natural sight radar and a strong throwing arm to boot. But just like any other player, Boisey was just an asset, and he was traded for better hitters at the end of his first season from North-Am to the Pak-Indostan Alliance League on the other side of the world. Boisey knew his mom would make a fuss over him leaving, so he spoke to her softly and said, "Don't worry, Mom; I won't die on you in baseball." This would become the truth, as our story progresses, for Boisey would not die playing baseball.

The chances of the boys playing against each other in the Major Leagues were slim, since they were assigned to different regions, but it was possible.

Now, our story looks at how the four boys coped with being split apart as they entered into the Major Leagues on different teams, at different levels of play, around the world. They understood the possibility that they could face each other someday. They knew that they might one day have to try to injure or even kill each other in the high drama game of World Alliance Major League Baseball.

CHAPTER TWO
A KILLING LONELINESS

AT THEIR HOME IN HYDER, THE PEECHEHS WERE A SLAP HAPPY kind of family. They joked around a lot amongst themselves and with their close family friends. These jokes either led to delightful laughter for everyone watching, or to embarrassment for the individual caught in a 'punked' situation. Lenny's father, John, loved to watch the 'old' vaudeville movies of the early 20th century, and he tried to make his family laugh, with his antics, to keep his working world woes at the North Arctic Launch Tower repair factory at bay.

John would read aloud science fiction stories that would enthrall Lenny's imagination. Lenny knew that if he didn't make it as a baseball player, he wanted to become an astronaut explorer for anyone that would have him. He wanted to be like the explorers of old. He dreamed of discovering new lands (interstellar planets) for the Earth, of planting the flag for the Alliance, and of having places named after him. He wanted to go to school and take up space. But a faint familiar voice would always come into his line of audio senses and his vision would clear. His mom would tutor him in the athletic ways of his grandfather as she steered him towards baseball and their family's prospective retirement. Lenny eventually saw Alliance Baseball as his way to space exploration.

"Okay, Len, it's time for you to get your chores done, please. No more daydreaming," said his father, calmly backing up what his mom had said earlier. "Up and at 'em, young man. You know what happened the last time you ignored your chores."

Lenny sighed as he got up from his comfy atmospheric pulsing lazy sky chair. He was just a few days from his seventeenth birthday, but his dad still treated him like he was ten, always reminding him of his chores. It's not that Lenny minded doing his chores, for he knew if he did nothing on his days off he would become 'a lazy little thing', like his mom always admonished in her cute voice.

Lenny knew that things had to get done, or else the yard would start to look like a 'redneck park' and the city's by-law administration would come around and give Lenny's dad a warning for not keeping his property neat and clean, like all the other well-kept homes in his neighborhood. The grass would discolor if it got too long, and that was the giveaway.

The long grass in Lenny's yard wasn't really grass: it was a mixture of dyes made up of biodegradable plastics and organic fibers pumping through a series of fine carbon nano tube mats placed on their sandy/arid lot. The nano tubes had grass-sized holes in them that allowed the gel-like grass to be pumped through it and out the small holes, and the result was a full thick green lawn. The gel, which dried instantly when it was exposed to air, would be pumped out at a rate that simulated grass growing specs. One could make the simulated grass grow slowly or quickly, simply by adjusting the rate of the gel pump that was situated in the foundation of the house. But the gel-like grass was weather-sensitive and would discolor if it wasn't cut regularly or if it grew too slowly. This was the local government's way of getting residents to keep up the polished appearance of their printed authentic properties. Other organic-looking things like trees, flowers, hedges, vines, or anything else you wanted to 'grow' in your yard could be easily purchased and made to grow through the same pumping processes, because everything was made up of the same gel materials as the grass. Computer programmed file cards inserted the shape, color, and style of plant you wanted to have appear in your yard, and then it came out of nano tubes looking exactly like the real thing. Palm, apple, pear, exotic, pine, or hardwood trees could be made to simulate the real thing. Real plants were a rarity in cities and a luxury in urban areas, because of the global catastrophe. The Earth had dried up into deserts, and the native plants and animals had disappeared. Only the super-rich could afford 'real plants' which required expensive clean water and a gardener to tend to them, for the real plants would easily wither away if they were not pampered, watered, and pruned promptly by an Artificial Intelligent (AI) or human gardener.

All that Lenny had to do was set the automatic, magnetically-operated disc lawn mower in motion by touching the pre-programed panel for the mower. Out went the mower to cut the lawn in the per-programed patterns it was instructed to follow. Lenny thoughtfully got twelve-year-old Two Wheel involved by teaching him to punch the code into the mower with his dog nose. As the lawn mower cut the grass Two Wheel loved to bite at the mover as it glided over the lawn making it go the directions it felt the mower had to go even though the mower was pre-programed. The mower also sucked up the artificial grass, leaves, and any other matter on the lawn. After the mower finished its work, it automatically returned to its enclosure and dumped the materials it had gathered into a central bin. The yard waste would be cleaned and re-processed. The cleaned, gathered, and processed materials from the lawn would then be put into their proper containment modules. Biological materials would be meted out to clean and diversify the artificial materials, then the cleaned artificial leftovers would be sent to material combining units. These cleaned materials would then be compressed and pumped back out into the yard as a tree, a vine, hedge grass, or whatever it was programmed to be. This very Eco-friendly system wouldn't leach into the environment, and it was 99.9% efficient!

Lenny did a few other chores while the lawn mower hummed away. He checked the windows for real insect smudges, and made sure that the skylight interlocks worked so that the searing heat of the sun wouldn't upset the normal inner house environment. If the house environment was off by even two degrees, his mother would chide him for not properly allowing family harmony in a house that was too hot or too musty. *"Real trouble for a young rising Alliance Baseball star like me,"* Lenny thought to himself. He smiled as he watched his old friend Two Wheel march diligently behind the AI mower, biting it and willing it to do its duty with an occasional bark.

Once Lenny had completed his chores for the day, he called Ray Tenner over and asked if he would help him ready his baseball gear for his inevitable trip to the Major Leagues in a few days. Ray and Lenny had played Alliance Baseball together since they were very young, over ten years now. They had also done a lot of shenanigans in their neighborhood like reprogram their neighbors' lawn mowers, those neighbors with huge luxury real grass lawns, to carve out swear words or deprecating crass slogans on their lawns that would get noticed right away by the by-law enforcement. Then, the offending owner got slapped with a verbal warning to clean up the offending prank Lenny and Ray had played on them. Oh, they always got caught eventually, but then the two of them had devised other plans like spilling real rotten eggs that they had purchased with their allowance onto their neighbors' lawns. Their neighbors' lawn mowers would pick up the eggs that would inevitably turn fetid in the storage tanks, much to the smelly dismay of the owners that recycled them. The owners knew who the culprits were, even though Ray and Lenny emphatically denied it was them when asked by those in authority. "They are young gentlemen," Lenny's mother would protest to the accusing neighbors, defending the boys who knew they were guilty but wouldn't admit to it. "You wouldn't do such a thing, would you, boys?" Lenny's mom would ask the boys earnestly. Lenny and Ray played the game, emphatically denying their involvement in the local hijinks.

When Ray arrived at Lenny's house, Lenny got up from his atmospheric sky chair without saying anything and he motioned for Ray to follow him out to his father's garage with the pull of his finger. Two Wheel panted enthusiastically as he followed the two teens.

Lenny looked at Ray mischievously and said, "Ray, what can we do to upset someone today?"

"Don't you think we're a little old for that, Len? Besides, we've got to keep our reputations intact as upstanding young citizens and great baseball players of this community of Hyder. You don't want our neighborhood thinking that we're still little twerps around here, eh?" asked Ray slyly.

"Aw shucks, Ray; I'm bored. We haven't played baseball in a week. The Luthberts aren't home, so we can't antagonize Boisey or even throw a ball. Two Wheel is bored too, aren't you, boy?" said Lenny. "I gotta have some fun, sometime, before I leave. I'm getting real antsy for some good old Ray and Lenny fun!" said Lenny loudly.

"Shouldn't you be preparing yourself mentally before going to the Austro-Asian League, Len? You are facing a life-changing event, and all you want to do is play some pranks?" asked Ray.

"Yeah, I think about my future a little, but it will come soon enough and I'll deal with it then. Here, help me adjust my running gear so I can go above the gear's speed limit. I've got something planned." Two Wheel barked anxiously, for he knew Lenny was excited.

"Don't you ever give up, Len? What have you got up your sleeve now? Are you sure we won't get caught? Are you...?" Ray was asking when Lenny cut him off.

"I think I'm going to get By-Law-Billie just one more time for posterity and for Two Wheel, eh Two Wheel, old boy?" said Lenny. Two Wheel barked and did a wheelie for Lenny.

"And just how are you going to do that? You know she's onto all of your tricks. You won't even get within a mile of her and she'll be all over you like a fly on poop, Len," said Ray.

"I've got a whole new idea and approach figured out that she'll never catch onto. I need you as a decoy, Ray," said Len, smiling giddily.

"Oh no you're not. The last time you used me, By-Law-Billie haunted me for a year. No way!" said Ray, backing away from Lenny with his hands up in front of himself. "She got me extra chores that I thought I was never going to get out of, and my mom said she wasn't very proud of me for the longest time, and..."

"Aw, come on, Ray; it'll be fun," wheedled Lenny, cutting Ray off again. "All I want to do is scrape By-Law-Billie's butt on the roadway for a few hundred yards so she'll have to take time off of work. She'll never bother you again, Ray, because you'll be gone playing baseball just like me. It'll give you some vengeful respite from her and we'll both have a good laugh. What do say, Ray, old pal?" asked Lenny, imploring Ray to go along. Two Wheel yipped and pawed the ground with his front feet in agreement.

"Okay, Len, but don't scrape her ass too much. I don't want her to sue us if we get caught for butt slaughter. What's your plan?" asked Ray, now smiling like a Cheshire cat.

Now Billie-By-Law just happened to be in their neighborhood measuring the height of the grass on private properties to see if the grass was too high with her resonance grass-sensor recording gun. The homes that were in breach of the by-law by letting their grass 'grow too high' would be given a citation for a first offense, or a fine for a second offense. From out on his lawn, Ray watched her take out her resonance recorder. Then she pointed the recorder at the lawn he was standing on.

"Anything wrong with my lawn, Billie-By-Law?" Ray asked nonchalantly.

"Not this time, 'Rat'. I see you've been a good boy and aren't as sloppy as you were the last time I was here. Your dad must have been happy for that fine I gave you for letting his grass grow too long, eh?" said Billie-By-Law mockingly. Two Wheel growled at Billie-By-Law and stood in front of Ray.

Ray looked up the street. He could see Lenny setting up his home-made graviton laser. Lenny gave the thumbs up to Ray, and then began running down the street towards them. That was Ray's signal to get started. "Yeah, my dad said that he wasn't sure whether you were a real cunt or you just sat on one," Ray said, laughing.

"You can't talk to me that way, you little shithead Tenner! I'll fine your ass off if you say another disrespectful thing to me," said By-Law-Billie loudly.

Just then Lenny went running by at a high rate of speed and said to Billie-By-Law, "Ray, she's not sitting on a cunt, she's a cunt that talks. Catch me if you can, bitch! Ha ha ha!" Lenny breezed by, knocking her hat onto her nose with the wind of his passing.

"That's it! I've had enough of you two little pricks. Peecheh, you're not supposed to be using running gear in the street at that speed! That's an offense. And Tenner, I've got you recorded calling me names. You're both going to get fines right now! Peecheh, you stop right now!" Billie-By-Law yelled to no avail. Now Billie-By-Law's vehicle was an open concept servo unit. It had a round, metallic-looking seat which she sat on while her feet operated

39

two smaller, round, similar servo pads. Her vehicle was run by the graviton-induced layer of metal placed under the road. This graviton layer also put a protective magnetic shield around her so that she would not be harmed by weather, bugs, dirt, grit, or the air as she operated her servo vehicle. The technologically advanced vehicle also gave her the magnetic power to make the modern lightweight vehicle move quite quickly. By-Law-Billie pressed her feet down on the two-foot pads of her servo unit to go after the quickly disappearing Lenny Peecheh. She jumped forward on her servo vehicle, went ten feet, and suddenly her seat stopped. At the same time, her footpads kept on going, with her feet attached. This effectively pulled her butt off her seat, and before she could react, her butt was bouncing and scraping off of the hard pavement of the street. She yelped out in pain as she bounced down the lane way of Ray's street after Lenny, who was out of sight. Lenny's graviton laser had attached itself to the seat of her servo unit and stopped it dead. The two smaller pads were allowed to continue on their way, dragging the yelping By-Law-Billie down the street on her now tender ass.

Afterward, when the authorities investigated the incident they couldn't find any evidence as to why her servo vehicle had fallen apart like it had. Lenny had run back to Ray's place, took off his running gear, and removed his homemade graviton laser from the stopped seat that split Billie-By-Law's servo vehicle in half. Then he had called the medical rescue unit to come and take the screaming, butt-scraped, By-Law-Billie away. Lenny was right: By-Law-Billie didn't get out of the hospital for two-and-a-half weeks. It took that long for the genetics hospital to grow enough skin to replace what she lost to the road by Lenny's little prank. Her recording of Ray calling her names was also mysteriously erased by Lenny's graviton laser. So, Lenny and Ray pleaded innocence, claiming that they were only watching Billie-By-Law do her job of checking lawns when she started harassing them. It was the classic situation of her word against Ray and Lenny's. The incident was recorded as a malfunction of her servo. Ray and

Lenny were mere bystanders who had witnessed the dysfunction, and they were commended for their heroic actions of immediately calling the E-Med rescuers to help a government employee in distress. By-Law-Billie screamed for hours at the authorities for complimenting Ray and Lenny. Though she swore that the two teens were responsible for what had happened to her, her claim was to no avail.

Lenny Peecheh, being the oldest, was the first of his group to be taken in the World Alliance Major League Baseball players' draft. He went to the Austro-Asian Alliance Minor League halfway around the world, 'Down Under', from his home in North-Am. Lenny played on the southernmost part of the island of old Australia, called Tasmania. Now a province of the Austro-Asian Alliance, Tasmania is where the leftover populations migrated south from 'Old' Eastern Asia when the global deserts claimed their lands.

Lenny was picked third overall in round one of the draft. This made his parents very happy, since being picked high in the draft would get him into the Big Leagues sooner. High entry draft picks were given extra training and groomed to be stars in the majors. If he could survive his first year on the team, he would be considered a 'money-maker' for the owners. With Lenny getting to the majors, Lenny's parents felt that they would get to retire thirty years sooner than they had expected. Lenny wouldn't play on a farm team in the minors for long. Many players floundered in the minor farm teams, and did not move up to the majors very quickly. Lenny steeled himself to the new reality that he would soon have to try and kill men his own age, and that they would try, with just as much vigor, to get him. He knew it would be a shock for him to leave his comfortable home, Two Wheel, his team, friends, and parents, but joining a major league farm team was what he wanted, even if it wasn't what he expected. Lenny was sent to play for the North Coast Eagles farm team in the Eastern Division of the Austro-Asian Minor League's 'A' team in the minor leagues on the island of Tasmania.

It was the players' pettiness for each other that surprised Lenny the most. The silly little 'bitches' between all of his new teammates baffled him. Lenny basically 'had' to get to know the players, but their attitudes gave him doubts. Did he really want to play Alliance Major League Baseball? Over his playing career there would be times he would have to depend on them for his life, and it made his inner conscious sick that there was no camaraderie between his fellow players to make their team the best it could be in the Austro-Asian Minor 'A' Farm Team League. It was like he had left reality and entered a surreal world of people who did not recognize each other as human beings, but rather as objects to be used for each others gain — no matter the emotional or physical consequences.

There were sixteen teams, or two divisions of eight teams in the Austro-Asian Minors, Eastern and Western Divisions. If you played the game well, you could get called up to the majors to play 'the real thing' at any time. Once you had been called up to play, played, and survived to come back to the minors to tell your home team all about it, you were considered a 'god' by your teammates. Superior treatment was awarded to that player by his teammates, and even by the coaches, for it meant more credits in the coaches' pockets every time a player was sent up to the majors from their farm teams. Usually, that chosen player who went up to the 'big leagues' didn't survive. The stark reality was that all of the players on this and any other minor farm team were considered fresh meat, or fodder for the majors to practice on (to kill).

At first, Lenny tried to play just a little under his abilities, as he did not really want to move up to the majors right away. But the coaches picked up on his slack. He was immediately ostracized and warned that he'd be sent home quite quickly if he did not play up to his potential. Going home was not an option for Lenny, as that would mean a life of shame and ridicule for 'cowing out' just when he was close to getting into the 'big leagues'. Also, he would have to work for the rest of his life at a spaceport, like his father and mother, making 'peanuts' for wages on an endless line of spaceships needing repair. Being a working goon was not what Lenny wanted. Rather, his goal in this short life was to be a real professional ball player. He wanted to survive and move on with his life. Lenny was determined to get ahead and live in the real world as a free and prosperous man, and so he forged positively on.

Well, there were several 'god' players on Lenny's team who formed 'cliques' or groups. They helped each other if the right things were done to make themselves look better on the playing field in front of the coaches and scouts. This wasn't Lenny's 'cup of tea', and so he went it alone, putting his best effort into every game to get himself out and off this whiny team and up to the majors as quickly as possible. Unfortunately, Lenny's ascent to the majors was quite slow because of one lucky 'triple god' player by the name of 'Bear'.

Bear's real name was Robert Osgood Bearonson. Bear was a great base runner and a medium-skilled batter/hitter. Running bases, that was Bear's calling card to the majors. Since his batting and hitting skills were not good enough to keep him steadily in the majors, he was used mainly as a pinch runner to fill in for the more important players of the major league team he would be called up to run for. Bear was designated fresh meat. Another rule in the majors was that if a star player got on base by batting, he could be immediately exchanged for a pinch runner to run the dangerous bases for them. Once the pinch running was done by Bear, the player he had replaced would go back onto the playing field in their regular position none the worse for wear. This was Bear's job. Although Bear had been put out there as fresh meat for the opposing teams, three times now he had managed to elude being killed, crippled, or seriously injured. He had experienced a few close calls when he got single beaned twice, running, but this beaning was not serious enough to stop him from playing and running the bases like he was hired to do. The adrenaline rush from getting hit (beaned) by the ball instilled in him enough desperation to make it safely around the bases. This was what Bear lived for — that adrenaline rush and playing in the big leagues — not to mention the incredible increase in earning power when the major team he played for won. Bear even got a 'kill' taking out a second baseman in a slide that stopped a double play. His coaches were very happy to know that Bear was ready to go the extra mile playing Major League Baseball.

Little did Bear know that of the thousands of past base runners who had played in Alliance Baseball, only three had ever made it to retirement. This was not a good percentage, but Bear was determined in his mind to make it that far. He would retire from the game of Alliance Baseball a rich man. He wanted this for his parents, who, just like the long line of other parents, had paid everything they had to get their son to the Major Leagues of Alliance Baseball.

When Lenny was officially introduced to his new teammates of the North Coast Eagles, he was given the reception worthy of a road-killed skunk. You see, it was bad luck to associate with a newcomer, rookie newbie, or neo-boy as he was called, for it was taken for granted that whoever associated with a newbie would die with that newbie if they were called up to the majors together. So, until Lenny could make some new friends, he would be on his own as a designated hands-off 'newbie'.

Bear and his clique did not give Lenny any slack. Bear would bad-mouth Lenny at every turn, and Bear's followers did the same during games and at their team practices.

"Hey, Peecheh, I hear the coaches are going to send you up to the majors so they can get rid of you pronto. They say that you swing the bat like a girl, and we all believe the coach, eh guys? Ha, ha," Bear said condescendingly to Lenny with all of his chums chiming in with laughter.

"Don't worry, 'Bruno', I'll be rid of you soon enough; and when I'm in the majors, you'll be sucking up to me!" was Lenny's retort as he stared them all down. The laughter of Bear's friends slowed to a trickle and eventually stopped as they gaped at the rebellious Lenny.

Lenny's hitting and running skills proved to be his good gains. It wasn't long before Lenny was in the starting lineup for his team, the North Coast Eagles, in the minors. Bear was always put ahead of Lenny in the batting lineup, and more than eighty percent of the time Lenny would get Bear around the bases with his improved hitting or at least to a scoring position during the game. This made Lenny and Bear look good on the field together.

After a couple of weeks of this productive-type play, the coaches called Lenny and Bear in for a meeting in the team conference room.

"Well, it seems that your play has improved a lot as 'mates' in the past while," said the head coach, Milton Wheelhouse, in the old Australian accent. Milton came from a long line of 'ball' players dating back to the old Hyundai-sponsored footy rugger leagues of old Australia, where you ground it out in the 'Aussie's Rules of Football' rugger leagues smacking heads and trying not to get too involved in concussive plays. Milton Wheelhouse was over a hundred and fifty years old!

Lenny just looked at Wheelhouse and the other staff present with a forced smile as his acknowledgment. Bear had a beaming smile, knowing he would make more credits. He wanted a chance to get up to the majors again and possibly stay there this time.

Coach Wheelhouse went on, ignoring Lenny's silence. "We want you both, Mr. Peecheh and Mr. Bearonson, to go up to the majors, in two days, to play for the Central Coast Knights of the Eastern Austro-Asian Major League in the province of Queensland. The city you will be going to is called Brisbane.

The Central Coast Knights are in a divisional final against the Zealand South Alliance Giants there. My good friend Oliver O'Sullivan, affectionately known as 'Oh Oh', says his scouts have had their eye on the both of you and they like the way you have been playing as of late. O'Sullivan feels that the two of you may be of some help to his team because they have lost several of their prime star hitters and runners. They have lost their last two games because of it. O'Sullivan's team could possibly lose their series because of his personnel losses. You see, the young men on that team were leading their series because of their outstanding play, but the opposing team has now tied that series up. O'Sullivan's team doesn't want to fall behind. They want a trip to the World Alliance Series Finals. Your stats have been good for the last two weeks, and you're both on your way to the big leagues to fill in where you can. Hopefully you will help that team win their series. Good luck to you, and may the sand winds be at your back," Wheelhouse finished in a congratulatory tone with his hands above his shoulders. He looked at the two rookies from behind his large wooden desk, and then waved them out of the room.

Lenny thanked Coach Wheelhouse for his confidence in him, shook his hand, and left the staffroom as quickly as he had entered. Bear, after shaking hands with the coach, met Lenny in the hallway with a scowl on his face. He gave Lenny another glare and said, "You'd better make bloody well sure that you don't screw up, mate, because I'll make sure that you will rot on the field when we go to play for the Knights. I know the coach there, and he likes me a lot. You're a rookie newbie, and I don't want that bad luck of playing with a newbie to get me killed. You hear me, Rat?"

"Don't worry, 'Bruno', I'll get you around the bases so you can sit on your fat butt and get your suck ass cronies to spoon-feed you when we get back," said Lenny as politely as possible, pushing his way past Bear. Bear was spouting obscenities and trying to assault Lenny as he left, but Lenny ignored him and quickly put distance between them before Bear swung at him with closed fists. Lenny went to his room and called home to tell his parents about his temporary posting to the majors. He reassured them that he was ready to play in the big leagues.

His father was happy for Lenny, but his mom had regrets about his playing in the deadly major leagues. Lenny's mom no longer wanted the financial gain; she just wanted her son "to come home!" His parents both wished him luck. "Two Wheel died the other day, Lenny," said his mother on the vid-phone just before Lenny hung up. Lenny had tears in his eyes when he tapped the end button on his videophone. Right now, he felt more alone than he ever had since leaving North-Am.

"This is what I came here for, and I'm going to do my best, no matter the results!" Lenny said in his mind as loudly as he could think. Then Lenny tried to get his mind off of his upcoming events and Two Wheel's demise by exercising, listening to his favorite music, and resting. Eventually, he drifted off to a fitful waking sleep that was filled with dreams of bears playing baseball on the opposing team and Two Wheel trying to bite his leg while he was at bat. *"Probably for leaving him to play baseball,"* Lenny thought miserably in his weird dreams.

The next two days were a blur for Lenny as he and Bear flew by rocket to Queensland and got settled into a new culture with new food. Lenny then immersed himself into honing his batting and running skills. Their first game was scheduled in two days. Bear also worked on his running abilities doing exhaustive workouts. He then went around the clubhouse, sucking up to the veteran players for advice. This was probably a good thing for Bear's mortality. Lenny and Bear both worked out for five hours on the day before they were to go and play for the Knights. They both packed their players' bags with only their personal playing gloves and cleats. Everything else, including all of their playing gear, was digitally made and supplied to them personally. They would have brand new top-of-the-line gear which all of the pros used. All of the pros displayed their sponsors' logos at their place of play.

They were flown by grav-plane to a city called Brisbane. Brisbane was the closest city to the ringed protection forest near the global desert. Lenny and Bear were sent directly to Oliver O'Sullivan, the coach of the Central Coast Giants. When he said "Oh, oh," you knew he had something up his sleeve that a player wasn't going to like.

O'Sullivan was an old grandpa-looking type of guy with fiery brownish-green eyes that seemed to burn a hole into your soul when he stared down at you from his high desk in the team's boardroom. It was as if the devil himself was looking out from the inside of O'Sullivan's skull and putting his mark on you. He spoke in a smooth controlled baritone voice, but his tone was all business.

"You boys have been called up to play in tomorrow's game. I have lost some good men the last little while because they got a little too cocky thinking that they could get by on their past performances. That is, they thought that the other players would spare them because they were such good players around the league and they were all friends with the opposing teams as well. Well, that fucking kind of attitude doesn't work around here in the majors, see!" stated Coach O'Sullivan. "You play for your own soul that I control, and you play for me! I don't care how many friends you have around here; I hate to lose! Play the game just to get by, and you will die when you least expect it, or even when you do, I'll put you out there to die! Play the game to win, and you keep a step ahead of the Grim Reaper, me! And, like others, you'll continue to prosper in this league, if you so happen to get away from me," said O'Sullivan, making his point by flashing a great yellow-toothed grin at the pair of young players facing him.

All that Lenny could do was nod his head in agreement, but Bear got right in there and said, "I'll do anything you ask, Coach; just put me in the game."

Coach O'Sullivan looked at Robert Bearonson and smiled. "You've done good here, Sonny Bear; just do as you're told and you may get to stay here awhile longer."

Ray didn't have a good feeling about tomorrow's game, and playing with that 'suck ass' Bear caused him to feel a strong foreboding that didn't allow him much sleep that night. As they left O'Sullivan's office, it was Lenny's turn to admonish Bear. "I've seen how you suck up to O'Sullivan, Bear. Suck up to him and get me in trouble tomorrow, and I'll make sure you get hung out to dry. I have a hunch that O'Sullivan will put you up first ahead of me. Unless you are a better man to me, you'll be a deader man than me. You see, I won't mind taking a bean if it means you'll take two!"

Bear, realizing his situation, said to Lenny politely with a Cheshire cat smile, "You'll do good for me, newbie, and I know you will because you want to stay here just as much as I do."

Lenny looked at Bear with slight disgust, but then realized that he should at least be a gentleman about them playing together. He said, "Look, Bear, I want to succeed as much as you do, but we have to stick together and make the best plays we can. If you play for me, I'll surely give you my best." With that, they tentatively shook hands and went their separate ways.

It was game time, and the stadium was packed with seven hundred and fifty thousand noisy fans from the city of Brisbane and surrounding outback areas. The weather was great and the roof of the monstrous stadium was open. There was no wind to bring in the bothersome sand of the great global desert from the north to the stadium. The fans hadn't seen a win by the home team Central Coast Knights in the last two games. Their team had lost miserably to the Zealand South Alliance Giants twice in these semi-finals.

Lenny could feel the excitement and electricity in the air, as the game he was to be involved in was about to start. In the dressing room, just as any young player would, Lenny marveled at the players he had only read about in sports magazines back home. He was here, dressing and rubbing shoulders with them! There was the great Beau Wirrapanda, with arms that rippled with muscles like the big branches of a solid oak tree. He was the current Eastern 'A' League batting leader who played first base. Beau, who was in his fifth year in the majors, could retire soon if his luck held out. Lenny also saw Tyson 'Shoe' Shuey, a great outfielder that Boisey liked the most. Shuey was a guy to watch when you ran the bases, for he could take your ear off at nine hundred feet with the ball and it would look like it had been done with a knife. Then there was Tim Swift, whose name implied his status as a great base runner. Tim Swift was Rob Bearonson's favorite player. Bear stuck to him like glue to get any hints about running and who to watch out for on the opposing Zealand South Alliance Giants team. The top stats pitcher, Josh 'Billie' Kerr, was the starting pitcher for Lenny's team, the Knights. Josh Billie, the second-best pitcher in the Austro-Asian Leagues, could throw a fiery fastball that sizzled at a hundred and eighty-two miles an hour!

Lenny wanted to ask Josh for his autograph before the start of the game. A bit of a loner, Josh sat alone at one end of the dressing room and concentrated on the upcoming game. Feeling some empathy for Josh in the 'alone' department, Lenny gravitated to him to try and pick his brain for ideas as to how to get ahead in the upcoming game.

The opposing team, the Zealand South Alliance Giants, had just as many great players. After the anthems were played from each Alliance Region and the starting lineups were introduced, the game got seriously underway. Lenny's team were the visitors and they batted first. There was a rumor going around that this game would be a bloody one. Apparently, there was some animosity about the Zealand Alliance Giants being extra vicious in their last two games. Injured players who could have been spared on their second bean because they were already injured beyond playing again for the day were deemed as being able to run by the field and electronic umpires. They were the veteran players who Coach Wheelhouse had mentioned were killed off in the last two games that the Central Coast Knights team lost. Because his team had been losing the series, Bradley Butler, the coach of Zealand, saw to it that those players on the Knights team perished. He cruelly wanted them eliminated to make himself appear the victor and a comeback coach in this series. In semi-final play his team was behind two to nothing, and he had to do something to shake up the poor play of his team. Recognizing the easiness between the two teams, he stopped it, for any friendliness made it look like he didn't have control of his team. Losing this semi-final series would result in fewer credits for his future retirement, and it could even cost him his job as coach of the Zealand Southern Alliance Giants. Coach Butler said that if his players didn't start playing like an Alliance Baseball team, it would be really easy to eliminate certain individuals. The team obviously didn't take him seriously, and so he engineered plays that got rid of those players that had offended him on his own team. Even some of his most protected players that bucked Butler were left on the field of play to perish.

Lenny was in awe with all of the hype and the noise of his first big league game. The arena shook with the weight and noise of the huge crowd.

As the game began, the game's announcer came in over the sound system. "The first batter up for the Central Coast Knights is a young vet by the name of Ben Kennedy."

Ben got a hit on the very first pitch, and as he ran feverishly to first base, the infield of the Zealand Giants gunned him down viciously. The ball was fielded by the second baseman who threw it forcefully at Ben's head. It hit Ben right in the throat, separating his windpipe. Ben went down on the first baseline with his hands clutching his severed throat. His eyes were bulging in his head; Ben knew his end was near. The first base umpire deemed Ben able to try and scratch for first base, because he was still moving towards first base. The first baseman picked up the loose ball and simply let it drop lightly on Ben, uncaring, for the second bean and the first out. Ben groped for first base, slowly dying on the ball field, gasping for air. The media cameras zoomed in on his young face, contorted in terror, so that all could see Ben's anguish as he suffocated into unconsciousness. A raised red halo surrounded his limp body, designating him out by the second bean. This is what the fans wanted: to see someone die in horror on the very first play of the game, right before their very eyes. They cheered the Zealand Giants home team loudly and zealously for this cruel kill. A speedy clean up medic clayon robot dispatched of the young dying player into a body bin so that the game could resume without delay.

Next up was Beau Wirrapanda, the league's leading hitter for the Knights. Ben took a ball on his first pitch. He got a hit on his second pitch and made it safely to first base. He was taken out of the game temporarily and a pinch runner was put in for him by the name of Chad Cox. Chad, or 'CC', was the fresh meat rookie that everyone talked about. Sent up from the minors from another farm team of the Central Coast Knights, he was to run the gauntlet for Wirrapanda and the Knights Team on the bases. Tim Swift was next at bat. Swift got an infield hit that sent CC desperately running for second base. Now the second baseman for Zealand fielded the ball. He quickly fired it at CC's body, striking him in the hip, and shattering his hipbone just as CC was taking a swipe at the second baseman with his razor-like gloves. CC was trying to prevent the second baseman from getting to the ball, but CC missed. Getting to the ball very quickly, the second baseman knew he had CC down and going nowhere, so he went after Tim Swift, trying to bean him before he reached first base. The Zealand second baseman picked up the loose ball that caromed off of CC and sighted his next target: Tim. The ball struck Tim's helmet and went into the minor infield area. This blow by the ball momentarily disorientated and slowed Swift down, but he managed to get to first base safely before the second bean could be effectively applied. However, he lost his helmet on the play. The ball was thrown at him a second time by the first baseman, who had gotten it from the minor infielder, but Tim made it to first. The ball went soft as it hit him on the head for the second time because he was now safe, according to the electronic field umpire. Now the injured CC still lay on the second baseline, squirming in agony from a shattered hip. He was still trying to crawl to second base, even though it was a hundred feet away. The first baseman received the now hardened ball thrown to him by the minor right infielder who was lurking behind first base. The first baseman threw it at the downed CC, hitting him in the back of his exposed head and effectively killing him for the second bean and out of the inning. CC's blood and brains spilled onto the field. Again, the fans went wild, because this game seemed to be going the way the last two games had gone. Lots of play with lots of gore, early, was what they wanted. Lots of savage play early in the game meant lots of money for the owners and players. Two Knights players were lost in the first inning of play, but the outs made credits for the defensive players who had killed them, as well as for the coaches.

The game continued on like this, with each team losing a player or two each inning. Others struck out or took double beans, but were not injured enough to be knocked out of the game. Runners on both teams also eliminated some of the defending Zealand team's veteran infielders as well as the Giants' veteran defenders on the bases. Mostly it was the young drafted players who had been called up like Lenny and Bear that were killed on the field.

It wasn't until the sixth inning that anything really serious happened. Tim Swift, up again, got another hit that gave him a stand-up double. Tim also took out the replacement second baseman who had possession of the ball for Zealand by driving his knife-like blades from his armored gloves deep into the second baseman's intestines as he dove for second base. The second baseman's intestines spilled onto the infield just as Swift crashed into second base. That hit and that savage play by Swift, at second, drove in a run that put the Central Coast Knights in the lead one to nothing. But in his exuberance, Swift took a gamble and went for third base. He was gunned down by Zealand's great center fielder, Sam Hurn, who had been getting at least one kill per game. Tim Swift, true to his name, swiftly took off from second base after eliminating the second baseman. He went flying for third when the ball got him in the lower neck, severing his spine. He instantly became a paraplegic who was unable to move anything below his ribs. The only thing that moved on Tim Swift was his mouth and arms. He tried to yell for help, but his lungs wouldn't push up any air. Tim was lying about twenty feet from third base, scratching his arms in the dirt in his attempt to get to third, when the Zealand third baseman picked up the loose ball that came to him from a minor infielder. The third baseman raised the ball high above his head and waited for the screaming fans to tell him what to do. The fans wanted more blood, and they chanted, "Kill him, kill him, kill him!" with a thumbs-down sign, and that was exactly what the third baseman did. Tim Swift's helmet had come off when he went down from his first bean, and the Zealand third baseman threw the ball at his exposed head. Again, the cameras zoomed in on Swift's head and illuminated the blow by the spiked ball. The ball literally squashed Tim's head like a watermelon crushed by a large rock dropped on it from twenty feet above. The hit by the ball to Tim Swift's head made his arms and legs spasm out like he had been given a final electric shock. All of the people watching around the world took in this gruesome reminder that no one was exempt from the savage play of future Alliance

Baseball, not even the great base runner Tim Swift. Swift had thrilled them with his play for years, right up to his death on today's field of play. There was no pension to be had by Tim Swift.

Coach O'Sullivan was losing players at a rate faster than he had anticipated, and he would now have to use his rookies Lenny and Bear. The players on the bench who knew O'Sullivan began to say "Oh oh," "Oh oh," which meant that O'Sullivan was looking for 'fresh meat'.

O'Sullivan looked at Lenny and said, "You, Peecheh, I need you to play second base where Swift played; think you can handle that?"

Lenny basically didn't have a choice: it was say no and go home, or play the game he loved but with the deadly major league rules and all of its stark realities to the utmost.

"I'm ready, Coach," said young Lenny with what he thought was confidence. This was it. Lenny was given the green light to play in his first big league professional game. He smiled nervously as his name was announced to the stadium home team fans. They booed him as he trundled out to second base wearing his new electronic playing gear. Lenny didn't see any action until the third batter came up for Zealand. The first two batters didn't make it to first base. One was taken out by the first baseman Beau Wirrapanda. In the first at bat, the out produced was a crippled runner: both legs were broken by the first baseman in two separate throws with an assist from the right side minor infielder. The second batter was killed by the third baseman, who made it appear routine to take out a player in one throw to the neck (the one bean rule) and snuff out the life of a young rookie. Before Lenny knew it, the ball was hit to him and he instinctively threw the ball at the runner trying to make it to first. Lenny hit the runner in the left arm, almost severing it off of the runner's body near his shoulder in a powerful smash. The first baseman got the ball from a minor infielder and beaned the runner a second time, breaking the other arm of the screaming incapacitated runner to cruelly make him the third out of the inning. With no useful arms to play with, the injured batter was quickly brought off the field by the AI clayon robots. It almost made Lenny sick. He had seriously maimed a man he didn't know, but at least he hadn't killed someone on his very first major league play.

Coach O'Sullivan was pleased by Lenny's play, and asked him if he could bat. Lenny said he could, and O'Sullivan promptly put him in the batting order for the seventh inning to replace the deceased Tim Swift. Lenny was second up that inning.

The pitching was like nothing Lenny had ever seen. The ball came at him at least twenty miles an hour faster than he was used to. The ball seemed to flame by him! Not wanting to show his fear, he swung at anything that came his way. He managed to run the count to three balls and two strikes, desperately fouling off five other pitches from the demonic pitcher from the Zealand team. Now this long at bat kind of tired out the opposing pitcher a little, and this gave the quick young Lenny an advantage when a slower fastball/slider came his way. Lenny gauged the pitch with his electronic sensing device over his left eye. The device relayed that the ball was moving towards him at a hundred and sixty miles an hour and it was a straight fastball that would pass directly into the middle of the strike zone. Smack! Lenny got his first major league hit with his first at bat, a blooper to center field. He easily reached first base, but was immediately taken out of the game by O'Sullivan. He was replaced by none other than Rob Bearonson. Bear was not happy about having to run for Lenny, but hey, a job is a job. Lenny was tickled pink knowing that all of his teammates back on the North Coast Eagles Minor team would see that Bear was running for Lenny. As Bear went out to first base, he scowled at Lenny and said, "You lucky shit, newbie."

Lenny retorted, "Don't get killed out here, Bear; who are your buddies going to suck up to if they lose you?" Lenny twisted around to get on to the magnetically hovering servo plate that brought him to his home team and to the safety of the dugout. His teammates congratulated him as Lenny took a seat in the dugout. O'Sullivan nodded at Lenny and gave him a thin smile as his teammates patted him on the back. Lenny didn't want to get too excited, but he was nonetheless happy that he made it out of his first major league debut unscathed.

On the very next play, the batter that came up for the Knights got a hit, making it a hit and run play. The batter made it to first. Bear, running to second base, killed the second baseman while running to second. His sharp knife-like protrusions coming out of his gloves drove into the second baseman's head, right beside his left ear. The second baseman fielded the ball and tried to bean Bear, flying into second base, but to no avail. Bear's quick cruel actions saved himself from a deadly bean.

The next batter hit into a long single bean play while trying to get to first base, and he was eliminated in a gruesome face-smashing single bean play by the Central Coast Knights' third baseman. Bear got the jump on the hit pitch, which got him down to third base much faster than the play had developed. Coach O'Sullivan just harrumphed to himself when Bear made his lightning-quick play for third. He said, "I knew that kid was going make it; he's got the right speed and toughness to continue in this league. He can stay here for the next little while, and then I'll see what he can do."

Bear managed to get to home plate on the next play before the batter was stopped by a double bean and score a second run from third, for the Central Coast Giants. That particular play seemed to convince Coach O'Sullivan that Bear should stay for the next playoff game. The Central Coast Giants went on to win the game two to nothing. The Giants devastated the Zealand South Alliance's lineup with five more kills, one of them a veteran player of three years. The Giants won the game two nothing. Coach O'Sullivan was quietly pleased with Lenny's and Bear's plays.

Lenny was sent back to his farm team, the North Coast Eagles, not for his play on the field, but for Coach O'Sullivan's own intuition that Lenny would soon be back permanently. Lenny wasn't too disappointed with that decision, because it gave him time to reflect on his recent experience. He felt that he could play the game in its savage fashion. And he was rid of Robert Bearonson, for now. As the new young 'god' on his team, Lenny formed a clique of his own. Lenny made them take pride in their team and their play. He set examples for newbie players to follow. These positive changes made Lenny's life more bearable for the time being. As his team began to feel somewhat proud of themselves, they played with camaraderie. This made the team play better overall as a group, and not just as a bunch of petty playing individuals.

Lenny had made up his mind to stay and play Alliance Major League Baseball, no matter what happened ! He wondered how Dean, Ray, and Boisey were doing. Would he ever get to see them again? Lenny felt in his heart that Ray Aloyisius Tenner, the 'Rat', was his best friend from home in North-Am. There were over ninety World Alliance Baseball Teams on Earth so the odds, Lenny felt, of ever seeing his friends in a game or playing against them were pretty small if he stayed in the Austro-Asian League.

When Lenny phoned home, his parents were relieved to hear that he had made it past his first serious test in the majors. His mother cried her eyes out, hoping Lenny would change his mind and come home to her after his first professional game. Lenny's mom said they had buried Two Wheel out in the country near a favorite picnic spot. Lenny listened to his mom, and lovingly told her not to worry: he would play his best for her every time he went out onto the field. He said his manly goodbyes to his dad and promised to try and get home as soon as possible. He reassured his parents that he would survive for the next little while playing Earth Alliance Major League Baseball.

CHAPTER THREE
LEARNING QUICKLY TO LIE BUT NOT DIE!

AFTER HEARING OF RAY AND LENNY'S 'FUN' THEY HAD WITH Billie-By-Law, Dean chuckled to himself. He wished he could have been there to see By-Law-Billie skidding her butt across the pavement. He wasn't too fond of her. Dean liked playing tricks on other people, but his shenanigans were mostly aimed at his favorite target: brother Boisey.

Dean thought back to his younger days, when he had a self-styled enthusiasm for unbridled fun.

Before Dean's parents got work for the Earth Alliance at the North Pole's North Alliance Launch Tower, they had been a very poor family that had little in the way of entertainment for their boys. Dean's father had collected and sold scrap metal that was sent to the deep Earth smelters twenty-five miles underground, where the heat from the Earth's magma could be harvested for the smelting of these recycled metals. It was a hard and busy life for his dad, who would be underground for many days at a time just to put food on the table for his family. After Dean's parents got jobs at the Northern Launch Tower's military factory repairing interstellar ships, his dad was home every night. That brought their family much closer together.

Dean, being the industrious type, had dreamed of being an Olympian before he was put into Alliance Baseball. Naturally athletic, Dean had made a homemade pole vaulting set-up in their meager back yard just after the family had moved to Hyder. It was his childhood dream to become an Olympian pole vaulter and set world records. His teachers and mentors said that he had the athletic frame of a pole vaulter.

So, Dean managed to collect four worn out/discarded synthesized poles from the construction of their new home. He cut two of them to eight feet long, dug two holes about six feet apart, and buried the cut poles to a depth of two-and-a-half feet into the ground in an upright position. He then managed to find some discarded rivets on a pallet of building scraps. He drilled holes in the uprights, starting at two feet above the ground, and he put holes every two inches as high as a ten-and-a-half-year-old boy could reach. Dean set another synthetic pole horizontally onto the rivets. Next, he found some foam scraps and piled them up on the far side of his vault to land on, and voila: he had a pole vaulting set-up!

Dean had saved two sturdy poles for pole vaulting over the horizontal bar which he had set at the lowest level on the uprights. A triangular hole pole trap, encased in synthetic wood, was dug in the ground about a foot before and in the middle of the uprights for the insertion of the pole. Next, Dean cut his vaulting pole to about four inches higher than he could reach with his outstretched hand. That would be the length of his vaulting pole. Dean stood back about forty feet from his vaulting set-up with his vaulting pole raised, the bottom end of the pole above his head, and then he dashed towards his pole vault set-up as fast as his feet could go. Upon nearing his set-up at a fast running clip, Dean skillfully inserted his pole into the hole trap he had dug, stiffened his arms as his pole stopped his forward motion, pulled his legs upwards while twisting his body inward to face the horizontal bar he wanted to go over, and sailed easily over the two-foot height he had set for himself on his very first vault.

Happy at his success, on his next four attempts Dean raised the bar to over three feet high and successfully soared over again and again. Missing on his fifth attempt at three-and-a-half feet, he tried again and made it over the bar on the next successive try. Happy with his endeavors, Dean called Ray and Lenny to come over and try their hand at pole vaulting in the Luthbert's back yard. Dean showed them the essentials of pole vaulting and encouraged his visitors to try their hand at it. Ray and Lenny were successful, though they didn't get as high as Dean. After a while the pole they were using began to show signs of stress. It could be heard cracking as they tried vaulting over the horizontal bar.

By this time, Boisey had found them. He was always intrigued by what Dean and the older boys were doing. Dean, wanting some fun and a little action, called Boisey over to their set-up. Winking at Ray and Lenny to be quiet about the stressed pole, he told Boisey what they were doing. Dean easily convinced Boisey to take the cracked pole and try his luck at pole vaulting. The older boys used the other sturdy pole to demonstrate to Boisey the technique of getting over the horizontal pole. Dean said, "Boisey, this is how it's done. Me, Ray, and Lenny have gotten over the bar easily. It should be a piece of cake for you. We want you to be on our pole vaulting team!" They then gave Boisey the cracked pole and let him try his luck at going over the horizontal bar. As luck would have it, Boisey made it over the horizontal bar twice before Dean said, "Hey, Boisey, you're pretty good at this. I'll bet you can go really high."

"You think so, Dean! You think I can do it?" asked Boisey enthusiastically.

"Why sure, Boisey, I'm sure you can go as high as me, Ray, and Lenny," said Dean, pumping up his unsuspecting brother's ego. "Why don't you give the highest level a try? I'm sure you can get over it, just like us. I'm sure you can do as good as us, Boisey," said Dean coyly.

So, the energized Boisey took off down their makeshift runway, mightily planted the faulty pole, and drew his legs up over his head in an impressive heave. It looked like Boisey would clear the highest level on the pole vault set-up made by Dean! But it was not to be. The defective pole snapped, then buckled under Boisey's weight at its zenith. Boisey didn't get over the level bar. Instead, Boisey sailed uncontrollably under the bar. His feet were over his head with his body twisting wildly under him. His left arm fell behind his back as he landed on the hard ground, missing the scrap foam heap, and Boisey, to his spectators' delight, crashed to the ground with a thump. He had fallen onto his arm with the full weight of his body.

Dean, Ray, and Lenny howled with laughter at the funny scene that had just unfolded, but their laughter soon turned to dismay and then panic as the shocked Boisey began to howl at the pain his limp arm gave him. He lay splayed out on the ground with his wounded arm under his body.

Dean's mother immediately came out from the kitchen door at Boisey's loud crying and asked sternly what had happened to Boisey. Ray and Lenny just stood there, shell shocked, not wanting to incriminate themselves nor Dean. Dean was quick on the draw as he knew the consequences if he told the truth. Dean said, "Mom, me and the boys were playing pole vaulting out here. Boisey wanted to try it. We let him, but the pole he was using snapped and he hurt himself, Mom, honest." Dean's mom accepted the explanation but made Dean, Ray, and Lenny take down the pole vaulting set-up, much to their relief. They were not punished for their misdeed of letting Boisey vault with a cracked pole.

"I'm telling your father, Dean, about this mishap, but I'll tell him it wasn't your fault. Boys will be boys, won't they," said Dean's mom, shaking her head. She took the howling Boisey into the house to tend to his sprained shoulder.

Dean loved playing Junior Alliance Baseball and his parents liked watching him. It gave the Luthberts a sense of community as they attended their sons' games together with their neighbors, the Peechehs and the Tenners. They all felt a sense of pride that their sons could play baseball together with such intensity. The three families enjoyed themselves immensely, watching the boys play Junior Alliance Baseball over the years. Whimsically, they forgot the reality of the big leagues that they wanted their sons to play in when they became of age. Being drafted into the big leagues was like being conscripted into the military.

Being the second oldest of our four boys after Lenny Peecheh, when Dean turned eighteen, he was drafted and sent to the Euro-Russo Alliance Major League to play for the Celtic Spartak Attack. Because of his size and skills Dean was selected first overall in the major league draft the next year after Lenny. That was the highest a Hyder junior league player was ever drafted — even higher than Mike 'Sliver' Le Courd, and his friend Lenny, who had both been chosen third in their time. Dean's hometown fans cheered gratefully and followed his career diligently.

Dean spent only two weeks in the minors with the Celtic Spartak Attack, as he outdid all of the other younger players by magnitudes of ten in the skill category required to be a major league player. He was quickly sent up to the majors with great expectations. Alliance Baseball wanted its best players right away, as the best seemed to get knocked off faster than they could be brought up to the big leagues. The Euro-Russo continent was a very arid place, devoid of organic shrubbery, and it was also a cruel place to play Alliance Baseball. As soon as you came to fame, your flame of stardom was usually snuffed out. But Dean determined to remain a lit flame!

Since the Earth had warmed up, ice hockey had disappeared due to the expense of keeping ice around. Many mainstream sports such as soccer, tennis, Olympic winter favorites, road racing, triathlons, swimming, and others had disappeared because of their costs and the hot dry weather that forced them out of regular play. It was a major drain on an Alliance's resources to fund other major sports leagues. The Summer Olympics were still held, but on a much smaller scale, and they don't get half the attention as Major League Alliance Baseball.

Alliance Baseball had been brought in as an entertaining sport to keep the interests of a troubled human race occupied and potential terrorists placated. People all over the world watched the gruesomeness of the violent play that Alliance Baseball afforded. Why go out and fight costly wars, when killing could be watched so inexpensively? Hundreds died playing the sport every day!

Terrorists didn't have to wage war on the world. The world did it for them by making baseball the ultimate violent pastime.

The Euro-Russo Alliance Baseball League that Dean was drafted into had flourished with tens of thousands of wannabe players joining their league farm teams every year. Their one wish was to become a world-class player in the Major Alliance Leagues, earn millions of credits, and live happily ever after. The talent was unending, and so Dean would have his work cut out for himself if he wanted to survive futuristic baseball. He would have to stay ahead of the young talent rushing with him to the major leagues, just like the young men from other generations who had gone off to brutal wars, not knowing what their adventures would bring them. The young men of today played Major Alliance Baseball with the sense that it would be fun and profitable. Profitable yes, but fun, not in the least!

Dean's minor league coach for the Celtic Spartak Attack, Romeo Tarkhanov, saw money potential in Dean right away with very little training needed. Romeo saw at a glance that Dean wasn't just ground beef to be sent to the majors, chewed up, and spit out. Romeo Tarkhanov knew in his heart that Dean would become a great player, given the right coaching and protection.

At first Dean didn't like the attention, but after two weeks and the promise to be sent up to the major leagues, Dean quickly settled himself down to the business of becoming a trained stopper and super killer in the game of Alliance Baseball.

As promised by Coach Tarkhanov with his benevolent eye, Dean made his entry into the big leagues with the Bremen Gyor Titans in the Euro-Russo Eastern 'A' League. The Titans were near the top of their league in standings, and Coach Tarkhanov wanted his cut for sending a well-trained young rookie to the majors. Coach Tarkhanov had put his best trainers on Dean to make him a great rookie, and Dean had certainly played with gusto. Dean was accepted by his fellow players as a man who could help them in their quest to get farther into the game for their own economic gains and maybe win a World Alliance Baseball Series.

In his debut game at third base, Dean made a good impression on his major league coach by eliminating four players from the opposition with single beans. His new coach for the Titans was Toni Zwanziger. Zwanziger was impressed by the newbie Dean, but Dean didn't at all like his role on the team. The coach used Dean in 'live' practices to push his players to their ultimate limits. That is, any player that didn't play up to Coach Zwanziger's standards was 'beaned' by Dean with the hardened dangerous ball. Though they were only struck by less damaging hits and not crippled, their injuries reminded them that they had to play sharper for their wanting coach. Soft rules did not apply in practices by Zwanziger's ruthless standards. He either wanted the best at all times from his players, or nothing but their deaths in real games! This was Coach Zwanziger's first opportunity to make serious credits towards his pension, and he was going to take full advantage. Dean would make him and his team winners in their league and maybe even a World Series winner! That would make Zwanziger a very rich man indeed!

The Titans rose quickly in the Euro-Russo Eastern standings to become the top team to advance to the World Series Alliance

Major League Baseball finals in their region. Dean wasn't bothered by the fact that his coaches were grooming him to become a super killer, because he was really enjoying himself as a major league player. Most of the time he was only crippling players instead of outright killing them.

The Titans didn't win in the World Alliance Series finals, but for Dean it was an eye-opening experience to get to the finals of World Alliance Baseball in his first year. Dean was a protected player, and so his career would be protected too. He would last for the foreseeable future in the professional leagues, if he played up to his coach's standards. He hadn't yet had the chance to see or play against Lenny or Ray, as their teams had not made it to their respective regional finals.

Dean was pampered in his role as a designated killer. He rarely batted. When he did bat, he always had a runner substitute so that he could be spared running the dangerous gauntlet of the bases. All he had to do was play third base with vicious accuracy for his home team, the Titans.

In his debut season at third base for the Titans, Dean set a regular season team record for the most 'outs' on just one bean onto base runners by a rookie third baseman. That is, he killed or incapacitated runners with just one hit from the ball so they could not continue in the game. He had set the sensational team record at eleven in one game.

Dean was always put on the roster to start a game for the Bremen Gyor Titans. The fans of the Euro-Russo league would pack the stadiums in droves just to witness the carnage Dean Luthbert would inflict on the opposing teams. Dean became affectionately known by his fans in Euro-Russo as the 'Tiro-Confuto', or Young Stopper.

Tiro-Confuto was mobbed wherever he went by young and old alike for his autograph. Every adoring fan wanted to take a selfie with him. Fame came easy for Dean. He soon forgot about the world he had left behind, including his friends and family who supported him. Over time, Dean began to indulge in the lights and glitter that surrounded him in Alliance Baseball.

As Dean Luthbert progressed in this game of futuristic baseball, his mind and body sank into that of a serial killer. The game became more of a live video session for him. Dean would pick his victims that gave him and his fans the most horrific of pleasures. That is, Dean would intentionally do things like crush a skull, disfigure a face, or intentionally take out a knee. Then he would let his team members finish off the runner with deadly precision. His fans would watch young players die on the field of play and they would cheer Dean on like a gladiator of old Roman times. Dean exercised his body and mind until nothing seemed to faze his mind and concentration while playing, even when he lost friends and teammates to the game. His protection by the coaches of his team meant that he could continue in the game with a ninety-five percent certainty that he would not be stopped, at least not in a physical fashion. In short, Dean was regarded as the fantasy killer in the Euro-Russo League. Riches and fame followed Dean wherever he went.

Dean also became a trendsetter in the Euro-Russo League with his major league team the Bremen Gyor Titans. He was one of those rare individuals who could do almost whatever he wanted. He was immensely popular, and so whatever he did or wore, others would copy him. Dean and his handlers soon realized this, and they cashed in by advertising whatever fashion or fad Dean dictated at the time.

In the fashion department Dean would wear his regular home team black uniform, with wide gold striping, and the number thirteen emblazoned on his back and shoulders for home games. For charity events that raised money for the poor of the world, and for 'soft' all-star games, Dean would wear a showy gold uniform with black pin striping. This uniform really made him stand out from his fellow players. In crunch playoff games when a win was needed, Dean would wear an almost black uniform with very thin gold pin striping. This uniform, which made him look almost scorpion-like, let the other team know his intentions of not losing that particular game. The opposing teams would suffer extra losses whenever he wore the distinct black uniform, much to the delight of his adoring fans. His nickname was evolved from 'The Stopper' to 'The Scorpion'. Many coaches and players of the Euro-Russo leagues feared the day they would play against Dean and his Titans.

If Dean's team was winning by a large margin of runs, say eight to one or ten nothing, he would set trends like hitting opposing players in the butt for their first or second bean. This would draw great cheering and laughter from his stadium fans and provide relief for the runner(s), who would not be killed by Dean, though they would have dandy keepsake bruises on their butts to remember him by.

Dean's star was high in the major league baseball sky. He was approached by the very rich, famous, and politically powerful for his fame on the field of baseball. He met politicians like Ricardo Narzani, from the World Alliance Council, that controlled the trade and transportation of most of the interplanetary star ships and Earth to solar inner planets. Ricardo Narzani liked being seen with Dean, because in the fans' eyes Dean looked like a 'good guy' in the game of Alliance Baseball. Being near Dean made Narzani feel the same. Investors of all kinds like Collin Bendshaw, an interstellar financier and partner of Narzani's, began to take up a lot of Dean's time. They got Dean to do their bidding on the political scene by championing their political agendas with his bravado talk of how good the Euro-Russo Region was for the leagues there, just like the Euro-Russo Alliance was for its people. Dean's ego began to get the better of him in what he did both on and off the field. As he put more hours into what the investors wanted, his playing performances on the field began to suffer. He didn't get enough rest. Dean began making mistakes on routine plays due to his fatigue from spending hours on video broadcasts. His coaches let these (little) mistakes go for a while, but when game losses began to mount, his handlers got very angry with him. The politicians who had touted Dean as their hero and leaned on the coaches to protect Dean, even more than the average star, began distancing themselves because of his floundering play. Dean didn't abuse drugs or anything like that, but he was becoming emotionally unstable. His poor play began to make those politically powerful people turn away from him when he asked for their help. Dean began an emotional slide, with his team, that would take him on a long road back home to North-Am. Dean's star in baseball fell hard on himself, and he had to pay for it with bad publicity wherever he went.

The Alliance Baseball world raised its eyebrows when the news hit the digital sky way networks with the blaring headline: **BIG NEWS!!! Dean 'The Scorpion' Luthbert traded to a South-Am Alliance Team due to faltering play!**

It was the end of the season for the Bremen Gyor Titans. They had performed poorly, and Dean was becoming a liability. The Titans didn't win their regional playoffs that would have sent them to the World Alliance Series playoff finals for the second year in a row. The finals were being played in the Pak-Indostan Alliance area. Unfortunately, the Titans finished second last in their league standings due in part to Dean's faltering play. The Titans blamed their missing the playoffs on certain players' performances, and they also mentioned Ricardo Narzani's influence as part of Dean's stellar collapse. Ricardo had not backed him up in the media frenzy. Dean was traded to the Porte Allegra League in the Eastern 'A' division in the South-Am Major Leagues, located on the southeast coast of the old country of Brazil in the old province of Rio Grande Do Sul.

Dean ended up in a city called Pelotas and a team called that by the same name. The city of Pelotas, with a population of six million great star ship workers, was a hub of interplanetary ship repair for the South-Am Launch Tower. The people of Pelotas were the great innovators of cutting edge research. They were geniuses in inventing the newest technology for adapting interstellar military applications to military uses in the Earth Alliance trade, while maintaining the Earth's interests such as reversing the global desert's expansion.

Dean's newest coach for Pelotas, in the South-Am league, was Carlos Vieira. Vieira told Dean in no uncertain terms that here in the South-Am leagues, "We expect our players to follow the tradition of hard work and forget the bright lights of stardom. Only hard work will get you the proper recognition you want as a baseball player, not schmoozing with politicians or showy stars." He scolded Dean lightly, determined that Dean would not dominate his coaching style.

Dean practiced with his new team and got to know his teammates a little, over time. Now Pelotas had some 'old country history', and so when Dean came to his new team, he got hazed. He had to drink a shot of pure 'Amazon-made' liquor, kiss a large, live, wild boa constrictor on its head, and address the snake as 'Bullo-Grande', his great mentor. Dean had to put up with the hazing from his teammates for a few days, but soon the hazing stopped because of his hard, industrious play. Dean settled into his new team as a first line starter at third base.

It had been a great blow to Dean's ego to be traded, as it felt like a step down from the notoriety he had enjoyed in the Euro-Russo league. He knew deep down that he had to endure the media frenzy if he wanted to play on in Alliance Baseball. Dean could have quit the game; all of the riches he had garnered from his fame through product sales and sponsorships would make an Earth Alliance Government Pension look like lunch money. But Dean wasn't about to go quietly from the baseball scene just yet; his ego wouldn't let him. He told himself that he would give it one more kick at the can here in South-Am, and if he didn't fare well, then he would leave the game on his own terms. He wanted to be able to say he had played five years in the major leagues without retiring on riches that he made before his five years were up. This would have looked like he took the money and ran, and Dean did not want to further tarnish his reputation as a great Alliance Baseball player.

HOMECOMING FOR DEAN

During the off-season, Dean kept as low a profile in the public eye as he could. He visited with his wildly happy and now well-off mother and father. Boisey, his adopted brother, would drop in from time to time to see his long-lost brother also. They had been apart for two years while playing Major Alliance Baseball. Dean, who had always been taller and bigger than Boisey, thought he'd pull his old trick of hiding behind the door and jumping on Boisey. Dean laughed to himself, predicting that Boisey would yell in terror as he fell to the floor with the bigger Dean on top, just like in the old days when they were kids. Dean's mom and dad warned Dean that playing tricks on Boisey wasn't a wise thing to do anymore. They knew Boisey had matured a lot, and tried to warn Dean. Dean just laughed and said, "Little ole Boisey is gonna get the biggest surprise he's had in two years when he sees me!"

When Boisey walked through the door, he looked at his mother and father. He smiled graciously and asked, bewildered, "Where's ole' Dean? I thought he was home."

His parents just kind of stared at Boisey and tried not to look at Dean, who was crouching behind the open closet door.

Boisey, speaking like the great gentleman he had been taught and brought up to be, asked again, "Where's Dean, Mom?" There came no answer.

Boisey asked again, but then the commotion started before anyone could answer. Quickly Dean jumped on Boisey's back with great glee and enthusiasm, thinking he would scare the pants off of Boisey and have a great chuckle at terrorizing him. The only thing that crossed Dean's mind though, when he jumped on Boisey's back from behind the door, was that this wasn't the little ole Boisey that he had known and tackled in the good ole days! The smile and glee melted from Dean's face quite quickly and transferred itself to his parents' faces, who kind of knew what was going to happen next.

Boisey didn't move a muscle, nor did he fall down in terror from Dean's old ruse of jumping on his back. Boisey simply remained standing. Then he reached a huge right hand over his right shoulder and easily brought Dean over his head with a mighty pull. With his other hand, Boisey gripped the belt of Dean's trousers, raised Dean up in a mighty lift, and began to spin his brother's gangly body around and around over his head. The tables were turned in this brotherly meeting with Dean yelling for mercy, "Don't hurt me, Boisey; please don't hurt me!" And with that plea, Boisey flopped Dean down on the plush carpeted floor in a heap. Then he sat on Dean saying,

"Nice to see you, Scorpion bro." Dean's parents didn't laugh, though they had broad smiles on their faces at the boyish antics of their two grown sons. They were very glad to have their children home. Boisey had grown a foot taller and gained about eighty pounds of pure muscle, going from one hundred and fifteen pounds to a hundred and ninety-five pounds since Dean had seen him last. Dean was still taller, but Boisey was now much stronger. All Dean could think of at the moment was that another situation was happening to him that he couldn't control, for even his little brother had put him to shame. But Dean quickly forgot what had just happened because his parents, who had quickly erupted into laughter, brought him back to reality. Dean was home and that was all that mattered for now. He got up and hugged Boisey and his parents tightly with joy. Dean laughed with them, glad that they were back together as a family once again. He re-established his family ties and temporarily forgot about the big bad world of Alliance Baseball.

"Dean, Lenny and Ray are coming for a visit. We'll all be together again for a little while," said Boisey. "Maybe we can all go out riding into the dunes, eh Dean? Wouldn't that be fun? Just like old times?" asked Boisey.

"I think that's a great idea, Boisey. We did that a few times a long time ago, didn't we. We had a great time racing around in the sand," said Dean.

Dean's mom said, "The dunes have become quite dangerous lately. The sand lizard population has grown significantly over the last few years. The military are planning a cull because there have been too many incidents of the lizards coming over to areas where the sand has overrun the forests and fences. The lizards even destroyed a neighborhood near the ballpark area here a few months ago. They killed over fifty residents and ate several people before they could be stopped. I don't think it is a good idea to go out there just yet. Also, they say that the sandstorms in the dunes are getting stronger. The provincial politicians have been trying to lessen the storms by putting more water onto the desert with spaceport freighters, but fueling the deserts with water has only made the sandstorms stronger," she said, very concerned.

"Don't worry, Mom, we'll get the newer heavy-duty dune buggies that the lizards can't harm. I've checked them out. So far, they haven't revoked anyone applying to go out into the near desert with these heavy-duty dune buggies. We'll be okay," said Dean reassuringly to his mother.

After the Luthberts had dinner, Dean and Boisey sat together in their parents' large dining room and talked about old times. Boisey asked Dean, "That Lenny always played jokes on me. I wonder if he's going to be the same when he gets here?"

"Well, I've heard that Lenny has become quite a gentleman where he's playing, and he's got all kinds of girls around him. Treats them all very nice, as well as everyone else, from what I hear," said Dean. "I think he's gotten over his boyish pranks."

"Well, I remember the time I asked him to introduce me to Sheila, one of his girlfriends that I really liked. Lenny stood behind me after he introduced me to her and I told her that I liked her. Lenny cut the belt that was holding my pants up just as I was saying, 'I really like you.' My pants fell down past my knees, she turned red and slapped my face, and I couldn't get a girlfriend around here for a year after that," said Boisey.

Dean laughed and said, "Well, I'll be here to protect you, bro, just like old times."

"That's what I'm afraid of, Dean: the old times," said Boisey. "Things are different now that we are all pro players. Even with so many teams in the leagues, we are eventually going to meet up with each other in a game, and I'm afraid we may have to eliminate each other," finished Boisey sadly.

Dean looked at Boisey and realized that he was right. Boisey had put some thought into his play over the last three years. Unless they could all be drafted onto the same team, they would indeed face each other at some point. Then they would have to do the unthinkable and try to kill one another in the game of Alliance Baseball.

"We'll have to cross that bridge when we get to it. For now, let's just enjoy our time at home and we'll have fun, eh Boisey?" said Dean.

Boisey nodded in agreement and smiled at his brother. "Yeah, well, we will have some fun, but you can't jump on me from behind the door no more, Dean; I'm on to ya for that one," laughed Boisey.

Boisey and Dean talked about how Boisey made it to the majors and where he was presently playing.

"I got picked two hundredth in the first round, Dean," said Boisey. "I played here in North-Am my first year, and then they sent me to the Pak-Indostan Leagues. Them guys there are pretty skinny and fast. I wasn't the tallest player over there, but I was the heaviest. It was hard trying to take them guys out, from the outfield, because they are smaller targets than the guys here at home. They are downright skinny, and it's like throwing at a running two by four," chuckled Boisey. "But I would set up targets after practices that were the same size as the Pak-Indostan runners and I got pretty good at hitting them smaller, skinnier guys from center field," boasted Boisey. "I know I talked to you about what I should do, Dean, after I got drafted, but them coaches didn't like me a whole lot, so I had to work really hard to try and zero in on them smaller runners there. I got traded six times in the minors and three more in the majors in the Pak-Indostan League before I finally settled down with the Chandigarh Bengal Tigers of the Pak-Indostan Western League. I really worked hard on my hitting and throwing, and finally got into a rotation to start almost every game. My team often plays against the teams in the Euro-Russo Eastern leagues because those leagues are so close together. I even got to see you play once, Dean. I was sitting on the bench that day when your team came to town to play against us. You hit three guys in the butt that game cuz your team was winning seven nothing. I laughed a lot and told everyone that you were my big brother, but they didn't believe me and said I was just bragging. I was real scared that day because I thought I would have to play against you, Dean, in that game. But my coach said that I wasn't going to play that day cuz my arm was hurting and he wanted me to rest it. It was the arm I hurt pole vaulting a long time ago. Do you remember that, Dean? So that was a great relief for me, and I got to see you play, bro," finished Boisey happily.

"That's great that we didn't have to play against each other, Boisey, but the coaches from my team won't let me bat or run most of the time anyway. They just want me to play third base and take out runners; that's my job. So, the probability of us playing against each other is pretty slim," said Dean.

"I hope it stays like that, bro, cuz I sure would hate to have to hurt my big brother," laughed Boisey, "'specially when he can't scare me no more by jumping out from behind a door," laughed Boisey again just as Dean surprised Boisey and tackled him to the floor in brotherly love.

CHAPTER FOUR
BEING THE GRUNT OF THEM ALL

RAY ALOYISIUS TENNER 'THE RAT' GOT DRAFTED INTO THE Africany Alliance League the year after Dean was drafted. Ray was drafted twenty-third in the first round — not a top ten pick, but high enough to get him to a major's farm team considering his phenomenal play as a rookie. There were sixteen teams in the Africany minors that were split into two leagues north and south. Ray played in the minors for six months for the Bafana Chiefs of the Southern Africany Minor League in the city of Cap-Ste-Marie on the southern tip of the island of Madagascar. The Southern League of the Africany Alliance had eight teams. The other league, which was in the old country of Morocco on the northwest side of old Africa, also had eight teams in the city of Tangier. These were the only two surviving countries of the Africany Alliance, for the global deserts had annihilated all other countries, people, and animals on the old continent of Africa. There were one hundred million people living in Madagascar and another million living in Morocco. Before the climatic catastrophes, the old African continent had over two billion people. These two provinces of the Africany Alliance had given the world the best minds for converting materials brought back from other star systems. The people turned them into the best working items the Earth could ever utilize, like new and improved star ship designs with diamond alloyed hulls, chromatic safety space suits, Diamoond Iron power plants, and Diamoond Iron batteries to run small cities on the Moon and other solar system bases. They had produced Diamoond Iron generators the size of an old car battery that could power a base of fifty thousand people and last a hundred years without replacement. Purification systems were invented that never needed replacing, along with all-purpose printers that made cars, houses, tools, and furniture. The list of inventions was endless from the ingenious people of the Africany Alliance.

Early in his career someone in the Africany media had noticed that Ray's initials spelled rat, and that is what he was called. In fact, no one on his team even knew his real name, and the fans of the Africany Alliance reveled in his moniker. Ray joked to himself, *"Hey, bad publicity is better than none at all. At least they know I'm here, even as 'The Rat'!"*

Ray's minor league coach, Nelson Rimet, wasn't too impressed with Ray when he first arrived and used him mainly as a base running grunt for the stars on his minor league team. From the bench, all Ray heard was his coach saying, "Hey, Rat, you shit ass, get out there and relieve so and so on the bases." Once Ray got the hang of running the dangerous bases, he also got the knack of always using his body armor or helmet to protect himself from the vicious hits by the ball. It got to be boring for Ray, for all he did was run. But he certainly could run, and so after a while his running attracted the attention of the scouts from the Moroka Town Spurs of the Northern Africany Alliance Major League in Morocco. They wanted him to play for their team in the majors. The scouts called Nelson Rimet and told them of their intentions to draft Ray onto the Spurs in the North Africany province of Morocco as soon as possible.

Coach Nelson Rimet expressed himself none too lightly: "I want you to do good up there, Rat, because if you come back here for of a lack of performance, your bed and pillows will be made out of Alliance baseballs that I will personally turn on, and the spikes from the balls will pierce your flesh until you want to die! And before I allow you to die, you will be abandoned in the desert to be eaten by the sand lizards," he said. "You get what I mean, young man?" Rimet grinned sarcastically.

Ray looked at Rimet, smiled, and said, "Once I start running from here, Coach, I ain't ever coming back, especially if I'll be sent into the desert!"

His coach smiled his usual crooked wry smile and said in the old South African accent, "Good. Now, go up there and make me some credits, son, and don't come back."

As a team member of the Moroka Town Spurs in Morocco, Ray was used mainly for running bases, but hey, it was the majors. The job paid well and you had to start somewhere. The team was what he expected. There were guys just like him, mostly grunts used by the coach as fresh meat for the killers of the game. Ray's base running abilities kept him where he wanted to be, playing major league baseball and earning rich credits every time his team won a game. As a rookie you didn't make many friends, because they would all end up getting killed or maimed from the game. Ray did what he had to do. He got beaned hard a few times and had some close calls where he and the other runners could have all been killed on the same play, but he always managed to get through a game, taking out a few defenders in the process.

After games Ray would always frequent a bar called 'Space Junkies'. In this bar he met a young molecular genetics doctor by the name of John Ignatius Germane Stehl. His initials spelled his moniker 'JIGS', and that's what he liked to be known as.

Jigs was studying at the Gia Earth Academy of Medicine and Science in North-Am and he was on holidays in Morocco. Jigs was mildly interested in Alliance Baseball. He said that he was working on cutting edge genetic molecular manipulations that could change a man's head into a real live carved Halloween pumpkin and many other human/plant and animal manipulations, as well as breakthroughs in DNA transposin disease controls and many other physical barriers of healing that had previously been thought impossible. Jigs and Ray became good friends, meeting frequently at Space Junkies after his home games.

After his workouts and games, Ray enrolled in a few spatial sciences online and hands on, in school courses at the prestigious Gia Academy in North-Am such as radiation protection, sub-light speed ion engine designs, physics, and spaceship logistics. He got his Earth-to-Moon freight ion rocket-flying license in the off-season of baseball and took on a second job, because he didn't have a girlfriend to occupy his time. He flew high-powered freight ion rockets from Earth's orbit to the Moon and back as something to do when he wasn't playing baseball. He visited his parents on his rare days off and assured them that he would try and play baseball as safely as he could. His mother always worried enough for the both of them, so he made sure she was always placated on his visits and vid calls before he left her to play baseball.

In his travels to the Moon and back, Ray met another young man by the name of Ian Shelton on one of the space elevator platforms he was loading from on Earth. Ian, who worked as a geological astronomer/astrophysicist for the Earth Alliance Science Group. studied past and present supernova occurrences in the Milky Way as well as enhanced digital spectral analysis of many kinds of star systems and their surrounding planets for hints of Diamainium, a new super metal sought by man in his travels not on the periodic scale of elements. Ian investigated whether other materials could be garnered from distant places in the Milky Way from occurrences such as supernova events. After the supernovas exploded in the Milky Way Galaxy, Ian studied that defunct star system's spectral analysis to see if there were any materials worth developing to bring back to Earth for processing. He looked for cesium, heavy metals like iron, nickel 54, free-floating diamonds, osmium, leftover gases like oxygen, and rare Earth elements. He tried to determine if these exploded systems had flung out planets that contained fuels like ethane that could be used in the freight rockets and manufacturing on Earth. Ian was especially interested in Diamainium, the most sought-after metal by the Earth Alliance because of its power yields, but Diamainium was a rarity throughout the galaxy. These materials would be gathered by long-distance flights of star ship freighters that would be sent out by the EABVs (Earth Alliance Business Ventures). Huge ships would gather these materials for the major businesses like 3D Printing and Earth Alliance Powers Systems to be traded with other Earth-friendly systems. Trillions of tons were always in the process of being transported, and someone was always making a lot of Alliance credits because of it. Through enhanced digital spectral analysis, one could send a fleet of automated huge star ship freighters to a positively identified system that had usable materials. This was far more efficient than exploring, which was time-consuming and cost great amounts of credits. Ian was just a finder for the well to do in this respect, although he himself invested heavily and quietly in these companies that retrieved materials from supernova remnants and planetary systems. Over time, Ian had become a rather rich man.

Ian had kept a secret from EABVs. He had found a large, dense concentration of Diamainium in the Large Magellanic Cloud about a hundred and sixty-eight thousand light years from Earth. The concentrations of Diamainium was way off the charts; Ian was certain of it! He had hoped to find someone he could share this information with, for whoever got their hands on this mother lode would change the political and power-wielding course of the Earth Alliance. After Ian shared his secret with Ray, Ray let Ian know of his ambitions to own his own space shuttling company from the credits he would make when he retired from Alliance

Baseball. The two of them could go to the Large Magellanic Cloud and find out for themselves what was there.

Ray and Ian became good social friends. To make conversation, Ray would often query Ian about what was 'out there'. Ian was a bit of a geek in the sense that his work gave him solace. Ian kept to himself mostly and was a one track-minded man in his work. He liked what he did and was a sought-after astrophysicist because of his findings in enhanced digital spectral work. Ian would look at certain areas of the sky and be able to tell his business contacts, through digital spectral analysis, what was in that specific part of the Milky Way. This avoided the need to send off expensive exploratory missions that would find nothing and require expensive fuel to move on to the next system. This was how Ian had discovered his mother lode of Diamainium. Not wanting to divulge its position, he was trying to figure out a way to go, himself, to the Large Magellanic Cloud to investigate firsthand this dense concentration of Diamainium.

Ian introduced Ray to a close friend, Pamela Jay. Pamela was an Earth Alliance Council politician. Ian said she was working on trying to become an Earth Alliance Executive Member for the North-Am Alliance. Ian and Pamela had been friends since their last year of university when they were studying to become specialists in their own fields of work. Ray didn't have too much of an interest in politics, but Pamela spoke with intelligence. Plus, she was a good-looking woman. Ray did like that good-looking quality in a woman, and he thought Ian was a lucky man to have someone intelligent like Pamela around.

During Ray's third season with the Moroka Town Spurs, he got banged up pretty badly in a game against the Cape Town Swallows. His injuries were so bad that he had to sit out the last ten games of the season plus the playoffs. His hip had shattered and his neck had gotten sprained in one play, but he still managed to get to a base safely before being taken out of the game. The doctors who patched him up said it would take a couple of months for the nerves and connective tissues to heal, but he would play major league baseball again next year. When a player like Ray got hurt and had to take time off from baseball as long as he did, he had to prove to the league that he could recover and play again. Then his retirement seniority (if you will) would not suffer for his pension.

Ray got Jigs to apply some genetic variant processes to help speed up the recovery rate of his injuries.

During his recuperation period, Ray went back to his second job of piloting freight rockets from the Earth to the Moon and back. *"Can't get hurt doing that,"* Ray said to himself.

Ray's work entailed hauling loads of materials between the Earth and the Moon. On Earth, space elevators were erected to a height of fifteen thousand miles high so that freight rockets could dock in space, high above the Earth's surface. At the elevators' top platform, where Ray's ship was docked, a huge three-foot in diameter magnetic cable two miles long would be attached to his ship then to a one-million-ton-bale of garbage to the freight ion rockets that Ray would operate. Ray's operation kind of looked like the tugboats of old with one powerful but tiny looking ship pulling a huge log boom down (or up) a river to its required destination. This bale would be towed to the Moon by the freight rocket, unhooked, and deposited into a designated crater via direct dumping. Next, a one-million-ton-bale of ore concentrate, mined on the Moon, would be picked up from a space elevator at a height of twenty-five thousand miles above the surface of the Moon. The return trip would transport the metal bale to a designated space elevator on Earth. This elevator would lower the metal concentrate to the top of the Southern Launch Tower and then to the surface of Earth and the Moon, to be manufactured. You see, the Earth scientists had perfected the numbers so that Earth could process billions of tons of economic materials brought from other star systems. As well, manufactured goods would be sent out to other star systems. One million tons of waste would be sent at a time to the Moon, and one million tons of metal concentrate would be brought back to Earth. In this way, the weight transfers from the trips between the Earth and the Moon would not put the Earth's or Moon's natural orbiting weights out of balance and cause the Earth or the Moon to go out of orbit. The Moon was essentially used as a huge garbage dump because of its many deep craters, and it was also was mined for its mineral wealth. It would have cost too much to settle the Moon to any real extent, so the economically viable solution was to establish a mining colony and a garbage dump there. Since water had been found on the Moon, putting a mining colony there was easy. These round trips to the Moon and back took about two days to complete, and Ray would do two a week. This travel included getting fueled up at the elevators because the rocket's fuel was brought in by fuel freighters from other solar Jovian planets. These fuel freighters gathered fuels from planets that contained methane/ethane, just like the fuels gathered from Jupiter, Saturn, and their moons. The ionic fuel was separated from these gathered fuels and then put into the ionic engines of Ray's vehicles. Garbage was also being hauled to Mars' moons, but by faster freighter ships. The ships would return with mining concentrate. A round trip to Mars and back would take ten days. The Mars flight was too long of a run for Ray; he preferred the short trips to the Moon. Ray liked the idea of owning a business, and he told himself that someday he would either buy or start a freighter star ship business. He would do this after he was finished with Alliance Baseball, if he made it the mandatory five years to retirement. He would use the credits he had saved from baseball and his pension credits, and he would use his experiences as a ship's logistics coordinator to organize his business. He had it all planned out. Ray thought he would like to work with Ian Shelton. He especially liked the idea of operating and commanding the star ships himself. Prospecting for valuable concentrations of Diamainium would be very interesting work indeed.

One day, Ray was dozing instead of watching his approach to the South-Am Launch Tower on a return trip from the Moon. Suddenly, an alarm went off on his bridge panel, indicating that he was on a collision course with an incoming star ship! He had accidentally wandered into the star ship lanes. While he had been dozing, Ray's incoming message panel had lit up and a direct order had come through to him. Ray suddenly became aware that he was in dire trouble.

"This is second officer Nina Cutoff of the Military EASS-20 to EAFR-1313; you are in our flight path to the South Am Launch Tower. You must move out of our way in thirty seconds or my ship will hit you. Respond, EAFR-1313!" said Nina Cutoff.

Ray almost choked on the beef jerky he must have left wadded in his mouth when he was asleep. Surprised, he hit the emergency thrusters systems button and tried to make a ninety-degree turn out of the way of the incoming star ship. Well, it was too little, too late, and Ray had a problem on his hands. A star ship is huge compared to a lowly freight rocket towing a million-ton metal concentrate bale. He was on a collision course with the star ship! Ray's ship barely grazed the military star ship, but the concentrate bale that was attached to Ray's ship by a magnetic cable bounced off the stars hip's hull. The bale's chain reaction with the star ship hull made Ray's vehicle take off like a stone from a slingshot. His ship looked like a water skier being towed behind a fast-moving motorboat. Ray tried desperately to regain control of his ship and cargo, but he was light on fuel and only had enough to dock at the South-Am elevator. He needed ten times the fuel he had left to stabilize himself and his cargo and to get out of the star lanes. Ray was in deep trouble, and all he could do was watch his own inevitable destruction with eyes and mouth wide open. "Oh shit!" was all he could say, over and over.

Again, his incoming message light lit up in front of him. It was that girl from the stars hip again. "EAFR-1313, this is Nina Cutoff of the EASS-20. We will put a drag beam on your ship and cargo. Once we have you stabilized, you will report to the South Am Launch Tower and fill out a space collision report for the Control Tower management."

Ray called back to the EASS-20 and said desperately, "You had better hurry up with that drag beam, lady, I'm about to get tangled up with another freight rocket. He's fully loaded with garbage and fuel and it ain't going to be a pretty sight if we collide!"

"Do you have a chromatic suit on?" Officer Cutoff asked Ray.

"A what suit?" Ray asked.

"A chromatic suit to protect you against the 'g' forces we have to apply with the drag beam to stop you and your cargo from smashing into another freighter," answered Officer Cutoff.

Now Ray had one, but he never wore it. He'd never needed it. He had only used it once in training two years ago when he first got his freight rocket license. "I've got one, but I don't have time to put it on just now, sweetie. I need to stop right now, or there will be a big mess. Right Now!" yelled Ray. "Right Now, Right Now!" he yelled again. His ship was on top of another freight ship and was about to smash into it.

"As you wish, EAFR-1313, Drag beam being applied now," answered Nina Cutoff.

Star ships, with their huge amounts of power, could make a strong magnetic drag beam from the separated electron molecules of hydrogen atoms. In this beam, the electrons essentially had a negative attraction to the positive atoms of any object they were projected on to. In Ray's case, it was him, his ship, and his cargo, together weighing millions of tons, that were to be stopped in about a fifty-yard space, just moments before colliding with another freight rocket and its cargo. Several hundred 'G's of force were applied on Ray's body, his ship, and his cargo. The stopping of Ray's ship and cargo was like the force of being hit with a giant Alliance baseball bat. Wham!

After the drag beam was put on Ray's ship, the stopping 'G's' made him smack into his bridge's observation window. Ray's mind and body felt as if he were floating after his sudden stop. He felt like he didn't have a care in the world. He noticed that there were a lot of ringing phones inside his head, like a hundred old phones that he had seen in old movies as a boy. Burring, burriing, burring went the sounds in his muffled brain.

Next, all Ray could hear was a female voice saying, "EAFR-1313, do you need assistance? …Do you need assistance? …Assistance? …Assistance? …Assistance?" trailed off as his mind and eyes slowly faded from the reality of his ship's small bridge area to darkness.

The next thing Ray saw was a familiar looking guy who was trying to ask him his name, and how many fingers he could see, and he soon he realized this was Jigs, his doctor friend. "He's starting to come into consciousness. He'll hurt for a little while, but he will be okay," Jigs said to his assistant. Again, Ray's mind faded from reality only to wake up again with a bright light shining in his eyes. He had a terrible headache, and the rest of his body was telling him it didn't feel good either.

"You are a very lucky young man, Mr. Tenner," said the male voice. "Not many survive a drag beam term stop without wearing a chromatic suit. As a matter of fact, of the many collisions that have happened above the Earth's South-Am Launch Tower, I think you're the first survivor that I know of."

Ray tried to say something, but his tongue and voice would not work together. His words came out like baby gibberish. "Fleagy grownderded brommm cuuxt glabf," Ray tried to say.

87

"That's okay, Ray; no talking for now," Jigs said politely. "The swelling from your accident will go down in a couple of hours and you can talk then," said Jigs. "Do you remember me?" asked Jigs.

Ray focused his eyes and saw Jigs. He tried to smile, but it came off as wrinkled lips, and even that hurt. Ray tried to look around and see where he was. He knew he was in a hospital of some kind, because there were all kinds of tubes emanating from his body.

"It's not very often I get to treat a celebrity baseball player such as you, Ray, as a patient," said Jigs. "I managed to save a few hundred thousand of your body's stem and blood cells that weren't destroyed by the drag beam stop and I got them to immediately start duplicating themselves." Jigs explained his medical processes to save Ray. "After a few minutes, we had enough good cells to put back into your body so it could stabilize itself. Then, we prompted them to regenerate via the stem cells rooted in the good cells. Next, we had the regenerated cells replace your damaged body tissues. Believe me, you had a lot of damaged body tissue from the traumatic swelling you experienced from your sudden stop by the drag beam. Here, I'll show you what you looked like before we treated you. Now this is why you wear a chromatic suit, even in ion rockets. It's like the seat belt rule from a long time ago; you never know when you're going to need it," admonished Jigs.

Ray's eyes opened wide when Jigs showed him a video of what he looked like after the drag beam stop was put on his ship.

"We got to you just about two minutes after the drag beam stopped your ship. We put you on the genetic repair plate right away and then into my sick bay for immediate treatment," said Jigs. "There was no time to swab you down and pump anti-death agents into you. I had to do radical genetic replacement therapy immediately, and this is the procedure we used on you. This is the first time I've ever had to do something this radical right away."

Ray couldn't believe the sight of himself in that video with his head, hands, and feet barely visible in that round swollen ball. They were like little nodes on the bloated periphery of the smashed, swollen apple of a body that was him! Next on the screen, Ray saw a robotic nurse with about fifty hypodermic needles piercing him on the repair plate. He watched his bloated body reduce to about a fifth of its swollen size as these needles removed liquids, which were then deposited in a spinning separation chamber. The robotic nurse hooked him up to life support at the same time it was recouping retrievable genetic materials. Ray looked like an experiment from an old show called *The Good Doctor*, where high-level med internes visualized treatment and stabilizing procedures before they even happened.

"Once we got the fluids out of you from the swelling, Ray, we had a bit of a chore finding 'good' stem cells. All of your vitals were just about on flat line, but our good robotic anesthetist nurse, Nurse Nelly, kept you alive. It was touch and go with you for about a half hour, Ray, until we got you genetically repaired. You'll be up and moving about in about twenty-four hours and as good as new in about two weeks," said Jigs. "For now, you must sleep, for the genetic repairs won't work as well unless you doze off." With that said, Jigs motioned for Nurse Nelly to give Ray an intravenous shot that would put him to sleep.

Ray's sleep was a fright-filled vision of post traumatic nightmares that repeated themselves over and over again. He dreamed of his collision with the star ship, the repeated callings of the female officer, and his endless medical repairs. He screamed and yelled in his mind over and over again for help. It was like he had willingly committed himself to an inescapable torture chamber. Ray was subjected to needles, sutures, gallons of intravenous vile liquids pumped into his body, and square yards of skin applied to his body that would peel off right away. Many more frightening procedures twisted, ebbed, and flowed in his Frankenstein dreams. In his sleep he could feel the sweat pouring off of his body. His heart felt like it was going to burst, feeling like it was beating hundreds of times a minute. It seemed that his taut muscles were at a breaking point, like pulled frayed cables. All he wanted to do was collapse and give in to his unconscious pain, but he couldn't: he was trapped in a live dream.

Ray woke up to a real human nurse who told him that he had rested quietly and his recuperation had gone well. Ray just groaned and thought, *"Yeah, well, that's not how I saw it."* He asked the nurse, gingerly, "How long have I been out?"

"Oh, about two days," she answered.

Jigs came into the room and told Ray that he could leave now. He would have to take it easy for the next week to allow things to heal properly. Jigs gave Ray a skin pressure needle of antigens and said, "That will help the healing processes going on in your body while it is still repairing itself. After a week of rest, you will have to undergo a physical conditioning regimen to harden you up, and then you will be as good as new."

"Can I still play baseball, Doc?" asked Ray.

"Why, of course you can. Just make sure you go through the physical training regimen I've set out for you. No baseball for the rest of this season though until you pass the Alliance Baseball Re-Entry Medical with me. You'll be able to run a marathon after that, if you'd like," said Jigs.

A tall, strapping woman walked into the room. She wore an Earth Alliance star ship uniform and she wasn't smiling. "Doctor, is this the operator of EAFR-1313?" she asked Jigs rather pertly in a military tone.

"He is my patient, and yes, he is that operator," said Jigs, smiling at Nina.

She turned to Ray and said formally, "I'm second officer Nina Cutoff, of the EASS-20. Please sign here." She handed Ray a digitized clipboard.

"Sign what? For what?" asked Ray, surprised by Nina's forwardness.

"It's for the damages and costs you caused when you went into the star ship space lanes, including my space lane. You caused a collision that could have had catastrophic consequences for the South-Am Tower and other ships around you," she said.

Ray looked at the digital clipboard and read that he was at fault for the collision. Any and all credits in his Africany Alliance Baseball account were to be turned over to the captain of the EASS-20 Star ship immediately to pay for damages. Otherwise, he would go directly to the South-Am stockade for processing.

"Those are all the credits I've got! I'll be broke! Those are all the credits I've made over the last three years playing baseball! You can't do this to me; I'll be broke and have nothing!" said Ray, incredulous. "I've got plans, a business to run, and you can't take that away from me. I've worked too hard for the things I've got. I have rights, I have…" Ray tried to shout, but Nina Cutoff cut off Ray's verbal expulsions and firmly said,

"You're lucky we don't put you in the South-Am stockade right now, Mr. Tenner. My boss, Captain Smiths, said it was only a minor bump and that I did the right thing to get you stopped. It's the law and rules you broke that are costing so much, and someone has to pay. Would you rather be broke now, or have money and be in the stockade for the next ten years fighting a space lanes lawsuit? And then you'd be broke anyway when you got out," reasoned Nina. "If you refuse to sign now, I'm authorized to take you, by force if necessary, directly to the stockade," she threatened.

"Yeah, well, I'd like to see you try," said Ray glaring at Nina. "I'm not signing anything." Disgusted, he threw the digital clipboard onto Jig's medical table where it bounced up off of it, almost hitting Nina in the chest.

Nina moved forward without hesitation and said to Ray, "Have it your way, Mr. Tenner." She grabbed Ray and gave him a shoulder throw over her tall frame. Ray landed flat on his back in the bed he had just gotten out of with a loud thump.

"Hey hey, easy there, Miss Cutoff. You'll undo a lot of good work I've done in the past seventy-two hours that I want to get paid for," said Jigs.

Nina ignored Jigs and said, "One more chance, rocket man. Sign, or I'll drag you away to the stockade." Nina clamped down on Ray's neck and arm with a judo submission move.

Ray hadn't fully realized how banged up he was until he landed on the bed. He couldn't even stop a woman from pushing him around, and he knew it. He said quickly, "Gimme the goddammed clipboard." He groaned and winced in pain as Nina let him go.

As soon as Ray signed the digital clipboard, Nina snatched it away, turned, and walked out the door without saying another word. Click, clomp, click, clomp went her standard issue boots on the hard-marbled floor, her bottom wiggling vigorously as she left.

Ray looked at Jigs and asked, "Who the heck is that brutal, good-looking woman who just clobbered me?"

"That, my friend, is Nina Cutoff: the toughest second officer in the Earth Alliance Star ship Fleet. You couldn't meet a nicer person when you're on her good side," chuckled Jigs. "Also, she is the only woman to play on an Alliance Baseball minor league farm team right here in North-Am. She could have turned pro, but she liked operating star ships better. 'They treat you better, the ships that is, and they always do what you tell them to do, unlike men,'" said Jigs, quoting Nina.

Changing the subject, Ray asked Jigs why he hadn't applied to work as a baseball doctor in the Earth Alliance Baseball Leagues. Jigs could earn a more lot credits helping a baseball team's injured players than he would earn by working for the government. Jigs said that he was on contract with the Earth Alliance Council because they were having a lot of trouble with exotic, interstellar, diseases that the explorers were getting in their travels. His expertise in genetic molecular altering was needed to help stop human explorers from getting these diseases, bringing them back to Earth, and passing them onto healthy people. Discovering cures for the maladies would take up most of his time. He was working on viable research that would result in breakthrough healing for all involved.

Thanking Jigs for his services, Ray said that he would pay him when he got back to playing Alliance Baseball in the upcoming season and when he had money in the bank. Jigs asked for Ray's autograph and said to keep in touch. Keep in touch they did, for Ray went to Jigs for bodily repairs several more times over his career in baseball. They remained good friends, as the future would attest.

With his fine paid, Ray went back to regular duty as a pilot for the Earth-to-Moon garbage runs. He took a quick crash course on chromatic suits and their benefits. Wearing one was just like getting used to a seat belt. Once it was on, you didn't even know it was there!

CHAPTER FIVE
A FAMILIAR MEETING WITH A BAD ENDING

AFTER HIS ENCOUNTER WITH NINA CUTOFF FROM THE EARTH Alliance Star ship Fleet and his subsequent physical recuperation, Ray felt a little depressed. To cheer himself up, he decided to call his parents and tell them he was coming home for a rare visit. He had some spare time, since he couldn't play Alliance Baseball until the next season. His mom and dad were ecstatic. In Ray's three years away since he started playing professional baseball, Ray had come home a total of only four times. Talking via vid phone was not the same, as there was no physical contact. Ray's visit meant a lot, especially to his mother.

At home, Ray got the royal treatment from his 'retired' parents. He didn't tell them he was now broke following his encounter with a star ship at the South-Am Launch Tower, because he didn't want to burst their bubble of financial well-being. Before Nina Cutoff had confiscated the remainder of his baseball savings, Ray had made sure that his parents would have enough credits to last them for at least another ten years. Ray's mom and dad were only in their seventies, and had at least another seventy years or so to go before they passed from this Earth. They had a long retirement ahead of them, and so Ray needed to get more credits for them as soon as he started playing baseball again. Ray had wished to give them the retirement they always wanted, so that they could travel the solar system and view the interplanetary sights they had always wanted to see before they were too old to do so.

Ray's mom informed him that Dean, Lenny, and Boisey were also home, visiting their parents at the same time as Ray.

Ray told himself, *"Think on the positive side. The boys I grew up playing baseball with are in town. It's been more than three years since I've seen them. I can forget my credit woes for now and have some good clean fun with Dean, Lenny, and Boisey."* Ray had heard through the grapevine that his three friends were now stars in their respective leagues. After dinner with his parents, Ray called up Lenny, then went to visit him next door at his house, where they used to play as children.

Lenny was waiting for Ray in his back yard, just like 'old times'. They exchanged cordial greetings with each other, but Ray couldn't help but wonder at the eerily familiar scene. Ray looked over at the yard next door, the Luthberts' place. The blue electronic fence still separated the Peecheh's yard from the Luthberts' yard. "Where's Two Wheel?" Lenny asked, looking for his dog of old as if his childhood companion was supposed to be here.

"What's going on, Lenny?" Ray asked. Then it happened: out walked the mature Boisey from the back-door of his house. Boisey stopped and just stared at Lenny and Ray with the same blank stare he had worn fourteen years earlier when they had first met. Boisey had the same original 'Alliance Baseball' in his hand; his mother had saved it for him. Boisey walked up to the electronic fence to face Lenny and Ray. "Where's your funny dog?" Boisey asked.

Seeing the ball in Boisey's hand, Lenny, on cue, echoed the past, "Bet you can't throw that ball over this fence."

"Bet you ah can," said Boisey, in a much deeper manly voice that kind of put Lenny and Ray on alert. "My brother is the best throwing third baseman in the Hyder league, and I can throw almost as good as he can." Boisey threw the ball over the fence. It landed at Lenny's feet, just like before, and Lenny picked it up. There was no Two Wheel to bark at Boisey. Lenny was about to say "Nice shot, Bozo," just like before, but before Lenny could get the words out, Boisey switched off the electronic fence between the yards and tackled both Lenny and Ray to the ground.

"Only this time I don't need my big brother to help me get my ball back from you bozos," said Boisey, laughing. He had pinned both Ray and Lenny down to the ground with his much bigger frame. Boisey said, "I wish Two Wheel were here to help us out."

Dean then entered the scene, on cue, and repeated the same words he had said fourteen years prior: "What's going on, Boisey? What's going on, bro?"

"He's got my ball, Dean, that I threw over the fence, but I thinks I can get it back without your help this time, bro," said Boisey, smiling. He got up, and the three of them dusted themselves off with Dean looking happily at them.

All of the boys were glad to see each other. They marveled at how much they had each changed from teenaged boys to grown young men, deep voices and all. The guys talked for hours about old times playing in the Hyder Minor Leagues in their younger years and of all the jokes they had played on each other. Boisey admonished Lenny for the Sheila incident, and Lenny promised he wouldn't pull any jokes on Boisey while they were together for this short time.

They talked about the possibility that they might have to play against each other one day. "Well, we'll just have to cross that bridge when we get to it, eh guys?" said Dean. "I wouldn't like to be in that position, but we as professionals have to play the game as it is meant to be played. I sure as hell wouldn't want to be taking out even my brother Boisey here, but if I had to, I would. Don't worry, Boisey; I'd only hit you in the butt, though," said Dean laughingly. Lenny and Ray gave a quick laughing grunt to Dean's rhetorical joke, but each of them agreed they would try to spare each other, if possible, in the event they did meet on the ball field in their future.

"I've got an idea, guys. Let's go riding in the dunes," suggested Ray. "I hear they have the latest dune buggy models down south in Red Deer at the northern edge of the global desert here in North-Am. The newest buggies are armed with mounted fifty-caliber machine guns and Terra-watt lasers. They are rocket-powered now. They can even operate in sandstorms because they don't need oxygen. The cabs are completely enclosed with spare fresh air. These new models are much safer in the face of sand lizards and storms than the old gas-powered, open rattletraps our parents used to rent for us. How about it, guys, are we on?" Ray asked.

They all agreed that they would take a gravi-plane together the next day to the ball arena near the city of Red Deer (in Mid-Central old Canada) where the southern entrances to the dunes were situated.

Going on to the dunes was a very popular pursuit for the adventurous, but there were huge, dangerous sand lizards living in and around the ring forests that separated the deserts from the arable land of North-Am. Sand lizards, though few and far between out into the dunes, were ready to attack anything that moved in their domain.

The sand lizards had been brought to Earth from another planetary system to help prevent the advancement of the deserts on Earth due to unchecked 'global' warming. These lizards were specifically bred for extreme desert conditions. The large lizards hunted each other for food, and fed on leaves which had dropped from the tall trees or anything else that happened to stray their way. They would also eat the seeds of the huge protecting trees. The lizard dung was super fertile in that it made the trees grow quickly, close together, and to a very large size when the seeds were passed through the sand lizard's digestive system. To the lizards, humans were like a hamburger without the bun, and much tastier than bland tree materials or other lizards.

Large sand tornadoes were the other danger out in the dunes. The sand tornadoes could bury a buggy in one hundred feet of suffocating sand in minutes, or fling it high into the air and carry it for hundreds of miles out into the ever more dangerous dunes, thereby making rescue difficult. Large boulders were a dangerous part of the sandstorms, as they would be flung up into the tornadoes and wreak even more damage to anything they were slammed into.

The large trees functioned as a barrier to the global desert, and also stopped the sand lizards. They were essentially a wall between the arable land/people and the deserts. The trees grew close together to over seventeen hundred feet high, and they contained the dust and sand that was constantly on the move from the hot winds that were created from the relentless heat of the sun onto the sand. The trees protected what living space that man had left on the Earth from the all-encompassing sand, sand lizards, and killing heat.

To enter the dunes there was a reinforced, underground, ceramic-alloyed tunnel which had been built underneath the three-mile thick forests' roots for safe, easy access to the desert. The trees grew so close together that humans could not walk through them. Only the lizards could, the smaller ones that is. The smaller lizards crawled and hid in the forests from their bigger nemeses on the sands. The smaller lizards could multiply in the safety of the trees. The bigger lizards could not move around in the thick trees because of their size. Instead, they patrolled the inner desert while the trees keep them penned in from the human encampments on the other side of the forest.

The big sand lizards were about fifty feet long, stood approximately ten feet high on all fours, and weighed in at ten tons or more. They could run up to sixty miles-per-hour in about two or three bounds, and they could endure over a mile at that speed without tiring. Some lizards were even larger and faster. There were millions of small lizards in the forests, but only the large ones lived on the dry sand. They foraged as far as fifty miles out in the open hot desert. They survived the midday heat by burrowing deep into the sand for protection.

When a large sand lizard reached maturity, and could no longer move freely in the protecting forests, it would venture out into the desert and challenge bigger males in a 'to the death' fight to try and take over their territories. The loser would be ripped to shreds and eaten by his vanquisher. Other lizards that happened to be in the area of dispute would eat up the vanquished remains once the winner had his fill.

This happened many times on a daily basis, as there were millions of medium-sized lizards reaching maturity every day in the forests. By day, the huge lizards either buried themselves, traveled slowly, or slept in the sand to protect themselves from the baking sun. At dusk, when things cooled down, they would emerge from the sand and turn into nocturnal terrors. Their smaller male siblings were always trying to get at the females that frequented the inner edges of the ring forests. The larger males were always trying to mate with the females, who would only venture out into the sand areas when they wanted to mate. If a sandstorm came up during the day, however, the big lizards will emerge from the sand to prowl the forest's edge under cover of the blowing sand. They would hunt for the smaller venturesome males. The larger lizards were territorial, had an acute sense of smell, and would viciously attack each other if they met at each others boundaries. The younger males that lived in the forests would constantly compete with each other, even driving each other out into the openness of the sand desert where their larger counterparts would eat them. Females were allowed to move freely about near the inside of the forest edges and were somewhat protected by the huge males lingering there, though if there were more than five or six females together, they would attack in unison and eat the younger males who were trying to mate with them. Sand lizards were not a very forgiving breed of animal when it came to their own survival. Even the large males had to be wary of injury by females, as it would mean a quicker death if they could not defend themselves properly.

On the outside of the protecting forests, where man lived, a large, fortified, electrified heavy duty alloyed chain fence, fifty feet high, was used to contain any lizards that may stray in search of human food or domesticated livestock. A clayon robotic military patrol constantly moved up and down the fences to stop any lizards if they should get over the fence or though it into where the human populations are. On rare occasions, a large lizard would happen to crash the fence, get through, and use its quick speed. If it couldn't immediately be stopped by the clayon robots, then there would be chaos, for the lizards preferred human meat to most anything else. At times, and this was a rare occasion also, a huge tornado-sized sandstorm would send the sand hundreds of feet high over the forests in narrow lane ways, burying the trees and protecting fences. These conditions would allow the huge male lizards, from the inner desert, to cross over the buried forests on these sand lane ways to encroach on human settlements. When the sand buried the forests, patrol gravi-copters, equipped with the latest in warfare ordinance, were sent to make sure the large lizards did not get into human settlements. New fences were immediately erected in front of the overrun forests for human protection, and the smaller lizards were allowed to roam this new open sand area. The smaller lizards would deposit their dung, which contained seeds from the forest's trees, on the new sand. Large amounts of water were poured onto the new sand areas from space freighters, and in a year or two the forest would recover with huge high trees as if the blown sand had never even been there.

Now the tunnels under the forests to the dunes were situated near the baseball arenas that were also near the dunes, because it was convenient for business owners to rent out sand dune buggies as well as run their baseball parks. Between games, the arena owners made their livelihood by renting sand dune buggies to locals and tourists alike. Many people derived enjoyment and thrills from being in a dangerous place while ninety-five percent protected by technology.

Our four friends, Ray, Dean, Boisey, and Lenny, showed up just before sunrise at the arena venue. Each rented a new, sleek, state-of-the-art dune buggy. These new buggies were modern technical marvels. They had large, fifteen-foot-high, thick, monster rubber tread tires, lizard-proof struck glass, and a light but powerful twelve-cylinder, two thousand horsepower, water/hydrogen drive engine for the get up and go needed on the desert sands. There was emergency rocket power to get from point 'A' to 'B' in a hurry, and all the bells and whistles like GPS, AC, sunblock bubble glass, fleet radio contact, automatic 'home' cruise, automatic one fifty caliber repeating weapons, and many more options to rave about. There was even a fridge, with all of the drinks and snacks one could ever want.

"Today we have an extra high heat warning where there is a likelihood of possible sand tornado because of the unsettled weather conditions out there in the dunes. It is ten degrees above normal at over a hundred and sixty degrees Fahrenheit out in the open rock-strewn dunes. So, if you boys see a sand tornado or I call you guys because I have one on my screens, you get the hell back here right away, got that? I pay high enough insurance premiums without losing a buggy because of someone's stupid mistake," said the rental owner. "If you don't come back when I call you, then I'll call the South-Am Tower. They'll pick you up with a drag beam ship and bring you right to the stockade where you'll sit and rot for a month if you don't pay me; got it, guys?"

"Wow man, chill out. We just came for some fun, not to be chewed out by the likes of you!" said Dean. "We'll be careful and get your toys back to you before they get too used up," added Dean, smiling like a sly fox with his super white teeth grinning at the dune buggy owner.

Dean paid for everything. "My treat," he said, to Ray's relief, as Ray did not want to be embarrassed about his financial woes, and he did not want to have to put all this fun on credit. The boys had a quick snack at the arena cafe, then got suited up for their day of fun.

Hydrogen/water-fueled engines, huge tires, and bigger egos were the norm of the day. Boisey had the lead foot as usual, and roared off ahead of the other three. He laughed into his mic, saying, "See you pokes later." He sent a plume of sand out the dune entrance hundreds of yards long. The others waited for the dust to settle from Boisey's exuberance and then went through the entrance together in a little slower fashion.

"Hey Boisey, you gonna run out of gas again like last time?" laughed Ray into his mic.

"Nope, that'll be Dean this time," laughed Boisey.

The desert south of Red Deer had mountaintops sticking out of the sand, much like the ones that stuck out in the old pictures of 'glacial Greenland'. They were actually the tops of the 'Lower Rocky Mountain Ranges' that extended right from North-Am down to South-Am Andes, buried in the sand!

The guys used these mountain tops to gauge their speed and distance. They had their fun cutting each other off or seeing who could get around these mountaintops the fastest in an all-out speed-fest to their predetermined GPS point at the end of their race. After about an hour of hooligan driving, they decided to stop and stretch their legs in the hot shade of a protruding mountain peak. Each grabbed a 'Hyderized drink'. They played the old game of rock, paper, scissors out in the hot dry desert air to see who would have to guzzle half of their 'Hyderizer' first. In turn, they each had to pay the penalty of taking a drink at certain points in their rock, paper, scissors drinking game.

While the boys had played this drinking game before, they somehow went just a little too far this time and inebriation began to cloud their judgment.

Lenny began with the teasing (which he had said he wouldn't do) and said to Boisey, "You want me to see if I can find a female lizard for ya, Boisey ole boy?"

"Yeah," laughed Dean. "You're a little bigger and wider than before. You should be able to handle one easily, eh bro? Ha, ha, ha!"

Boisey retorted, "If you can take me now, then I'll take the lizard later, Lenny." Now Dean wanted to get back at Boisey for embarrassing him at home in front of his mother and father, so he jumped on Boisey's back when he wasn't looking. Next, Lenny dove at Boisey's feet, knocking him to the ground. Ray came over with a half-full bottle of 'Hyderizer' and quickly poured some of it into Boisey's opened protesting mouth. After the three of them had the immobilized, gagging Boisey subdued, Boisey begged for mercy, and they let him go. Boisey was still sputtering for air. Ray ran over to Boisey's dune buggy and relived himself by urinating on Boisey's tire. Lenny ran over to the other side and did the same. Ray climbed up onto Boisey's dune buggy and opened the canopy.

"You guys always pick on me!" fumed Boisey, wavering and inebriated in front of his dune buggy. "Well, I'm going to make you guys pay for your fun. Ray, you get away from my buggy!"

ordered Boisey. Things seemed to be getting out of hand now for our four friends.

Ray laughed, got down off of Boisey's buggy, and said, "Ah, come on, Boisey; it was fun, and you know it."

In the distance the sky began to turn brown and darken. Suddenly the radios of each of their buggies belched out a warning: "Hey guys! You four ball players get into your vehicles and get the hell back here, now! There's a big sand tornado heading your way and you've only got about sixty seconds before it runs you over. Move, move, move!" shouted the owner over the dune buggies' radios.

Well, this was a first, as the four boys had never contended with a sand tornado before. The situation went from hot and clear to hot, windy, and dusty in about thirty seconds after receiving the warning call from the owner.

Dean thought he saw Ray jump off of Boisey's dune buggy in the dusty air, but he couldn't be sure who it was.

"Quick, Boisey, into your buggy," said Dean, trying to help his drunken brother into his dune buggy. "Here, I'll set it to automatic return, Boisey; you don't have to do anything. The buggy will get you back to the tunnel by itself. You hear me, bro?"

Boisey looked up at Dean with a drunken smile and said, "Sure, bro, anything for you." Within seconds, the wind picked up to over fifty miles an hour. The sand tornado, which wasn't very far off, made a howling sound like a giant wolf on steroids. Large walled sheets of sand began to swirl with the driving wind.

Buffeted by the hot gritty winds of the sand tornado, Dean jumped off of Boisey's buggy and ran to his own dune buggy as fast as he could, while trying to keep the stifling sand out of his eyes and lungs. The winds were getting stronger by the second. Ray took off first, and Lenny was right behind him. Lenny paused momentarily to let his dune buggy shield Dean from the ever-increasing sand tornado winds. This allowed Dean to just make it into his dune buggy. He took off using the emergency rocket power, heading for the tunnel entrance several hundred miles away. Lenny waited until Dean was underway, punched his emergency rockets, and followed him along with Ray. The storm was moving at about a hundred and fifty miles an hour. The only way the guys could get back to the tunnels in the blinding sand of the storm was to use their GPS to retrace their way back. They had to avoid running into the hidden mountain tops. It was a harrowing return ride. Instead of going straight back to the tunnel entrance, the dune buggies went on the zigzag racing route the guys had taken on their way out to the 'fun' spot, this time at much faster speeds.

But when the dune buggies finally made it to safety at the other side of the dune entrance, there were only three of them. Dean yelled into his mic, "Boisey, where are you?"

The owner of the dune buggies came out and said that he had tracked all of them. He said, "Three of yous came the right way, but one went into the storm. I tried to contact him, to tell him he was heading the wrong way. All I got was a bunch of loud garble. Then I heard several loud smashes and he went off of the radar."

Dean, very angry, said to Ray, "Hey Rat, just what the hell did you do to my brother's dune buggy?" Dean pointed his finger accusingly at Ray.

"I didn't do anything; I just made sure that Boisey's cab was open when the storm got near us so he could get in quicker. You were the one who helped him get in the buggy!" said Ray, defending himself from Dean's accusations.

The owner, who was also agitated, looked at Dean and asked, "Who's going to pay for the buggy that's lost? My insurance doesn't cover me for storm-related losses!"

Dean ignored the owner and continued to accuse Ray. "I saw you up on Boisey's buggy. What the hell did you do to make his rig go back into the storm?" Dean asked, moving menacingly towards Ray.

"Nothing," Ray said. "Nothing," he repeated as he backed away from Dean.

The owner had called security while Dean and Ray were arguing. Security separated Ray and Dean as they were near blows. The security team asked the dune buggy owner what had happened. Lenny was strangely quiet through the security man's questions, and he left without saying anything to the other boys except that he was sorry for what had happened. Meanwhile, Dean and Ray were embroiled in a heated argument over Boisey's disappearance. Ray kept saying that he had done nothing wrong, and that maybe Boisey had taken manual control of his dune buggy in his inebriated state and drove it into the storm, disorientated, because of the booze he had consumed. Dean retorted that he had set the GPS rockets for Boisey's dune buggy to return back to the tunnel entrance. He was positive he had set Boisey's dune buggy on automatic homing with his GPS on.

In the end, the security team recorded their stories. Dean couldn't prove that Ray had done anything wrong, and Boisey's disappearance was deemed an accident. The sand tornado had most likely claimed Boisey's life. A search by gravi-copter would be sent out once the area was safe and clear of the sandstorm, beginning at the point where Boisey's dune buggy went off the owner's radar screen.

Dean told Ray, "You killed Boisey, and I'm going to kill you if I ever get the chance. I'll make sure it's on the baseball field. You just wait and see, Rat; I'll get you." Dean was still yelling as security led Dean and Ray in opposite directions.

Ray was still feeling the effects of the 'Hyderizing' liquor they had consumed while out on the dunes. He went to a local pub in Red Deer, not believing what had happened to his friend Boisey. His childhood friend Dean, Boisey's brother, had accused him of Boisey's death. Ray got sloshed at the bar in Red Deer, all the while hearing Dean's voice echoing in his drunken brain, *"You killed Boisey, Rat, and I'm going to kill you!"*

"I didn't do anything. What am I going to do?" Ray asked himself. *"Dean doesn't believe me. I don't know if Lenny saw anything. I don't know what happened."* Ray began to sob at the break up of his friendship with Dean and for the death of Boisey. He wondered why Lenny had left without talking to him. The world had turned topsy turvy once again, and Ray didn't know what to do. *"There must have been some kind of glitch or mistake; there had to be!"* Ray thought to himself. Soon, Ray's vision was absorbed by a female face that he had sidled up to and that was the last thing Ray remembered that night.

CHAPTER SIX
A CLIMBING RAGE

DEAN BECAME A VERY ANGRY AND DETERMINED MAN AFTER Boisey's disappearance from their dune buggy expedition in the global desert at Monterrey in North-Am, with his so-called friends. He made it his new mission to get the Rat, Ray Aloyisius Tenner. Dean thought Boisey's death was Ray's doing, yet there was something unexplained that still nagged at Dean about the day Boisey disappeared. He had recurring dreams about who was where at the moment when the sand tornado came speedily upon them. In his dreams Dean always tried to get to Boisey's cab to set him on a safe course, but he could never be satisfied that Boisey would come back to Monterrey. His dreams always showed that there was something on Boisey's cab, a shadow of someone familiar to Dean that would always steer Boisey out into the raging sandstorm. But Dean, in his gut, knew it was Ray that had done the unthinkable by sending Boisey on a reverse course to his death. It was shown in the investigation that Boisey's GPS was set at exactly one hundred and eighty degrees off of the automatic homing signal. Dean was certain that Ray had done this. He knew that Boisey had not been in the best of shape, for they had consumed a lot of alcohol that day. Had the homing device been set properly, the buggy's homing device would have automatically brought Boisey's dune buggy back to safety at the tunnel entrance. Boisey would have survived the killer sand tornado that carried him and his buggy hundreds of miles away. The tornado literally tore Boisey's dune buggy apart, for the sand tornado had carried within it large boulders that acted like a grinding mill. No device, except a twenty-foot-thick titanium wall, could stand up to a torrid sand tornado's barrage and the rocks it carried. Boisey's body was never found, even though he had worn a homing device. It was thought that the great sand lizards were responsible for his disappearance, because lizard tracks had been found around the remains of Boisey's wrecked dune buggy.

Dean went back to training camp with his team Pelotas, in the city of Porte Allegra in the South-Am Alliance's Eastern Baseball League district. Dean played hard, he got along with his teammates, and he stayed out of the media spotlight so he could focus his attention on getting his team to the World Alliance Baseball Series Finals. There, in the finals, Dean had a feeling that he would run into Ray Tenner. He would finish him off, legally, once and for all in an official Alliance Baseball game. Dean's name and passion for vicious play became known in the South-Am leagues, and he once again became a wildly popular player. His fans adored him, just as they had when he played in the Euro-Russo Alliance League.

Dean's coach, Carlos Vieira, saw to it that Dean was a continually protected man in the game because of his dedicated play on the field. Dean put a lot of credits in his coach's bank account because of his style of play. This was Dean's fourth year in the major leagues. Dean knew that if he could make it another year, he would have a rich pension from Alliance Baseball. But in his enraged heart he knew that wasn't possible until his wanting of revenge had been settled. Ray Aloyisius Tenner had to die!

Dean followed the play of Ray's team, the Morouka Town Spurs, from the Africany Alliance League in Western Morocco. He found that Ray's team floundered somewhat. They never seemed to get very high in league standings or even to the finals. Dean had the feeling that he wouldn't face Ray in a game any time soon unless both of their respective teams made it to the Alliance Baseball World Series Finals. Dean worried nervously that Ray would probably get killed or retire before Dean could exact his revenge.

Dean began an undercover process using his financial prowess to influence certain people in the game of baseball. To try and get Ray and his team closer to him, he began bribing low-paid league officials in the Africany Alliance Leagues who were involved in the league drafts and trades. He bribed them to get better players on to Ray's team so that the odds of them meeting in a game at the World Series Finals would become a reality. Dean also ensured that Ray became a more protected player through offering bribes to Ray's coaches. Dean wanted the pleasure of killing Ray himself. It wasn't the winning of the World Series that Dean wanted; it was Ray's life. Only vengeance for his brother Boisey's life would satisfy his hungry anger!

Dean's first move was to get in touch with Ray's coach of the Morouka Town Spurs, Nelson Rimet, to see if he would bite on the large amounts of credits that Dean dangled in front of him. Rimet's team wasn't giving him very many wins. Dean's public personae had brought him great financial gains, and he now used it as a weapon to get what he wanted. Once Dean started his web of deceit and saw that it would work, he became tireless at trying to fix baseball so that he could meet Ray in a future game and kill him on the field of play.

Ray, on the other hand, had noticed that things were mysteriously going well for him in the Africany Alliance Baseball League, but he never suspected that Dean was behind it. Dean covered his devious financial tracks very well. Ray's team, the Spurs, was getting better by the month. They were climbing in their league's standings because of Dean's illegal bribery. A good crop of new players had come in from the Africany Minor Leagues. Ray enjoyed the luxury of getting to hit while being relieved from running duty on the dangerous bases. He even enjoyed a rare visit with his mom and dad back home in North-Am during a lull in seasonal play. All the while, Dean was in the background, quietly pulling the strings to make these progressions happen for Ray. Dean was slowly drawing Ray to him, like a spider inching towards its prey on the web that it spins.

But then things took an unexpected turn for the worse for Dean when Nelson Rimet passed on from this world due to old age. The new coach of the Morouka Town Spurs, Rex Thembi, didn't want Dean's bribes, nor did he want all of the accompanying controversy. On a Q-Phone private channel Rex Thembi told Dean that if he persisted in trying to bribe him or anyone else on his team, he would expose him, and that would be the end of Dean's quest for Ray. As time went on, the better-quality players were no longer sent to Ray's team, and the Spurs soon went down in their league standings. The good players who remained were being killed off on the field of play. Even Dean's credits couldn't keep up with the financial burden of getting better players onto Ray's team. Dean found that his chances of getting at Ray, in a game, were dwindling. His bribes were not working anymore. Dean reasoned that a plot to kill Ray outright, outside of the game, would surely be discovered, for the leagues around the Earth were closely watched for these kinds of actions by league officials.

Players killing each other off the field as vendettas was a big no-no. Alliance officials vehemently frowned upon these types of killings. If it was discovered in any way that a player had tried to kill another player off the field because of an on-field dispute, then the offending player was disbarred from the league and all of their years of credit winnings were confiscated. If caught, Dean would be made a poor man by the league of governors who would confiscate all of his economic accounts. He would be left with a lifelong court battle to prove himself innocent. The ensuing jail term would be another consequence of his action.

So, killing Ray off the field was not an option. Instead, Dean employed another strategy. Even though the tragic event which had turned Dean against Ray had occurred off of the field, Dean made Ray's demise his on-field passion. He would use Lenny, Ray's best friend, to get the three of them to meet in a game in the future. Lenny was Dean's lure to get Ray. This would mean Dean would have to get Lenny and Ray on the same team as soon as possible. Dean set into motion a rifle-like maze of cunning and deceit, and he was the bullet!

Lenny now played for the Perth Roaring Jets in the old state of Western Australia on the west coast of that large, arid, island continent. Dean sent complimentary salutations to Lenny's coach, Brett Cahill, and a credit bundle equaling a year of the coach's salary to his bank account. Coach Brett Cahill was pleasantly surprised that someone would be interested and willing to pay for a medium grade player like Lenny Peecheh. Coach Cahill took the bribe and kept the undercover actions of Dean's solicitations quiet. Dean continued to spin his web of deceit again to try and draw Ray Tenner, The Rat, closer to him. He would use Lenny Peecheh, Ray's best friend, to exact his revenge.

Dean wanted Lenny and Ray to play together because he knew that they would play harder if they were on the same team, just like old times in the Hyder Minor Leagues when all four of them played together as kids and teenagers. So, Dean set about getting Lenny traded first, and then Ray, to the same North-Am team. This process began to exhaust the financial prowess of Dean's economic holdings. It took the entire playing year, but Dean managed to persuade the Bafana Chiefs' coach, Coach Rex Thembi from Ray's team, and Coach Brett Cahill from Lenny's team to trade Ray and Lenny to the North-Am team called The Labrador Redmen, from the Eastern League of the North-Am Alliance. The old city of Goose Bay was home to the Labrador Redmen, and it was still a fly zone for the Earth Alliance military of North-Am. After some expensive arm-twisting, Dean finally got Rex Thembi and Brett Cahill to come into his web of misfortune. To his great satisfaction, he spun the enclosing web that would lead Ray the Rat to him.

Now that Dean had Lenny and Ray on the same team, he began working even harder to get his team, Pelotas from South-Am, into the Alliance Baseball World Series finals by racking up win after win. Dean would consistently kill ten or more players a game in his regular season play. Dean's play on the field inspired his teammates to do the same by playing better and more aggressively, no matter who got terminated. The Pelotas climbed to the top of its league's standings in the South-Am Alliance Leagues. Dean's team went on to win both the South-Am finals as well as the Alliance Major League World Series championship that year. Unfortunately, Ray and Lenny's team did not make it that far. But Dean was patient. He knew that Ray and Lenny would eventually find a way to win, just like the old days when they played together on the Hyder Barmen minor league teams. Dean was sure they would meet at the end of the next upcoming season.

During the off-season Ray and Lenny started what would become their own local solar and interstellar transportation company with Ian Shelton. They studied the markets, looked at loans for purchasing ships, went over the personnel lists of the people that they would employ, and asked Pamela Jay, Ian Shelton's friend, about the political and governmental hurdles of making an upstart business of star goods transportation a success. Pamela Jay said that the governmental regulations shouldn't be a problem for them, but she warned that Ricardo Narzani would be a tough cookie to deal with. Narzani controlled most of the space transportation businesses associated with the Earth Alliance. The mouse-sized business of Ray and Lenny would be up against the elephantine juggernaut of Narzani's. Ricardo Narzani could quickly drive them out of business. However, Ray and Lenny weren't fazed by Narzani's political power. They knew they could be more efficient than Narzani. They could slowly win over customers with more personal attention. One-on-one meetings with customers would provide reassurance that their transportation company was the better choice for goods transported with cheaper prices and better service. They tried to convince their clientele that they as a company could grow to rival Narzani over time.

The new baseball season was Dean's sixth and Ray's fifth year playing Alliance Major League Baseball, the years they could officially retire if they made it to the end of the playing season. It was Lenny's seventh year. Boisey would have been in his fourth year, if he hadn't lost his life in the desert dune buggy accident. Dean added this fact to his revenge portfolio of Ray Tenner.

Lenny hadn't retired after his fifth year, because he wasn't married and had nothing to retire to. He played on, while knowing the dangers of continued play in the Alliance Major Leagues. Dean had now played five years in the Majors, and he could have retired if he wanted to, but he wouldn't. Dean played on, knowing deep down that he would find a way to get to Ray in the upcoming season.

Now Dean knew that Ray and Lenny liked their women on their off days, and so he set about hiring women who could get close to Lenny and Ray. This way Dean's female plants could follow Lenny's and Ray's actions more closely through video and audio recording devices. Dean could fine-tune his plans of getting Ray and Lenny to play against him as they cajoled with their women friends. The season stretched on, and both teams performed exceptionally well — so well that Ray and Lenny felt that they could make it to the World Alliance Baseball Series finals with the Labrador Redmen.

Dean had employed the use of a certain Alliance politician by the name of Ricardo Narzani whom he had met many times before when he was playing for the Bremen Gyor Titans in the Euro-Russo League. Dean wanted Narzani to help him pull some strings in his quest to get Ray. For this purpose, Dean used the military's highly secretive 'Uncertainty Principle' of communicating. This is what was called a 'Quanta-Phone' lent to him by Ricardo Narzani, borrowed secretly by Narzani from the Earth Alliance Government. If it was discovered that Dean was fixing games, he would be thrown out of baseball, lose ninety-five percent of his accredited wealth, go to jail, be disbarred from any events connected to 'Alliance Baseball', and have all records of his play deleted from the history of the game. This was indeed a very steep price to pay if he was caught in his quest to get Ray Tenner. The Quanta-Phone was Dean's secret line to the crooked politician, Ricardo Narzani. It was Dean's perfect instrument of deceit to get to Ray.

This uncertainty principle of communicating, called quantum entanglement, was the only method ever invented by man that could not be eavesdropped. As soon as any kind of listening or spying was initiated, the communication wave on the quanta-phone, in that specific connection, would collapse and the spying party would be left without a single shred of evidence that a call had even taken place. While the would-be eavesdropper wouldn't even know where the signal had originated or where it had gone, the eavesdropper could be tracked. If caught listening to a government call, the offending eavesdropper would be charged with treason. Treason warranted the death penalty as imposed by the Earth Alliance Government. This type of communication could be done over very long distances, even across the galaxy, almost instantaneously, and not be detected or recorded in any way. So, Dean could spy on or talk to anyone he wanted, whenever he wanted, with impunity, just so long as his political contact, Narzani, didn't spill the beans about his inquisitive ways. Ricardo Narzani would use every means at his disposal to get the upper hand on anyone so that he could run any of his operations with an ace in every hole he dug. Narzani could turn the tide on anyone he was in collusion with, know he would not be blamed for the electronic 'wiretapping' he sponsored, and be assured that he would not get hit with a bucket of political shit when it hit the fan, so to speak, with the Quanta-Phone.

Narzani covered all of his bases as well as Dean's. Narzani had much loftier goals than just killing Ray. He wanted to snuff out Ray, Lenny's and Ian's bid to become players on the interstellar trading markets that he mostly controlled.

On the upper side of the Earth, in North-Am, things began to come together for Ray and Lenny's team, the Labrador Redmen. They were winning and moving up in their league standings. Lenny played first base and Ray played second base. Ray and Lenny were a deadly duo on the defensive side for the Redmen. Next to nothing got by them. Ray and Lenny basically mowed down ninety percent of the runners who tried to get by them on the bases. The coaches from other teams dreaded the days that they had to play against the Redmen, because they always lost their 'filled in' rosters of good drafted farm team boys. The other teams would lose up to thirty rookie players in almost every game, not to mention losing the game and making little if any credits at all to their bank accounts. The Labrador Redmen rarely lost a game when Lenny and Ray played at the same time. They were 85 and 5 in the current season. The Redmen went on to the North-Am finals and got a birth in the World Alliance Major League Finals.

Ray and Lenny made credits by the tens of thousands by playing game after every game using their great defensive and offensive skills on the field. The more 'outs' they made, plus wins, the more credits they got paid. So did their coaches and teammates. The whole team became wildly rich, and the fans came in droves to watch the Deadly Duo perform every game.

Ray and Lenny furthered their great wealth by their sales of off-field merchandise, marketing, and advertisements. Life had finally begun to pay off for the two friends after years of dangerous play. Their success would also look good for their star ship business when they retired from Alliance Baseball. They each invested heavily in 'hard' hardware needed to get their business 'off the ground', so to speak. They bought equipment like the newest spaceship hull steel, enhanced launching fuels, and cosmic radiation protection so that Ray, Ian, and Lenny could travel safely in their ships through interstellar space. They even got their own personal space elevator to get their products into the upper atmosphere. Ray and Lenny asked Pamela Jay to help them secure real estate for their ships on the SALT launch pads, a space elevator contract, and the required licenses with the Earth Alliance Government. It looked like they were well on their way to becoming up and coming businessmen with Ian Shelton as their geological astrophysicist. Would this all come to be? Would this be a positive go for their futures? *"Let's hope so,"* Ray, Ian, and Lenny said to themselves.

Ray asked Lenny when he was going to retire from playing Alliance Baseball. Ray had researched the historical records of players who had played beyond five years, and none had survived as long as Lenny. Lenny was the record maker, but as the odds would have it, the record maker would become a record marker if he continued playing in the dangerous professional Alliance Baseball Leagues of Earth.

"You've got almost seven years now, Lenny. Don't you think it's time to retire before something happens to you? Don't you want to enjoy your life, instead of being here 'popping off' young guys every second day? You're not getting any younger, you know. You're twenty-five years old now and that's real old for baseball," Ray laughed as he said this, being as he was only two years younger. "Don't you ever think about finding a nice girl, settling down, and seeing the galaxy? You know you could quit at any time, eh Len?" Ray asked nicely.

"Yeah, I think I'm going to call it quits at the end of this season, but see the galaxy? I'm not really interested. Yes, I'd like to go to a nice recreational planet called Edenia I've heard of, out near the Large Magellanic Cloud on the outer rim of the Milky Way. I'd take my parents there to make them happy. They deserve it for all of their hard work they put in for the North-Am Alliance and for me," remarked Lenny. "That is what I want for them and me. As for finding a female to like me, I'd like to know if there really is anyone who would try to get to know me as well as you know me, Ray."

Ray harrumphed with a smile and said, "I'm not going to become a girlfriend of yours, that's for sure! But you can be bet we'll be together in the best business endeavor that Earth has ever seen, my friend," expressed Ray. He then proposed an idea to his 'slightly' older partner. "Why don't you and I open up a second local space transport company? I know a few people that we could hire that have the smarts about going to places to get materials for Earth while keeping Narzani in check. Our new company would make a bundle. I understand the Earth-to-Moon exchange runs. I did them for years, and I saw the moola that Narzani makes along with Ian. You and me could make a mint, so to speak, even without trying that hard. Narzani is just a tyrant when it comes to charging his customers exorbitant fees for freight just to the Moon. That way you could just work from that fancy planet Edenia you're talking about near that large cloud, and you could visit us here on lowly Earth once in a while, eh? The game isn't everything Lenny, is it?" asked Ray.

"I'll just be the investor, Ray. You're right: I don't want to be tied down with running a company. I'll leave that up to you, Ian, and the team that you hire," said Lenny. "I kind of want to be alone for a while if and when this baseball nonsense ends. I'm thinking that I'll need some space," said Lenny, looking at Ray with a bit of uncertainty. He thought back to Boisey's end in the dunes, and felt the guilt in his gut weighing him down.

"Good ole Lenny," laughed Ray. "Can't pigeon-hole you down, eh Len, just like the women can't either. Always avoiding responsibility but keeping your finger in the pie at all times, so to speak."

"If I've got my finger in the pie like you say, then you must have your whole fist in it for the girls you go around with," said Lenny, giving Ray a friendly shove and laughing.

After their home games in the North-Am province of Labrador, Lenny and Ray would frequent a bar in Goose Bay called 'Kiss the Fish'. The name came from an old fishing tradition that the locals still used to haze wannabe East Coasters from North-Am, especially baseball players. The tradition went like this: when newbies like Ray and Lenny came from places in western North-Am, like the isolated town of Hyder, they had to drink screech, a shot of pure alcohol. Then, to be accepted by the local folk, they had to kiss a freshly-caught raw fish. There, at this 'Kiss the Fish' bar, Ray and Lenny met a young quantum electron engineer by the name of Bill Hill.

Bill had originally come from the backwoods of the Ozark Mountains in North-Am, an area that had been taken over by the global deserts. Bill Hill still had the old Southern drawl that punctuated the Ozark people's annunciations, and so at times he didn't sound too intelligent at all to Ray and Lenny. But Bill Hill was very intelligent indeed. Affectionately known as 'Hill Billy' to his friends, Bill was an up-and-coming QEME, or Quantum Electron Mechanical Engineer. These types of Quantum Engineers worked on developing technology for star ship engines that would take these ships to significant gradients of light speed for interplanetary travel. This type of technology piqued Ray's interest, considering his plans to expand his own star ship transport business. It seemed to Ray that a man who knew a lot about star ship engines might just fit into his plans of setting up a competitive, interstellar transportation business.

Bill Hill was studying and working at the North-Am Gia Academy in Goose Bay on North-Am's easternmost coast. The academy, considered the most prestigious of any in North-Am, taught the brightest minds. At the Gia Academy, cutting-edge technologies for man's interstellar space missions were either invented or improved upon. Bill was working on experiments for the government/military by testing the new 'Mag-Hydro-Electron Drive' engines, for faster interstellar travel entering into double lensing wormholes. Double wormhole lensing was another name for the proven invention of the Alcubierre "Warp" drive. Bill Hill had brought the Alcubierre Warp Drive to today's interstellar travels by altering space time in front of a space-faring ship, 'shrinking' the space so to speak, thereby causing a quantum vacuum in front of a ship while enlarging space time behind it. This enlargement behind the star ship would initiate a quantum compression to drive the ship forward at faster than light speeds. By this method the ship would be traveling in a warp bubble, and not in direct space. The laws of physics would not be broken by a ship going faster than the speed of light in a quantum bubble, which was not possible in normal space.

Ray asked Hill Billy if he could fly a star ship with this Alcubierre Drive and Bill said, "Ah's not only can fly them but ah can build them their engines, too. There's a few other things ah can do besides the star ships. Ah likes to participate in 'Mag-Saber' tournaments, and Ah'm just getting into quantum communication reviews, so maybe Ah can try to crack the uncertainty principle of the secretive 'Quanta-Phone' that uses the uncertainty principles, but the muons, up-quarks, neutrinal cascade and..." Bill would have gone on, but Ray cut him short. He wasn't about to go into a quantum sub molecular physics lesson with Bill.

"Would you be interested in working for me and my buddy Lenny, operating those star ships with the Alcubierre Warp Drive you say you're working on, Bill?" Ray asked. "We need someone who can give us an edge when competing with Ricardo Narzani."

"Well, Ah have to finish my stint at the Gia Academy, here in North-Am. Ah need to complete my degree in Advanced Electron Mechanics like my grandpappy wants me to. Ah has to do a mandatory six-month contract with the Alliance Government Council once Ah get my degree, but sure, what the heck. Ah'll get to see the galaxy faster if Ah work for you, Ray. Look me up in a year or so and we'll talk about it over a pig-sty sip at Kiss the Fish," said Bill.

Now a pig-sty sip was a newly-invented Earth Alliance drink made up of pulped overripe peach flesh, an ounce of sweet pink wine, one-and-a-half ounces of pure Goose Bay screech, and an ounce of whatever liqueur you wanted to dilute it with. It was served over crushed ice with a rich, peppery sugar on the rim of the glass. After you'd downed a few of these pig-sties, you began to snort giddily, like a pig. You'd want to go to back the trough for more, and you'd have hot lips from the peppery sugar. Grunting became the norm after you'd had more than three pig-sties.

After the impromptu business meeting with Hill Billy, Ray and Lenny got his address, said their goodbyes, and went back to their home team's dorm. Ray and Lenny had to get themselves ready for a tough game the next day with the Brattleboro Bulls. The Bulls were a rival team of the Labrador Redmen in the North-Am East Coast League. Each team was battling for the top spot in their league and vying for a chance to go to the season's World Alliance Baseball Series Finals. Tomorrow's game would be played in the city of Torreon, just north of where the great Earth-encircling forests touched the global desert in the old country of Mexico. This game with the Brattleboro Bulls could get their team, the Redmen, to the Earth Alliance World Series finals. But Lenny and Ray didn't realize that if they won, they would be meeting Dean's team. The only thing on their minds was tomorrow's win against the Bulls.

The game the next day was a bloody one, as expected. Both teams lost their relief backup roster of twenty-one men after seven innings, and the veterans like Lenny and Ray had to play full time on the field against the other team's veterans for the remainder of the game. That is, they had to hit, run the gauntlet of bases, and play the dangerous defensive part as well. If they got on base there was no relief, because all of the relief call-ups were made dead on the field. Only the bull pen pitchers, ten on each team, were left in relief players.

Cito Gaster, the Redmen coach, wasn't about to forfeit the game, and neither was Ed 'Eddy' Frenette, the Brattleboro Bulls' coach. Each coach desperately wanted to win this game. The credit payout for the coaches would be huge, and the winning team would get a chance to go to the World Series Alliance Baseball finals in a blaze of glory. It would also be a great payout game for the players, for there were over eight hundred and eighty thousand paying fans in the stadium watching this premier final game. This meant a fat payout for the winning coaches and players by way of the media coverage and extra bonuses in sales of player paraphernalia. The fans could sense that the latter innings would be much more entertaining than the previous seven innings.

In the eighth inning, the visiting Brattleboro Bulls were up. In the run scoring department, they were up two to one. The first batter for the Bulls was a four-year veteran by the name of Jerome 'Slapstick' Hickey. Jerome wasn't the Bulls' fastest player, but he was one of the cagier ones. Jerome would always try for the blooper/slap hits like hitting the ball anywhere there was a hole that he could see in the defensive team's infield positioning. And that was what he proceeded to do on his second pitch at bat, hitting the ball to center field in front of the outfielder for the Redmen. This four-hundred-foot blooper that dropped in front of the center fielder of the Redmen safely gave Jerome first base for the Bulls. The home team tensed.

The next batter for the Bulls was John 'Boom' Thome, a tall, lanky player with a loud booming voice and a booming bat to match. John always wore a trademark bushy mustache, and so his moniker in the advertisement industry was an Alliance bat with a bushy mustache attached to it under the bat stub handle. Fans loved it. Like Eddie Shack supporters from the long ago National Hockey League, fans gave their allegiance to John Thome. His smiling mustache appeal awarded John many millions of Alliance credits in advertisements. John Thome modeled his character on Eddie Shack, who had been a volatile player in the old NHL hockey leagues. Shack could race away from you at a moment's notice, but could also fight on a dime, when the conditions warranted it. John never fought in baseball, but he always acted like he wanted to.

Ray knew John from the North-Am minor leagues. John had already put four years into the Major Alliance Leagues, and in the off-season, he had frequently expressed to Ray his desire to retire from baseball.

But this would be a retirement he wasn't expecting. John Thome hit a brutal one-bounce line drive right to Ray that sent Ray reeling back ten feet before he could stop himself from the ball's momentum striking his ball mitt. Ray couldn't get the runner, Slapstick Hickey, running from first to second, but he knew it would be close. He was sure he could get John Thome before he reached first base. Ray looked through his digital eyepiece, calculated John's speed, and threw for John's left leg. If he got him there, John's other leg would not get him to first base. Desperate as he was, John Tom knew his only chance was to try to dive for first base. By pulling his legs under himself and stretching his arms out, he would be a smaller target. John hoped that Ray's imminent throw at him wouldn't put him out of league play completely. Well, the small target must have had a bull's-eye on it. Ray hit John in the upper thigh area, shattering John's major tibia leg bone near his upper hip. John fell in a groaning heap about five feet from first base. Lenny picked up the loose ball and just dropped it onto John's writhing body for the second bean and the out. Lenny didn't want to cause John any more pain, but the fans booed Lenny and Ray for their compassionate play on John Thome. They wanted blood, and they wanted it now. John's leg was terribly smashed. This would undoubtedly be his last game, for his leg would never heal right for him to play professional baseball again. At first Ray felt bad for grievously injuring his 'off-season' friend, but he soon shook off any feeling of guilt and was ready for the next batter. *"That's how the game has to be played. No compassion to cloud your judgment, just hard-hitting play after play until you win the game. Sorry, John,"* Ray said to himself.

One out, one on second base was the game situation for the Redmen against their opponents. Next up for the Brattleboro Bulls was another veteran, 'Rocky' Moorges. Rocky played the game like Dean Luthbert, deadly all the way. Rocky was another protected player on his team, but with all of the 'fresh meat' rookies gone, he had to play the whole of the game now and not just the batting part. Rocky, a bundle of nerves, battled himself in the batter's box against the Redmen pitcher. Rocky ran the count up to three-and-two from the Redmen's pitcher whose name was Big Dave C. Dave C. let a rocket of a fastball go chest letters high but in the strike zone at Moorges. Rocky hit a deep infield line drive to the shortstop of the Redmen. The shortstop for the Redmen caught the line drive; held the runner, Hickey, at second; and threw the ball at Rocky who was heading to first base. The ball hit Rocky on the helmet when he was ten feet from first base. The blow stunned Rocky and knocked the helmet off of his head that was now exposed. This first-time bean blow sent Rocky careening off his running lane and falling down into the foul ball area of the minor infielder's domain. The minor infielder rushed to get the ball that careened off of Rocky. She fielded it to Lenny, the first baseman on the Redmen's team, but the minor infielder was cut down by Rocky, who had quickly gotten up from the first bean. The minor infielder died a quick but bloody horrific death. Her mistake was being too close to Rocky in the active field of play as she fielded the ball.

Girls in Alliance Baseball were an integral part of the minor infield system. They took their chances in professional league play as seriously as the boys. In their youth, the boys were always wanting to become professional league players. They usually started their careers as minor infielders. The girls, however, were rare. When girls played the game, they worked through the ranks of minor leagues. Then they worked their way into the major leagues as minor infielders, but they didn't last long in the pros because of the gruesome play. Getting hurt was not an option as a minor infielder, but hey, if you could get near and out of the way of play for tens of thousands of credits a year, heck why not. Both the boys and the girls could do a dangerous job as well as an effective job of getting an out for their hometown team.

Rocky knifed the female minor infielder in the throat with his razor gloves as she tossed the ball to Lenny. Rocky then tried, wobbling and with teeth exposed in his grimace of pain, to get to first base. Rocky hadn't seen Lenny run in from first base as he got the ball from the dead female minor infielder who had dropped onto the ground.

This time, Lenny didn't disappoint the fans. He threw the ball, point-blank, at Rocky. The blow from the ball caved in the whole of his face, causing blood and brain matter to come out of his ears as the ball squashed his head in. Rocky Moorges fell onto first base, dead, but he was not safe due to the second bean on him by Lenny. The runner on second base, Jerome Hickey, who managed to get to third safely while this was going on, winced at his teammate's demise.

So now there were two out and a man on third for the Brattleboro Bulls. Hickey, for Brattleboro, hoped that he could get to home plate, but he knew his odds were well under thirty percent during this type of play. The infielders and out fielders for the Redmen were determined that 'None Shall Pass'.

The next batter for the Bulls was a second-year vet by the name of Rolly Boudrow. Though a bit chubby to be playing the game, he had managed to keep himself alive by his consistent hitting. Rolly was a smart player who always waited for the right pitch to come to him. The Redmen's pitcher was up to eighty balls pitched in this game when he faced Boudrow. The throwing arm of the

Redmen's pitcher, even with the enhanced robotic throwing gear, was getting tired. Rolly Boudrow waited him out during seven pitches of intense fouling and sizing up pitches for called ball. Boudrow finally got ball four and he got a walk that sent him jiggling and smiling to first base. Rolly hadn't fully run the bases in months, and so he was a bit out of breath when he got to first base. Rolly looked desperately at his coach. He wanted a relief runner out here for himself. He knew he'd have trouble running the bases quickly because of his plump size.

Rolly's coach, Eddy Frenette, looked at him and motioned that there were no more bodies to put out onto the bases. Chubby Rolly would have to do his own honors of running the bases in this intense time of play.

Cito Gaster, the coach of the Redmen, came out onto the field and relieved Dave C., his tiring pitcher. Gaster put in a fresh throwing arm, Don Le Blank, to face the best batter for the Bulls who was coming up next. Ace Kring was a rare individual in that he pitched and hit at the same time in Alliance Baseball. Pitchers were usually a protected commodity, but with no fresh meat left to put into the game, Frenette had no choice but to put Kring up to bat or forfeit the game.

Now Ace was another protected veteran who enjoyed batting, because if he got hits in previous innings, the rookie runners would run the bases for him. Running the bases made him a little nervous. Ace proceeded to strike out in his attempt at bat, and that ended an otherwise positive inning with the score still two to one for the Bulls.

Ray's team, the Redmen, were up in the bottom of the eighth. Up to bat came a player named Luc Breaultt, a relief pitcher from the bullpen. Batting was fairly new to him, for he was only a relief pitcher in the bullpen and there was no one left to bat on the bench. Luc proceeded to strike out. Next up was Ian Adams, a two-year protected vet who could run like a deer.

Ian ran the count to two and two. A blistering fastball came a little inside from the Bulls' pitcher, and Ian hit the ball for a fourteen-hundred-foot home run. The fans and the players on the Redmen bench went wild, for now the game was tied two to two. Ian was the hero of the minute for his great clutch hit. Ian received lots of high fives when he got to his team's dugout.

Stark reality quickly returned, for the next three batters for the Redmen were swiftly dispatched. All three had their brains splattered on their way to the first base on single beans by the third baseman for the Bulls, the great throwing third baseman Giles Peelltier.

At the top of the ninth the Redmen even had to put their trainers into the game to replace the dispatched players. They were desperately hanging on, trying not to lose this game. The Bulls' first batter up was none other than the deadly third baseman Giles Peelltier. Giles knew that this was crunch time and that his life would be on the line if he didn't get a hit. He was a good hitter, and striking out was not an option. If he struck out, he knew that his future with the Bulls would be as good as finished. His coach would surely 'hang him out to dry', so to speak. Giles managed two long foul balls that looked like home runs but were not to be. Then he got two pitches called balls that were put past him by Le Blank to run the count to two and two. As Giles began to sweat, the eyepiece of his digital viewing display fogged up. A batter could call time to get a bat boy to come and help him un-fog his eyepiece, but Giles waited a second too long and the pitcher let the ball go before he could call time. He suddenly realized that this pitch would cross the plate in the strike zone. With the pitch coming towards him at a hundred and eighty miles an hour, Giles desperately swung and managed to hit the ball off the top of his bat. The ball went so high into the air that it seemingly disappeared up into the rafters of the huge enclosed playing dome. All of the defending players of the Redmen looked up in disbelief, thinking that the ball wasn't going to come down, but down it came. It was caught by the third baseman for the

Redmen, but Giles Peelltier was already on first base, smiling like the Cheshire Cat from *Alice in Wonderland*. This was indeed a lucky break for Peelltier, for it was classed as an infield hit by the infield umpires! Fly balls were no longer counted as outs in Alliance Baseball. The media and the fans hadn't seen Peelltier get to first base, because they had been watching the ball go up into the high steel-girded rafters. Giles sighed a great relief, for his job as a player was kept intact. Everyone had a great laugh about how Giles floated, ghostlike, safely out to first base while the ball floated in 'nowhere space', as comically reported by the play-by-play commentators. The game needed fun and comedy, because the stark reality of death was always there. The comedy quickly turned to reality as the next batter for the Bulls hit into a double play. Giles and the young vet hitting were both beaned and knocked out on that play. Giles wasn't seriously injured. He got hit in the shoulder and the buttocks, which resulted in severe bruises, but his partner was blinded by the ball and had his rib cage shattered on the second bean. This effectively eliminated him from any future play. Lenny and Ray were both a part of the carnage inflicted on the Bulls' two players taken out of the game this inning.

It was now two out for the Redmen. The next batter for the Bulls was a tall, lanky man by the name of Dave Holmes. Dave played outfield for the Bulls and had quite an arm on him for beaning runners on the bases, much like Boisey Wallers had been, when the ball came to him in the outfield. Like all the other vets, he liked being protected, and he didn't like the fact that he was now playing full time because of the shortage of players at this juncture in the game. The Redmen's pitcher didn't let up on Dave. Le Blank kept the ball high and in tight to Holmes, which caused Holmes to swing wildly with his articulated bat on the first two pitches that came at him. Holmes called time to slow the pace down. He needed to get his concentration back, because he was behind zero and two in the count. Digging his heels in the sand at the plate, he stepped into the batter's box. He was determined to get a hit. Holmes fouled off two more pitches, swinging aggressively with his pivoting bat so the Redmen's pitcher would think twice before putting the ball into the strike zone for Holmes again. Two more pitches zoomed past Holmes, but the home plate electronic umpire called them balls. The fans, aggravated about these long counts in the batting schedule, began to catcall Holmes in an attempt to distract him from his play at the plate. Not to be deterred, Holmes stood his ground and hit a home run that just cleared the twelve-hundred-foot mark on the outfield wall. Holmes trotted the bases and thumbed his nose up at the catcalling, booing fans of the Redmen as he ran down the third baseline to home plate. It was now three to two for the Bulls.

The next batter for the Bulls was quickly dispatched with a single bean to the runner by none other than Lenny Peecheh playing first base. He did it with a ball to the throat area of the Bull's runner who had been trying to get to first base. The fans gave an appreciative roar of approval for Lenny on the last out at the top of the ninth inning.

At the bottom of the ninth inning, the Redmen were up to bat but down a run with the Bulls threatening to take the game and the series. The Bulls only had eight men out on the field, not nine as required by league play, but the rules stated that you could field no less than eight players if you had no more replacement players. First up for the Redmen was Donny Brodsseau, another bullpen pitcher inserted into the lineup because of the lack of young bodies. Now Don hated to bat, because his pitching was what kept him out of the regular batting lineup and in the game of Alliance Baseball. Don didn't last very long at bat. He hit to the third baseman of the Bulls and was quickly dispatched with two beans that shattered his ribs and his spine. These blows caused him to slowly roll over like a snake that had been run over by a car on hot pavement. Don had blood gushing out of his mouth. The fans cheered the Bulls on for their brutal play as Don Brodsseau was carried off the field by the clayon health

A FUTURE PASTIME – A COMPLICATED BASEBALL STORY

robots that gave immediate first aid to injured players. Would Don play another day? Only his doctors knew for sure.

Next up for the Redmen was Ray Tenner. Now Ray knew what was expected of him, and he was determined to go out and make things happen for his team. Ray stepped aggressively into the batter's box and eyed the Bulls' pitcher with the tenacity of a cheetah after its prey. The incoming pitch was high and inside, a flaming pitch that almost hit Ray in the head. Protesting to the levitated umpire above him, Ray said, "Hey, Ump, don't you think that was intentional? A little close, eh? He threw it right at me!" The home plate umpire agreed with Ray and issued a warning to the Bulls' pitcher that if any of the next pitches were in the same area, he would be ejected from the game. If a pitch were to hit Ray, then the pitcher would be subjected to a year in jail. So, the gauntlet was laid down for the pitcher of the Bulls to play to Ray.

Not to be outdone, the Bulls' pitcher sent in a fastball, that sizzled past the swinging Ray with no contact on the ball, traveling at a hundred and eighty-two miles per hour. The replay on the jumbo tron clearly showed Ray closing his eyes and swinging at the ball as it went over home plate. Ray reset the pivoting bat around his body and said to himself, *"Come on, Ray, calm down. You can hit this guy!"* Sure enough, the next pitch was a twisting, corkscrew of a ball that Ray lunged after, but he hit it just foul. The count was one and two now. Ray wasn't nervous at all, and his confidence was evident to the cheering fans. With his pivoting bat curled around his body, Ray stood his ground at the plate. He waiting menacingly for the Bulls' pitcher to try and get the ball past him. The next pitch was to be in low for a ball that the Bulls' catcher had signed out to his pitcher. But the next pitch came in just a bit higher. Ray blasted the ball to the wall in center field, over a thousand feet away, for a safe stand up double into second base. The home team fans roared their approval for Ray's success at hitting the ball in such a pressure-filled situation.

The next batter for the Redmen was a good friend of Ray's: young but enthusiastic Dan Jolettey. The pitcher was too much for Dan, and he hit into what looked like a possible double play. Ray held on at second base and watched in horror as Dan was gunned down by the second baseman of the Bulls with a first 'bean' to his head. Dan was then surgically finished off by the first baseman, who got the ball from his minor infielder and hit Dan full in the face with the spiked ball. No mercy was given in a game that expected none. Home team Redmen fans watched again, horrified, as the young Dan Jolettey was removed by the clayon clean-up team. The Bulls' fans roared their approval for the gruesome play.

It was now two out with Ray on second base and Lenny Peecheh up to bat. The fans in the stadium were on their feet cheering their home team Redmen, but the Bulls' pitcher was determined not to let the Redmen score. He did not want to send the game into overtime. Lenny pointed to the center field wall, making the fans cheer loudly, but the Bulls' pitcher shook his head in disapproval, showing that he wasn't about to let Lenny get a hit that easily. Lenny stepped into the batter's box. His snake-like bat was tethered like lace over his right shoulder and extended down around his ribs on his left side. Lenny eyed the pitcher with his digital eyepiece, trying to decipher what kind of pitch would be coming at him. Lenny caught the faintest hint of the pitcher feigning a fastball, but what was really coming in was an off-speed pitch. This caught the hard-hitting Lenny a little off guard, and he looped a clumsy swing at the ball, not quite getting the swing he had wanted as the ball dropped off into the lower strike zone, and he missed the ball completely. As he spun in circles over home plate, he thought to himself, "Not bad, not bad pitching." Lenny contemplated the Bulls' pitcher. Very determined, Lenny composed himself by stepping out of the batter's box and then smiling like he hadn't a care in the world. Then he stepped quickly back in the batter's box for the next pitch. *"Okay, stretch, let's see what ya got,"* Lenny said to himself.

While Lenny was at bat, Ray had been bad-mouthing the Bulls' pitcher in an effort to distract him from getting the ball past Lenny. Ray would do anything for Lenny on the ball field. If Lenny got a hit, then Ray could try to score from second base.

An alarm went off in the stadium stating that a sand lizard attack was a possibility, but not a probability. This potential event was only in the ten percent range of happening, and the Earth Alliance Clayon Military of North-Am was being dispatched to handle the situation. The fans and players were not to be alarmed. This was just a medium low alarm warning. The game would continue with a low level yellow alert being displayed on the jumbo tron.

With this minor distraction past him, Lenny again inserted himself into the batter's box. He let a ball pass him by, low and outside. The count was now one ball and one strike on him. Lenny readied himself again in the batter's box. The Bulls' pitcher fired off a fastball that Lenny was ready for. Crack went Lenny's bat! It was a line drive past the shortstop into the outfield, but the left fielder was on it right away. Ray rounded third base quickly and got the signal to go for home from his third base coach. As Ray rounded third base, the left fielder anticipated this. He threw the ball with all of his might and accuracy at Ray's head to prevent him from scoring the game-ending run. The ball came in at Ray, who had rounded third and was going for home. The Bulls' catcher blocked Ray's path twenty feet from home plate. The ball just missed Ray by one-tenth of an inch and went into the Bulls' catcher's mitt. Ray dove for home plate while the Bulls' catcher threw the ball at Ray, who was only ten feet in front of him. The ball hit Ray on the top of his helmet and popped the helmet off his head in a dramatic fashion, but Ray maintained his cool and kept moving forward. Ray drove his razor gloves into the neck of the Bulls' catcher, almost decapitating him. This opened his way to home plate, even as the minor infielder got the ball and threw it to the incoming pitcher. The pitcher got the ball and drove it at Ray for the second bean, but it was not to be. Ray managed to slide, touching home plate a fraction of a second before the ball hit him in the neck. The ball went instantly soft, according to the rules of play. This was made so by the electronic field umpire, so as not to injure the safe Ray Tenner. The ball gingerly bounced off of his exposed neck. This allowed Ray to score the run for the Redmen that gave them the win and the advancement to the World Alliance Baseball Series Finals.

A great roar went up from the home team Redmen players and fans for their win. Underneath the roaring of the crowd, the warning of a sand lizard incursion was upgraded to 'Red/Yellow', or imminent. This was not noticed by the celebrating players or the home team fans, because of the noise. The alarms were barely audible above the celebratory cheers of the crowd. Once they realized that danger was at hand, the fans began to stream out of the stadium. They knew that if they did not get to protective shelters, the sand lizards would get to them. Just then the alert changed to red and a full-scale incursion of lizards descended over the outfield wall.

All hell broke loose in the fans' frenzy to get out of the stadium as the sand lizards freely launched themselves onto the playing field. The lizards had crashed a gate at the outfield wall and were now in the stadium, hissing and roaring their want of human flesh.

Ray got to Lenny and quickly congratulated him on his hit that got him to home plate. As they were trying to get to the safety of their team's bunker, two huge, male, eighty-ton lizards broke over the center field wall onto the field. Players as well as fans scrambled for safety. This was the reality of the new global desert world: no one was safe, no matter where you lived or who you were. The military clayon robots quickly marched in through the infield gates and began firing on the monstrous lizards. Pandemonium was the order of the day as the lizards charged the human-run military vehicles that fired on them. One lizard was cut down just before reaching its intended target, a gravity-run 'Hummer'. The second lizard was successful in crushing its antagonizer by grabbing the gravi-hummer, clawing at it, and literally ripping the whole front end of it open with its mighty serrated teeth. It picked the exposed human occupants out of the hummer with its snake-like tongue, and promptly ate them. Three other gravi-hummers converged on the threatening lizard that had eaten their colleagues. The menacing sand lizard was immediately cut down with punishing laser fire that made the area stink of rotting flesh as the giant lizard writhed in its death throes. Three more smaller lizards entered the arena but were quickly dispatched by the clayon guard.

The news media had a field day filming this unprecedented event and broadcasting the happenings to the rest of the world, much to the delight of the violence-hungry viewers that were not in attendance at this particular game. Clayon robots and human-run attack vehicles finally stopped the sand lizard incursion with five sand lizards dispatched and only three human deaths. No fans had died, just military personnel, so it was basically a victory for the government in their protection against the mighty male sand lizards.

Ray and Lenny had managed to reach safety inside their players' bunker. Concerned for their fans, they called a press conference to convey their hope that everyone was safe. If anyone was hurt because of the sand lizard attack, they would help pay for any medical expenses. Today's win had made a lot of credits for Ray and Lenny, so they wisely used some of them to keep their fans happy and coming out to games. The generous offer of these two compassionate individuals was broadcast far and wide, for it was rare for players to be so concerned for their fans in light of the suffering players had to endure on the field.

Ray and Lenny had brought their team to the Alliance World Series Finals today with their win. They were quite excited about this turn of events, but their excitement would wane when they found out that they would be going against Dean Luthbert and South-Am's Pelotas in the upcoming World Series tournament.

CHAPTER SEVEN
LEADING UP TO A SERIOUS MEETING

WHEN LENNY AND RAY WERE SUITING UP FOR THEIR NEXT important game, they got a loud heads up jolt from their trainer who had just entered their dressing room with a message they couldn't refuse: "Coach wants to address you guys right now. He'll be right in, so listen up you bunch of 'here be now's," the trainer kind of cussed.

"Listen up, you hard playing meat heads," said Coach Cito Gaster of the Labrador Redmen to his team. "You've all played well in the last little while, but today you are going to have to dig deep into yourselves, deeper than you've ever had to dig before, to advance into this tournament of the World Alliance Series of baseball finals. To advance, we have to try and keep our losses down, preserve our team's core strengths of vets, and play the game the way it was meant to be played, with heart, but with no mercy to our opposition!" With that short motivational speech imbued into his young players' minds, the players gave a rousing cheer to their coach that was deafening to the ears in the team's sequestered dressing room.

Cito Gaster was fair with his young charges. He listened to his players' suggestions in the way they played the game of Alliance Baseball without giving up control of his team. If something wasn't working right, if the team was losing, or if the team was losing players excessively to ordinary plays and Gaster's sub-coaches couldn't see what was going wrong, then Cito would ask the players what they thought should be done to elevate the teams' style of play and win those close games that would otherwise be lost. Cito Gaster was a good listener and was a richer man for it in both credits and friends around the baseball league. He truly wanted his players to win. He had no wish to be seen as 'the tyrant' that most coaches became. Most of the coaches around the leagues resorted to bullying their players, and they were not a popular figurehead with their charges.

Dean Luthbert couldn't have been more delighted with the Labrador Redmen's advance to the world finals. This meant he might get a real chance to finally exact his revenge on Ray Tenner for his brother Boisey's death. Dean wanted his brother's demise avenged by Ray's death, displayed for all to see. His team wouldn't play against Ray's until later in the tournament at the World Alliance Series finals. For now, Dean had to focus his attention on his upcoming games so he wouldn't lose his chance at revenge on Ray Tenner.

Ray became aware that Dean's team was in the finals when his batting coach posted the team rosters up with their game schedules. As soon as he saw Dean's name, Ray knew that there would be an inevitable meeting between them on the playing field and that each would have the chance to eliminate the other. Ray didn't want to kill Dean, but he knew that Dean wanted to kill him. Ray steeled his mind to the fact that he would have to stop his childhood friend from killing him. To defend himself, Ray knew he would have to take out Dean with deadly force!

When Ray told Lenny about Dean's presence in the finals, Lenny just kind of gave Ray a cool "Oh ya." Lenny's sullen silence and the down turned look on his face confused Ray. Lenny was usually an upbeat kind of guy who would be happy that Dean was in the same finals tournament as them. They all had the competitive spirit of wanting to play against seasoned players like themselves. Lenny often planned strategies with Ray on how he could get a player but not kill them, just hurt them, so he and Lenny could play on. But this time Lenny just said, "Hope we don't have to kill Dean."

There were six teams in the World Series Alliance Baseball Finals, one from each Alliance Territory established on the Earth. This year's teams were The Labrador Redmen from the North-Am League, Pelotas from the South-Am League, Spartak Locomotive from the Euro-Russo League, Bengal United from the Pak-Indostan League, Purple Sanga from the Austro-Asian League, and the Morouka Town Spurs from the Africany League. All of these teams had worked hard and sacrificed hundreds of players over the course of the season to get to the big payout finals of the World Alliance Baseball Series. Each team had to play each other once in an entertaining round-robin style of play for the bloodthirsty fans. Each team would be rated first to last according to wins, kills made, and runs scored. First place from the round-robin got a buy (free pass) into the finals. The other five teams battled it out in a repechage series for the other spot in the final series game. This is where all of the teams that didn't make the final spot in a tournament playoff battled it out. The winner advances to the final where they would meet the team who got the buy into the finals. A lottery was used for the first round of games, and then a schedule was drawn up for the rest. The finals were being played in North-Am, in the port city of Mazalta, from the old country of Mexico that had merged into North-Am when the global deserts took over most of the southern parts. The protective forests were also near this city of Mazalta that had ten million residents. Being this close to the global deserts, giant sand lizards were always a probable threat.

The Redmen played the Morouka Town Spurs in their first game of the slated round-robin tournament. The Spurs were the home club of the minor team, the Bafana Chiefs, that Ray had played for when he first got drafted. His old coach, Rex Thembi for the Spurs, was still coaching. Ray remembered how Thembi had told him to run from him and keep running. Thembi knew his team was in trouble when they had to play against Ray and Lenny, so he tried desperately to knock them out of the game early. Thembi put his top pitcher out on the mound. In making this pitcher start, Thembi hoped that he could get Ray and Lenny killed or at least knocked out of the game early so that his team could get ahead of the Redmen for the win.

Ray and Lenny would not have any part in their early exit of this game. In fact, they made the opposite happen. Between the two of them, Ray and Lenny single handedly took out twenty of the Spurs' runners on ground ball hits. To their embarrassment, Thembi's team was forced to forfeit their game due to lack of players on the field. Too many had died or been injured as a result of Ray's and Lenny's aggressive offensive and defensive play on the field. Even several minor infielders had been lost on the Spurs team. Thembi cut his losses and forfeited the game, because he didn't want to lose the pitchers in his bullpen or his core of protected players in the first round of the tournament. His protected players were the only players left that could pull his team forward in the next game. He would have to call home and get at least another eighty players sent up from the Africany League to bolster his team's roster back to playing strength. Ray and Lenny got second and third star of the game, respectively, for their formidable style of play.

Dean's team, Pelotas from South-Am, played their first game at another nearby enclosed baseball dome against the Purple Sanga from the Austro-Asian League. Due to Dean's popularity, there were over eight hundred and fifty thousand fans present. It was a close affair but Dean, the determined player that he was, ensured that his team pulled through by hitting the go ahead run home and stopping twelve batters from Purple Sanga from ever seeing the light of day again. Not to be outdone by Ray and Lenny, Dean got first star in the game he played. The media gave our star players the royal treatment in that they were hailed as three of the top ten players to be watched in these Alliance Baseball World Series finals. The media also gave a slight blurb about the rivalry between Dean's team and Ray and Lenny's team. They told the fans to watch for a momentous meeting of these players in the games to come.

With their respective teams winning the all-important first game in this first round, the coaches of The Redmen and Pelotas gave their players a two-day rest. Feeling restless without practices or games, Dean, Ray, and Lenny wanted to check out the nightlife here in Mazalta and let off a little steam of pent-up tensions. Ray and Lenny got female dates to act as guides for them in Mazalta, to show them around town. They sampled the local culinary cuisine with these girls. Dean went out with an entourage of his adoring fans and bodyguards. As fate would have it, our two groups happened to frequent the same establishment and an inevitable clash occurred.

They met at the popular Fiesta Grande, a large venue with lots of room to move about. Ray and Lenny, to their surprise, ran into their friends Dr. Stehle, 'Jigs', Ray's doctor friend who had patched him up after his Moon haulage rocket run incident; and Bill Hill, 'Hill Billy', the quantum electron mechanical engineer who designed star ship engines for the Earth Alliance Government. Ray invited both Jigs and Bill to sit at their table and enjoy the nightlife. When Lenny asked them why they were here at this particular nightclub, both Jigs and Bill explained that they each had enough leave time from their respective jobs with the World Alliance Government in North-Am, and they had agreed that coming to the Alliance World Series Baseball finals was in the cards for them.

Bill Hill asked Ray if he was scared of getting killed in this deadly game of baseball. "Don't you feel that at some point you're gonna get it?" Bill asked, matter-of-fact.

Ray just said, "Well, I know the dangers of playing this game are real, but if I play good enough to be a protected player, I have a ninety percent survival rate. By playing with old fart Lenny here, I'm sure I'll be able to get through even the worst of times."

"Who you calling old fart, you young punk?" Lenny joked, taking a swing at Ray's shoulder.

"You old man, you are a year and a half older than me, aren't you, and the truth hurts, eh?" Ray said mockingly to Lenny.

"Yeah, but I can do it with the best of them!" said Lenny, looking at his beautiful date.

"More than once a night?" asked Ray with a smirk on his face.

"Now gentlemen, we have women present; mind your manners," said Jigs. "And I do believe that is your friend over there, isn't it, Mr. Tenner? Isn't that Mr. Luthbert, a couple of tables over?" Jigs pointed out who he was talking about.

Ray and Lenny looked across the hall of this fancy restaurant to see Dean laughing with his friends amongst his entourage following. Dean did not notice Ray or Lenny, for he had his back to them. Lenny called a waiter over and asked if he could send Mr. Luthbert a certain kind of drink. The waiter asked what kind of drink it was that Lenny wanted to send to Dean. Lenny told the waiter to look up the North-Am drink called 'Hyderizer', and he proceeded to give the formula of the drink to the waiter. Lenny and Ray watched with bated breath as their hometown drink went to Dean.

At first Dean wasn't sure what to make of this familiar concoction that had been given to him, but when he turned around and saw where it had come from, Dean obligingly drank it down within five minutes to his friends' surprise. Dean usually abstained from any kind of stimulant or depressant when he was in a serious ball tournament situation. But being in a giving mood, Dean sent

Ray and Lenny the same kind of lambasting liquid refreshment. Ray and Lenny each drank down their drinks in five minutes, just like Dean had done. Then, according to Hyder protocol, another round of drinks was called for to see who would pay for the second round, seemingly given in friendship.

Bill Hill asked Ray why they were consuming large amounts of alcohol, and Ray said, "It's just a little hometown friendliness. You should watch what hometown boys do when they meet away from home." Ray and Lenny watched as Dean forced himself to down the second 'Hyderizer', and then Dean made sure that Ray and Lenny got their drinks right after he finished his. Ray and Lenny were not as fast as Dean at getting their 'Hyderizers' into them, but as they were trying to gulp them down, Dean came over to their table in a kind of tipsy staggering fashion and said sarcastically, "How are you doing, Tenner, you murdering bastard!"

At that point Lenny stood up in Ray's defense and said to Dean, "I might be smaller, but being older, I'm tougher, Luthbert!"

Lenny tried hitting Dean's jaw with a drunken roundhouse but missed. That made Dean step back. Lenny then pounced on the staggering Dean, knocking him down. Lenny put his head beside Dean's and said in a lowered voice, "You leave Ray alone; he's not to blame for Boisey's death in the desert!"

"Yes, he is!" yelled Dean. "And there's nothing that will convince me otherwise. That asshole is the one that killed my brother!" Dean gave Lenny a mighty shove that sent him sliding under a nearby table. Dean stood up shakily and was ready to take a run at Ray.

Pandemonium was about to ensue. Each party's bodyguards tried to get into the affair between Ray, Lenny, and Dean with deadly force as they brought out weapons that would have easily silenced the Kodiak grizzlies of the still wild northern regions of North-Am. Ray got a hold of Lenny and pulled him up from the floor, and they went back to their table as their two lady escorts fled the scene. Meanwhile, Dean gave his thugs the order to beat the hell out of the two culprits who had assaulted him. Ray's and Lenny's paid protectors stood in front of them, ready to take whatever came their way.

What happened next was a scene out of an old space movie. Bill Hill, or Hill Billy, got between the two groups that were about to do battle. He had a mag-saber at the ready; the extended cruiser tip indicated that it was ready to be used. Hill Billy pointed it at both warring parties with the intent to use it on whoever wanted to start a ruckus first.

Dean shouted, "You can't use that thing here; it's illegal for anyone to have a mag-saber!"

"Not if you have a license to carry one like Ah have, and not if you work for the government that gives me the right to use it right now," said Hill Billy threateningly. "Now, Ah'd likes to see us folks get along here right nicely so why don't yous all just sit down and try to enjoy the rest of the evening, eh boys?" finished Bill Hill in his Ozark Mountain drawl, standing tall with the mag-saber at the ready.

Both groups slowly moved back behind their respective hired bosses. Hill Billy did not move a step. He kept his position between the two confronting groups until he saw both sides sit down. After staring them down Hill Billy was satisfied that nothing else violent would happen, and he re-holstered his mag-saber.

With that, the two sides about to war on each other backed off and a bloody confrontation was averted. Dean left the Fiesta Grande waving his arms, yelling drunkenly about Ray with his bodyguards supporting him as they went out of the lounge. "Don't you worry, Tenner, I may not have roughed you up this time, but I will get you on the field, you can be sure of that!" said Dean in a vicious but slurring drunken voice, waving his arms in the air.

"Good show, Mr. Hill," said Jigs. "You did a fine job of not letting heads roll, and you made my job as a doctor tonight much easier."

"My pleasure, Doc," smiled Hill Billy, bowing as he put his mag-saber away in his hidden hilt.

Ray and Lenny were in awe at what had just happened, but, like Dean, they were pretty inebriated. "Well, I'm impressed that a guy I hardly know would come to our defense, Mr. Hill," said Ray, kind of slurring his words. "How the heck can we ever repay you?"

"Mr. Tenner, Ah knows yous highfalutin ball players face death every day of your playing lives, but letting people get hurt or killed foolishly goes against me and my grand pappy's ways. I like a good fight, just like the next redneck, but it has to be for a purpose, and not be a grudge bludgeoning affair like this one was gonna be," said Bill Hill. Ray and Lenny opened their drunken eyes in stark recognition of what Hill Billy had said.

Lenny and Ray expressed their gratitude to Bill Hill, and they agreed to get together again soon.

Ray joked, "If we can get you and Jigs to come with us more often, we won't have to hire bodyguards, eh Lenny? Ha, ha," Ray laughed. He slumped into a chair, chuckling drunkenly to himself. Lenny just smiled a lot and waved goodbye pleasantly.

Before he left, Hill Billy went into a reprimanding kind of speech, "Ah do think you've got one mad wet hen that wants to peck on yous guys. It seems to me that yous boys have had a tussle before and Ah hope you can settle it amongst yourselves on your own terms. Ah'll tell you something, though: Ah don't want to be friends with anyone or be invited to a scrap of friends every time they meet because that only gets me on the wrong end of things. Ah want to be there as someone who's defending a right, and not committing a wrong like that feller did. He is mad at yous. So, Ah bid you goodnight, gentlemen. Mr. Tenner, Ah will be taking you up on that offer you made awhile back about me working for you in your star ship transportation business. Like yous guys, tonight Ah almost made a mistake of doing a wrong. Ah wish you two the best in this final baseball series. Ah really likes the way yous guys play the game and Ah hope yur the same to work with as you play ball: serious. That means that Ah'd like to be happy where I'm doing what Ah do. Goodnight, and good luck, guys."

"Bravo, Mr. Hill, bravo!" said Jigs. "Well done, old chap; I'm impressed with your demeanour and your machismo style of fair play." Jigs patted Hill Billy on the shoulder as they walked out of the Fiesta Grande.

"Whut did you say, Doc?" asked Bill. "Ah am not great with those fancy words of yours, but Ah do think it was a compliment, wasn't it?" asked Bill. He wore a crooked questioning look on his face like an innocent farmer from the old 'American West'.

"That'll do, Mr. Hill, that'll do," said Jigs reassuringly.

Ray and Lenny were dumbfounded at the events that had just transpired. They had expected an all-out bloody scrap with Dean and his entourage, but were now left kind of empty-handed. They were headed into an alcoholic stupor because of their foolish decision to drink two 'Hyderizers' in just over an hour. "Well, my good friend, we're all dressed up and nowhere to frecken go, so what the hell should we do now, eh, old fart Lenny?" Said Ray. Lenny seemed a bit distant at the moment, and did not respond. "Hey man, what's the matter with you? You had Dean down, and you let him go! I know you're the better man, Lenny. You should have pounded him when you had the chance," insisted Ray.

Lenny said, "Ray, I really don't want to hurt Dean, but I know in my heart that someday I will have to. If I don't, he will hurt me. He's our best buddy from our early days. We have to find a way to make sure he gets through this year so we can all retire and make amends to each other later. Besides, it's against the rules for ball players to fight with each other off the field. I feel really tired right now and I want to get back to my room and crash. We've got a game the day after tomorrow, and we'll both feel like shit when we sober up later."

Ray knew his best friend was right about getting some much-needed R and R. He didn't want to press his friend's veiled protection of what seemed to be an archenemy of theirs, and so he left his inquisitive questions for another time. The bodyguards helped Ray and Lenny get back to their rooms without any further incident.

CHAPTER EIGHT
MAKING A PLAN AND A PLAY

WHEN DEAN AWOKE LATE THE NEXT MORNING IN HIS HOTEL room bed, everything was still spinning from the previous night's events. It felt as if the full Moon was sitting on his head, he had swallowed a viper that was coursing through his gut, and a monkey had crapped in his mouth making his breath unbearable even to himself. As he remembered what had transpired the previous night at the Fiesta Grande, he knew he had let his emotions get the better of him. Next, he noticed something unusual for his morning wake up ritual: his aides weren't present, and his room was a mess. He felt that maybe this scene was his doing. There was a message on his vid phone from the World Alliance Baseball Director, Hector Versacruz, who was directing the World Series finals here in Mazalta, North-Am. Dean was afraid to listen to the message. When the commissioner called, it was either to congratulate you on your win at the finals of Alliance Baseball, which hadn't happened yet, or there was trouble attached to his call. Dean knew it was the latter, and a feeling of dread came over his already hungover body. Dean rolled over onto his side, pushed his bed covers off of himself, and touched the vid phone replay to review the message.

On the vid-phone screen Versacruz's face appeared. He said, "Mr. Luthbert, this is Hector Versacruz, Director of the Alliance

World Series Finals here in Mazlata. It has come to my attention that a transgression took place between you and two other players at the Fiesta Grande last night. It seems that no one was hurt, but I must remind you that if players from different teams are going to frequent the same entertainment areas together, they must do so peacefully, respectably, and with etiquette. Players must refrain from violence off the field, no matter what happens on the field. I was told that an unknown government official stopped the situation before it got out of hand. For that I am thankful, as it has saved me a lot of digital work on your behalf, not to mention the costs that you would have been responsible for had your situation escalated. I don't know who this government person is, because he has an encrypted code put on him by the World Alliance Government Council that we are not allowed access to. He's a member of the military, and I'm going to look into why he was at the hotel last night. It seems that he has played an assuming roll in last night's incident, and I'm at a quandary. I can't reprimand you unless I have an official report, which I do not have, but I am trying to obtain one. I am trying very hard to get this incident out of the way, especially since the media are trying to blow it out of proportion. All I know is that we, the Alliance Baseball Council, only allow violence between players on the field of play and nowhere else. These are the rules set down by the Alliance League Executive, and I expect you to abide by them. If anyone had been hurt because of your actions, then you know the consequences. Let me reiterate these consequences: you will be disbarred from baseball if I find that violent actions are being conducted against other players, off the field, at these tournament finals by you or your entourage. All of your assets will be seized upon justification of your actions by a tribunal I will head! If another incident occurs that you are deemed responsible for while these final games are being conducted, you will be dealt with according to these rules that have been set forth. For your own information, I have sent this same message to the other two players that were involved in this incident at the Fiesta Grande, and I have let your respective coaches know about the basic circumstances. I have instructed them not to penalize any of you, as there will be no actions taken by me in this matter, at this time. Versacruz out." A slight click on the vid phone and silence signaled that the call was finished. Dean rolled back onto his pillow and groaned until he felt better.

Dean thought about how lucky he was that that skinny hillbilly had got in his way to stop him from getting at Ray. He also wondered why Lenny hadn't roughed him up when he had him down under the table at the Fiesta Grande. He recalled that Lenny had said that Ray wasn't responsible for Boisey's death, but Dean knew otherwise. Dean knew he'd get his chance soon enough. After a shower, he went to his team's dressing room. He checked the schedule and saw that the next team they were going to play was the Euro-Russo team, the Spartak Lokomotiv. Then something unexpected happened: he got a text message on his wrist vid from Ricardo Narzani. He wanted to meet with Dean. Dean hadn't heard from him since he had been traded from the Euro-Russo League to South-Am two years ago, and so wondered what this abandoning, political, ex-friend wanted. He was instructed to meet Narzani at a scheduled rendezvous that no one else could know about. Dean was to come alone with no media poking their noses after him. Narzani said to meet after his team practice, at around 6 pm.

Later, Dean sat across from Ricardo Narzani in a meeting room in the baseball dome, that Narzani rented, that held the games. "So, how are you doing Mr. Luthbert?" asked Ricardo sincerely.

"Forget the niceness, Narzani; what is it that you want?" said Dean, in an agitated tone.

"My, my, such a bad attitude for such a fine baseball player," Narzani remarked.

Dean had a bad hangover from the Hyderizers he had unwisely consumed the night before and was justifiably grouchy, but his real feelings of aggravation were for Ricardo Narzani. Ricardo hadn't supported Dean when he went through his downward spiral with the Gyor Titans, three years ago. Dean had been traded in a media scrum that he couldn't get away from. At the time Dean had asked Narzani to help him, but Narzani had distanced himself from Dean. Narzani hadn't wanted his reputation as a top dog politician for the Euro-Russo Alliance tarnished. He didn't want to be seen dealing with a mixed-up ball player like Luthbert.

"I'm here to help you with your problem," said Ricardo, trying to make Dean feel more at ease.

"And what problem is that?" Dean asked suspiciously.

"Oh, you know, Mr. Tenner, alias 'The Rat'. I have it on credible authority that he's going to retire after this season and you may not get a chance to kill him like you want. Like you, this is his fifth year in Alliance Baseball, and I have heard that he wants to retire from baseball and start up a business that will see my profits in space transport take a loss. I can't have that happen, especially if my creditors know that it may put me out of business, so to speak," said Ricardo. "I may be able to help you eliminate him here at these games. I could help your team win the Alliance Baseball World Series. This would send you onto a glorious retirement with all the riches you deserve, and you would never have to deal with 'The Rat' or the world again. You would be scott free of everything, even me. You would be rid of Mr. Tenner, and I would be rid of Tenner's business ventures," Ricardo finished.

"You know that I can't be involved with anything like that, Narzani. I'd be kicked out of baseball and made a pauper," said Dean, truthfully for once. "I've already been warned by Commissioner Versacruz not to take any actions against Tenner except on the field. How are you going to get rid of him without involving me?" asked Dean.

"Well, I've got interests other than baseball that should exempt you from what I'm about to propose," said Ricardo Narzani. "I know of a certain North-Am engineer that may put a damper on my industries with the introduction of the 'Uncertainty Principle Telephone'. It is a technological advancement on the 'uncertainty principle' where if a telecommunication call in our day and age is eavesdropped on, the eavesdropper won't ever be able to reconstitute the communications signal on today's vid phones because of the quantum entanglement principle. Once the wave is eavesdropped, it collapses; and no record of the wave call can be traced. But this person, this 'Hill Billy', has figured out how to use the uncertainty principle to his advantage in that he will be able to intercept any and all calls of mine, or anyone elses for that matter, via the 'uncertainty principle phone', anywhere in the known galaxy. He has figured out how to eavesdrop on the invincible uncertainty phone's anonymity. This makes my businesses prone to eavesdropping by people who will expose what I do in the interplanetary space transportation business. I need secrecy to keep my industries going, or I'll be toast," finished Narzani.

"How am I involved in all of this technological goulash, Narzani?" asked Dean rather rudely. "I know nothing of this uncertainty principle phone you speak of."

"Well, it seems that you have ties to all of the people who are involved in what I want to propose to you," said Ricardo.

"And that is…" trailed Dean, wanting to know.

"Let me put it this way, Mr. Luthbert. I want you to try and get these people together in one spot, and then I'll deal with the situation as it arises. You will be part of it, but you will not be blamed for anything. I give you my word that the actions I'm planning will never show you in any way responsible for what I propose," said Ricardo.

"I need more info before I agree to anything for you, Narzani," stated Dean.

"Well, I will tell you what I want, but not everything. I want a get-together of the people you know, so I can direct the complications I'm proposing onto them," said Ricardo, evading Dean's inquisitiveness.

"What do you mean by 'complications onto them', Ricardo?" Dean asked.

"I mean to eliminate them so that they won't interfere with my business and political dealings that I've built over the years as the head of the Euro-Russo Alliance. There are interstellar productions that will be largely inhibited if these people you know continue to exist and expand their business into the interstellar transportation business, which is my realm of expertise. Also, I want to become the nominated head of the World Alliance Council next year and follow through on my proposals to make the planet a better place to live, for the people of the world, that is," said Ricardo, keeping his language intentionally vague.

Dean knew he was in over his head at trying to get back at Ray Tenner for his brother Boisey's death. He was at a loss right now as to how to get back at Ray Tenner since the hotel incident. Narzani's proposal seemed inviting, so Dean decided to play the part of Narzani's unknowing sidekick.

"I tell you what, Ricardo: it seems I'm a bit naive as to what you really want here, but I am game to get rid of Tenner '*if*', and that is a big '*if*', you make sure that Tenner's not around to make my life miserable anymore. And if I get barred from baseball, you will make sure that I'll be okay financially," said Dean.

"I will put sixty million credits into an unnamed account which only you will have the access codes for you today, on condition that you make sure that Ray Tenner, Ian Shelton, and Bill Hill are in the same place, at the same time, that I designate. Bring

Tenner's best friend Peecheh. I will most graciously attend to your monetary needs once things have been completed, Dean," said Ricardo Narzani on a most friendly personal note.

"Who is this Bill Hill, and why are you so interested in him?" asked Dean.

"Well, let's just say that I know that Mr. Hill will be joining forces with 'The Rat' Tenner in the foreseeable future, and from what I can gather on him, he is a bit of a rogue when it comes to working for the Earth Alliance Government. This Mr. Hill has a reputation for bucking the systems that are in place that regularly help the downtrodden situations of the of the poorer people of this world, to the detriment of the more affluent people, like me. He seems to be today's Robin hood, using government funding to help the lower classes. I want to help the more affluent, so that my nomination to the head of the World Alliance Council will not be jeopardized. The intellectuals of this world have forecasted that this Bill Hill will not help the establishment in future government actions. In short, he's a rogue that the inner workings of the Earth Alliance Council do not want to deal with, as Mr. Hill cannot be trusted with the secrets of the Council," said Narzani. "Also, there is a certain woman who is part of this, but she is not important right now. My concern with her is that she is treading on my political aspirations. It would be nice if she could be included in this group that I want eliminated. Her name is Pamela Jay."

Dean knew he had a real hard decision to make. He could wait to kill Ray himself on the playing field, though the odds were it might not happen this year in baseball or ever, or he could trust Narzani, who may just be his 'easy answer' to his bitch with Ray Tenner. Finally, knowing that he would like to make sure his parents were taken care of if anything happened to him, Dean agreed to Narzani's proposals. Dean had realized that it was a win-win situation for him. He would get paid either way, even if this mixed up soap opera didn't happen, because of Narzani's payout to him. Plus, he could make a lot of credits by winning the World Series. Dean felt more at ease now that his goal of killing Ray Tenner was closer to being fulfilled.

Narzani went on to say, "Baseball, for me, is the forum through which I can approach the people of my region in the Euro-Russo Empire, Mr. Luthbert. I have the political strength and fortitude to press on with my plans to become the leader of this planet as Head of the Earth Alliance Council. I have access to hundreds of millions of people watching the game. They will vote for me if they see me as a great leader. I need you, Mr. Luthbert, to help me achieve my goal of becoming World Alliance Council Head," finished Narzani.

Dean knew he was being played, but his role as a pawn in this high-stakes political chess game was a major one. He, the powerful pawn, would set up the two rooks and a knight, Ray, Bill, and Lenny, to be taken out by the main bishop, Narzani, in this dark chess game. Dean made up his mind to strike a deal with Narzani.

"If I set these individuals up for you to knock off, Narzani, then I want the sixty million credits put into a bank account for my parents, not me. That way no one will know about anything, no matter what happens this month," said Dean. "As for your plan to get this Hill Billy person, that is your own doing. I know I can get Tenner and Peecheh together, but I don't know about this 'Hill Billy' character, or the others you're talking about," said Dean.

"So, do I have a deal with you, Mr. Luthbert? Will you bring these individuals together for me at a certain gathering I will oversee?" asked Ricardo Narzani.

"Yes, I will, but it may take some time to 'get them together', as I'm not on their 'good persons' list as of yet. I'm going to have to try and be the nice guy here, but I don't think they are going to go for it. I'll need to make up an excuse to meet with them. Then you will need to find a suitable place for them to come to, trusting they'll come," said Dean.

"Take your time, Mr. Luthbert. The cost of helping you will be a steep price that I will have to bear for both of our sakes," said Ricardo, trying to make Dean feel as if the payout was a great financial burden to him.

In regards to Dean's payout, it was a pittance in comparison to what it would really cost Narzani if his exposure to the world was made known through his shady dealings by the new 'uncertainty principle vid-phone' that was being improved upon by Bill Hill. Also, Ray Tenner's efforts to try and start a company that could cost Narzani everything he had worked for in the past twenty years, as chief of Interplanetary Transport Systems, was his other business concern. Ricardo Narzani could lose billions of credits if his business adversaries were to succeed. In the political arena, Pamela Jay was another concern. She was the only one who could really expose him through political channels. He also wanted her present when his 'elimination plans' were put into play and finalized, for she was the political 'thorn in his side' and Narzani wanted to be rid of her too.

When Ricardo left, Dean started to formulate a plan for getting Ray Tenner and his friends together in the same place. He would invite their families to come and visit them here in Mazalta at the Grand Festival of Alliance Baseball Players at the Conquistador Palace. He knew that the parents were still good friends, even though their sons played on different teams. Dean would throw a formal party for his 'old friends' in an effort to make it look like a reconciliation of sorts, and thereby fulfill his deal with the devil, Ricardo Narzani.

CHAPTER NINE
CROOKED POLITICS

RICARDO NARZANI WAS CONSIDERED BY HIS PEERS TO BE A VERY dangerous man, politically, for he would do almost anything to get his way in the Earth Alliance Government. There were a few politicians in the government that openly opposed him without fear, for they knew if they were to 'disappear', Ricardo Narzani would be in great trouble politically and rightly so. That is why Narzani tolerated them.

One of his opposing critics was an outspoken up-an-coming politician by the name of Pamela Jay. The poorer people in her region wanted to vote Pamela Jay onto the seat of the Euro-Russo Alliance Council, because they felt that Narzani was getting too powerful for their good. Nothing had ever really seemed to change since the global deserts came. The people of the lands had never been supported by the government in power, and now they felt that change was in the offing. Credits were never sent to the right places to help the poorest regions of Euro-Russo. The poor always bore the brunt of the environmental changes in the old Europe and Russia regions. It seemed that the 'political' always stepped over — or on — the 'peasants' and vaulted themselves to power as elite rulers of the land (same old, same old, was the saying by the rank and file). History had repeated itself in the poorest regions, even though the rest of the world had changed for the better with diverse races and cultures putting aside their differences and getting along to the betterment of their regions. The people realized that they would suffer ever harsher realities because of Narzani's rule of law. They needed a champion to democratically help them in their cause for a better life in the Euro-Russo Alliance. This champion was Pamela Jay, and these desperate people wanted her as head of the World Alliance Council so that their concerns could at least be heard.

Now Pamela Jay was an oratorical woman who felt that the rights of the individual were more important than the rights of the group. She wanted people to be able to choose for themselves and not have someone do it for them. This philosophy differed from that of Narzani, who, as head of the Euro-Russo Alliance, made the decisions for everyone. Narzani always spoke majestically of making the lives of the common people simpler, so that they did not have to worry about decisions his government could make for them. Everyone in the Euro-Russo Alliance would have a good life (a chicken in every pot, so to speak). No increase of taxes, more credits for infrastructure, blah, blah, blah... This kind of political rhetoric had made Narzani a lot of credits. Yet the people of the Euro-Russo Alliance knew for a fact that Narzani only said he was helping them when the opposite was true. He was slowly milking them for their hard-earned credits. He was silently stealing from them. So, Pamela Jay had made it her quest to help the people of the Euro-Russo Alliance. She did this by constantly trying to expose Narzani and his cronies like Collin Bendshaw, head of the North-Am Alliance, for what they really were. They were trying to control everything while making it look like the local governments had sided with the people for their benefit. You see, Pamela had grown up in a poor family. When her political star began to rise, she made a promise to herself that the people, not the governments, would get her support.

The game of Alliance Baseball was a backdrop for the World Alliance Council Government head politicians. Its propaganda for the crooked politicians (from videos aired during baseball games) was garnered from the Earth Alliance council member states who took full advantage of this publicity because the game was the draw of the people, the votes they wanted. Many a political speech was made to the huge crowds that attended the games. Politicians never missed a chance to say at least a zestful hello to the people at the games, and they touted their accomplishments over the airwaves to the people via the games. Alliance Baseball attracted interest worldwide, and so the politicians were naturally drawn to the large numbers of people (and potential 'votes') at the games. Subtle messages were usually presented by each Alliance's Government region's heads of state to try and persuade the people to vote for them. Here in North-Am, Collin Bendshaw was the Head of State, and Ricardo Narzani was his counterpart in the Euro-Russo Alliance. They both had their dark dealings in interplanetary and interstellar trade that had made them super rich, but power was their ultimate ego-quencher, not economic gains. They always sought to spin webs of deceit that made them look better when presenting their orations to the masses.

When Bendshaw and Narzani found out about Ray's quest to undercut their Earth-to-Moon-to-Earth haulage business, they knew they would have troubles in their futures economically and possibly politically. Along with Bill Hill's discovery of how to eavesdrop with the 'uncertainty principle' vid phone and Pamela Jay's political meddling, they had their hands full trying to control the accusations and rumors of their shady dealings in the solar system and beyond.

"So, Collin, how do you think we should proceed against the efforts of those who are going to run us out of business?" asked Ricardo Narzani.

"First, we have to silence Miss Jay. I'm at a loss at how to do this, for as our most outspoken critic she will surely rail against us for control over the Earth Alliance Council. As for Mr.

Tenner, Shelton, and Bill Hill, I'll leave that up to you, Ricardo," said Collin.

"Well, I have an idea for Miss Jay, since you're at a loss of how to help me rid her from her bid to get elected to the Head of the Alliance Council," said Narzani. He continued, "There is a certain young astronomer/physicist who may unknowingly help us. Ian Shelton works for the Earth Alliance Government, and he finds most of our interstellar commodities using our highly touted "chroma scope" orbiting a trillion miles past Pluto outside the Kupitr Belt. We think he is in a relationship with Miss Jay or once was. I've recently found out that he also secretly works with Ray Tenner, and is in the process making future business dealings with him. I have it from reliable sources that this is happening right now. So, if I can get Tenner, Jay, and Hill together by using Mr. Shelton, I have hatched a plan that will be to our benefit. I will use sand lizards to accidentally burst into where they will be, and then let the sand lizards do the eliminating for us. No suspicions will point towards us. It will all be accidental, of course. This occurrence will take place in two days, after the final game of the first round-robin set of games in the Alliance Baseball World Series Finals," Ricardo informed Bendshaw.

"Don't you think that's a bit morbid to have them eaten by those monsters?" asked Collin in a serious tone. "Besides, how are you going to use sand lizards? No one has ever caught a large one alive. They're usually destroyed on sight for the damage they inflict when they are on our side of the global ringed forest. They are very unpredictable and as ferocious as hell, from what I've heard. They can easily outmaneuver the clayon guards. Human guards aren't that much more effective if they don't get to the sand lizards quickly. This could make a very bad scenario for us, especially if your plan doesn't work properly and the media sees right through your ruse," finished Collin.

Ricardo continued after Collin's interruption. "It's always the males that intrude and cause damage, never the females. I've studied the sand lizards mannerisms in the last little while. The females don't come here because of the attention they get from the males out in the global deserts. They are usually a lot more docile and smaller than the males, but when they are upset they can be deadly, scaled down from the males of course, but they still exhibit deadly aggression when agitated. They'll more than do for what I want done," said Narzani. He proceeded to show Collin a video showing a threesome of female lizards tearing apart a single male not much larger than them. "You see, I have three of these ferocious smaller females in my custody. I have raised them since they were very young. They were only three tons apiece when I acquired them. I can put them in the vicinity of our selected guests, aggravate the hell out of them, and then let the female lizards do the rest. They weigh twenty tons apiece now, and I've been starving them for this occasion," said Ricardo, smiling.

"How are you going to move creatures that big without anyone noticing?" asked Collin.

"There is a facility near the baseball domes that the players use for R and R during lulls in their schedules. The Conquistador Palace is used by dignitaries or V.I.P.s for private functions. I've set up an underground bunker attached to the Palace for this specific function. I'm almost certain that Tenner's team will make it to the finals this year, by the way they are playing. There is a three-day layover for the two teams who make it to the playoff finals, and according to league rules, the two teams have to spend their time there so that the players can be supervised as they relax. I've already got the three female lizards there in a lower concrete bunker. They are sedated so they won't get out of hand until I need them. When we are ready, they can be quickly revived and moved upward along the vehicle entrance ramp without anyone finding out. I have a plan that will make it look like they have overrun the main fences and clayon guards at the ringed forests and have them ambush the populated areas at the Conquistador Palace," finished Ricardo Narzani after revealing his diabolical plan.

"That will catastrophically disrupt the World Series Finals Tournament! You'll kill a lot of players, not to mention anyone else who's around, including you and me!" said, Collin, exasperated. "That has never happened in the history of baseball. There will be no finals, and a lot of people will die unnecessarily because of your plan." Collin looked very worried indeed.

"My point precisely, Collin. A few will be sacrificed for our greater good. We will keep our enterprises going at the expense of Jay, Tenner, Peecheh, Hill, and even Shelton if necessary. So the games will be momentarily stopped, so what. The people will be disappointed, but they'll get over it. It will all come together next year with a few condolences, tears, and moments of silence and then everything will be as before, eh Collin?" said Narzani slyly.

"If you can pull this off, I'm all for it, Ricardo, but you have to make sure that I don't get caught up in the repercussions. Getting caught will mean a treason charge against you and me. The penalty for treason is death. When proven, death is always the result for anyone involved in treason. You know the constitutional rules!" said Collin, terrified.

"The only way I'm going to pull this off is to have you introduce Ronald Messtier, the Master of Ceremonies at the R and R festivities, at the Palace. I'm going to organize it," said Ricardo. "That way it won't look like you've done anything wrong, and you can plead innocence all you want."

"You mean you want me to be there when you let those awful sand lizards loose in the Palace?" said Collin incredulously, looking at Ricardo as if he were crazy.

"Don't worry, Collin, old buddy; you'll be right by a fortified exit that will lead you to safety. The sand lizards will never even get near you. I'll also be there with ten, laser-armed, clayon guards who'll protect you and me. The lizards won't even come near us. It is the only way I can pull this off without you or me being implicated. It will make you look like you are a victim. Our escape will be deemed miraculous. I need you to do this for me, for us, and for our businesses. This is the only way I can eliminate those who are trying to stop or expose our business dealings as controllers of the delivery systems we now dominate. And I'll finally be rid of that witch, Pamela Jay. I know I could never kill her myself, for if I did, it would be the end of me politically," said Ricardo, matter-of-fact.

"How will the sand lizards get to the R and R facility?" asked Collin. "There is a twenty-four-hour watch by the clayon guards near the global forest. They watch for the lizards' presence at the forest's edge. When they are seen, an alert is initiated which draws an instant response by the reserves who'll cut them down like hamburger," finished Collin.

"In the past there have been a few times, three if I'm correct, that the clayon guards have made mistakes in trying to find and stop the giant sand lizards that have escaped from the edges of the great global desert. No matter how much trust we have put into them, the clayon guards have failed us on occasion. I have studied the times when they have made their mistakes, and I'm going to devise my plan around one of these 'mistakes' that they have made in the past. I will change the dynamics slightly so that the clayon guards won't be able to stop my 'princess lizards' from accomplishing their mission," said Ricardo. "I can cause a large enough disturbance to prevent detection of any traces of my plan, Collin. Then we will be better off. Our economic/political futures will be a lot brighter once we eliminate our enemies!" Ricardo ending his speech to Bendshaw with a bit of gusto.

"I'm completely unwilling to give up my political position as Head of State in North-Am. My family has a long history of governing there, twenty-three generations to be exact. I don't want to be seen as someone who has gone amok from my actions. Are you sure you can pull this off without getting any crap on me?" asked Collin.

"I can guarantee with ninety-nine percent accuracy that this 'function' will be carried out without a hitch, Collin. I've got a baseball player on the inside who is going to help me make this happen. He asks a small price, but I am able to pay him what he wants for his actions and silence. He will be my star player in this set-up of historical consequences that will make, by my say so, 'our' world a safer place to live," said Ricardo sounding like a truly crooked politician.

"Who is this player you refer to, Ricardo?" asked Collin.

"That is my business, and not for you to know, my friend, because the less that is known about others involved in this plan, the better, if you know what I mean," said Ricardo putting down a synthesized puffer.

Ray and Lenny's team, the Labrador Redmen of North-Am, went through to the final round-robin game. They had eliminated the four other teams to face one last opponent, Dean Luthbert's team, the Pelotas from South-Am. This final game of the round-robin tournament would determine who would finish first and who would be second. Winning this top dog rating at the World Alliance Baseball Finals was a great ego-appeaser for the players, who would get a needed rest from competition. These two teams in this semi-final had beaten all the other teams to meet in this round-robin final. In this game, there would be but one loser. The losing team would have to go through the long and arduous journey of eliminating all other teams to get back into the finals against the team that defeated them. This was called repechage.

MEDIA HYPE BY NORTH-AM BROADCASTING

The vid media hype of the North-Am Alliance world vid broadcasting network hyped up this game through a preview of what was to come when these two teams met in the semi-final of World Series Alliance Baseball. Billed as the 'Scorpion' against the 'Deadly Duo', this preliminary game could see some big names snuffed out before determining who would advance from this semi-final to the World Series of Alliance Baseball.

Who would be played? Who was most likely to die? Who would be left out at game time, and who would play? Who was on the most 'exciting' list? Exposure of all the players' nuances was the topic of the day for the media and the adoring crowds, for they wanted to know everything about everybody. These questions were asked of the public to make them come out and adore their heroes. These questions made the people, the fans, want even more of their heroes' actions on the field of play displayed so that they could decide upon their villains or heroes from the list that the media gave to them to decide upon.

Ricardo Narzani talked to Dean in his limo in the stadium underground preferred parking lot. "Mr. Luthbert, I have informed you of my plan to eliminate Mr. Tenner and his friends. What do you think of it?"

"I think it's a great plan," said Dean. "That way I can lure Tenner in and then watch as he gets eaten like a fly by the meanest lizards on Earth," said Dean in a determined monotone.

"That's my man and I'm glad you are in agreement Mr. Luthbert. I will see that you are rewarded handsomely with sixty million credits into your parents' accounts," said Ricardo, smiling slyly. All the while the wheels of political power were turning in his head at his beastly plot. "Just make sure that they sit by this entrance at the Conquistador Palace right here," said Ricardo, pointing to a floor plan, he was showing Dean, of the facility that would host this so-called party.

"Collin Bendshaw will be introducing the Master of Ceremonies Ronaldo Messtier. Both of us will be located near a fortified exit, right here, so when things start to happen, your escape will be quick and safe. I will have a squad of ten clayon guards ready to help you escape when things turn nasty," said Ricardo. "I'll be right beside both you Mr. Luthbert, when we make our exits. I will have cameras rolling while the events unfold, and we'll make heroes out of our eaten friends as they try and get away," laughed Ricardo happily.

Now more than ever Dean felt that he could accomplish his goal of eliminating Ray Tenner without further family prejudices. On the playing field it would be a hit and miss situation where Dean could possibly be the one gone from the equation instead of Ray Tenner, according to the rules of play. Using sand lizards had a more of a 'hit' reality to it, and Dean liked those odds. Dean began to formulate his words of mock apology to Ray and Lenny, in his head, for the upcoming function. He was a good conjurer of apologetic rhetoric in that he knew Ray's and Lenny's softer sides from all the years they had spent together in their youth.

CHAPTER TEN
GAME ON!

"THIS IS YOUR ALLIANCE COMMENTATOR, J. D. BOWER, ANNOUNCing the game between Pelotas of South-Am and the Labrador Redmen of North-Am. It's the final game of the round-robin play to determine first and second place at the World Alliance Baseball finals from Mazalta, the southern most city of North-Am. I will be broadcasting live over airwaves all over the Earth. As all of you fans know, today will be a great game between the two top undefeated tournament teams in this round-robin World Series Alliance Baseball Finals. The outcome of this game will determine who will have a rest, and who will have to doggedly go on to try and retake their place as top team… or die trying," enthused the North-Am Games' commentator.

"We have the Labrador Redmen from North-Am against the South-Am's Pelotas playing here in Mazalta today for you fans who have just tuned in to our broadcast. In this last game of the first round, we have the Scorpion against the Deadly Duo. As you can see, this is a sold-out stadium with plenty of fans to cheer the teams on. There are over eight hundred and eighty thousand anxious and noisy fans here today wanting to see a brutal, high-scoring, deadly game. The whole building here feels like it's alive and literally vibrating with excitement. We'll get our camera to show you the throngs of people here," said the commentator.

From the commentator's booth the camera panned out over the human sea of spectators in the enclosed baseball super domed stadium. "It is mind-boggling to have so many people in one place, at one time, and they are all under control!" extolled the commentator. "Of course, strict rules are set out for the fans to behave, or else the consequences would not be a happy ending for the offending parties. Sixty thousand armed clayon guards are ever present among the spectators surrounding the infield during the game. Another ten thousand clayon guards are stationed above the crowd at the top of the seats on a circular eves section, built specifically to hold the guards above the spectators, each with a camera imbedded in their bionic bodies that scans the crowds for trouble in the stands. If a fight between rival fans occurs, then the clayon guards are immediately dispatched, usually a hundred at a time, to quickly arrest the feuding individuals and remove them from the premises. The clayon guards always take more than just the guilty culprits. A ring of twenty or so innocent fans is also removed from the offending area. They are all put out into the streets with the indicated troublemakers whose heads are marked with permanent paint, and the rest is history when it comes to taking care of troublemakers in the stadiums. The law has never convicted any fans that have caused trouble in the stadiums, by the way, yet the troublemakers never seem to return once they are put out with the innocent fans. So, rowdiness is a definite no-no. Only unbridled enthusiasm is welcome, and the fans are usually self-controlled in that respect.

"Many fans come bearing cloth or paper banners. Huge amounts of people come wearing face or body paint or fancy masks. The home team is always represented by the home team fans wearing their home team's colors. Fans of the Redmen home team wear red and white. Fans of the Pelotas visiting team wear black and gold. Yes, there are a few tens of thousands of dedicated fans here to represent the visiting team, but usually the home team fans' jerseys color them out. If a spectator gets too boisterous and looks like they may cause a disturbance, then a non-harmful laser light is shone onto them by a clayon guard as a quick reminder to not get out of hand and to settle down. So, as you can see, an Alliance Baseball Game is quite an event. It's great fun for all," finished J. D. Bower, the game's broadcasting commentator.

"Now, on with today's game." And with that comment, the commentator began giving the starting lineups of each team over the broadcasting system to the watchers in the stands and over the vid-vision networks all over the Earth. Other stations cut to commercials and life drummed on at this World Series Alliance Baseball game.

In the dressing room before their game, Ray looked at Lenny and asked if he was ready for today's match. Although this was their usual ritual, Lenny looked like he was worried that something bad would happen today. He was pacing, which he usually didn't do. So, Ray said reassuringly, "Hey, Lenny, it's going to be a good game today, even if we are playing against Dean. I mean, as long as we can get onto base when we bat, I'm sure the coach will send out relief runners to get you and me off of the bases. We won't have to worry about Dean beaning us."

"Right now, all I want to do is get through this game with us intact. I've never played against Dean before, and that kind of has me scared, especially since he's gunning for you. I've had a great run with my time in this game, and a great time with you, Ray. I want our good times to continue after we retire, but I'm afraid of today," said Lenny lethargically.

"Well, old man, you can't have it your way all time; you of all people should know that by now. We've both played a lot of games. We've been injured many times and we've also taken a lot of young, good ball players down, so let's just enjoy ourselves and let the game take its course. I know we'll get through it. Don't worry, we'll be just fine," said Ray reassuringly.

After Ray's comment, they both smiled. At that moment their coach, Cito Gaster, summoned the team for their pregame pep talk.

"I want all of you guys to be as sharp as possible out there today, for if we lose this game, we will have to go back into the system and play every team again in the repechage. That would mean four more gruelling games of brutal work to get back at this team we are going to grind it out with today, which almost never happens. It has only happened once in the over two-hundred-year history of Alliance Baseball that any team has fought back to play the team that has gotten the bye into the finals. If we beat them today, then it's the same for them. So, what would you meat heads rather do: win and rest, or lose and work your butts off, all over again?" asked the coach, eying them menacingly. He expected an answer from his charge of young players.

At the top of their young lungs, the team answered with a resounding, "Win, Coach; we want to win, we want to win, we want to win!"

Gaster put his hands up to quieten the team down and began, "They've got the best pitching stats in the tournament." Coach Gaster went on, "So now that means our own pitchers and batters will have to be, as I said before, sharp, when they are in the play. As for running, batting, and base playing, we are the better team and we've got that all sewed up. So, let's dig deeper than we've ever done as a team and give these South-Am bastards hell!" finished Coach Gaster in a crescendo of his rhetoric rant, pumping his fist into the air over and over.

"Redmen! Redmen! Redmen!" shouted the Labrador Redmen team members as they filed out of their dressing room and out onto the playing field. The cameras sent images of the enthusiastic team parading onto the field. The home team crowd erupted into a loud cheer that instilled pride into every Redmen team member as they trotted out onto the field shouting their team's name.

Dean's team, however, was not as boisterous as the home team Redmen. Their coach Carlos Vieria may have been more of a laid-back type of man, but he never let his guard down with his players. If you didn't do your job on the field, you would certainly hear about it from Vieria. So, in that respect his players gave him what he expected: one hundred percent respect while playing on the field.

"We are playing the second-best team here in this tournament. What does that mean to you men?" asked Coach Vieria. "What do you think they can accomplish?" he said, raising his voice a little while speaking in a controlled tone. "I'll tell you the answers to both of these questions. They can beat you at any moment of the day, and before you know it, it's you who will be the dead man and your team will lose!" He emphasized the word 'lose'. "You have your leaders, the vets on this team that have done well. As for the rest of you rookies, you can't depend on the vets all of the time to carry the team. You, as a whole team, must gather your true strength as ball players and rise above our adversaries so that we may be victorious together. If you do not win today, you will either have a long road ahead to get back at our enemy, or you will have a long road back to your home Alliance, in South-Am, to face the people who will jeer at you as you walk past them with your heads down. They will call you losers until the day you die. Many of you will become space workers, or peons, and will never play baseball again!" finished Carlos. He had emphasized the word losers in a caustic tone, while pumping his fist into the air. Then Carlos then just stood there, staring at his players. That signified he was finished his pep talk and it was time for the team to have their say.

Dean stood up as the representative leader of his team and said, "Coach Vieria is right, men. We are the top team here, and we have to stay the top team so we can take the Alliance World

Series crown home with us, for South-Am! We do this for our team and our coach, Vieria!" shouted Dean.

With that, the Pelotas' players jumped to their feet and loudly chanted, "Carlos, Carlos, Carlos." Their chanting continued as they marched out onto the playing field to do battle with the Labrador Redmen knowing the home team fans knew who they were chanting for.

The home team crowd made the ground rumble like a minor earthquake when they started jumping up and down in unison, over eight hundred thousand strong booing the visiting Pelotas team as they first appeared onto the field. Then their cheering almost made you go jet-roaring deaf when the home team Redmen stepped out onto the field.

The field's turf color was the usual white, which signaled that the game was about to begin. The levitating field umpires came down to the field of play level. They spoke to the team captains about their conduct on the field, and wished the representatives of each team good luck in their endeavors in this game. The Redmen were shown on the jumbo trons as the home team because they had scored more runs than Pelotas during the tournament. Once the umpires rose to their positions above the field, the home plate umpire signaled the field computer umpire to turn the playing turf from white to green. The game was on!

"Play ball!" shouted the home plate umpire. The old original chant instilled fear into the players, for the deadly dance of Alliance Baseball had begun and reality was here!

The levitating servo discs brought the Redmen, the defensive players, from their respective dugouts to their starting positions on the field against the visiting team. The batter for Pelotas was brought to home plate. The levitated servos made sure that no one had to expend any unnecessary energy, as the distances to be covered were literally thousands of feet on the larger playing fields of Alliance Baseball.

A promising young rookie batter, Edgar Rodriguez, was first up for South-Am's Pelotas. Edgar took the count to two balls and one strike, but the home team pitcher challenged him with a fastball that sailed one hundred and seventy-two miles an hour right over the plate. Edgar swung his jointed bat for all he was worth. He connected with a mighty ground ball that should have went through the infield like a hot knife through butter, but the second baseman for the Redmen, Ray Tenner, knifed at the speeding ball as it was about to go past him and got the sizzling grounder to meld with his glove. The ball's built up momentum dragged Ray for over ten feet backwards on the field before Ray could get control of himself. He got up off of the turf quite quickly and eyed his opponent through his electronic eyepiece, gauging Rodriguez's speed going to first base, and then he threw the ball at the runner. As the spikes came out of the ball, it cleanly hit Edgar on the jaw, crushing it, spattering blood over his face, and knocking him out before he reached first base. The field umpire signaled an immediate one bean out rule, and a raised red halo encircled the downed runner to signify that he wasn't able to continue to first base. The single bean by Ray was an official out for this first batter of the Pelotas Team.

The home team fans roared their approval for Ray, and the clayon medic robots removed Edgar Rodriguez's motionless, bloody, still alive body off of the playing field. Hopefully Rodriguez would heal and play again at some point in the future. This was the tone of the first two innings of the game, during which no one got past the infield of either team. The coaches knew that if the younger rookie batters could get onto base in the early innings, they would have a chance to score and get the advantage of staying ahead. But this was not to be. The six young men who took turns at bat were either killed or brutally crippled trying to get to first base: four by the Dynamic Duo, and two by Lea Loocke, the third baseman of the Redmen.

At the top of the third inning, Dean came up to bat. As nervous as he was at facing Ray and Lenny, Dean didn't let them know it. Dean even pointed his finger at Ray as a warning that he was coming for him if he got on base. Dean was an experienced, cagey batter, and Coach Cito Gaster knew it. Dean had a sixty-six percent average of getting on base with an infield hit, and a ninety-nine percent average with an outfield hit. Coach Gaster immediately brought in a fresh new arm that could steam the ball over the plate at over a hundred and eighty miles an hour. This change of pitcher wasn't new to Dean, as this pitcher, Stoney Bruch, had pitched against him before in another league. Dean took it all in stride as he set himself in the batter's box. Dean actually let two great fastballs go by him over the plate for strikes to make his count 'O' and two. His strategy was to get the pitcher over-confident enough to put a pitch near the plate, and that was exactly what happened. The third pitch, from Bruch, came in a little outside but at waist level. It was Dean's favorite pitch. He swung at it with the precision of a pro and sent the ball zinging just over Lenny's head at first base into right field for a double base hit. Then he comfortably strode into second base where Ray was playing.

Dean merely said, "Well, this is nice. We are actually near each other legally, and nothing is going to happen, eh Rat?"

"The game isn't over yet, and I'll get my chance at you, Dean. You've had it too good for too long, and I'll make sure that it won't last," was all that Ray had to say. Dean jogged off the field and was relieved by a pinch runner under the 'protection of vets' rule of the game.

The next two batters for Pelotas each hit singles that put two runners on and scored the pinch runner at home plate who took over for Dean on second base. Now with only one out,

Coach Cito Gaster changed his pitcher again to help improve the chances of his team getting out of this inning with only one run scored. His hunch to replace his pitcher had been right, for the new pitcher got the fourth batter up for Pelotas to hit into a double, single bean, play. The Deadly Duo were key to stopping the Pelotas' base runners from scoring.

The play-by-play commentator, J. D. Bower, said, "We have one out with two men on base in the bottom of the third. Now it doesn't look good for the Redmen. One of the best hitters for Pelotas is up to bat: John Elton Thomas, otherwise known as the 'Jet'. This right-handed hitting veteran with over four years in Alliance Baseball can really push a ball. And by that, I mean he is a consistent hitter who is a threat at any time in the ball game. All that is needed is just a hit of any kind, and Pelotas will easily score another run or two in this inning. The home team fans have quieted down quite a bit, for they feel this situation may not turn out in favor of their favored Redmen. John 'Jet' standing tall in the batter's box is ready for anything to be thrown at him. In comes the first pitch, and it is a sizzling fastball," said the play-by-play commentator.

A loud crack sounded over the P.A. system.

"It looks like that one is going out of here over in left field. I've not seen a ball hit so high in a long time!" said J. D. Bower.

Now a loud clunk was heard, and everyone knew what that was. The left field foul pole had been hit so high by the ball that no one could tell where the ball was. Stadium cameras zoomed in on the left field foul pole as the ball fell on the left side onto the ground. The levitating third base field umpires signaled a foul ball to the home plate umpire, much to the relief of the home team fans and the Redmen.

"Well, how about that? It's just a long phantom strike ball. After a strike that traveled an estimated four hundred feet high and fourteen hundred feet long, the 'Jet' has to bring himself back to the batter's box," said the commentator, matter-of-fact. A new ball was given to the Redmen pitcher and the commentator announced, "The next pitch is outside. The Redmen catcher, Johnny Brench, a great Hall of Fame name, quickly sends the ball back to the pitcher and the cycle begins again. The pitcher wastes no time in delivering to the 'Jet'. A sizzling slider is thrown down and in. The 'Jet' hits the ball hard on the ground to the second baseman, Ray Tenner. Tenner magically scoops up the ball and gives the runner coming from first to second a full-face smash with the ball. This blow sends the young Pelotas player down to the turf. The red 'out' halo around the base runner signifies he's out. Lenny Peecheh, for the Redmen, gets to the loose ball from Tenner and puts the bean on the 'Jet' for Pelotas coming to first base by hitting him on the helmet. Then Peecheh gets the ball again from the minor infielder who sends the errant ball to his first baseman. Lenny pumps it at the downed 'Jet', hitting him in the upper leg, smashing his femur, and getting the second bean for the second out of this double play masterly performed by the Deadly Duo to make it three out. What a dramatic end to this third inning with no more runs scored by Pelotas. My, how an inning can change when it looks bad for the home team," reflected J. D. Bower. The home team crowd roared its approval as the writhing 'Jet' was removed from the field by medical clayon robots. "The teams now change positions and we have the Redmen coming to bat to finish off the fourth inning," finished the commentator.

"At the bottom of the fourth inning and it's to the top of the Redmen's batting lineup to start at bat. Lenny and Ray, who did not start at bat, are now inserted into the batting lineup to start the inning off. They are expected to try and get that run, scored against them by Pelotas, back. Ray is first up to bat. In the previous innings Ray has kept himself warmed up in the virtual warm up batter's box behind his team's dugout. He has swung his bat many times to keep his swing at the ball as fresh in his mind as possible. Nervously, Ray steps onto the field. He is then brought out to the home plate by his flat servo-disc, and he finally steps into the batters' box. With his hand up so the pitcher won't throw, Ray quickly glances at Dean, who is playing third base. Dean has a big smile on his face. To Ray, it looks like Dean is saying, *'Come on, Rat; hit it to me and see where you get on this field,'"* surmised the commentator.

"Play ball!" shouted the levitating home plate umpire from above, and with that, the Pelotas' pitcher threw a high and inside pitch. While it was within the limits of a pitch not being thrown at a player, the pitch still made Ray jerk back from the plate in an automatic defensive move. "Inside ball one!" shouted the home plate umpire from his lofty position.

Ray, in his mind, quickly told himself, *"Come on, Ray, you've been here a thousand times. Settle down and watch for your candy pitch to come in."*

The next pitch was a fastball across the plate for a strike that Ray let go.

"Strike one! One and one is the count," called the home plate umpire.

Ray watched the pitcher and tried to guess what he would deliver next. Ray's guess was wrong. He had expected a low pitch, but the ball came inside across the plate faster than he had anticipated. Ray tried to get his bat around, but the power of the pitch hit near his fingers, and because of the pitch's power, the ball bent his favorite-hinged bat in half. After a slight delay, a new articulated bat was brought to Ray. The count was one ball and two strikes. This was not where Ray wanted to be. He hunkered down for his next pitch, but he fouled off. As he began to feel more confident in his batting abilities, he readied himself for the next throw. This time, Ray was ready, and a pitch came at him that was slightly on the outside of the plate, but nonetheless, it was a pitch in the strike zone. Ray set his jointed bat to the pressures he felt that would give him a hit, and that is exactly what happened. Ray hit the ball over the first baseman, right down the right field line, to give himself at least a double. By the time the right fielder got to the ball, Ray had rounded second base. His third base coach signaled Ray to come for third. Seeing that Dean was waiting for him on third, Ray took a quick glance over his left to see if the right fielder had thrown the ball towards Dean. He had. Ray thought he would get to third base comfortably, but to his surprise, the third base coach urged him to dive for third as the right fielder had thrown the ball perfectly to Dean. If Ray didn't dive, he would be beaned, possibly fatally. Ray desperately dove for third base. He couldn't use his knife-like blades on Dean, because the rules stated that if the opposing defensive player didn't have possession of the ball, the base runner could not use the blades in his armored batting gloves or cleats. Ray half flew at Dean and attempted to touch third base safely with his right arm. Ray put his shoulder into Dean's forward left leg, just as Dean caught the ball. This collision made Dean go off-balance. The force of their collision knocked Dean down and forced him to drop the ball. The minor infielder had to get possession of the ball and give it back to Dean to keep the ball in play.

Safely on third base, the dust settling around him as he lay on the ground, Ray wondered if he had hurt himself.

Dean and Ray had been this close only twice since Boisey's death in the desert sands. Ray could feel electricity from their proximity as Dean stood up, in possession of the ball. Dean looked menacingly at Ray and said, "You're a lucky shit, Tenner, but shit only lasts so long until the smell wears off and goes away."

Cito Gaster motioned for Ray to stay as the base runner. When he had made it to third base, Ray had a better scoring average than replacement runners.

"Well, Rat, you're on base. I may still get a shot at you after all before this inning is over," said Dean, as he passed the ball to the minor infielder who threw it back to the Pelotas' pitcher.

"Don't count on it, Dean; Lenny's up next, and all you'll see is my dust when Lenny hits me home," said Ray, scowling at Dean.

"Play ball!" shouted the home plate umpire from his levitated position.

"And the next batter is none other than Lenny Peecheh, the other member of the Dynamic Duo, for the Redmen," extolled the commentator over the airwaves. The crowd gave a round of enthusiastic applause as they roared for their home team favorite at bat.

The play-by-play commentator went on, "Lenny Peecheh is second in this tournament in batting averages. He is the top hitter for the Redmen. The only other player to better him is none other than Dean Luthbert, the 'Scorpion' for Pelotas, on third base." The fans booed when they heard Dean's name.

"Here we go. Now there is none out and a man on third with the top batter for the Redmen at the plate," said the commentator. Lenny stepped off of his levitating disc and, in an almost gentlemanly fashion, entered the batter's box. He smiled and signaled to the umpire that he was ready.

"Play ball!" shouted the home base umpire.

"Here's the pitch, and it's a fastball, low and inside," said the play-by-play commentator. "The Pelotas' pitcher appears hesitant to give Peecheh any kind of hittable ball. He seems to want to keep the ball away from him, but I don't think that will deter Peecheh. He'll go after anything. And, true to form, the next pitch is low and away by the Pelotas' pitcher. But Peecheh hits at the ball by sending the ball just over the first baseman's outstretched glove. That hit by Peecheh gives him a single; it sends in Ray Tenner to score from third base, and the game is now tied," said the excited commentator, J. D. Bower. "Peecheh glides easily to first base as the ball is scooped up by the speedy right fielder for Pelotas and sent quickly to second base to hold Peecheh at first," said the commentator. The home team crowds went crazy and they cheered wildly for their team.

Ray took a good look at Lenny on first base, and gave him the thumbs up sign for getting him to home plate safely.

"Now with his batting duties accomplished, Peecheh is relieved at first base by a pinch runner by the name of Lonney Cameron, and rightly so, for the coach of the Redmen, Cito Gaster, wants to preserve his prized hitter Mr. Peecheh. His mates in the dugout are full of praise for this fine hitter and slaps on the back and butt are given to him from all on Mr. Peecheh's team," stated the play-by-play commentator.

"Next up for the Redmen is a young rookie by the name of William Wentworth Winterberg," said the commentator. "He comes from a long line of Winterbergs who gave us our first star drive engines that got us to the next nearby star systems. The Winterberg Star Engines are slow as a snail compared to today's Mag-Hydro-Electron-Drive Engines that bring us all over this wonderful galaxy of ours. Bill, as he likes to be called, steps up to the plate. The first pitch is a high fastball clocked at one hundred and eighty-two miles an hour that flies past the young batter," said the play-by-play commentator.

"Strike one!" called the home plate umpire.

"The ball goes by Winterberg for a strike. Time out has been called on the field. Cito Gaster floats out to home plate because he wants to talk to his young charge up at bat to let him know what to expect from the pitches to come," said the commentator.

"Since we have a few moments here while Coach Gaster talks to Winterberg, why don't we do a short info session on William

Wentworth Winterberg," suggested the play-by-play commentator. "What makes a young man with a rich ancestry and wealth want to play the fatal game of Alliance Baseball, you ask? Well, here is a clip from Mr. Winterberg's interview yesterday with our chief North-Am sports correspondent John Morgans," finished Bower, the play-by-play commentator.

The clip played over the airways and William Winterberg's words began: "My father begged me not to play Alliance Baseball professionally, as I'm his only son. But I don't want to live in my father's shadow doing corporate work like space business transactions," said the young Winterberg. "I want to do something on my own that shows I've done something for myself. I'm the first Winterberg to set aside my family's wealth and protections. Instead, I've found a wealth of friendship and camaraderie with my team, the Redmen. It gives me great pride to represent my Alliance Region of North-Am and all of the great people that live there. I would not give up this chance to play Alliance Baseball for any other opportunity, even my family's wealth and power," said young William Winterberg at the end of the video clip.

"Well, there you have it from the horse's mouth. A young man ready to make his mark in the world of Alliance Baseball on his own two armored feet. Let's hope he gets out of this inning of high home team drama and is able to play on, for the Redmen need dedicated players like Winterberg," said the commentator exuberantly.

"The time out has run its course and the high-flying home-plate umpire has just bellowed 'play ball'," said the play-by-play commentator. "Cito Gaster has returned to the Redmen's dugout on his designated servo-plate. The young Winterberg steps back up to the plate, steeling himself for the next pitch. The Pelotas' pitcher launches a fastball that blows right by the swinging batter, William Winterberg, for strike two. The crowd is apprehensive at what may happen to this young man. Is the young batter going to strike out, or is he going to all out try and get a hit?" asked the commentator. "The Pelotas' pitcher gets his sign from the catcher. The pitcher winds up, and it looks like he's going to send in another fastball. The batter, Winterberg, sets himself for the pitch, but the cagey veteran pitcher sends in an off-speed screwball that catches the young batter off guard. Winterberg swings his jointed bat for a miss, 'Strike three, yer out!' calls the home plate umpire, and the stunned batter, William Winterberg, hangs his head in shame at striking out. The home team fans boo and harangue him for his faux pas at bat. Now striking out in Alliance Baseball when you have all of this technology at your disposal is a no-no. Usually batters will risk getting beaned rather than strike out in front of the home team fans, hoping they will feel sorry for you if you get injured, because they have no mercy for you if you strike out. And on top of that, Winterberg's coach lets him know he's not in his good books for striking out. I guess William Winterberg's musings of trying to do things on his own are not happening for him today," said the commentator. "Let's hope the next time he's up at bat in this game he'll do better. One out for Pelotas as we await the next batter up. We will go to a quick commercial break," said the play-by-play announcer.

"Well, what did you and Dean have to say to each other when you were flirting with him at third base?" Lenny asked Ray, chiding him with an elbow.

"Well, let's just say our next meeting out on the field won't be as cordial as the last two. Dean said he kind of wants to kiss my butt," said Ray, laughing comically.

The play-by-play commentator came in, "Okay, fans, we have one out and one on first for the Redmen. Up next, we have Mark Gaucthier, known affectionately by his teammates as 'Dark Mark', and I can see why," said the play-by-play commentator. "Mark's skin color is so dark that he makes his white and red uniform actually glow in contrast. Gaucthier is another home team favorite. A two-year veteran of the highly regarded Redmen, Dark Mark is usually inserted into the lineup because of his slap-type hitting and for moving runners on the bases. Where will Dark Mark put the ball today?" asked the commentator. "Okay now, Gaucthier is at the plate with his jointed bat furled around his lithe body and the Pelotas' pitcher, Martinez, eyes Gaucthier. The pitcher hurls a fast-breaking ball that Gaucthier swings at, and he fouls it off."

"Foul ball! Strike one!" called the levitated home plate umpire.

"The home team crowd is cheering loudly for Gaucthier, who always has a gleaming white-toothed smile at the plate. Next pitch is a fastball right down the heart of the plate. Gaucthier swings his jointed bat and connects with the ball, but it goes directly to the second baseman of Pelotas in one hop. Looks like a double play coming up here, folks," said the play-by-play commentator. "Oh my, what a throw by the Pelotas' second baseman on the fervently running Lonney Cameron going to second base. Down goes the rookie runner, Cameron, with a hard bean to the stomach, but he's up right away. He's making an honest effort to get to second base, when the first baseman abandons his post at first base and lets Gaucthier get to first safely. The first baseman for Pelotas picks up the loose ball that has bounced off of the rookie runner Cameron while struggling on for second base, and hurls it at the back of the head of the rookie runner, Lonney Cameron, who is the pinch runner for the vet Peecheh," said J. D. Bower, the commentator, with candor.

A loud smack was heard over the noise of the crowd, and down went Cameron, the young aspiring runner.

"Oh wow! This has got to be one of the most vicious hits so far this game," said the play-by-play announcer. "Did you fans at home see that second bean by the first baseman for Pelotas? The spiked baseball has literally impacted itself into the back of the head of rookie runner Lonney Cameron, and it's made the eyes of the now deceased Cameron pop right out and spill onto the field. The home team crowd is appalled and silenced at the sight out on the field as a red raised holograph forms around Cameron, the sprawled out Redmen runner," said the announcer.

"A faint cheering can be heard from the few Pelotas' fans for their team's kill on the young Cameron, but the hometown crowd is mostly silent and beside themselves at the horror of young Cameron's death. I think that this is one of those plays that reminds us why there are no more wars in this world. Extreme violence is the show of this game of World Alliance Baseball, where vicious play shows us the uselessness of war. This is why we have no skirmishes between Alliances, only a war of baseball," the announcer philosophizes. "Now there are two outs, as young veteran Mark Gaucthier who made it to base safely is relived on first base by another rookie runner for the Redmen."

Ray looked at Lenny, and then both of them looked down the third baseline at Dean. Dean lifted the protective clear visor over his face. He had a big smile as the home plate umpire bellowed, "Play ball!"

Dean looked directly at Ray and Lenny for a few seconds, pointed his finger at them, and mouthed the words, "You see that, Rat? You'll be dead soon, just like that young kid." Then Dean lowered his visor and positioned himself for the next Redmen batter.

"The next batter up is a rookie by the name of Helmut Leompert. He was recruited from the Euro-Russo Alliance League from a team called the Byern Munchen. That team hails from the city of Munich in the old country of Germany, now a province of the Euro-Russo Alliance. The Allianz Mega-Dome, the largest Alliance Baseball stadium in the world, is situated there, with a capacity for over nine hundred thousand people," finished the play-by-play commentator, J. D. Bower.

"Now that you have that tidbit of history under your belts, we'll continue with our calling of the game here in Mazalta. Helmet Leompert stands up at the plate and quickly hits his first pitch on to the ground. The ball hit by batter Leompert goes right to third baseman Luthbert, who wastes no time in gunning down the young runner trying for first with a bean to his ribs that crushes the left side of his rib cage and sends him to the turf. The ball goes into the minor infielder's first base zone. The minor infielder then fields the loose ball to the first baseman of Pelotas, who quickly dispatches the struggling runner with a second bean to the left shoulder. This causes further physical damage to young Leompert's body on the ground. This is signaled as the third out by the electronic field umpire, who raises a red holographic red circle around the injured, writhing, and out runner of the Redmen.

"Well, that was a rather bloody inning for the Redmen, who lost two promising young players, Cameron and Leompert, to the great plays by the Pelotas' defensive team," said the commentator. "Now up next in the top of the fifth for Pelotas is…"

The game went on for another three innings with many plays, hits, and gory outs. A few runs were scored by Pelotas.

"Now at the bottom of the eighth, the score is Pelotas three, Redmen one," said the play-by-play commentator. "The Redmen have lost over twenty players in the game so far, and Cito Gaster, the coach, is worried that he's going to lose this game. Cito Gaster is afraid that his team will have to go back into the repechage system and play all of the other teams again, just to get back to the finals and play Pelotas again. He feels that his grip on the World Alliance Finals is slipping away. He has come up with a strategy to use all of his veterans in the batting lineup. No rookies. Cito Gaster feels that he can get the runs back and win this game with his best players. Now it just so happens that Ray Tenner is up to bat first for the Redmen this inning. Let's see how the events unfold in this second last inning of play."

The play-by-play commentator stated, "Well, now it's do or die for the Redmen in this eighth inning, and 'The Rat', Ray Aloyisius

Tenner, is up to bat. It's three to one for Pelotas of South-Am over the Redmen of North-Am, and Coach Vieria has put in a fresh relief pitcher named Ben Cossa, from his bullpen, to start the eighth inning. He's down to his last two relief pitchers, so this is where Pelotas has to hold the line for the win in this crucial game. Tenner steps up to the plate and signals to the home plate umpire above him that he's ready to play. The first pitch is a smoker, by Cossa, that goes by Tenner who doesn't even move on that burner across the plate for a strike. The Pelotas' pitcher, Cossa, means business, for the speed on that last pitch was a hundred and eighty-three miles per hour. Tenner sets himself in the batter's box. Here's the pitch: it's a loping slider that Tenner fouls off. The crowd has become tense and silent in these eight innings of play; there is very little cheering going on for the home team. The Redmen need a hit from their vet Tenner. The next pitch from Cossa is a ball, and the count is one and two. In comes the next pitch, and Tenner is on it like a sand lizard after a human. The ball is hit hard and it's a line drive between third base and the shortstop. The ball squirts into the left field area and Luthbert just misses fielding the ball."

The commentator continued, "We have a man on base for the Redmen, and up next is the wily veteran Lenny Peecheh. Tenner is left out on first base with no relief runner to replace him. His coach, Cito Gaster, has faith that Tenner can run the bases and hopefully score," said the play-by-play announcer.

The Alliance commentator chimed in with the following trivia: "Lenny Peecheh has seven years in the World Alliance Baseball Leagues, and he knows what's needed to get his team through for the comeback win in this game. Peecheh digs in at the plate and the first pitch is a fastball, which he hits over first base. Tenner heads for second, but wait, his third base coach signals Tenner to go for third. My, this is going to be close. Are we going to see the vet Tenner get gunned down?" asked the play-by-play announcer. "The ball gets fielded quite quickly by the center fielder, and he surgically sends it at the running Ray Tenner. Or will the ball get to the third baseman, Luthbert, so he can put the bean on Tenner? Now Ray knows that his signal to continue to third is a gamble by his third base coach to try and gain an advantage for the Redmen. Ray surges for third base, where Dean Luthbert, his archenemy, is waiting. Ray looks at his third base coach who tells Ray to get his blades out from his gloves, as the throw will be here before he gets to third base. Ray has to take out the third baseman, Dean Luthbert, to reach third base safely. As soon as Ray sees the ball go over his head, he steels himself to the fact that he's going to have to take out Dean, his childhood friend at third, and maybe kill him. Dean catches the perfectly thrown ball from center field. Dean knows he's got two seconds before Ray gets to him, and he aims right for Ray's face. Dean's throw makes the ball's spikes come out as it sails mightily at Ray's head. Ray at the same time has launched himself at Dean, knowing he might be able to get to third, even with the two of them just five feet apart and Ray about seven feet from third base and safety. The ball goes directly for Ray's face, but luckily Ray has his two gloved hands out in front of his face. The ball is miraculously impaled onto the blades that have come out of Ray's armored gloves, and Ray punches his knife-like gloves into Dean's midriff. The ball is between the blades and Dean's flesh. Down go the two opposing players in a dusty heap, and the crowd anxiously awaits the call by the third base umpire and the outcome of this stunning collision of these two top veteran players. 'Safe!' says the third base umpire. Both players are uninjured following that jaw-dropping play. I can't believe there are no injuries, and there is no blood to speak of, from that play!" said J. D. Bower, the play-by-play commentator, in exasperation. "Tenner should have had his face smashed in and Luthbert should have had his innards splayed onto the field, but as luck would have it, only a few bruises have come out of this rare play at third base. I can't believe that these two great ball players did not draw blood, or inflict any serious injuries upon each other. The ball has actually gotten in the way and prevented injury to both players. In all of my days as a sports announcer,

I've never seen a play like this where two opposing players did not get hurt. We'll review this play right after the break. Cito Gaster for the Redmen has called time out, giving his runner Tenner some time to recover," said the play-by-play announcer.

Dean lay on the field. The wind had been knocked out of him by Ray's flying hit with the ball imbedded in the blades on Ray's armored gloves. Ray also lay on the ground. His right arm hugged third base, and it felt like Tweety birds were flying around his head singing in unison after his collision with Dean's rock-hard body. Ray could kind of make out the voice of his third base coach praising him for his humungous effort to get to third base. The crowd had jumped up and roared their approval on the play. Lenny Peecheh was safely on first base. As Ray looked at Dean, their eyes conveyed surprise that they were both uninjured.

Ray spoke first. "Are you okay, Dean? I had to do what I did because we are professionals. I really don't want to kill you. I want us to be friends. Let's try and get out of this game alive, and have a future. It's so close. We both have five years in baseball; and after this series is over, win or lose, we can both live out our lives in peace," said Ray, trying to win Dean over.

"Yeah, I'm alright," groaned Dean, realizing that they, as past friends, had almost ended each others lives just moments ago. "This doesn't change things, Ray," said Dean. "I'm still going to try and get you," added Dean, but now in a much friendlier tone.

"If you don't get me, Dean, then maybe we can get together and talk?" asked Ray.

"Maybe," is all that Dean said, knowing full well he had another plan to get Ray if he couldn't get him on the field.

Now, as fate would have it, Ray got batted to home plate, making the score three to two. Lenny got as far as third base. The next three Redmen batters went down in a flurry of beans, trying to attain first base, and the great Lenny Peecheh was held at third each time. In the end, the Redmen lost this all-important semi-final game, to get the bye into the finals, by the final score of three to two in the ninth inning. Ray's Redmen were thrown back to the lions to see who would come out on top to play the Pelotas team from South-Am in another round-robin style of play. Three gruelling games to get back to the top was the Redmen's challenge in this murderous game. To the players, this felt like climbing Mount Everest once in a race and then having to do it all over again because someone has already beaten you there, in that race to the top of the mountain.

CHAPTER ELEVEN
THE LONG ROAD BACK TO THE TOP

AS THE REDMEN TEAM FILED INTO THEIR DRESSING ROOM FROM the immediate moments of play, dejected after their loss to Pelotas of South-Am, they realized that their trek was a long road of vicious baseball to even get back into contention with Dean's team from South-Am. But dejection wasn't in their vocabulary. The players looked at each other, regenerating their conviction that they could do the impossible. They slapped each other on the back, and cheered each other non-stop. The self-determination of their play on the field today had shown that even losing was a good thing, for they were not invulnerable. They could be beaten, but not stopped. The players felt that they could overcome adversity. Even though getting back at Pelotas was a seemingly impossible task, they knew they could do it. Gaster told them that the way to win back the losses they suffered today and get back into the World Alliance Series Baseball Finals was through really hard work and dedication. "If you men do not work hard, you are finished!" stated Coach Gaster.

After the team's own reconsideration and their knowledge that they would have to determine their own destiny, they looked to Gaster for steerage of their team's future.

Coach Cito Gaster gave them some disheartening words. "Yeah," he said, and paused. He continued, "All of you guys should hang your heads in shame, because you let the most important day of your lives slip through your hands and mine. I am your coach, and you have let me down. As your coach, I stand here with my hands open to all of you players, and I ask you to win. You haven't won yet. You were near victory, but now we must begin again this trial. It is of the utmost importance for you to go on. I will be here to help you through your letdowns. I don't want letdowns, but they are inevitable. No more letdowns, boys." With Gaster trying to stare at all of his players at once, his next words bluntly reiterated his message: "I doubt very much that you lowly baseball players can muster up the balls to even win another baseball game! I'm fucking disgusted with you guys. All of you! Look at yourselves. Can you win? I'm not here to do it for you. You are here to do it for yourselves! The Redmen Rule. You have to win without thinking of yourselves as individuals, but as a team! Each and every player has to do it for this team! I'm here to give you shit for it! If you lose, you will get shit. If you win, you avoid the bucket of shit." With his scalding words ringing in his players' ears, Gaster left the Redmen players in their dressing room to think things out for themselves.

Ray Tenner stood up, and walked into the middle of the dressing room. Holding his hands up, emphatically making a halting motion, he defiantly railed against Gaster's words and said ever so slowly, "Who....the....hell....does....he....think....he....is?" The rest of the players, even Lenny, looked at Ray as if he had lost his mind. "I'm here to play baseball, not listen to some old man rant about how we played today! We are important, not Gaster! You sons-of-bitches have played the best baseball I've ever seen. I'm proud of all of you, and I'm not letting one loss or Gaster's words stop us from getting back at Pelotas, no one, you hear me?" shouted Ray. "Who's with me? Because if I have to go out on that field and play the next three fucking games by myself to get back in this, I will!" finished Ray, yelling defiantly.

Well, that got a bug, a fire, or whatever you want to call it lit inside or under all of the Redmen, and they all joined hands in the middle of their dressing room and made a vow that their team would get back into the Alliance World Series finals, no matter what. They chanted, "We will win!" over and over again for a good ten minutes.

The North-Am's home team, the Labrador Redmen, had definitely put themselves in a pickle by losing their final round-robin tournament game to the South-Am's Pelotas. They would not get the rest they so deserved and that Dean's Pelotas's team would surely enjoy. It was a tough grind battling the other teams again, because all of the other Alliance teams were just as desperate in their fight to get to the World Series Alliance Finals as the Redmen. Each game was a hard-fought battle with many leaving the game and never coming back. Many died on the field of play. Some were crippled because they had not received treatment in time, and some just quit because of the horror of the game — you might say that the shell shock got to them.

Ray and Lenny both suffered several damaging injuries during their long-fought comeback in the second round-robin. Ray got a broken leg and crushed ribs in the second last game on a double bean against the Purple Sanga from the Austro-Asian League, and he had to sit out the last game of the repechage series to heal from his wounds with genetic stem cell transposin treatments from Jigs. It was a nail-biter to watch his teammates play such important games from his team's dugout and not be able to play. Before Ray got injured, Lenny suffered a broken collarbone and a severe concussion during the game against the Spartak Locomotive from the Russo-Euro League. Even with the Deadly Duo stuck on the bench, the Labrador Redmen were up to the task and played demoniacally to get the wins they so desperately needed to continue on.

Both Ray and Lenny were able to return to their team from their injuries and get back into the final game through quick-paced treatments and genetic therapies given to them by Jigs. Now since the Labrador Redmen had battled their way back into the World Series Alliance finals by winning three games in a row, they were given three days extra rest before the final game against Pelotas. They needed time to heal up and get ready to play.

During this rest period before their final game, when their coach, Cito Gaster, didn't have them practicing, Ray and Lenny met up with their friends Ian Shelton, Bill Hill, Doctor Jigs, Oscar Duhalde (Ozzy), and Pamela Jay at a local eatery in Mazalta. Oscar was the star ship pilot that Ray and Lenny have hired to operate their ships in their aspiring business. The group engaged in a lively discussion about their futures in a secluded booth where their conversation wouldn't be overheard.

"I didn't think you guys were ever going to pull off this comeback to get at Pelotas, Ray. I was thinking more along the lines of I'd have to cremate the two of you and spread your ashes from here to Andromeda, but realistically maybe in a crater on the Moon," laughed Jigs.

"Well, I think it's a good thing that Lenny and me got busted up. We were very tense from being out there too long. We needed the time off, and we probably avoided being 'ended' out there on the field. Luck has been on our side, that's for sure, eh Len?" said Ray.

Lenny just nodded affirmatively to Ray, and took a sip of the drink in front of him.

"Can't says ah've really been enjoying watching yous guys playing ball out there. Kind of like sending pigs to the slaughter, jest like back home in the Ozarks. My grand pappy told me not to be too friendly with the hogs I used to watch because Ah might be the one to 'put them on the hook' so's to speak when they got slaughtered. Ah never watched them pigs again after Ah saw 'Hoobie', a real character pig Ah liked, getting put on the hook. Ah stuck to my books instead. Hopes you boys can 'get off the farm, so's to speak, soon, so Ah don't have to see yous go on the hook neither. Then we can run your business for you, Ray," said Hill Billy, sipping on his special mountain berry wine.

"Don't worry, Bill; I'm sure Ray and Lenny will get through this last game and then we'll all enjoy our futures with them," said Ian Shelton happily.

"Speak for yourselves," said Pamela Jay, looking around the table to make a point. "I'm in politics. Even though you ball players are in a dangerous line of work, there is a light at the end of the tunnel for you, so to speak, in that you can quit, be killed, crippled, or retire, and then you'll be free from your obligations. I have to put up with some of the worse characters in the Earth Alliance Government every day, with no end in sight. It's like I'm watching the pigs at the trough all the time," joked Pamela Jay. Everyone at the table chuckled.

Lenny stood up and proposed a toast. "Pamela Jay may be right about politics, but here's to our futures! And here's to the doc who's helped us live a bit longer so we can get to retirement and avoid getting put on the hook!"

"Here, here!" said each in unison and they clinked their glasses and sipped on their interplanetary imported wine from a system in the Orion Nebula. Hill Billy stuck to his mountain berry wine.

"I got a call from Dean today," said Ray, informing his friends as they sipped their drinks. All eyes turned to Ray.

"Dean congratulated us on our comeback victories, and he said that he is really looking forward to seeing us in the finals in a couple of days. He also requested that all of us would be his guests at an Alliance private dinner at the Conquistador Palace. It's a social gathering of all of the baseball teams' players, their wives, and invited family before the final game. I think it's his sarcastic way of giving Lenny and me our 'last supper', so to speak," said Ray, lightly sarcastic.

"Can't says Ah really trust that fellow Luthbert to think of your well-being, Ray. 'Specially since he's friends with that Narzani politician. Ah'd say they both really wants you and Lenny dead.

Wouldn't trust them two politicians as far as Ah could spit into a howling wind," said Hill Billy. "And if Narzani is in cahoots with your rival Luthbert, Ah'd really be looking into why Luthbert wants having yous as his special guests."

"Why would you say that about Ricardo Narzani, Bill? I know he's a bit of a shady character, but I think he does have the Alliance's and Earth's well-being at heart. I have to contend with him every day when the Alliance Government is in session. He seems to want what everybody else wants, albeit in his own stubborn way," said Pamela Jay.

"Ah will tell you why Ah don't like that Narzani fellow. Ah works for the government too, and Ah have more of an inside track on what the government is doing than anyone here, especially with the military these days because that is where most of my work in experimental electron mechanics is done. Ah don't like what Narzani's business dealings are doing to the people of the Euro-Russo Alliance," said Bill.

"And how do you know about Mr. Narzani's business dealings, Bill?" asked Pamela Jay. "I can't even get a truthful digital readout on his everyday affairs, and I'm going to be the next Assistant Governor of the Euro-Russo Alliance. I know exactly what the Euro-Russo people want, even with Narzani plotting his strategies."

"If you can keep a secret, Ah have got a secret or two to tell," said Bill to Pamela Jay in an honest tone.

Those gathered at the table were all ears, awaiting Hill Billy's secrets. "Well, all's Ah can say is that Ah have perfected a way to eavesdrop on the 'Quantum Entanglement Uncertainty Principle' vid-phone or the Qeup vid-phone. This type of eavesdropping is from the old BB84 Quantum Cryptography (QKD) information transmissions where no one could infiltrate quantum super position emanations. Quantum super positions is the most secretive method the Earth Alliance Government has to conduct business transactions among themselves and with others like them in this galaxy. They have a lot to hide," said Bill. "And I've also been working on how to safely store negative antimatter by the kilogram. Got a few sizable credit grants from the North-Am government's military to continue my work in electron mechanics. But Ah have been spying on the guys that are spying on me, cuz I don't want my working experiments to fall into the wrong hands. The antimatter would change the outcome of power between the Alliances and this world, as we know it. One Alliance would rule instead of all of them co-operating, as they do now. Ah don't want this singularity to happen with only one government. It could cause a dictatorship and lead to wars between our Alliances. Ah'm for the people. If I Ah have to die for the people, then these innovations Ah have put forth to you will die with me," finished Hill Billy.

"The Qeup vid-phone is the government's way of keeping secrets safe," Pamela Jay informed them. "It, the Qeup vid-phone, has a natural barrier. Once an intrusion on the communication wave is made, the wave immediately breaks down because the electron spin, its wave, is affected. No record of the ongoing or previous communications can ever be recorded or tracked down. This is what I have been told by communication experts. How have you managed to bypass that natural breakdown barrier, Bill?" asked Pamela Jay.

"Like Ah said before, Ah will tell a secret if you guys can keep a secret, especially you, Pam. Ah feel that Ah can trust all of the people here at this table. Do you all agree to hear me out? Nothing can go beyond this table," Hill Billy said.

Everyone at the table nodded in agreement. They anxiously awaited Bill Hill's groundbreaking secret of how to monitor the Qeup vid-phone.

Bill got out a piece of blank paper from a folder he was carrying and began to write out a formula. As he wrote, he explained the Qeup vid-phone principle. "This here is the original mathematical equation that states how the wave of the uncertainty principle, for a Qeup vid-phone, works. The uncertainty principle states that it is not possible to simultaneously determine the position and momentum of a particle in a wave-like pattern. In quantum mechanics, 'quibits' of information can be sent through regular communicative venues, but they cannot be listened to or overheard by anyone. But in quantum mechanics communications, the more the *position* of the communicating electron is known, the less the *momentum* is known, and vice-versa. This is an original quotation from a well-known and innovative professor by the name of Heisenberg, who long ago invented the 'Heisenberg Uncertainty Principle'," said Hill Billy. His formula looked like this: $\Delta x \Delta px \gtrless 1/2 \hbar$. "This is the formula that makes the cryptology system for the Qeup Vid-Phone work. This formula tells you whether the spin of the communicating molecule is up or down in the communications wave signal, and if it is working. Once the spin of the electron has been interfered with in the quibit quantum state, then the wave signal naturally shuts down. The spin and the momentum cannot continue in the wave packet that is sent in because of interference from the eavesdropping signal, and the eavesdropping on the communications wave beam between Qeup vid-phones stops. In general, when measuring an unknown, I have figured out a way to keep the communications signal on Qeup vid-phones operating by removing and stopping the spin of the communications molecular electron signal before the vid phone is used. Knowing the wave pattern, with minute application patterns of sub-atomic sized nano-magnets, I can apply my sub-atomic sized nano-magnets into the telecommunication signal to alter the position and momentum of the communicating electron signal. These nano magnets will slow the electromagnetic actions to the wave pattern in the photon packet that wreak havoc on the signal, and make it stop. These nano-magnets then suppress the spin of the communicating electron, thus slowing the spinning electron molecule to a full stop. No wave is allowed to appear in the signal of those communicating with the Qeup vid-phone. At the same time, Ah keep the non-spin of the communicating electron active by agitating the now non-spinning electron, that has no wave action, to only an up and down agitated motion. This gives the false impression of a wave pattern, when in actuality the electrons are just jumping up and down and not spinning. It's kind of like moving your arms in a simple up and down motion, as opposed to swinging your arms wildly in circular motions. Ah can now eavesdrop on a communications conversation at will, because the wave action of the photon packet is in a linear, straight line motion, rather than in a wavy, curve-like motion due to the up and down movements of the electron. However, no wavy motions are made, and so the signal doesn't stop. Is anyone understanding any of the things Ah have said so far?" asked Hill Billy.

Ian understood because of his background of in astronomical physics. The rest of the people at the table seemed interested, and kept their attention glued to Bill Hill. Bill continued his explanation, "This action of keeping the position of the communicating electron in its non-spin mode unknown to those who are using the communications beam allows me to tune into them. Ah may eavesdrop on a conversation, at will, without the original signal beam being disturbed and collapsing due to the regular wave altering eavesdropping interference signal by someone else. The packet of photons, in which the original signal is being sent, is undisturbed by my eavesdropping signal because the pressure of the nano-magnets prevents the slowing of the communicating electrons wave from being disturbed in a unified fashion. The uncertainty principle electron molecule isn't sensitive to simple up and down motions of the communicating molecule being governed by my sub-atomic nano-magnets, nor is it sensitive to the eavesdropping of a minute power slowing the beam using atomic nano-magnets to slow its electrons to a stop. Only the spin of the molecular wave is sensitive. So once the spin of the communications electron has been slowed to a stop by my secret outside monitoring forces, then I can listen undetected and know what they're saying. My monitoring of their conversations doesn't alter the communicating beam, and it doesn't collapse the quantum signal. Now, the pressure of the agitating sub-atomic nano-magnets on the Qeup vid-phone signal slows and stops the spin of the communicating electron to a key point (signal pressure) that can't be detected. The electron molecule is now with the stopped spin and continuing up and down momentum. Ah can keep the communicating electron signal active by agitating it up and down. The electron molecule is kept agile with the up and down agitation replacing the spinning/wave actions of the electron in my eavesdropping signal from my newest Qeup vid-phone. Ah can now listen in on any communication anywhere in this galaxy, even when ships are entering in a double wormhole lensing gate using enhanced Alcubierre Drive **and** even in sub-space. The formula for the newest Qeup secret listening vid-phone is: **$\Delta x \Delta px ? 1/2 \hbar\text{-}(\text{-}E_s + E_{a\pm})$**. The **$E_s$** in the formula represent my insertion of sub-atomic nano-magnets in the signal's beam (wave) to remove and stop the spin/wave of the electron in the communications beam without collapsing the communicating signal. The **$E_{a\pm}$** in the formula is the sub-atomic nano-magnets agitating the electron to an up and down motion, keeping it active but removing the wave action. This up and down action again gives me its exact location and its non-spin location in the signal, thus not allowing the communicating signal to break down when the spin of the electron molecule is stopped. Ah've dumbed down the pulse amplitude of the original telecommunications signal by eliminating the peak amplitude, the root mean square (RMS) of the communicating wave of the electron, and the oscillating variable. There is no more sine wave to the communications signal in the spinning electron. There is only a flat line, like when a person's heart stops and the heart monitor shows the person is deceased. But that is not the case here in my 'dead signal' detection. Ah still have a pulse on the original signal and any other signal in the communications stream by now agitating the electron only up and down. Ah can fool the detection services by providing a false wave pattern to the signal being monitored," finished Bill, looking at his friends.

Everyone appeared very confused when Hill Billy gleefully peered up at them after his long-winded explanation.

Again, Ian Shelton was the only one who understood the jargon of what Bill Hill had just said because of his background in physics, astronomy, and quantum mechanical applications.

Ian said, "With this kind of technology, Bill, you could virtually shut down all of the Earth Alliance Government by listening to whatever they are saying anywhere in the known universe! What are you proposing to do with this newest technology?" asked Ian.

"Ah was just going to keep it under wraps until Ah found a politician Ah could trust with this information, and then Ah would make this world a better place for the regular slogs like us," said Bill, looking at Pamela Jay. "Ah am hoping to help eliminate governmental shady dealings, help the layman live better, and shrink the global deserts by using the things Ah have made today, through better communications," said Bill.

Oscar Duhalde (Ozzy) asked Bill Hill a question, "What is the other secret you have, Bill, in regards to the antimatter?"

"Well, again, there is another thing Ah have found out. Ah can now isolate negative antimatter, but only in minute quantities. I need more time to find a suitable containment field for more than an ounce at a time. A thousandth of an ounce of this antimatter has the power to completely sizzle a person to nothing, to dust, if in the wrong hands and applications. It also has a very dangerous military application that Ah can see from my position as an innovator of this very volatile material. Ah am sure Ah can make a containment module for a kilo at a time of this volatile stuff soon, but Ah have to be sure, for it is billions to one in annihilation of matter when it comes in contact with regular matter. This is much stronger as an energy producing medium for Earth, but it could also be used as a planet-busting weapon if it got in the wrong hands," said Hill Billy. "Ah have stumbled upon a process of how to separate excess electrons on larger 'isotopic' molecules on the periodical scale. Kind of like carving a wart off of a whale: it's there, but you don't really need it. When Ah collect enough of these separated negative electrons, Ah have the finished product of pure antimatter. Ah have, in my possession, the knowledge of how to physically hold all of the power of the atom theoretically in containers from the size of a grain of sand to the size of a cup with only a barrier of a lead-lined unbreakable Diamond Iron glass globe," finished Bill in his Ozark's slang.

"I'm impressed, Mr. Hill, at what you've accomplished and how you have kept these real innovations secret from your employers," expressed Pamela Jay. "But now that they are working, how are you going to show them to the governments of the Earth Alliances? Aren't these inventions technically their property, since they sponsored them?" she asked.

On cue, all eyes went to Bill Hill. He wasn't used to all of this attention, even if it was in private. "This is why Ah want to tell all of yous here about what Ah want to do. Ah don't have the finances, the political powers that be, or the 'smarts' to do this alone. Ah recognize that Ah need help, and Ah feels that the right people are here, at this table, who kin help me give these inventions of mine to the world in a peaceful fashion. Ah don't want to be known as the inventor of mass spying or planet-destroying technology like the scientists of old who got nuclear science to flower but used it mostly in military applications," drawled Hill Billy in his Ozark mountain slang, candor shining in his eyes.

"Wow, it seems like I'm sitting in on a bit of Earth-shaking history, and I haven't even done a thing," said Ray. "All I know is I want me and Lenny to get through this final game, and then

I hope I can help you guys sort out this quite confusing political info that Bill here has given us," said Ray.

"That's the thing about this info, Ray. Ah need you and Lenny to commit to helping me along with any politicians we trust to protect these vital innovations from falling into the wrong hands of guys like Narzani or Bendshaw. Ah am also assuming it will affect even the outcome of World Alliance Baseball Finals in some way if it gets known," said Hill Billy.

"Okay, I know it's premature, but I have the feeling that our team will win the World Alliance Baseball Finals. I will commit my winning credits to your inventions for the betterment of man, Bill," said Lenny. "I've got so much, I'll never be able to spend it all," laughed Lenny.

"I will second that," said Ray, backing Lenny up. "My credits are on you, Bill."

Pamela Jay said, "I'll third that. I will strive to the best of my ability to help you use your inventions to the betterment of mankind. We will keep your secrets until the right moment is at hand to release them."

"What are Ian and I supposed to do here?" asked Oscar. "Just sit around and act like bed bugs? We want to contribute too."

Ian started in, "I have a conflict of interest with the people I work for in that I use inventions made by government employees to my advantage, seeing that I'm a government employee right now," said Ian Shelton. "But in this case, I think I can turn a blind eye and wait this one out before I let certain politicians know about these inventions," said Ian.

"Hey, I'm just a dumb star ship pilot who is listening to shit I really don't understand. I probably couldn't explain it to someone who could do something about it anyway. What the heck am I supposed to say, I'm in?" asked Ozzy with his hands in the air.

"You're in no matter what, Ozzy. Now that you know everything, Ah'm gonna have to kill yah if you don't wants to be with us. What do you say, Ozzy?" said Bill, holding his mag-saber and putting the joker pilot on the spot.

"I'm in," said Ozzy. "And you can put that thing away now, Hill Billy!"

Bill continued, "Ah have also had an incident at the Gia University with a professor of mine that Ah don't want to elaborate on just yet. All Ah can say is that it involved a clayon robot, and I just barely got away with my life. Ah have had to move all of my data on to these two mega-tera-byte flash drives. Ah have got one copy for Pamela Jay and one for myself of all the things Ah have explained to yous all tonight. If anything happens to me, my flash drive that Ah have on me will self-destruct because Ah have it tied into my brainwave functions. But the other one that Pamela Jay has will stay intact, and you may use your discretion to do whatever you want with it to help the people of Earth. Just make sure it stays in peaceful hands," said Bill.

"Okay, I don't want to be a spoiler here, but what are Lenny and me supposed to do about Dean and his invitation to 'the last supper'?" asked Ray to his table of new found secretive friends.

"Well, Ah will keep your 'ball friend' Luthbert and the politicians Narzani and Bendshaw monitored by my new vid-phone. Ah will try to keep yous updated," said Hill Billy.

"Thanks, Bill," said Ray. "Hey, how about we have a few more drinks, play some team virtual vid games, and forget the world for a while, eh? Hey, Peecheh, I bet I can whop you and Hill Billy at Virtual Sand Lizard Ping Pong. I'll take Pamela Jay as my partner, because I've heard from a Hill Billy spy here that she's the best in the Alliance Executive at it," challenged Ray.

Lenny looked at Pamela Jay and asked, "Well, how about, Pam my gal?"

"You're on, Rat; and look out, Lenny, a sand lizard is on your tail!" smiled Pamela Jay.

As the friends played Virtual Sand Lizard Ping Pong, Dean Luthbert made a secret phone call, unmonitored by Hill Billy's Qeup phone, to Cito Gaster, and Dean began to spin his web of dealings to get Ray Tenner.

CHAPTER TWELVE
THE LAST SUPPER

IT WAS THE DAY BEFORE THE BIG GAME, THE FINALS OF THE Alliance World Series of Baseball between Pelotas and the Redmen. Dean Luthbert had made arrangements for Ray, Lenny, and their friends to dine, with him, at the grand estate that Dean had rented for the occasion. The three boys' parents had also been invited to the gala as special guests.

"I have it all set up, the 'Last Festive Dinner', before the final game of the series. The dinner will take place early this evening at six pm., at the Conquistador Palace. There will be tables, in your name, at the front of the hall," said Ricardo Narzani to Dean. "The plan I have made is to release the sand lizards during the festivities. Once things are underway, the escape route for you and your parents is guaranteed while your friends are taken care of by my biological pets," said Narzani.

"Are you sure this is going to work? I also want you to make sure that Lenny's and Ray's parents are taken care of. I really only want Ray the Rat," said Dean .

"It will go off without a hitch, Mr. Luthbert. I will make sure that the guests you have mentioned will be safely taken care of. And we will be rid of our rivals for good," said Narzani, clenching his fists by his side.

Ricardo Narzani made a Qeup phone call to his associate in politics, Collin Bendshaw. This would prove to be his mistake, for Bill Hill had his eavesdropping quantum vid-phone tuned into the frequency of this conversation: "Collin, just letting you know that that 'Jay' woman who's been giving us all the flak in the parliamentary proceedings won't be at the next session due to some gastronomic problems I've incurred for her," said Ricardo.

Collin Bendshaw spoke cautiously, "I really think this is a morbid way of dealing with issues that confront us, Rick. Don't you have a better way, like using rogue clayon guards that have their sentient chips altered by some exotic device accidentally turned on by an irate alien servant looking at gifts he didn't get from our Alliance Federation of Interstellar Under Planets or something?" asked Collin.

"No, I think this is the most natural way. If we use something like you just said, someone, somewhere will start an interplanetary war over where the gift came from. The Earth Alliance can't afford to take on another interstellar war at this time. The offended race would trace it back to the source and that would mean our departments would be under investigations and we'd never get anything done behind the scenes, if you know what I mean. The Alliance can ill afford an interstellar war at this time. Besides, a natural occurrence is better than a technologically induced one because there's less blame to go around. I'll get back to you on my plans," said Ricardo. He ended his link with Collin.

Bill Hill had overheard the conversation. He hadn't gotten the real gist of what Ricardo Narzani was planning, but Bill felt Ricardo was up to no good when Pamela Jay's name was mentioned.

The Conquistador Palace featured a museum display of all the history of the technological and medical advances man had made over the last three hundred years since the global deserts had expanded to engulf two thirds of the Earth's land surfaces. The museum showed how the Alliances were formed, how man had pooled his resources to invent star drive engines like the Winterberg and Alcubierie drives, and how these had progressed to artificial wormhole lensing using the latest Mag-Hydro-Electron-Drives for distant galactic travel at near relativistic speeds for the exploits and battles for supremacy with other races. Earth's interplanetary friends including Mars, Venus, Jupiter, and Saturn's moons had enabled further medical breakthroughs because of their isolation and experimental atmospheres to progress research into man's durability into galactic space.. Those who had been responsible for many of the historical venues shown here at the Palace were lauded for their efforts in setting up the displays. There was a display featuring the bringing of the sand lizards to create the great ringed protective forests with enough information to keep a person occupied just reviewing the posted historical data for weeks on end.

Visitors had the opportunity to explore displays of when Alliance Baseball had first started. Sports stars from the original first years of the inter-region leagues were featured, as well as examples of the old-style equipment that players had used to play enhanced baseball. The first stars of the new game wore piston-like attachments on their arms and legs and had a mini powered battery cells incorporated into the belts to drive the piston-like devices on their bodies. This made the early Alliance Baseball players run much faster than the players from leagues of old that followed the old rules of play. Original greats like Babe Ruth, Yogi Berra, Jackie Robinson, Shoeless Joe Jackson, Ty Cobb, Joe DiMaggio, and many others were enshrined on the hallowed walls. Alongside the old players, Alliance Baseball players were on display like Mike 'Sliver' Lecourt, Jerry the 'Ape'-man Loncheeay, Perry 'Backstop' Nayes, and many more.

Original baseball cards had been donated, and fans could buy re-prints of old, donated playing cards for their own collections.

Ray, Lenny, Pamela Jay, Ian, Bill, Jigs, and Ozzy passed under the great archway of the great Conquistador Palace together and entered the great room where paid human servants catered to their whims. Their outer apparel was neatly folded and placed by the specialized behind-the-scenes help. These efficient, service maid clayons tended to the players as they were processed into the banquet hall. Lenny and Ray waved to their parents and made motions with their fingers saying that they would come ever to see them in a little while.

Ricardo Narzani greeted them from his position at the head table once the players and their wives had been taken care of by the staff and the robotic maids. "Greetings to you, Mr. Tenner, and to your entourage. I hope everything is to your liking?" asked Ricardo, whose large toothy grin reminded Ray of an old predatorial Tyrannosaurus Rex.

"It is for now," said Ray, smiling back at Ricardo. "Where is Dean Luthbert? I thought he was going to be dining with us."

"Oh, he will be here shortly. He stopped to greet another group of players and friends, such as yourselves, and he is signing autographs before escorting these guests to their table," said Ricardo. "I'm sure he'll only be a few moments."

"*Odd*," thought Ray, and he asked himself, "*Why would Dean, a highly respected ball player, be placing people at tables at such a gala event? This Narzani fellow must have caught Dean playing with a pig the wrong way, and it's his way of getting high-priced help for free.*"

Just as Ray finished his musings, Dean appeared through the entrance way from the dining area. He too had the smile of a dark demon like arch devil. "Nice to see you, Ray and Lenny. Who are your friends?" Dean asked, pleasantly extending his hand to Ray. "I'm glad our parents are here to see all of this too," said Dean.

Ray thought to himself, *"Things are just a bit too weird. I've got not one but two Raptor cats grinning at me. One of them really wants to kill me, and the other looks like he's got something up his primortive sleeve. Narzani looks like he wants to make sure I don't get out of here alive. I'm really going to have to watch myself tonight."*

Not to seem ungracious, Ray took Dean's hand, shook it politely, and introduced his friends. "You remember Pamela Jay? She's a member of the Euro-Russo Alliance executive. And these are my new found friends: Ian Shelton, Doctor Sthel, and Oscar Duhalde," said Ray.

"Nice to meet you all. Let's get everyone seated and we can get this gala started," said Dean, acting like the perfect host as he guided them towards the dining room table they were to sit at.

As they moved to their table, Dean spoke to Ray quietly, "Let's us call a truce here, Ray, just for today. Let's both try to enjoy ourselves before the big game tomorrow. I'm sure you'll find the atmosphere here to your liking." Ray had an uneasy feeling that something terrible was going to happen, but he managed to smile graciously at Dean. "Okay" was all Ray had to say.

Ray and his friends were seated at a table just off to the side of the head table in a dead-end corner of the large dining room. They had a good view of the head table that would most certainly be occupied by Alliance dignitaries. Their parents sat on the other side of the dining room, near an exit.

"I'll be sitting beside Mr. Narzani on the opposite side of the head table tonight," said Dean. "Since my team is the first-place finisher in this tournament, he wants me, the captain of my team, to sit at the head table with him and the other VIPs. It's protocol, and one of the perks of winning," said Dean, almost chuckling as he unceremoniously threw a rival's light insult at

Ray and Lenny. "Anyway, enjoy yourselves, as this may be the last time we'll be this close without using a fork on each other," joked Dean. Then he hurriedly rushed off to sit beside Ricardo Narzani at the head table.

"Well, Mr. Luthbert seems to be in a joyous mood considering he wants to have you drawn and quartered in the near future, eh Ray?" joked Bill.

"Yeah, got to let the poor uptight fellow have some fun before I do the same to him, eh Bill?" Ray joked back.

There were enough tables to seat over four hundred people and a head table that could sit over twenty. Everything at the tables was first class, such as the fine compressed crystal glasses made of Conoxtain-Oxygen-induced minerals brought from the outer rim of the Milky Way Galaxy. Pressed into elaborate cup shapes rather than produced by heating actions. These fabulous urns sparkled naturally even in the dimmed light of this huge dining room. The fine cloth fabric coverings on the tables almost shimmered because of the chromatic technology woven into them as they oozed light in rhythmic and fascinating fashions. The artificial exotic, flowered central place settings adorning the tables looked and smelled like they had just been freshly placed. An expensive bowl of light champagne accompanied by small cuts of succulent watermelon graced each of the tables for the patrons' enjoyment. It seemed like the perfect setting for a perfect evening.

Bill Hill spoke up with a wry skewed smile on his face, "Well, Ah kin say that this is a real fancy setting. Much fancier than my grand pappy's old pig farm kitchen back in the Ozarks."

Ray and his friends all had broad smiles at Hill Billy's candor. Ray joked, "Maybe we can get a roast piglet on a spit for you, Bill. Would that make you happy?"

A FUTURE PASTIME — A COMPLICATED BASEBALL STORY

"Only if my grand pappy were here too," said Bill. "Ah would tell you one thing, though: this place does have a bit of a bad odor for me. Ah tried to listen in on that Narzani's vid-phone conversation he had last night with his political friend Mr. Bendshaw. Ah only gots a few words of it, but it sounded like he was planning a big splash for tonight's ceremonies. And Ah don't like where we are placed in this room for any kind of splash," said Bill.

"What are you implying, Mr. Hill?" asked Jigs, as all eyes at the table looked at the uncomfortable Bill Hill.

"Since Ah have had things happen to me at the Gia Earth Academy, Ah like having my back to a wall with a door on it. Neither of them are happening right now, cuz Ah am stuck in a corner. The vid phone conversation confirms that," said Bill suspiciously. "Look at Narzani and yer baseball friend Luthbert over there. They have the positions and the doorway that Ah would like to have."

"Oh, come on, Bill, you don't think anything violent would happen with this many people here and the media looking on?" asked Jigs, interested in what Hill Billy had to say.

Before Hill Billy could respond, Collin Bendshaw stood up and introduced the Master of Ceremonies, Ronald Messtier. Mr. Messtier stood up from his place at the head table, and addressed the crowd in front of him.

"Ladies and gentlemen, may I have your attention please. Let me introduce myself. As Head of the World Alliance Council, my name is Ronald Messtier. Welcome to the traditional gala dinner before the final game, at the wonderful Conquistador Palace. This event has been held every year for the past three hundred years. When our forefathers knew that the world had to come together in crisis......."

On went Messtier, giving praise to all of the Alliance Councils of Earth and all of their foresight. They had helped the people of Earth by eliminating war, bringing baseball to the forefront as a world pastime with all of its innovations, and so on.

As Messtier spoke, Bill Hill decided he wasn't having anything to do with this gala. He told Ray and his friends to get up. He wanted them to leave right now because of a premonition he had. The whole group at the table protested, saying it would cause a scene if they left while the Head of the World Council was speaking. They, especially Ian, wanted to know why Bill was acting so strangely at such a festive time. Nearby guests' eyes were on their table as Hill Billy got louder and louder, encouraging his friends to leave.

"Come on, Ah said we should leave, now! This Narzani fellow wants to hurt Pamela Jay," said Bill, with meaning in his voice. Ray's friends were beginning to react nervously by talking among themselves as to what they should do.

Just then, a warning was sent through the P.A. System: "Please be advised that the clayon guard has identified sand lizards in our immediate area. The local government apologizes for this inconvenience. This is a final warning of a threat that a sand lizard is in the vicinity. Everyone in this room should evacuate until the danger is gone. The proceedings will go on as usual after the alert has been rescinded."

While Ronald Messtier was apologizing for the inconvenience and people were filing past the head table, a terrible crash sounded and a menacing sand lizard appeared through the wall next to the main entrance. It was swishing its large head back and forth to make the opening in the wall larger.

There was instant pandemonium as the huge threatening sand lizard struggled through the opening. It made ear piercing hissing noises, struggling to free itself of the debris of the wall it had just crashed through on its way to get at the people in the room. It roared and hissed over and over again, as it moved toward a group of players and their wives from the Euro-Russo team. Quickly the sand lizard shot out its slimy tongue and pulled into its mouth one of the women it had cornered. She screamed manically until it quickly devoured her. The large female sand lizard then turned itself towards Ray and Lenny's table, its menacing claws and jaws moving in for the kill. The sand lizard again flicked out its deadly tongue and caught Ian by the leg. Pamela Jay screamed in fright as the huge lizard tried to draw Ian into its vicious jaws. A quick flash was all that was seen by the stunned onlookers and then half of the sand lizard's tongue lay bloodied on the floor, oozing reddish green liquid. Ian struggled to get away from the giant reptilian's appendage.

Hill Billy had taken out his mag-saber and sliced off the serpentine tongue of the sand lizard. That's where the flash had come from. Next, as the sand lizard hissed in agony, it turned to face its tormentor, Bill Hill. As it did, Bill drove the head of his mag-saber deep into the throat of the menacing lizard to expose its open, breathing organs. The sand lizard was now mortally wounded. It writhed in pain, swinging its head and tail back and forth and knocking people and furniture all over the ballroom. Bill Hill hung onto his mag-saber that was still embedded in the throat of the lizard. With desperation he pulled the mag-saber out of the giant lizard's throat as it thrashed its head and Hill Billy to and fro. With momentum from the sand lizard's thrashings. Hill Billy swung himself onto the back of the sand lizard by a loose piece of flesh hanging off of the giant reptilian's face. Bill then mounted himself behind the sand lizard's head and drove his mag-saber into the back of its skull, repeatedly, until the giant beast fell to the floor, slowly convulsing itself into death.

Bill dismounted the shaking sand lizard and told his group to head for the main entrance. They must get out as soon as possible. "Go, go because there must be more lizards".

Ray had been watching the head table where Dean and Ricardo were sitting, and just before the warning was announced, he had noticed their quick retreat out the nearest exit — even though the alert had not yet been announced. Their clayon guard stood in front of their exits with lasers at the ready, not allowing any other guests to escape through this particular exit. It was as if they wanted the people in that area of the dining room to remain there, at the mercy of the sand lizards.

Ray said, "You were right, Bill, something like the last supper was planned for us by Luthbert and Narzani. I think they were trying to get us all killed, especially me, so Dean wouldn't have to do it on the field. I don't know how I'm going to prove it, but I think Dean and Narzani planned this, as they were the first to get out even before the official notice, from what I saw. But to prove it will be another story," stated Ray.

The reserve clayon guard robots came rushing in to the ball room try and help those who were still in shock in the chaotic room to leave. Ray found out through a human servant that all of their parents were okay. They had been ushered out quickly and were on their way back to their respective hotels. Each couple was accompanied by ten clayon guards.

Then suddenly another sand lizard appeared through the same hole the first one had burst through. By now most of the people in the room had vacated. The sand lizard lashed out at the clayon robots that were there helping people get out. The clayon robots began firing their laser rifles at the tough hide of the sand lizard. The sand lizard swung its log-like tail and took out ten clayon robots like they were plastic toys, squashing them flat and rendering them inoperable, and stopping the laser fire directed against it. In came ten more clayon robots firing their lasers at the back of the sand lizard, only to enrage the monster further. The sand lizard eliminated its antagonizers in about five seconds by snapping them up in its vicious jaws. Ray and his friends were still in their corner of the ballroom due to events beyond their control. They had not been able to get themselves to an exit because of all of the pandemonium of people exiting. They simply had to wait their turn to get out. They were still in the ballroom's interior with no way out, and a second sand lizard was about to inflict harm on them.

Now, with no opposition, the second angry lizard moved closer to Ray this time, backing him into the corner with no escape. Ray backed up as fast as he could from the hissing giant sand lizard, fell backward against the wall, and sprawled out onto the floor. He moaned and cried out to himself, asking how he could avoid this eating machine that was about to devour him. Its solid black, hardened, shark-like eyes came at Ray like an emotionless dragon. It opened its serrated mouth to send its deadly snatching tongue at Ray. Ray darted behind an overturned table just as the appendage came for him. The sand lizard's tongue hit the table, knocking it away, and again exposing Ray to the vicious giant. Seeing it had missed its target, the sand lizard jolted itself forward to get a better position on Ray. Its talons dug into the granite floor to make sure Ray would become its next meal.

Lenny, Pamela Jay, Jigs, Ian, and Ozzy had cleared the room through the exit that Dean had used. Only Hill Billy remained. Now ready for the second sand lizard, Bill moved to the side as the lizard concentrated on Ray. Bill made an attempt to slash the lizard with his mag-saber, just like he had done with the first lizard. Its tough green flesh could pretty well stand up to laser fire, but not the cutting power of the mag-saber. With a roar and a quick swinging action of its head, the distracted sand lizard caught the attacking Hill Billy off guard and knocked him off of his feet. Bill sailed through the air and crashed into the wall in the corner. There he lay, in a heap on the dining room floor. The mag-saber lay there, unmoving, just like Bill.

Ray peeked over the top of the overturned table he had gotten behind and knew he was in real trouble. The clayon guard robots came to Ray's aid by putting themselves in front of Ray and the hungry sand lizard. The clayon robots drew out their mag-saber swords, knowing that their laser weapons only slowed the lizard and would not stop it quickly enough. They suicidally attacked the sand lizard in an attempt to protect Ray. The clayon robots were not as good as Hill Billy with their mag-sabers, and the sand lizard quickly ran them over, with its bulk, before they could do any effective damage to the hulk of its huge green body. The sand lizard thrashed about, taking out any nearby clayon robots with its agile tail, and in its quick movements, it went again to where Ray was hiding, behind the overturned table. It swiped at the table with a muscular taloned forelimb, sending it across the large room and through the wall and taking out a clayon robot in the process. Ray was splayed out onto the floor by the impact of the sand lizard's huge clawed forelimb removing the table. Now the sand lizard had Ray at its mercy and it stood over Ray, opening its mouth to directly devour him. Its huge serrated jaws, dripping bacterial saliva, opened and came at Ray to crunch him to lizard mush. Ray lifted his arms in a primitive defense, knowing his very end was at hand as he tried to struggle free. Ray mouthed the words, "Mom, help me as you always have, please." He closed his eyes, knowing this was the last breath he would ever take.

Then, a few things happened very quickly that Ray couldn't comprehend. First, there was a loud sound like electricity arcing in the open air with an accompanying bright light. Next, a terrifically bad smell surrounded Ray and he found himself covered from head to toe with bloodied lizard meat. Looking up, Ray could only see the back half of the sand lizard's body as it lay charred, still smoking, with its innards strewn about and leaking its fluids onto the dining room floor. Then Hill Billy's voice rang in Ray's ears, "You all right, Ray? Looks like you got enough supper on you to last a week, or a couple of Rat weeks, ha, ha," said Hill Billy, laughing reassuringly.

"Yeah, I'm okay, but what the hell just happened to that sand lizard?" asked Ray. "I thought it was going to have me for dinner, and now I find myself covered in lizard dinner."

"Well, Ah couldn't get at her with my mag-saber quick enough to help you, so Ah gaves' her a little antimatter medicine, about a hundredth of an ounce worth. That seemed to settle her appetite down. Ah gave her dessert before she had you as her main meal," finished Bill, sort of smiling and wobbling from his injuries put on him by the female sand lizard.

"I thought that you couldn't contain the antimatter," said Ray. He got up, sloshing the dead, sticky meat off of himself.

"Ah said Ah could not contain a pound or two of the antimatter, just an ounce or less of it. This is what Ah fed the sand lizard so it wouldn't eat you as its last supper. One hundredth of an ounce of the antimatter will combine with a billion or more ounces of positronic organic matter, and that is why the sand lizard's body was terminated in half," said Bill. "Now let's get you out of here and get this pork rind off of you and me before another one of those 'Interstellar Darwin' munchkins' comes a calling," jested Hill Billy. He paused for a moment, and continued, "Ah knew something like this was going to happen because Ah heard Narzani say he wanted us to be eliminated, especially Pamela Jay. Ah've recorded the conversation and Ah'll present it to the Alliance Council as soon as Ah can."

"Maybe you had better wait on that issue, Bill," said Ray. "I think the game should be played first, and then the political high jinks can start after it's over."

"Why, Ray?" asked Bill. "We've got him dead to rights, with what he's said."

"I think we should leave this one to Pamela Jay, as she would know best how to handle this political hot potato. She's more suited to exposing Narzani than we are, wouldn't you agree?" asked Ray.

"Yeah, Ah guess you're right, Ray. She's got more insights to this than what we do," agreed Hill Billy. "For now, let's get you outta here, clean you up, and try to put yourself and Lenny at ease. Ah think Lenny is waiting for you at the main door. Ah saw him there a minute ago. Ah will stick around to make sure this Narzani fellow doesn't try anythin' else against you here, Ray."

"Thanks Bill," said Ray in gratitude, heading for an exit.

The main camera for the ceremonial event had recorded all of these events at the Conquistador Palace. Ricardo Narzani, Dean Luthbert, and Collin Bendshaw couldn't believe their eyes when they saw that the ones they were trying to eliminate were still alive. They had met right away in a spare banquet room near the main festivities and began to discuss what had just transpired.

"I knew this was going to happen," said Dean. "That bastard Tenner is so lucky. I have to get back to my team and distance myself from this debacle. It's all yours, Narzani. Make sure I get paid. I got them here, that was our deal!" stated Dean, and he ran out of the smaller banquet room.

"What are we going to do now?" Collin Bendshaw asked Ricardo. "Surely someone will figure this out and we'll be ruined. That Bill Hill is a government employee and I'm sure he'll expose us," worried Collin.

"I'll handle this," said Ricardo. "You go on the regional vid-system, Bendshaw, and reassure the locals that the sand lizard alert is over. We'll make heroes out of the ones we just tried to eliminate to keep the spotlight off of us. I'll review the events of the sand lizard attack and give you some video to show the people how it happened, so it won't look like anybody's fault. I should have it ready in ten minutes. Go, go!" yelled Narzani. Collin Bendshaw left immediately.

Ricardo talked out loud to himself as he reviewed the video of the gala proceedings at the Conquistador Palace, trying to figure out how he could cover his tracks. *"I'd like to know what Tenner used on those sand lizards to stop them. Seems like pretty powerful stuff. And like Collin said, the guy who helped them is a government employee. I'll just have to look into this Bill Hill's history, eh? Rest assured, Mr. Tenner: I will get you myself if Luthbert doesn't. I own the interstellar trade deals and the interplanetary haulage. The future can't have two top dog businessmen in the one industry I am going to monopolize. The interstellar transportation loop is mine!"*

CHAPTER THIRTEEN
'ALL OVER' ACCUSATIONS

COLLIN BENDSHAW WENT ON THE REGIONAL AIRWAVES OF North-Am after the sand lizard incident at the Conquistador Palace in Mazalta, and he reassured the baseball-loving crowds that it was safe to attend tomorrow's Alliance World Series Baseball game. There had been a few injuries and only one fatality at the festive dinner for the players and their wives. After downplaying the upsetting news as much as possible, Collin quickly turned his words to praise for the man who had almost single-handedly stopped the sand lizards and saved many lives. He played an edited version of the murderous events at the Conquistador Palace and the reports that followed gave firsthand accounts of Bill Hill's gallant actions to save Ray Tenner and others at the Palace.

Ray, Lenny, and their friends gathered at the Redmen's team residence. Ray had just got out of the clayonic shower. After being cleaned and clothed by the shower bot, he asked what they were watching so intently.

"The media seem to have a hero that saved the day at the dinner last night, and that man is Hill Billy," said Lenny.

"Is that right, Bill? Are they saying that about you?" asked Ray.

"Ah don't consider myself anywhere near that kind of status. All Ah did was make sure that Narzani, his political friends, and your ball friend didn't get what they wanted. Ah am sure Pamela Jay as well as all of us were targets of the sand lizards last night. Narzani has it out for all for us. That is what Ah gathered from the Qeup phone conversation Narzani had with Bendshaw and Dean Luthbert," said Bill.

Just then a staff member of the team came to their room and said that there were reporters wanting to talk to Bill Hill.

"Tell them to go away. Ah don't want to give any interviews," said Bill.

"But they are quite insistent, Mr. Hill," said the staffer. "They are saying that you used a secret weapon at the gala festival at the Conquistador Palace, something even the government doesn't know about. The media think you have something to hide."

Bill Hill got up and went out into the crowded hallway of paparazzi snapping pictures. Journalists instantly crowed question upon question at him. Bill put his hands up to silence the crowd and shield his eyes from the bright lights of the cameras.

"Ah will not be taking any questions. Ah am going to give you a statement, and then Ah am going to leave," said Bill. He began, "Ah have it on authority that the sand lizard attack was planned to disrupt the games and politics of this region. Ah am not implicating anyone, for Ah have no real evidence to provide in that regard, and for me to name anyone would be setting myself up for a defamation lawsuit. A sand lizard attack usually occurs after a desert windstorm overwhelms the protecting forest with sand. No such storm has occurred in the last thirty-six hours to bury the protecting trees, and so Ah am wondering how the two adult lizards got past the clayon defenses undetected. As for any secret weapon Ah may be harboring, all Ah can say is that Ah have no comment on that. The sand lizards were stopped by a combination of the clayon defense robots and laser technologies the government has provided for them. If you have any other questions, Ah suggest you direct them at the powers that be who are in charge around here."

With his statement over, Bill quickly returned to the confines of the Redmen's team residence. The reporters shouted questions after him as he left the media scrum.

From his private viewing box Ricardo Narzani frustratedly said, "Did you hear what that Hill Billy said?" shouted Ricardo. "We make him out to be a hero, and he's throwing it back in our faces, the bastard! I'll make sure he never gets out of the Gia Academy alive!"

"This is where you said you would provide the details of how the sand lizards got through our defenses and show how the clayon guard made mistakes in that regard, Ricardo," said Collin Bendshaw. "Mr. Hill did single handedly stop two sand lizards, and he did it with a weapon we don't know about, even though we can't prove he has in his possession something that the Alliance Government hasn't told us about," finished Collin.

"I'll go on the airwaves and straighten this out once and for all," said Ricardo.

Just then, Ricardo's wrist vid-phone notified him if an incoming call from Dean Luthbert.

"Why are you calling me?" asked Ricardo. "Someone could be listening to us. If you want to talk, then either meet me somewhere or call me on a secure channel."

"I want us to have a nice conversation, in private, about what happened and how we are going to handle what happened," said Dean calmly.

"I'll make sure everything is taken care of, Mr. Luthbert, and you can continue to play baseball with peace of mind. I'll make sure the Earth Alliance Council makes a formal investigation into this matter," answered Narzani formally as he hung up on Dean.

Ricardo Narzani had a secret that only he and a select few on the Earth Alliance Council members knew about. He had an agenda to slowly take over the Earth Alliance Council's governing body's powers by gradually getting rid of politicians, like Pamela Jay, in ways that would not implicate him. This sand lizard attack had been carefully planned right down to the last detail, but the plan hadn't included variables like Bill Hill and he had secrets of his own to further his agenda. Narzani was using the clayon guard to his advantage. He had gotten millions of these variable robots to be under his command, so he could subtly control the armed forces as well as the populations of the Earth Alliance regions. He didn't want anyone but a select few to know about his planned takeover. He knew that the Earth Alliance regions would never go for this *coup détat*, and he understood that secrecy was the only way to reach his goals. The botched sand lizard attack made him aware that his planning processes for his takeover must be rethought. His wanting of supreme power had been set back because he hadn't gotten rid of Ray, Lenny, and Pamela Jay. They were three stumbling blocks to his next move on gaining control of the powerful Alliances, and now Hill Billy was the fourth. Bill Hill had stopped his plans, quite easily, and Bill Hill seemed to have the power to change chaotic events. Mr. Hill was now a target of Ricardo Narzani's in his ultimate plans to take over the Earth Alliance governments. Mr. Hill would become Narzani's newest target in his actions to become supreme ruler of Earth.

"Ah have to leave now," said Bill. "My boss, the Regent at the Gia Academy, wants me to come back because of what he's seen and heard. Ah am going to have to do some fancy talking to get myself out of this one. Ah think that Narzani fella may have something to do with me being called back. Ah booked a full week of holidays that Ah have wanted for a whole year now, and Ah have only been here four days. Ah was hoping to watch your finals game tomorrow, Ray. Looks like Ah am going to have to work a bit harder on my other teleportation experiments to keep my boss happy and out of my hair," drawled Bill.

"Is that another one of your secrets, Bill?" asked Pamela Jay.

Bill said, "Ah wasn't going to let that one out of the bag, but Ah guess Ah just did. Ah am working on making objects pass through each other by making each of their molecules line up in a parallel fashion so the molecules of each object don't entangle, or hit each others orbits. That is, all the masses, if they are not molecularily lined up, will crash into each other, thereby causing the teleportation beam to collapse and matter to be crushed into each other at the failure point. But if you can make it so that the molecules of an atom don't touch each others orbits, then they should theoretically pass by each other without so much as a scratch on them, and with no molecule out of place when matter is reconstituted. Ah am working on that scratching part right now. Ah can get things to pass through each other, but they don't come out in one piece at the other end just yet. Ah have to adjust my gravitational waves to a specific quantum frequency to start the teleportation process, then add an altering frequency that can withstand the outside degradation interferences. This should, if my calculations are correct, quantumly make something that will molecularily allow these objects to do just that: pass each other. Ah have got it down to several billion miles in distances, but Ah want to increase the range some so that travel by humans in star ships between stars will become a thing of the past. In the future, it will just be a short hop to another star's station to get to other regional interstellar places. Once Ah fine-tune my instruments, it will take only minutes to set up. You see, Ah have discovered a quirk in the Heisenberg Uncertainty Principle," finished Bill.

All in the room looked at Bill Hill in amazement at what he had just said. They remained silent, undecided on whether Bill Hill was just making things up as he went along, or if he was telling them he had something coming down the inventor's pipe that would change space travel in the near future.

"Don't worry, Bill; if you need our help, we'll be there for you. If you want to change jobs right now and work for me, you can. I'm going to retire, win, lose, or die right after this final game. If I live, we'll start a new life together as business friends," said Ray.

"Me too," said Lenny.

"Me three," said Pamela Jay with a smile.

"We'll all be here for you, Bill," said Ian, shaking Bill's hand as he was leaving.

"Me five and Ozzy six," said Jigs, laughing.

When Bill had left the room, Jigs said, "Poor Bill; it seems the more good he does, the more he gets into a bad snake 'pit' of situations and has crap piled on himself for it. He's a hell of a scrapper, though he doesn't look the part. He is so quiet and gentle in his own way. Also, he has an amazing mind that is one in several billion, I'd say."

"It seems we all have to leave," said Pamela Jay. "I've got to find some answers about that sand lizard fiasco and the scene in the video where the sand lizard seems to just blow up for no reason. Bill thinks it wasn't an accident that the sand lizards were there. I think Bill is on to something about Narzani. Narzani has been asking for political favors amongst his friends in the government's cabinet as of late, and it seems he has a quiet coalition deferring to him. I'm going to get to the bottom of his secret endeavors. How about you guys, are you leaving too?" she asked, turning to Ian, Jigs, and Ozzy.

Ian nodded his head, as did Jigs and Ozzy. "Ray and Lenny, we'll see you later. Good luck in the finals, eh guys," said Ian as they filed out the door.

With their friends gone, Ray looked at Lenny and said, "Well, old chum, I guess we should get our minds off of what happened and start thinking about baseball, eh?" Ray flung a wet towel playfully and it wrapped around Lenny's face. Lenny swiped the towel quickly off his face. Lenny then chased Ray with the wet towel and snapped it onto Ray's butt.

"Ouch! That hurt!" Ray cried out.

"Not as much as this next one is going to," said Lenny, an evil look in his eyes and the towel held tautly in his hands. Ray took off running with Lenny in hot pursuit, snapping his towel wildly. Ray howled with each snap of the towel that connected with his rear.

CHAPTER FOURTEEN
GAMES LEADING TO THE GREAT GAME

NOW THE NORTH-AM'S ALLIANCE REGIONAL MEDIA POWERS that be were quite interested in Ricardo Narzani's words on the world broadcast. They wondered just how a sand lizard attack could have happened, when weather conditions warranted that its occurrence should not have been. It was a story everyone with influence in the world wanted to hear, reminiscent of the Donald Trump of old times when everyone waited with bated breath on what B.S. he would come out with next.

Ronald Messtier, Head of the World Alliance Members Council, called Collin Bendshaw to ask him why the sand lizards hadn't been detected sooner. Why were the clayon guards not better prepared for the attack that almost prevented the World Alliance Baseball Series from continuing? It would greatly upset the voters around the world if better protection wasn't provided during events that even the politicians attended. That would be a political forum to discuss at another time.

"I regret to inform you, Head Council Messtier, that the clayon guard had a breakdown in its automatic chain of command. A clayon guard robot was accidentally disabled at a key moment when the sand lizards came bolting out through the protective forest. Hence, the detection wasn't recorded as immediately as it should have been. One of the sand lizards ate the clayon robot, chewing it to bits, and I was told that the strong stomach acids of the lizard stopped the robot from alerting officials. Its automatic responses were not displayed as quickly as we had hoped because of the strength of the sand lizard's destructive stomach juices on the clayon robot. This delay is the reason that the detection wasn't recorded. The giant sand lizards must have found a way through the global forest somehow and surprised the clayon guard, then continued on quite quickly before getting into the Conquistador Palace.

It has been shown that the two sand lizards got over the protective fence that protects the living areas around Mazalta and covered the five miles from the forest to the Palace in less than two minutes. With the initial clayon guard now disabled, the breakdown of protection was inevitable. There wasn't enough time to send out the general alarm fast enough to get everyone to safe enclosures because of the clayon that had been disabled. It wasn't discovered by the second line of defense until twelve minutes after the sand lizards had gotten through to the populated areas. At that time, a full impending alert was issued. It is regrettable that there was a fatality and that some people were hurt, but I've got a committee working on plans to better protect vulnerable areas like the Conquistador Palace and the Baseball Dome in the future, Council Messtier," answered Collin, reading off of a script that Ricardo Narzani had provided for him filled with lies that Council Messtier had to tentatively accept.

"Clayon guards are not supposed to fail, Mr. Bendshaw. We have assured the people that over and over again! They are made up of what's supposed to be infallible clayonic materials, as I understand. They are made to reconstitute themselves in almost any situation. Clayon guards are supposed to annihilate themselves one after another in their protection of us. I don't care about sand lizard stomach juices or such. I want a public inquiry into this matter, and I want answers into this incident as soon as possible. The people want answers that I need to provide them with, from important people like you. If I don't get the right answers that the people want, then it will be you who must answer to the people. I hope that an incident like this doesn't happen again, because it doesn't look good for your regional governments' safety precautions. That will keep people away from the game. When you keep people away from the game, which is the Earth Alliance Government's main source of entertainment votes, then the populations start to get other ideas which lead to law breaking anarchy and reduced votes at election time for people like you. And, it makes speaking the truth difficult for me. So, I want you to make sure that your region is safe, or else someone new will replace you!" warned Head Council Messtier in a rather stern voice.

"Yes, steps will be taken to ensure this doesn't happen again, Head Council Messtier. I will personally follow through with this inquiry. I will also have Mr. Narzani give a public statement ensuring that the North-Am and Euro-Russo Alliance regions are safe and that no one has to worry about any more sand lizard encroachments at any of the games or events," ended Collin in a conciliatory tone.

Just as Collin's vid-phone conversation ended with Alliance Head Council Messtier, Ricardo Narzani appeared on the world vid system to address all of the public news channels. He gave his version of what had transpired at the Conquistador Palace the night before. He was covering his and Dean's tracks, politely, so to speak.

From Ian's room at the Fiesta Grande Hotel, Ray and Lenny watched Narzani as he fudged the facts of the sand lizard attack. They listened to Narzani lie directly to the populace of North-Am. Ray and Lenny knew that he could alter the facts, but they had to hear Narzani's version first.

Ricardo Narzani began, "In my role as Vice-Head Council of the Earth Alliance Council and as Grand Marshal of the

Alliance Baseball World Series Finals, I reopen the games to begin the finals of this great pastime." The great crowds outside the stadium watching Narzani on a huge jumbo tron made a low cheer for Narzani.

Ricardo Narzani said, "I have asked the North-Am director Collin Bendshaw to look into the matter of the sand lizard attack at the Conquistador Palace last night. I also want to tell the people of the city of Mazalta, here in North-Am, that extra precautions will be put in place so that any future encroachment by the sand lizards will not cause another violent episode during the games. This is especially true when the final game is being played in such a wonderful city as Mazalta. During the game, extra clayon guards will be deployed, by the hundreds, for the well-being and protection of the local populace. The defensive zone from the ringed forest area and the electric fence where the clayon guard are deployed will be triple-enforced with robotic guards so that a sand lizard attack will not happen. If one does, it will be contained during the World Alliance Baseball Series. The people's protection will be totally ensured, or I will resign as the top executive of the Euro-Russo Alliance. You have my word on it," said Ricardo Narzani in his short broadcast. "Thank you all for your most kind patience. Our gratitude will always be to the people of Earth." Ricardo's image appeared at the end of the broadcast with his hands over his head, making him look like the disappearing Cheshire Cat.

"Come to think of it, Lenny, I think that last night was Dean's and Narzani's way of trying to get rid of me because they both know that I want something from them. They want me dead, badly, and that is why the sand lizards came specifically after me at the Conquistador Palace. I think that some kind of undetectable chemical attraction agent was sprayed in our corner of the banquet room, and that is why both sand lizards came that direction right off the bat. If it wasn't for Hill Billy, I wouldn't be standing here saying that I don't believe anything of Narzani's broadcast," said Ray.

"What are you thinking, Ray?" Lenny asked.

"Well, as I see it, Dean has a twofold excuse for wanting me gone. That is, he wants to avenge Boisey's death. That is the big one for him, even though I didn't cause his brother's death. Second, he doesn't want me to win the World Series of Alliance Baseball here in Mazalta, in front of the North-Am fans. Narzani wants me gone, and possibly you too, Lenny, because we're both going to cut in on his transportation business here on Earth, to the other Alliance of Planets, and then out to the stars," said Ray.

"If that's the case, then we had better be on our toes to make sure Dean and Narzani don't try something again before our game tomorrow," said Lenny.

"Yes," Ian spoke up. "Ray, I don't want you to be the scapegoat of your past. I believe that you did not cause Dean's brother's death because of the circumstances recorded during the sand tornado in the desert."

Ray reiterated, knowing that he was a target of deep discussion amongst his friends concerning Boisey's death. Ray said, "I tried very hard to get Boisey back to the Mazalta entrance. We all would have been sucked up into the sand tornado's clutches, had it not been for the quickness of the owner's call at that time. He was the real presence that we needed for our survival."

Nodding in understanding, Ian cordially said goodbye and then left Ray and Lenny to themselves.

"Before Bill Hill left he gave me a secret patch code to his government Qeup vid-phone, the newly invented quantum entanglement one, the one Bill wants to keep secret. He put the code onto my vid phone," Ray confided in Lenny. "Bill got the special signal made up for listening to secret government conversations without anyone knowing about it. Bill said he's got it linked to Narzani's private coded signal. My vid-phone is patched into his; it will give me a signal that he's in an ongoing conversation with someone and I can listen," said Ray.

"Wow! You mean we can spy on the government around here and not get caught?" asked Lenny incredulously.

"We can only listen; we can't record or say anything, or the signal will get cut off due to our interference. If we try to record it, then Narzani will know someone's on to him," said Ray. "So, all we can do is listen and try to outguess him."

"I think I'd rather be playing baseball than acting like a spy, Ray," said Lenny.

"Yeah, I know. I don't think I have the time for spying either. Maybe we can get someone else to do it for us," said Ray.

"Like who?" asked Lenny.

"I think I'll call Pamela Jay and Ian and see if they can put some time into our little situation here and leave us to play baseball," said Ray.

"You're playing with fire, Ray, if you want others to be involved. Government business can be quite sticky when they discover they have been spied on by someone whom they wouldn't have suspected. I'm pretty sure they will be watching us and will use any excuse to label us spies and take us out of the game. People disappear, no matter who they are or how prosperous they are. I think we should keep this one to ourselves," warned Lenny.

At that moment, the quantum vid-phone given to Ray by Hill Billy began to ring. Ray glanced at Lenny with a *"What should I do?"* look. He knew he either had to turn the vid-phone on, or not answer it. He chose the former, and put the vid-phone on one-way speaker so that both he and Lenny could listen without the caller detecting them.

Ricardo Narzani was speaking to Dean. "You have your credits that I said I would give to you. I trust your silence is assured, Mr. Luthbert," said Ricardo.

"Yeah, I can live with that as long as you keep giving me those opportunities," answered Dean.

"Then you will try your hardest to make sure that Tenner and Peecheh don't make it through tomorrow's game, Mr. Luthbert. There will be an added bonus for you if you can accidentally throw an errant ball at a certain politician for me also. I will give you directions tomorrow, as I will be attending the game. I will also make sure that this certain politian will be in the correct place at the correct time when this errant ball is to be placed beside her," said Ricardo rather sarcastically.

"Don't you ever get tired of knocking people off and using other people to do it so you don't get shit on yourself?" asked Dean, equally sarcastically.

"I'll ignore that last remark from you, Mr. Luthbert," said Ricardo Narzani, coolly. "The person I want you to target will be sitting in an open box seat just before first base. I will have a member of my staff point this person out to you. I will be there as you will see me in the stands just above her, but when the transaction takes place, I want you make a throwing error that will have accidental but regrettable consequences. Can you do that for me, Mr. Luthbert?" asked Ricardo.

"How am I going to get the ball through the protective electronic shield that surrounds much of the field from the ringside bleachers?" asked Dean.

"There have been freak magnetic disturbances around the Earth during Coronal Mass Ejections, or CMEs, that disrupt the electronic workings of our susceptible Earth communication systems. These CMEs have made even our best technological advances temporarily inoperable. I will provide the freak disturbance when the moment arises so you can make your errant throw and blame it on a powerful magnetic storm from the sun as the game is being played," said Narzani in a controlled tone. "Many times in the past three hundred years this phenomenon has happened with an event recording data point, such as a CME event that has been detected but not broadcasted to the media by our inefficient government," said Ricardo.

"So, who's this politburo hack in your government you want snubbed?" asked Dean.

"Never mind who it is; just do it! Also, I have been negotiating with a coach, Gaster from the Redmen, who may help you in your quest for the Alliance World Series Championship," insisted Ricardo.

"Alright, alright, just hold your family jewels in place and I'll see what I can do," said Dean, hanging up on Narzani. Dean had the feeling of dread coming over him as he sat on his bed in his luxurious hotel room. He felt like crying like a little boy, even though he was a grown man. The tears did not come. "All I want is Ray Tenner," said Dean. "No one else." His resolve hardened at that moment and Dean got up to go to his team practice.

What Ray and Lenny heard on the quantum vid-phone made their eyes widen as big as green, unripe grapefruits.

"Gaster is taking bribes from Narzani now," said Ray. "I don't think I want to listen to this quantum phone anymore. It's giving me information I don't want to hear. I'd rather play the game and take my chances than play the spy man. I'm sure it's Pamela Jay whom he wants eliminated, but how he's going to do it and when, we don't know."

Lenny shook his head and agreed with Ray. "You're right, Ray. We should get Pamela Jay to help us. She should be able to get to Narzani and control whatever he's planning, and we should be able to play the game without interference," said Lenny.

"Let's call Pamela Jay and ask her if she's going to the game tomorrow and where she's going to sit," said Ray.

"I think we should talk to her and Ian in person, as we will be listened to if we use any regular technology to contact them, Ray," reasoned Lenny.

Just as Ray and Lenny were about to get up and leave, Cito Gaster, the Redmen's coach, came into the room. "Hi guys," Cito greeted them. "I won't dilly dally around with you two. Here's what I've planned for the game tomorrow. I want both of you to start and play the whole game tomorrow. I'm not going to relieve anyone on the bases. I want everyone in the starting lineup to try and get runs as soon as possible. That way our team has a better chance of winning. It's the finals, and I think if I play my best players first rather than the rookies, we'll be able to win this final game and the World Series," said Cito with a fake looking smile.

"Sure, Coach, but why not take us out of the game if we get on base and let the rookies do the foot slogging until we're really needed. Isn't that what's usually done?" Ray asked.

"Well," said Cito, smiling, "looking into the archives of the last one hundred years of Alliance baseball games, the teams that start their vets are favored to win, rather than the teams that save them for later on in the match."

Ray and Lenny didn't question Cito's decision. They just knew that their game would be a whole lot scarier if they stayed in full-time rather than being relieved if they got on base. "We'll do that for you, Coach, and we'll try and keep ourselves from getting knocked off," was Ray's response.

"Thank you, gentlemen. I'm giving you two, as well as the rest of the team, today off to recuperate and get your heads around the idea that you're going to play for the greatest cup event ever in the history of baseball," said Cito enthusiastically. "By the way, since there was a sand lizard attack, I'm imposing a team curfew as of right now. No one will miss tomorrow's game," said Cito, getting up and leaving the team's meeting room. Coach Gaster's decision seemed unusual to Ray and Lenny, but hey, the coach was always right, or else they wouldn't be here.

"We are going to have to be on our best game tomorrow, ever, Lenny, or we'll be chicken fodder for Dean and the Pelotas," said Ray. Ray and Lenny left their room to go to the physio clinic. On their way to the clinic, they saw their coach being approached by someone they didn't know just outside the main door lobby area. This person handed the coach a thick brown envelope. Cito took the thick package, looked around suspiciously, turned, and quickly walked away down the street from the main doors.

Right then and there both Lenny and Ray knew they were being set up to be hung out to dry in tomorrow's game. It looked like Cito had just taken a bribe right in front of them, and there was nothing they could do about it. Break curfew, and they wouldn't play. Complain to someone about the coach, and they would be ostracized and not allowed to play — even if they were trusted stars in the baseball world. They would be sent home in disgrace, have everything they had ever worked for taken away, and never play Professional Alliance Baseball again. They would have to get lowly jobs in a spaceport repair shop and work for the next seventy years or more at a laborer's rate. They needed someone to help them, and that would have to be Bill Hill. But they were faced with the perplexing dilemma of how to get a message to Bill. Their vid-phone was only good for listening in on other conversations, not making a direct call.

"Hey Ray, let's use one of the trainers at the physio clinic to get a message out," said Lenny, but just as the words came out of his mouth, Coach Cito mysteriously reappeared at the physio clinic. He had gathered all the trainers in the physio room and was talking to them animatedly.

"I guess that's out of the question," said Ray, disappointed.

Just then a bat boy came up to Ray and asked, "Is there anything I can do for you today, Mr. Tenner and Mr. Peecheh?"

Ray and Lenny looked at each other, and they knew that the young teenaged bat boy was the out they were looking for. Cito never talked to the bat boys.

So Ray and Lenny talked to the bat boy, plied him with praise, and gave him a simple written message on a micro holo DVD, not much bigger than a little fingernail. They asked him if he knew who Pamela Jay was, and he said that he did know who she was. Ray asked him to deliver the holo DVD with the information they wanted Pamela Jay to hear. Ray gave advance payment to the bat boy of two thousand credits to make the delivery. This was more than the bat boy had received all year. He enthusiastically left the Redmen's physio training area, saying, "Thanks, guys. I'll make sure Miss Jay gets this, and no one is going to stop me."

"I think our world is closing in on us, Ray," said Lenny. "I want to get the game over with as soon as possible and get out of this rat race I've been in for seven years. It's now beginning to scare the hell out of me, and I think it's time to retire."

"I know what you mean, Lenny. On the ball field we can handle just about anything, but now that Dean, Narzani, and god knows who else seems to be after us, I'm with you, partner. We have to win that game tomorrow, or we're toast," said Ray.

Ray and Lenny took showers and were about to head back to their rooms for the night when the terrible news came in. The bat boy that they had sent out with their information for Pamela Jay was dead! A faulty door on the subway system, under the city, had accidentally killed him. Trapped by a closing door, dragged by the anti-grav train, and cut in half as it proceeded into the tight, vacuumed tunnel, the bat boy's remains were scattered beyond recognition.

Again, Ray and Lenny looked at each other and just knew in their gut that the bat boy's death was no accident. Someone was watching their every move. Worse, whoever had done this dastardly deed may have the halo DVD that they had sent to Pamela Jay! Waiting for tomorrow was like being tied, prone, to a moving platform that had a large rotating saw blade moving towards them. There was nothing Ray or Lenny could do as they were inevitably being drawn forward to the rotating, giant saw blade.

CHAPTER FIFTEEN
THE FINAL GAME

"WE'VE BEEN WAITING FOR THIS FOR A LONG TIME. IT'S GAME day!" shouted the play-by-play commentator J. D. Bower over the vid media echo systems to the listening throngs in front of their vid sets worldwide. "The size and roar of this enthusiastic crowd here in North-Am makes the ground tremble under your feet, shaking the foundations of this mighty enclosed modern baseball dome, here in Mazalta. The shaking feels like an earthquake. The shaking comes and goes with the roar and enthusiasm of the loyal fans of Alliance Baseball. We call that people aftershocks, and there are many of them! There are over eight hundred and thirty thousand strong here to see the battle of the best of the best, the titans of Earth Major League Alliance Baseball this year. The Labrador Redmen of North-Am have fought against all odds and ground their way back to the top of the Earth Alliance Series repechage style of play to do battle with the South-Am's Pelotas. This is the match up of the giants in the world of Alliance Baseball, a one game contest where the winner takes all the trappings, credits, and glory and the losers go home just as that, losers, with a pittance for pay and a likelihood of being ridiculed by their home Alliance regional fans. Anyone who has bets on this game says it is any team's game. The stats are so close that even the betters won't give good odds as to who will be victorious today.

"Who will win this mighty game? Will it be the Redmen? Or will it be the first-place finishers from South-Am, Pelotas? It will be a nail-biter if anything for all those watching and playing this great game of Alliance Baseball!" said J. D. Bower.

The vid commentator went on to say, "On this day of the big game, for the past three hours all of the players and staff of each team have been cloistered in separate sound- and vibration-proof rooms so they could not hear the noises from the outside world that may otherwise distract them before the final game. No roar of the crowds, no interventions of the media, and no autograph seekers are allowed near the teams. No visits by dignitaries or family members offering best wishes are allowed. No distractions at all to make the players' minds wander from their prize. The big prize they yearn for is winning this all-important final game and basking in the glory that goes with it."

To fill in time in his vid cast before the big game, J. D. Bower continued, "Early in Alliance Baseball, the owners of the teams noticed that if this type of internment were applied to the players and coaches, their performances on the field of play would be much better. It has been found that exposure to the loud and adoring world resulted in lowering the 'peak playing velocities in the players' minds' for the three or four hours that it takes to play this final game. A downturn in players' peak playing performance is clearly not desired. That was the reasoning given by the owners to the media as their excuse for not letting the fans see their beloved ball players practicing out on the field of play before the game. Much to the dismay of the players, the crowds, through their boisterous cheering, made many of the new rookies play very ambitiously, sometimes foolishly, and even fatally, and then they would die very quickly on the field of play, much to the delight of the gore-hungry fans. So, this is why the teams cannot be seen for three hours before their deadly final game."

Cito Gaster was given respectful applause by his team when he walked into the locker room. He stood before them and began, "I don't have to tell you how important this game is today for all of us. That thought should have sunk into you men days ago. No amount of my mouthing off to you players now will get you any farther in this game than it already has. This is the ultimate moment of your playing careers. You core vets know what's needed of you: you have carried this team a long way and now is the time to show your inner metal as professionals. You rookies who have survived over the past few weeks are now vets, and you must set an example to the newbies that follow. When we win, this will be our greatest day! You must now envision yourselves as great baseball players. See yourselves hitting, running, scoring, and eliminating the opposition before you even enter the field of play. That way all you have to do is step into your vision and complete this game. There is no other reality more real than that," finished Cito Gaster in an upbeat voice of enthusiasm for his players.

Ray, Lenny, and the others present nodded and said with some enthusiasm, "Here, here," to Gaster. They sounded like a British Parliament of old, patting themselves on the back.

The opposing coach, Carlos Vieira of Pelotas, had a similar pep talk for his team. He said, "We as a team have done very well. But very well will not get us to where we want to go as Alliance Baseball players. We are going to play against a team that has worked like **animals** to get back at us, and with that frame of mind, they will defeat us!" bellowed Vieira. Vieira's team was surprised at this kind of talk, for their coach had always talked of victory. Vieira quickly went on before the team could fully react to what he was saying. "This will not happen if, and that is a big 'if', you instill in your minds that we, as the great team that we are, shall tame those wild animals. We are the masters of our own destiny, not the animals! Do you hear me!?" shouted Vieira.

Pelotas' team members stood up and merrily cheered their coach and themselves as loudly as they could muster for over a full minute.

Dean approached Coach Carlos Vieira and said, "Let me be the first to say that I'm going to try and give you my best game today, Coach Vieira . I'm ready to take on the whole damn Redmen team if I have to, or give up my life in the process," finished Dean so that all of his teammates could hear. Of course, Ray Tenner's demise was also on his mind.

"Good, Scorpion, good," was Carlos' reply. "You will get your chance to shine today as well as our whole team. Our great Alliance team of South-Am and its people of Pelotas will be proud of you. It is time, my charges, to go to our glory," said Carlos Vieira, pointing out the doorway to the field of play.

Dean led his team onto the field holding the flag of Pelotas, with a scorpion emblazoned on it. Dean wore his dark black uniform with the yellow trim fringe and red highlights. From a distance, his long lean frame and his uniform made him look like a scorpion. When Dean came walking out of his dressing room onto the open field of the dome, the cheering crowds of North-Am became subdued. They oohed and awed at Dean's menacing-looking uniform along with his menacing grimace; today, he meant business. His look was posted on the big jumbo trons and on all of the vid sets of the world, for all to see. The Scorpion was here, not for a long time, but for a killing time. No one would get past Dean Luthbert on base or otherwise, if he got to the ball, and the home team crowd knew it. They gave him a pleasant ovation in hopes of cooling his vicious ways.

Next came the Labrador Redmen onto the field led by Coach Cito Gaster. North-Am's banner depicted an aboriginal man riding a white horse full tilt towards a blazing sun in a victorious pose. He brandished a spear, a traditional weapon of indigenous people. The home team crowd went wild and began to chant, "Redmen, Redmen, Redmen!" The fans hoped to give the Redmen the spark they needed to score early and keep South-Am's Pelotas out of the game.

"It is game time!" announced J. D. Bower loudly, in a cheery tone, over the airwaves and vid screens of the world. The umpires levitated down to field level and called for the team captains to come out of their dugouts on their servo discs. The team captains would carry out the ceremonial coin toss performed by the home plate umpire to see who would be the 'home team' and have the choice of batting or playing on the field to start the play of the game. Ray and Lenny, as the Redmen representatives, went out on their levitated servo discs to the home plate area. Dean and Vincent from Pelotas did the same.

"Okay, gentlemen, I guess you guys know each other well enough, so we'll bypass the introductions and get on with the proceedings as quickly as possible. The fans are waiting," said the home plate umpire.

"Yeah, we want to get things over with as soon as possible," echoed Dean. He looked straight into Ray's eyes, conveying that he wanted to nail Ray as soon as he could in this game to avenge his brother Boisey's death.

Ray just smiled at Dean and said to Lenny sarcastically, "You call it, partner. The opposition seems to want heads today, anyway."

The coin was tossed into the air by the home plate umpire. "Call it!" said the officiating umpire.

Lenny naturally called tails while Dean said heads. They watched intently as the coin twirled, flipped in the air, and bounced on the white turf several times before coming to rest at the umpire's feet. The cameras of the world zoomed in on the bobbling shiny coin as it stopped with the deciding side of the coin visible to all.

"Tails!" said the umpire loudly. "To the Redmen, they are the winners of the toss." The home plate umpire pointed to Lenny of the Labrador Redmen for all to see that the decision of the coin toss went in favor of the Redmen.

"It is your decision, Redmen: what start do you want for this game?" asked the home plate umpire, looking at Lenny.

Lenny said, "We'll take the field and let Pelotas bat." The captains ceremoniously shook hands as the crowd roared its approval, and the umpires levitated to their respective positions fifteen feet above the field of play.

"Sure thing, Tenner and Peecheh; it doesn't matter where you start, because I know that this day I'll have your heads on a platter," said Dean when the umpires were out of earshot.

"Good luck, old man, because you're going to need it when I take you out," was Ray's response to Dean's threat. Ray scowled at Dean as the servo-discs began to take them away from each other to their respective dugouts.

The home plate umpire again signaled that the Redmen were the home team and Pelotas were to bat at the start of the first inning of this all important final game where the winner takes all. The home plate umpire yelled the traditional 'Play ball!' The crowd began cheering in anticipation. The white turf was changed to green to signify the official start of the game, and then the crowd really began to cheer and roar in earnest. Hands covered ears to stop the aggravating reverberations of the adoring crowds. All was in order according to the lineups, and the spectacle of deadly Major League Alliance Baseball ensued.

The commentator for the inter-Alliance broadcast initiated his on-air task at hand of giving voice to the play-by-play analysis of the game. J. D. Bower began, "Okay, fans of the Earth Alliance Major League Baseball World, there you have it. The Redmen are the home team and they have chosen to take the field and let team Pelotas, from South-Am, start at home plate. The playing turf has been changed from white to green, signifying that the game is to begin, so here we go, and hang onto your hats. Having home field advantage means a lot to the Redmen, as they will have last bat, if this game is a close one, which we expect it to be. Now, for you interested fans, we have breaking news. Pelotas has been able to acquire Ziguro Hashimshita from the Austro-Asian League at the last minute following intense negotiations by Pelotas' executive who asked that Ricardo Narzani, from the Euro-Russo Alliance, be included in the baseball political wranglings for 'Ziggy'. It is purported that Ziguro Hashimshita, aptly named 'Ziggy', can throw the ball at over one hundred and ninety miles per hour. This is an unheard-of ball speed for this game. There have been only two other pitchers in the three-hundred-year history of Alliance Baseball that have ever been able to do that. It's been a hundred years since we've seen that kind of ball speed from any Alliance pitcher's arm on this planet, even with robotic enhancement. What happens here today with the best offense in the league, and that is the Redmen, against the best defense from Pelotas should be nothing short of exciting to say the least," said the game's commentator.

"Isn't that Ziguro Hashimshita?" Lenny asked Ray.

"Yeah, it's Ziggy alright," said Ray, crestfallen.

"Didn't you play together in the Austro-Asian League two years ago, Ray?" asked Lenny.

"Yeah, I did, but back then he was just a skinny rookie pitcher struggling to try and get the ball over a hundred and seventy miles per hour," said Ray. "From what I hear, he got an undetectable illegal genetic implant in his shoulder two years ago, and he's just now peaking with his pitching stats in Major League Alliance Baseball. The genetic implant will only last so long, and then his shoulder will blow up from the pressures he'll put on it. It's a gamble he's taken, but when that happens is anybody's guess.

After that, Ziggy will never play baseball again, let alone use his dead shoulder. He got the genetic implant for the monetary gain from the wins. He's super rich now because of the implant and his enhanced pitching abilities. We just have to try and get the hits we need and hope he fails in his attempt at being the big throwing speed pitcher that he is today. He's going to have to work real hard if he wants to get by us, because I know his pitching style. It hasn't changed; it's only gotten faster, and I think that will be his downfall today," said Ray, clenching his teeth and eying Ziggy.

Ray and Lenny both watched as Ziggy took his warm up pitches on the pitcher's mound. They could hear the ball leaving Ziggy's hand and whooshing into the catcher's glove a quarter of a mile away from inside their dugout. Ziguro smiled triumphantly as he threw the ball, then he looked down his nose at the Redmen's dugout with fire in his eyes. Ray and Lenny both knew that Ziggy would be hard to hit in this game. They would both have to really dig deep to try and get any hits or plays off of Ziggy if their team was to even come close to winning today.

Distracted, Ray looked dispassionately into the boisterous crowd near the dugout. Amongst the roaring and waving crowd, Ray noticed Bill Hill and Jigs sitting together over first base across from his dugout. They were with Pamela Jay, Oscar Duhalde (Ozzy), and a strangely familiar woman that Ray knew he had met before but couldn't quite place. Ian Shelton wasn't with them. Ian was probably working, as Ray knew he didn't have a great interest in baseball. Bill Hill and Jigs looked at Ray, who gave them an enthusiastic thumbs up. He was glad to see that Bill and Jigs were at this final game. He poked Lenny, showing him where their friends were situated. Lenny waved and acknowledged them with a smile. Ray wondered at Bill's presence, because he had said that he had to get back to work and his studies at the Gia Academy in Labrador City for the government and that he would miss this final game. Jigs had said he would be at the game because he had a few more days of leave to use up.

Bill Hill, acknowledging Ray's 'thumbs up', held up a four-foot-long box, pointed to it, and then pointed to Ray like the box was meant for him. Ray was puzzled at Bill's enthusiasm, but he acknowledged that he could see the box in Bill's hands. A bat boy from Ray's team ran into the stands, took the box from Bill, and brought it to Ray. Inside the box were two handmade, hardwood bats. Ray looked at the bats and felt puzzled. He hadn't used a wooden bat since his first junior days in the Hyder Minor Alliance Leagues when he was six years old. Since then, Ray had always used his modern, chain-made, pivotal bat. This must be a goodwill gesture on Bill's part to make Ray feel better during this big game. After he opened the box, Ray read the note inside.

"Ray, Ah knows you have the best equipment in the world to play baseball with today, but these two bats were made by Grand pappy Hill. Ah've only used them once when Ah played Junior Alliance Baseball in my younger redneck days. Grand pappy gave them to me before he died with the instructions to only use them if Ah really needed to, otherwise they won't last in the game. 'Ah knows they have at least one good hit left in them,' Grand pappy told me. Good luck to you and Lenny."

Looking the hardwood bats over, Ray could see that they were made of Ozark White Mountain Ash, one of the hardest woods in the world because of the pure mountain water the trees flourished in. The bats were perfectly handcrafted with Bill Hill's grandfather's initials stamped on them, BOH, (Bill Oliver Hill), and they had been shellacked with a very hard covering of some kind. Another curious feature on the bats was that they bore the World Alliance Baseball stamp of approval, which Ray had never seen on anything but chain-made Alliance bats.

Lenny came over, sat down beside Ray, and asked, "Where did you get those old things? I haven't heard of anyone using them in our profession in the past seven years. The year I started, a seven-year veteran like me used a wooden bat like these ones during one of his at bats in a game."

"What happened when he used the wooden bat?" asked Ray.

"George LeBonte was the best hitter around in those days," said Lenny.

"Wasn't he the great slugger for Pak-Indostan's best team, the Merdeka Marauders?" Ray asked. "We all wanted to be sluggers like him when we were kids, remember that? Even Boisey thought he could be like him. LeBonte was on two winning Alliance World Series Cup Teams, wasn't he?" asked Ray.

"Yeah, that's him. But when he used the wooden bat in regular play, it shattered into splinters from the force of the ball. LeBonte hit into a double play in which he and the runner on first base were killed on single beans. LeBonte never got to retire. Instead, he died from making the mistake of using a wooden bat at the wrong time in his career. He did it for showmanship, thinking he would 'get away with it' in his last fatal game of baseball," finished Lenny.

Ray looked at the wooden bats from Bill Hill, and thought that he wouldn't need them today. He asked the bat boy to put them aside. He would do something with them later. He would also thank Hill Billy after the game for his gesture of goodwill.

With the game started, Ray and Lenny had to set aside any distractions and literally put their life's focus on the game at hand. The Redmen took to the field at the top of the first inning with Cito Gaster yelling his usual obscenities at his players to play better, get the outs right away, and get back to batting as soon as possible.

Coach Vieira, not to be outdone, did the same, as it was the tradition for coaches to try and look as mean as possible to the players and the fans in the watching world. It was hoped that these displays of 'urgent' emotions would spark immediate aggression in their players' style of play.

The play-by-play commentator J. D. Bower began, "On the mound the starting pitcher for the Redmen is the crafty young vet, Jerry Dozey, who has three years hurling experience. His knuckle screwball is second to none. The knuckle ball comes in at you at a hundred and sixty-five miles an hour, which is kind of slow for major league pitching. The ball looks like it's writing your name in the air when it comes at you, that's how much movement Dozey puts on it. It stays within the boundaries of league play ninety-five percent of the time, which is why it is his bread and butter pitch," reflected the play-by-play commentator. "The ball has to remain within the pitching lane limits going to home plate, or else it is automatically called a ball. You see, the ball cannot move more than three feet up, down, or sideways when it's thrown towards home plate by the pitcher from two hundred feet away. When the ball is twenty feet from home plate, it has to be in the batting area designated by the league so it doesn't come in at the batter sideways near or in the strike zone. The home plate umpire sees this on his monitor when he makes his calls on each pitch. Some pitchers can make the ball bend more than ten feet from the mound, two hundred feet away from home plate, but the ball has to be in the delineated 'zone of play' twenty feet out from home plate — otherwise, this kind of fancy throwing is not allowed in Alliance Major League Baseball pitching. It seems we have quite a match up here of pitchers with the barn-burning thrower, Ziguro Hashimshita, the best fastball thrower in the world, for Pelotas, against the best knuckle ball thrower the majors have seen in a long time, Jerry Dozey, in for the Labrador Redmen," finished the play-by-play commentator.

"Now up for Pelotas is the great lead off hitter, Juan McDermott, a South-Am native who has played in the North-Am Leagues for a year. His last name comes from his dad's side and his first name comes from his mom's side. Juan, a three-year vet of

Alliance Baseball, can smoke the ball for base hits at any given moment, and he has done this many times against the Redmen pitching in other games over the years. He has a three hundred plus batting average starting today's game in this tournament," J. D. Bower, the vid commentator, informed the viewers. He continued, "Dozey starts his windup, lunges towards home plate, and hurls a fastball by McDermott on the inside of home plate for a strike. Next pitch is a screwball that Juan McDermott is fooled completely by as he goes after the pitch but fouls it off. The next three pitches are balls, which run the count full to three balls and two strikes," said the vid commentator, and he continued the play-by-play uninterrupted. "Dozey knows he has to get McDermott to go after the next pitch, or it's a free walk to first for the initial batter of this first inning. So the pitcher, Dozey, challenges the batter with a low fastball over the plate at the batter's knees. McDermott hits the ball hard on the ground to Ray Tenner at second base. With the ball bouncing into his glove, Tenner quickly lines up his runner and throws the ball into the ribs for a bean onto the running McDermott. But the throw is a little high, and McDermott takes the bean off of his helmet. McDermott is sent sideways on the baseline, still on his way to first base. McDermott quickly recovers, making it to first base safely before the minor infielder can retrieve the errant ball and get it to the first baseman Peecheh for the second bean. This is regarded as an error on Ray Tenner's part for not stopping the aggressive McDermott with the first bean to his helmet instead of to the body. Play is stopped and the wobbly McDermott remains on first base with no relief runner to take him out of the game. He gets his helmet back from his base coach as it was knocked off by the ball which allows him to put it back on. If the helmet had fallen off of McDermott's head while on his way to first base, the rules state that the helmet would have to stay off for the rest of McDermott's time in the inning while he was on base. In this case the ball knocked it off, and so it will stay on the head of the thankful McDermott.

"Now back to home plate where we are ready for the next batter. We're ready to start again as the home plate umpire calls 'Play ball'," the vid commentator reported.

"Pelotas has a man on base now with none out and an error is charged to Tenner of the Redmen," the vid commentator continued. "Up next is the wily right-handed hitter Gulshan Sibi. Sibi was traded to Pelotas from the Pak-Indostan Alliance two years ago, and he has made a name for himself playing for Pelotas in the South-Am leagues. He looks too skinny to be playing major league baseball. Sibi the swinging toothpick has really been a force for Pelotas with his great running and batting abilities," said the vid commentator. "But don't let his looks fool you. He's got hidden power in them bones and can really put a zing on the ball when he hits," added the game's vid commentator.

"The pitcher, Dozey, winds up and delivers a meandering knuckle ball that moves all over the map. Sibi swings wildly with a misplaced effort by his floundering articulated bat, and the fans on the first pitch reaching for the ball. The home plate umpire calls 'Strike one', and the home team fans roar their approval for Dozey's pitching. The next two pitches are balls, out of the strike zone, to Sibi. He waits patiently in the batter's box for Dozey to give him the right pitch so he can lay into it. These throws by Dozey are high mid-range velocity. These throws are easily recognized by most batters for their slower speeds, but the movement on the ball has a ninety-nine percent chance of the batters thinking 'Just where the hell will the ball be in the strike zone when I want to swing at it?' The batters can see the ball coming, but where it's going to be when it gets to you is anyone's guess. Dozey delivers a high moving knuckle fastball into the strike zone. Gulshan Sibi recognizes the pitch for what it is. He swings with confidence into the ball with his pivotal bat and sends the ball just low over third base, falling in fair territory onto the field of play, and rolling all the way to the left field wall. It's a long single base hit for Sibi. The left fielder running over thirty miles an hour gets the ball and heaves it to third base to stop McDermott from advancing, but to no avail. The hit easily allows McDermott to get to second from first. Sibi gets to first base safely and we now have two men on base for Pelotas with none out in this first inning of play," said the vid commentator. J. D. Bower continued without a pause, "The ball is fielded by the left fielder and thrown in from the outfield to third in one bounce to keep the runners from advancing. The Redmen are getting behind here early in the game. Oh boy, here we go, look at this: Cito Gaster calls a time out. Gaster's taking a servo disc out to the mound to talk to his starting pitcher, Dozey. Sibi at the same time is relieved of his base running duties. Sibi, the veteran, is replaced by Robert Bearonson, a young running rookie. McDermott stays on second. During this time out, we'll refer you out-of-stadium fans to our sponsors. We'll be back in two minutes to fill you in on the ongoing happenings on the field," ended the game commentator.

Cito Gaster was a fair man when his team was on the winning side of play, but a mean s.o.b. when his team was losing. Gaster went up to Dozey and said, "Look here, Dozey, you're fresh. You should be heaving like a demon out here. Why the hell have you let two men get on base this early?" he asked crabbily to his starting pitcher on the mound.

Dozey looked at Gaster like he was trying to get the batters out or at least get them to hit onto the ground for an infield play. "Well, Coach, I'll throw harder," was all that Dozey could say, not wanting to be pulled this early in the game.

"You're damn right you'll throw harder. We don't have time for your easy pitching. We've got a game to play, and I'll not let you spoil it by slacking off in the first inning. I want you to make the next three batters dead men, or it'll be you who'll pinch-hit in this game!" finished Gaster in a superior tone. That was a threat that Coach Gaster would follow through with if Dozey, the pitcher, didn't get the next three batters out. If he didn't, then

Dozey would have to bat in the game. Pitchers were generally protected from batting, so they could only pitch. Dozey wasn't a great hitter, and having to bat would certainly mean his death. A designated hitter was always put in for the pitcher when they came to bat in the regular lineups. This threat by Gaster did put some real fear into Dozey's mindset, and he vowed in his mind that he would do better.

"Okay, Coach, I got ya. Harder it is," said Dozey.

Cito Gaster returned to his team's dugout on the servo disc with a determined look. The fans had quieted down when Gaster was out on the field talking to his starting pitcher, but they cheered loudly when Dozey was left in the game.

"Well, it looks like Gaster put some kind of challenge to Dozey, the Redmen pitcher. Young Dozey has a determined look on his face," said the vid commentator. "Let's see if the fire lit under Dozey heats things up here in the top of the first inning in this great Mazalta Dome."

"Play ball!" yelled the home plate umpire as the Redmen's time out expired.

Throw like a demon Dozey did. The next two Pelotas' batters went down with consecutive strikeouts which made them look like the silly swinging rookies they were. Now into the heart of Pelotas' batting order the next man to bat was none other than the Scorpion, Dean Luthbert. Dozey knew Dean was a good hitter as well as a top infielder. Jerry Dozey again became fearful of losing his job. He formulated a plan for how he would pitch to Dean.

Dean Luthbert stood up to home plate looking ready. His confident smile said it all. Nothing would get by him.

The vid commentator J.D. Bower began, "Dozey has pitched like a madman to the last two batters, getting two needed outs.

Can he do the same to Luthbert, the top player for Pelotas? Dozey sends in a fastball in the strike zone to Luthbert, but it's outside on the corner of the plate. Luthbert lunges at it with his articulated bat but misses. His articulated bat was bent slightly the wrong way for the pitch. 'Strike one!' calls the home plate ump. Dozey tries his dependable knuckle ball, but it doesn't fool Luthbert. The Scorpion straightens his articulated bat and all you can hear is a loud 'smack'! It's over the center fielder's head to the center field wall. What a hit!" shouted the vid commentator J.D. Bower. "Luthbert makes first, goes for second, and gets an easy stand up double and a run batted in for Pelotas. McDermott comes in to home plate for the score with the rookie Rob Bearonson going to third base on the hit by Luthbert," said the play-by-play commentator. "What a hit by Luthbert. It went easily to the wall and the center fielder, for the Redmen team wasn't even close to getting to the ball. The center fielder made a quick recovery, though, and got the ball back into the infield to stop a second run from scoring from third," finished the play-by-play commentator.

Dean, now on second base, was only a few feet from Ray. "Looks like this is another time you and I can be close together and not stick a fork into each other, just like at the Palace, eh Tenner?" said Dean, eying Ray in an attempt to distract Ray's focus on the game.

Ray ignored Dean and his badgering. A relief runner came out for Dean on second base, and Dean deliberately brushed against Ray as he went by him, intimidatingly hard enough to make Ray move. "I've got my eye on you today, Tenner," said Dean as he trotted off to his servo disc coming to bring him off the field.

"You're just lucky, Luthbert, that you've got a sucky coach who won't let you play when it really means something. You're his biggest pet suck, I'll bet," said Ray. Ray kept his cool, knowing that he might have his chance to get back at Dean later on in this game.

"The next Pelotas' batter is a lefty, Toni Veracruz, a second-year vet. The rather young-looking Veracruz is a fan favorite of the females in South-Am. Dozey for the Redmen sends in a fast ball slider that stays over home plate. Veracruz hits the ball in a one hop directly to Lenny at first base. Lenny scoops up the ball, checks the runner Bearonson at third and the pinch runner at second, and puts the ball, spikes and all, into the young batter's face, sending him out of the game and terminating his life at the same time for the third out of the first inning. Lenny isn't going to fool around with just injuring Pelotas' players today; they are going down!" said the J. D. Bower.

This was a sign to Dean that the game wasn't going his way. The previously silent home team fans of the Redmen now roared their approval of Lenny's viciousness on the recorded play. On the stadium's jumbo tron, they watched the gory replay of the young Pelotas' batter, Veracruz, being put out of his misery by Lenny Peecheh. Lenny had provided the fans with what they wanted to see.

"Three out!" called the first base umpire as the red holographic light was raised around the dead Pelotas' batter that had tried for first base.

"That's three out; the inning is over," finished the home plate umpire as the red holographic light finished going up around Veracruz, the downed two-year vet.

"The Redmen and Pelotas exchange places on the field. The topof the first started with the Redmen committing an error. The Redmen are down a run early in this game. What mayhem will ensue at the bottom of the first inning is your guess, as well as mine. We go to break and leave you with the last play of the inning finished by none other than the great Lenny Peecheh," said the play-by-play commentator, J. D. Bower.

Pamela Jay and Nina Cutoff had become good friends through their mutual friendships with Ray, Ian, and Jigs. The two ladies arrived just as the bottom of the first inning was about to begin and the Redmen were to bat. Pamela and Nina seemed to enjoy each other's company, despite their vastly different jobs, as they settled into their seats on the first base line of the stadium, close to first base. Pamela was unaware of what was in store for her that day. Although Ray and Lenny knew, they couldn't tell her what they had overheard during Ricardo Narzani's vid Qeup Quantum phone call to Dean the day before. Ray and Lenny knew she was in some kind of danger, but they had no way of forewarning her.

"Okay, now that we're back to regular programming, we'll fill you in on the Pelotas' pitcher Ziguro Hashimshita. During the first inning against the Redmen, Ziguro didn't give the Redmen batters even a sniff at the ball for a hit. He pitched the first inning with the authority of a major league pitcher and struck out all three starting batters for the Redmen. He didn't even allow a foul ball during his pitching debut here at the finals. The ball zipped by the batters at over a hundred and ninety miles per hour, with each batter swinging only one time at bat. The ball went by them so fast that they swung on each of their third pitches, because during the first two pitches the batters had literally watched the ball go by them before they could even react to the ball. All of the three batters up for the Redmen looked bad in their at bats, and the fans began to boo their home team on the third batter because they couldn't even tick the ball as it zoomed by them at great speed," said J. D. Bower.

"Strike three, yer out!" called the home plate umpire on the third batter of the inning for the Redmen. Nine pitches by Ziggy Hashimshita was all it took to end the first inning with three strikeouts in a row to show for his efforts. A fantastic beginning for the starting pitcher, Hashimshita, the Pelotas' pitcher. His Pelotas' team looked good to continue their scoring ways in the second inning as Hashimshita shut down the Redmen to no hits at all.

"The Pelotas' pitcher looks like he can shut down the Redmen batters quite easily. It doesn't bode well for the Redmen if this is the theme that the game will follow. We'll be back soon with more play-by-play action of the game," said the commentator as the programming paused for another commercial break.

Fans at home watched a commercial advertising the newest servo vehicles that touted environmental conforming non-polluting stats. Next, new stem cell research was touted on the airwaves as offering cutting-edge improvements to people's future health. Lotteries, which were still allowed, were promoted as buying into the health of the planet to try and get the populace to buy environmental friendly products as well as health care benefits in the form of lottery tickets. These advertisements, which were apparently sponsored by the politicians of all of the Earth's Alliance Regions, were for the benefit of the viewers of the airwaves.

"Once again, the teams exchange positions on the field of play to begin the second inning," said the play-by-play commentator. "Now, the second half of Pelotas' batting order is coming up to bat. This is a roster which is quite well known to the coach of the Redmen, Cito Gaster. They are the best hitters the Pelotas' team has to offer. Cito Gaster knows this, and so he quickly changes his starting pitcher to Conyee (said like Connie) Harsnett, knowing that Dozey wouldn't be able to handle them.

The next three batters up for Pelotas are Rodrigo Rainho, Aurther Arante, and Waldimer Abbreto, aptly named the 'three amigos' as they are always in this batting order for their team. These three are a terror to a pitcher's ego because of their great hitting and base running abilities."

J. D. Bower, the commentator, said, "The first at bat is Rodrigo Rainho, and he steps up to home plate oozing confidence. He is ready for whatever Harsnett has to offer him. A little bit of info for you fans out there on Harsnett before he begins," J. D. Bower adds to his broadcast. "Conyee Harsnett is a homegrown Labrador boy whose parents came from a long line of earlier fishermen, back when fishing was the industry here in the province of Labrador in North-Am. Fans still call Labrador 'The Rock'. Harsnett's ancestors came as settlers from the old country of England, now part of the Euro-Russo Alliance. Later descendants became spaceport workers in the great city of Goose Bay on the east coast of North-Am. Now Harsnett is known to be a bit aggressive in his pitching style, as he doesn't allow very much time between his pitches when batters are up. You see, he lacks the great speed of the Pelotas' pitcher Ziguro Hashimshita. Harsnett's forte is that he can change his pitches abruptly and keep batters guessing as to what he is going to deliver next."

"Harsnett goes right after the batter Rainho by putting a medium speed pitch (139 mph) inside and on the hands of the Pelotas' batter. Rainho, thinking it was a speed ball heater, swings out in front of the ball as he pulls his articulated bat inward to his body and misses the ball completely," said the play-by-play commentator.

"Strike one!" shouted the home plate umpire from above.

"The pitch also makes Rainho flinch as he thinks it's a little too close to him, and he complains to the umpire above him. The home plate umpire quickly reprimands Rainho, saying that the pitch wasn't that close to him, and if Rainho makes another complaint, he will be ejected, because he, the head umpire, runs the game, not Rainho. 'Play ball!' shouts the home plate umpire." The camera goes to commentator J. D. Bower, where he is shown making the same pointing in the air action as the home plate umpire for the fans over the vid broadcast airwaves to see.

The commentator went on: "Harsnett quickly sets up and delivers a streaking slider that is low and inside, aimed near Rainho's knees. Rainho steps back from the plate as the pitch zings past him, and he makes a face that shows he knows it may be a strike."

"Strike two!" bellowed the home plate umpire from his lofty perch fifteen feet above home plate.

The vid play-by-play commentator went on, "Rainho really looks nervous now with the count zero and two, as he sets himself for Harsnett's next pitch. The cagey Redmen pitcher fools Rainho. He sends in a high outside curve ball that looks like it might catch the corner of home plate. Rainho, not taking any chances of striking out, goes after the pitch, straightening out his articulated bat to get as much extension as he can to get at the ball. Rainho hits the ball off of the end of the bat and sends the ball directly to Lenny Peecheh, at first base. Peecheh scoops up the ball and puts the Pelotas batter Rainho away with two vicious beans, one to Rainho's ribs. This slows him down. Rainho continues for first base, but Peecheh recovers the ball from his minor infielder and finishes the struggling Rainho with a blow to his upper right leading leg, which breaks his femur. Rainho goes down onto the field with a raised red holographic light around him to signal he's out, and the clayon medics clean him off of the field.

"The fans for the Redmen again roar their approval for the takeout by Lenny Peecheh. Lenny acknowledges the fans with a wave of his glove and a bow for the adoring masses. There are two more one bean ground outs made by Harsnett to end the second inning. All of the Redmen players hop onto their servo plates that are automatically sent out to them so they don't have to run the quarter to half mile to their dugout at the end of the inning.

"The game continues with the first batter for the Redmen, Fat Don Le Flanc, striking out with no fanfare involved in this play at the plate. Hashimshita just blew the ball right by him. The crowd boos Don Le Flanc's strikeout. He mouths a lot of words as he mounts his servo plate, yelling obscenities to himself and to no one in particular. Le Flanc is usually good for a few foul balls, but he goes down in three pitches delivered by Hashimshita. I guess Gaster won't be using Le Flanc again this game unless he really has to, maybe as running meat on the bases" said the vid commentator, J. D. Bower, dully.

The vid commentator continued his audio broadcast in a more upbeat tone, "One out now for the Redmen and up next is a left-handed hitter, Arthur Edison Arante, for the Redmen. I have some historical data for you folks at home on Arante. Arante is a very distant relative of the historical soccer player known as 'Pele'. Arante's nickname is 'Pele', so named by his parents in honor of his distant relative. So, Pele steps up to the plate and is ready for Hashimshita to make a delivery to him. The pitcher, Hashimshita, gives no ground to Pele and he again does the same to Pele as he did to other batters in the previous inning. Hashimshita puts a fastball inside on Pele, but the quick-thinking Pele takes half a step back from home plate and takes a full swing at the ball. Pele fouls it off, hitting the ball down the third baseline and hitting the head of the Pelotas minor infielder at third in the process. The minor infielder quickly stands up after the collision with the ball and immediately calls out, 'I'm good; I'm good.' And he bows to the laughing crowd and delivers the errant ball back to his pitcher. Looks like a future Alliance Baseball Player to me," laughed the vid commentator.

"The play goes on, with Hashimshita knowing Pele is on to him. So Zigouro Hashimshita throws a rare change up that flutters all over the strike zone and Pele, surprised by the change up, slaps at the ball and it goes right to Pelotas's man Jose Battina at second in one bounce. Battina puts Pele in his sights and puts the ball right into Pele's eye that has the optics mounted over it. The ball drives the eyepiece device deep into Pele's eye socket, putting him down into a tumble onto the turf. Pele is unable to continue, and the one bean mercy rule is enacted for the out. Pele is wheeled off of the field by the medical clayons with a red holographic light following him. His face bleeds profusely, as evident on the stadium jumbo tron to the bloodthirsty fans," says the vid commentator. "I hope his eye can be saved by the great med doctors of the game," he adds.

"Wow, ladies and gentlemen, the Redmenhave lost two veteran players in less than a minute this inning. Let's see what happens in the next minute," said the play-by-play commentator.

"Two out none on, play ball!" hollers the levitated home plate umpire.

The next batter for the Redmen is Marty Cavana. He is a new call up recruit with great batting numbers in the minor leagues. Cavana hits the very first pitch from Hasimhita which was a low fastball over the plate and Cavana hits it to the shortstop Jaun Elnido of Pelotas and Cavana is gunned down with a wicked throw from Elnido that hits Cavana right under his left cheek bone shattering it up into his eye and clearly knocking Cavana out for a one bean out.

"Three out" calls out the home plate umpire. "And with that the teams exchange places on the field with Pelotas coming up to bat after we check in with our sponsors" says J.D. Bower as the vid screens all over the Earth fade to commercial again.

After returning to the air waves J.D. Bower begins, " So up to bat first for Pelotas is Jose Heyman a second year protected vet that has made a lot of credits for his coaches and teammates with his great batting and superb and cruel base running. His nick name is 'The Slasher' for that is what Jose did to defensive players if they got in his running lanes. He would slash them as brutally as he could without killing them. All baseball teams always gunned for the very lucky but crafty Jose Heyman. Heyman steps into the batters box and Harsnnett sets and delivers a fast ball as hard as he can hurl at Heyman. The ball is low and on the outside corner of the plate and Heyman fouls it off."

"Strike one!" yells out the high flying home plate umpire.

Harsnnett can now see that Heyman doesn't like low pitches and he delivers a low but inside strike to Heyman. Heyman pulls his hands in and powers his articulated bat into the ball driving it to the Redman's third baseman Lea Loocke. Loocke scoops up the hard driven ground ball and delivers a blow to Heyman's forward running left knee that drives the leg sideways snapping his leg almost right off. Man what a devastating hit from Loocke on Heyman. Heyman is down and deemed incapacitated to continue and is out on one bean. The home team fans roar their approval of Loocke's dramatic bean on Heyman and also the demise of Heyman. Clayon medics have to sedate the traumatic, screaming Heyman before they can get him off of the field." Says J.D. Bower.

"Next up for Pelotas is the left outfielder and left hitting, Ramon Corrtezz, a one year vet with the potential to get on base with his great hitting stats. Corrtezz steps off of his servo disc and cooly gets into the batters box ready for the next Redman pitch. Harsnett obliges Corrtezz and challenges him with a chest high fastball. Corrtezz smacks a high fly ball out to the center fielder and he bolts for first base. The ball has been hit so high that the first base coach sends Corrtezz onto second base. I think that the aggressiveness of the Pelotas coaching staff will not bode well for the desperately running Corrtezz as Bill Bennings for the Redmen has fielded the ball as Corrtezz is rounding first. Bennings fires a laser like spiked ball to the second baseman Ray Tenner who gets the ball well before Corrtezz can reach second base. The Rat places a front right shoulder shattering bean on Corrtezz almost stopping him in his tracks. The injured and wobbling Corrtezz is still deemed able to continue to second base by the elevated umpire at second. The second bean rule will apply on this play. Lenny Peecheh, the first baseman retrieves the ball that caromed off of Corrtezz and delivers a second rear right shoulder bean causing Corrtezz to faint from the pain and is called out by the levitated second base umpire. A red holo grapic light encircles Corrtezz and he's quickly taken off of the field by clayon meds." Finished the play by play commentator.

"Two out and batter up" calls the home plate umpire in a howling voice for all to hear.

"The third batter this inning is Waldimar de Breto, another lefty who stands six-foot five. From the province of Paraguay, a province of South-Am, de Breto is native to the South-Am Alliance region. He was born in the outback of old south-western Brazil, a province of South-Am".

Ray yelled out to Harsnnett, "Come on, Connie, watch this guy. He's got a wider bat. Keep the ball away from him and strike him out."

The vid commentator informed the watching fans, "Now, players in Alliance Baseball can use a larger, heavier articulated bat if they can wield it. De Breto's bat, which is almost twice the diameter of normal articulated bats, looks like a large caveman club. But don't let the size of the bat fool you: de Breto can swing his huge bat just as accurately and swiftly as the smaller bats that other players use. The advantage of the larger bat is the surface area that de Breto will put in the strike zone. It gives him the advantage that he'll more than likely hit the ball in some way. The size code for bats in Alliance Baseball goes according to each player's size, and Waldimar de Breto, being a very big man, can wield this huge bat. Harsnnett has seen this kind of bat and batter before, and he plans his strategy."

"Play ball!" crowed the home plate umpire.

Harsnnett sent in a low outside slider that De Breto swung at and missed. De Breto's large bat made the air swoosh loudly as he swung at the ball that went out of the strike zone past him.

"Strike one!" shouted the levitated home plate umpire.

"The next two pitches are called 'balls'. De Breto patiently lays off and watches each ball go by with an eagle eye. Harsnnett challenges de Breto with a low fastball just in the strike zone, and de Breto pulls and slaps the ball down the third baseline. Lea Loocke, playing third for the Redmen, scoops it up, throws the ball on the run, and hits the big man, de Breto in the ribs. This slows the big man down on his way to first base. De Breto, for his size, has absorbed the bean well and continues, hurting, but loping for first base. De Breto has been beaned hard once by Loocke. Will he make it to first?" asked the play-by-play commentator. "The minor first base infielder grabs the ball that has deflected off of de Breto's ribs and sends it to Lenny Peecheh at first base for the Redmen. Peecheh finishes de Breto off with a devastating bean to the left shoulder that causes the tough de Breto a huge amount of pain. Man, that must hurt to get beaned twice and still be standing. De Breto is out with the red holo light around him. He waits, bent over, for a servo disc to come and take him off of the playing field. That's three out and two veteran players that Pelotas has lost so far. These losses since the first inning will probably hurt their team's skill level of play. With those great players now out of the game, the coach for Pelotas will have some very difficult decisions to make as to who will play outfield for de Breto. Waldimar de Breto being a veteran outfielder will surely be missed, as for his size he is very quick on his feet in the outfield for Pelotas," finished the play-by-play commentator as the teams exchanged places on the playing field.

As the Redmen come off the field, Ray looked towards his friends in the stands. Suddenly, he realized how he knew that woman who was sitting beside Pamela Jay. She was that star ship officer who had roughed him up. She had made Ray sign and pay for the collision he had caused when he was flying cargo ion rockets to the Moon and back. She didn't have her uniform on, and she was smiling at him. That was why he hadn't recognized her right away: she was smiling. *"Nina Cutoff,"* Ray thought to himself, remembering. *"And she likes baseball. Maybe she's not all that rough around the edges once you get to know her, just like Jigs said."* Ray then spotted Ricardo Narzani sitting three rows higher than his friends. *"Odd,"* thought Ray. *"Usually dignitaries like Narzani sit in protected box seats and not with the local rabble."* Quickly Ray took his mind off his friends and focused on his game, for he was first up in the bottom of the second inning.

"Okay, Tenner, I want you to get a hit this inning, and I want that run back that was scored on us," was all that Cito Gaster said to Ray in an irritated tone.

The underlying cause for Gaster's bad temperament was that Narzani had bought him off with a huge bribe. Gaster had been instructed to be gruff with Ray and Lenny to throw them off of their focus and possibly lose this game today. Also, Lenny and Ray knew that they were to play the whole game and were not to be protected by being taken off the bases if they got on base. Being taken off as a protected player brought your chances of injury down to only five percent. By playing full time, they each had a fifty percent greater chance of being killed. That wasn't a good thing for Lenny and Ray, for they wanted to retire after this final game free of injuries.

As Ray went out to home plate, his teammates and the home team North-Am crowd cheered him on.

The crowd's cheers sometimes made it very hard to concentrate, but Ray blocked out the noise of the crowd and focused on his task at hand. With his hand up as he stepped into the batter's box, Ray eyed the Pelotas' pitcher, Ziguro Hashimshita. Ziggy was well-known to Ray. They had both played on the same team in the Austro-Asian League a few years ago. Back then, Ray could easily hit Ziggy's pitching. All he had to do was wait out Ziggy until the right pitch came in to him. Ray lowered his hand, and the next thing he knew the ball went by him in a fiery flash, right over home plate, at a hundred and ninety-two miles an hour! "Strike one!" bellowed the home plate umpire.

"Man, that was fast," Ray thought to himself. *"I'll just get my bat out in front of the ball on the next pitch and run like hell,"* Ray told himself, but the next pitch sped by him in a flash, again. As he was moving his articulated bat off of his shoulders, the ball flew by just as fast as the previous pitch.

"Strike two!" called out the home plate ump.

"Ziggy quickly has the count to zero and two on Ray Tenner. Tenner, who has a reputation for getting on base, looks worried. Tenner doesn't have the count in his favor," said the play-by-play commentator. "Hashimshita looks every bit as confident with his pitching as he did in the first inning when he got the ball past these veteran Redmen batters. Here's the next pitch: it's another torch pitch to the batter, but Tenner manages to foul that one off up and back behind home plate onto the protecting electronic viewing field. Hashimshita has allowed two hits so far in a dozen pitches, and a foul ball for Tenner," remarked the play-by-play commentator.

Ray knew he had a lot of pressure riding on him to get a hit. He looked at Ziggy, trying to figure out where he'd put the next pitch. *"No more thinking, Tenner; just hitting. Clear your mind!"* Ray thought to himself as he faced this ominous pitching opponent that he thought he knew. Ray lifted his bat off of his shoulders and pressured the articulated bat to straighten it out in anticipation of the next pitch. The ball came more quickly than he had anticipated. The ball was high and inside on him, heading for his head, but Ray didn't move. The ball missed his head by an inch. If it had hit him, it would have killed him. By Ray not moving away from the pitch, it looked like Hashimshita was throwing at him. The home plate umpire called a ball on the play, and stopped the game momentarily to give Ziggy Hashimshita a verbal warning for putting the ball too close to the batter out of the strike zone. If this happened again, Ziggy, the offending pitcher, would be ejected from the game and the home team would be awarded a run. Those were the rules. This warning for throwing too close to the batter offended Ziggy, and he looked visibly upset. Ziggy had always been perfect in his deliveries, and he had never meant to throw at this batter, even if he did know that Ray Tenner was a great batter.

This was the break that Ray had been hoping for. The pitcher, Ziggy, was now a little off in his throwing game, and this was what Ray Tenner needed, to get a hit. The next pitch was a ball, low and outside. Now the count was even at two balls and two strikes. Ray stepped out of the batter's box to slow down the pace of the play and psych himself up for what he knew would be a barn burner of a pitch from Ziggy.

Straightening his articulated bat again with the pressure of his hands, Ray waited for Ziggy to get his sign from the catcher. Ziggy stared down at Ray for a few extra seconds before his delivery, and then he unloaded the mightiest pitch of the game: a hundred and ninety-six miles per hour fastball. Ray put his bat into the zone where he thought the ball would be, and missed the ball completely, "Strike three!" yelled the umpire. "Yer out!"

Ray couldn't believe that he had struck out in his first at bat. He hadn't struck out before in this tournament. The fans were silent. Some were stunned that Ray, their star player, had struck out. Others booed Ray as he left the batter's box, unnerved. With his head down, riding the servo disc back to his dugout, Ray noticed Ziggy grimacing and holding his pitching arm close to himself. *"He's blown up his shoulder!"* Ray thought to himself. *"I've got to tell Lenny."*

"Lenny, wait him out. Ziggy's implant has blown up his shoulder; I'm sure of it. Look at the way he's holding his arm. He's not smiling anymore. We've got him!" said Ray excitedly.

Lenny nodded to Ray as they passed each other and they slapped each others hands in encouragement. Lenny immediately stepped up to the plate and swung his bat in anticipation over home plate to warm himself up. Just as Ray had predicted, Ziggy delivered a fastball at Lenny high in the strike zone but well down in speed. Lenny moved up half a step in the batter's box and easily hit the ball over second base for a single on his first pitch. Suddenly the mood of the crowd picked up again as one of their home team Alliance boys got a hit off of the mighty Pelotas' pitcher Hashimhita. Lenny easily made it to first with a single, but he was not relieved of base running duties. Lenny was signaled by Cito Gaster to stay and run on the deadly bases.

Ray looked at his coach just as Gaster was looking up at Narzani in the seats, and Ray could see that they were making subtle, almost undetectable gestures to each other. *"Narzani really has Gaster in his pocket!"* Ray realized, but there wasn't a thing he could do about that right now. *"What the hell are they planning? This is probably why me and Lenny were told to stay in the game full time. This is what the phone call on the vid-phone was all about. Narzani is trying to affect the outcome of this game by getting me and Lenny killed!"* Ray saw that Narzani was also looking and nodding at Dean, at third base. *"What the hell are the three of them up to?"* Ray asked himself helplessly. He watched.

Cito Gaster then called a time out to talk to the officials about a lineup change he wanted to make. He wanted to put in a batter by the name of Rolly Boodreau, and scratch the player that was originally to come to bat.

Then it hit Ray in his mind, *"They are setting me and Lenny up for a kill. Right now, it's Lenny that's being set up! Coach Gaster is going to make a lineup change and put a rookie batter in. Narzani and Gaster are hoping that the rookie, Boodreau, who's up next, will hit into a double play, and then Lenny will be the first to go down,"* he thought. Ray, in his helplessness, steeled himself for what was to come next.

"Cito Gaster makes a lineup change and puts a rookie batter up to try and advance Lenny Peecheh to second base. Well, this is an unusual move by the home team Coach Gaster. He's putting Rolly Boodreau, who is not known as a good hitter, up to bat. A relatively unknown hitter for the Redmen, Boodreau made the Redmen's lineup from the minor leagues of North-Am just last week. Gaster must have confidence in Boodreau to put him in the game this early," the vid commentator chimed.

Boodreau stepped up to the plate, smiling and revelling in his chance to become a star in the World Alliance Baseball tournament. Ziguro Hashimshita, the Pelotas' pitcher, knew he had a rookie up to bat, and realized that he would have an easier time getting him to hit into a double play, even with his hurting arm.

Ziggy sent in a long slow curve that was going to break over home plate. Boodreau, smiling, just watched the ball sail by him over the plate. "Strike one!" bellowed the home plate umpire. Gaster in the dugout couldn't believe that Boodreau had let the perfect pitch go by him for a hit.

"Come on, Boody, hit the ball. It's right over the plate, you meat head!" yelled Gaster heatedly at Boodreau. Ray thought he knew what Boodreau was doing, but couldn't be sure. *"Maybe Boodreau also sees that Ziggy's arm wasn't any good to him anymore. Maybe Boodreau is waiting him out, just like I told Lenny to do,"* Ray reasoned.

Boodreau looked at Lenny on first base, winked, and smiled. Then he turned and faced the mighty Ziguro Hashimshita knowing that he, Lenny, and Ray knew Ziguro's arm was no good.

"What the hell is Boodreau doing? Does he know that Ziggy's arm has blown? He must know! Man, this game is getting weird," thought Ray, sitting nervously in his player's dugout looking on.

Again, Ziggy put another relatively slower pitch over the plate for Boodreau to hit, and again, Boodreau just let it float past him. "Strike two!" was the home plate umpire's call.

Gaster turned red in the face and called a time out. He got on a servo disc and zoomed out to home plate to rag on Boodreau for letting two perfectly hittable, good pitches go by. Gaster was fuming and he let Boodreau know it. "What the hell do you think you're doing, Boody? This is a World Series final game, you know! You're making us look like a bunch of idiots letting perfectly good pitches go by like that. I've put you in for a reason: to hit the fucking ball! The ball went over the plate, twice, perfectly for a sure hit, and you just stood there smiling, letting it go by. I want you to lay into that apple and get us a hit. Do you hear me, you fucking idiot!" said Coach Gaster. Veins were popping out around his neck and his arms were flailing as Gaster berated Boodreau.

Boodreau just stood there, smiling and nodding at Coach Gaster. He said meekly that he would do his best. Gaster got flabbergasted looking at the buffoon-like character he couldn't believe he had sent up to bat. He raced back to the dugout realizing that he may have made a big mistake putting Boodreau up to bat. He couldn't change that now. He could only hope that Boodreau would either do what he asked, or strike out.

Narzani was also wondering what the heck was going on in the field of play, as he had an interest in what was transpiring. Narzani looked at Gaster, but Gaster looked away in a kind of embarrassed way, knowing he might have screwed up in his choice of batter this inning.

Now no one realized that the buffoon Boodreau had an agenda of his own. He knew that Ziguro's shoulder was on the verge of collapsing. By letting him throw more pitches, Ziggy's shoulder might just give out. And that is exactly what happened. On the next pitch, Ziggy's shoulder went 'pop' as he came around with the ball and the ball landed on home plate. "Ball one," called the home plate umpire. Two more balls were delivered by the faltering Ziggy, bringing the count to three balls and two strikes.

Now Boodreau set himself at the ready in his batter's, box looking like the real ball player that he was.

Ziggy winced and groaned as he desperately told himself that he could get this batter out. Ziggy put all he had left into the last pitch, but all the ball did was float in at Boodreau. Rolly Boodreau lightly hit the ball so it rolled out to the second baseman that was in Lenny's running baseline. Lenny got a great jump on the play and made good ground with his speed going to second. As Lenny was nearing second base, the second baseman scooped up the ball to throw it at Lenny, but Lenny had the jump on him as the defensive player was in his baseline. Lenny put his knife gloves into the throat of the second baseman, severing his jugular and windpipe at the same time. This made the second baseman drop the ball where he collapsed. Boodreau made it to first in a trot, and Lenny charged onto third. The play was stopped by the second base umpire because of the elimination of the defensive second baseman. The home team crowd went wild, cheering at the wonderful planning of Boodreau and the gory offensive takeout by Lenny at second base.

Gaster was kind of embarrassed about his good fortune, but Narzani scowled at Gaster for letting things get out of hand. Narzani wanted Lenny dead, and he wanted the seemingly inept Boodreau hit into a deadly double play to cause the death of Lenny Peecheh, but it didn't fit into his plans. Gaster let the rookie Boodreau stay out on first base, and he sent up another rookie hitter. He hoped that this would cause a double play and Lenny would not score from third.

Ray felt a lot safer now with Lenny being on third, even if Dean was there scowling at him and giving him verbal jibes. "You are one lucky s.o.b., Peecheh, for getting this far," said Dean.

"I don't think so," said Lenny. "We've got players that think with their brains, and not their mouths like you. Boodreau did a great job out here, and Hashimshita is finished because of it.

You ought to know that by now," finished Lenny sarcastically, implying that Dean was a bit of a dimwit.

"Play ball!" shouted the home plate umpire.

The broken-armed Ziguro Hashimshita was replaced by a South-Am native pitcher by the name of Gamel G. Gonzalez, or 'G. G.' as he was known to the baseball world. G. G. was a good low-ball pitcher who rarely gave pitches high in the strike zone. This pitching by G. G. was turned into many infield hits that resulted in easy kills for the tight-knit infield of Pelotas.

G. G. was all business for Pelotas on the next few plays. He struck out the next Redmen batter and got the one after that to hit into a double play in which the crafty Boodreau was knocked unconscious with a single bean to the head. The batter was doubled beaned, crippled with two shattered legs. The first shattered leg was compliments of Dean the Scorpion Luthbert. Lenny stayed safely on third while the events unfolded to end the second inning. "Three out," called the home plate umpire to end the bottom of the second inning.

"Lucky shits; we didn't score, Luthbert," was all that Lenny said to Dean as the teams traded positions on the field. He and Lenny traded further verbal abuses as they parted.

The next two innings were a slaughter. Each team lost six batters who didn't even make it to first base. Four out of each of the six outs for each team were deaths, and the other two were career-ending injuries for the players trying to get on base. The baseball fans were loving the defensive play of each team. Today they had already seen twelve players exit the game due to deadly and crippling injuries. It looked like no one would be getting anywhere on the field of play today.

"It's the top of the fifth inning now, and Dean is up at bat leading off for South-Am's Pelotas. Harnsnett is still pitching for the Redmen," said the vid-commentator.

"Come on, Connie, get him to hit to me. I'll make sure he'll be taco material before he gets to first base," Ray yelled out, trying to distract Dean. And that is exactly what happened. Dean hit the ball to Ray, who scooped it up and waited for Dean make a real run for first base. Dean, knowing that he was in Ray's sights, just trotted towards first base, looking like he knew he would be seriously beaned with the ball. The minor infielder followed Dean along cautiously as Dean sauntered for first, watching for a pass ball or seeing if the ball would bounce off of Dean and to him, with Ray's inevitable throw.

Ray threw the ball at Dean's head, but the quick-thinking Dean made a quick surge of speed, fooling Ray, who missed Dean completely on the play. The minor infielder caught the ball as it went by Dean and threw it to Lenny on first. By this time Dean was bearing down on Lenny with his knife blades from his gloves extended to take Lenny out. Lenny fell to his side to avoid Dean, but threw the ball at Dean. The ball hit Dean, but it was not a crippling or killing throw that Lenny wanted to hit Dean with. The ball glanced off the side of Dean's helmet. Dean narrowly missed slitting Lenny's throat with his gloved knives going by Lenny's neck to touch first base safely. The childhood friends, Dean and Lenny, looked at each other and knew that they were deadly serious about killing each other in this game. Lenny nodded and acknowledged Dean for his crafty running, but Ray was really upset at himself for not getting Dean on his initial throw. This was another unforced error for Ray, and he was angry with himself for putting his best friend, Lenny, at risk. He had put Lenny in danger to make sure he could get Dean, but Dean had outsmarted Ray by changing his running speed. This was an old trick in the game of Alliance Baseball. Dean was made to stay on base by his coach, Vieira. As another good hitter came up, Dean hoped he would have another chance to take Ray out. He needed to get a jump on the play at hand, running for second base.

Dean looked up at Narzani, sitting about three rows up behind Pamela Jay. Narzani gestured to Dean, pointing slightly towards Pamela Jay. Dean nodded slightly to acknowledge Narzani. Ray watched this exchanging of signals and wondered what the hell they were planning.

"Why would Narzani point out Pamela Jay to Dean? Narzani must be trying to do something to her, but what? Dean's on first base right now," Ray thought to himself. *"How could he hurt her in an open setting like this while he's running?"*

Next up for Pelotas was a right-handed, three hundred plus percent hitter, Pedro Ramirez. Harsnnett, the Redmen's pitcher, knew he would have to keep the ball away from Ramirez or he would score a home run, and this would put his team further behind in runs. Harsnnett wound up with all of his pitching might and put his best fastball low and inside. Ramirez tried to pull his articulated bat in towards his body to get at the ball, swung, and missed the ball ever so slightly, fouling it off. The home team crowd oohed at the close call hit.

"Foul Ball. Strike one!" called the home plate umpire. The home team fans were becoming restless with just pitching. They wanted to see another gory play, especially with Dean Luthbert on base. The home team crowd would love to see Dean taken out at this time in this final match, for that would mean that their home team would have a much better chance of securing the championship.

The Scorpion had a streak of twenty at bats of getting on base without being injured. It was a streak he had bragged about, in the media, claiming that he could prolong it at the expense of the lowly Redmen's infield, but Dean knew there were much better players on the infield defending for the Redmen. Dean also knew his chances for survival at this time were very low due to this being the final game of Alliance Baseball this year along with the caliber of the players he was up against. This was it! Dean was playing against Ray and Lenny for the battle of their lives!

Harnsnett got his signal from his catcher. The catcher wanted an off-speed slider, but Harnsnett knew that the batter, Ramirez, would be looking for something like that, and so he shook the catcher's sign off. The catcher for the Redmen gave Connie Harsnnett another sign, and Harsnnett nodded in agreement. Harsnnett wound up like a top and he delivered a fastball as hard as he could throw. Ramirez fouled it off, hitting the fastball down the third baseline, just to the left of third base, and the minor infielder felt the flame of that zinger off the bat of Ramirez go by his head. The minor infielder blessed himself on camera and bowed to Ramirez for not killing him with that foul ball. The fans laughed and cheered the minor infielder for his respect and luck.

"Strike two!" bellowed the home plate umpire.

The next three pitches by Harsnnett were called balls. These close 'ball' pitches, which the experienced Ramirez eyed closely, ran the count to a full three and two. Harsnnett, being in for four innings, was beginning to tire. His arm was feeling the effects of heaving the ball at over one hundred and eighty miles an hour for over forty pitches. But he didn't let Gaster know this. On his next pitch, Harsnnett sent in an outside curve ball that came over the outside edge of the plate, and Ramirez slapped at it. The ball went slowly out to Ray at second base. Dean had a great lead off of first base when the ball was hit, and he got the jump on the play. Dean put on a burst of speed for second. Ray didn't quite have the time or the angle to field the ball and throw it at Dean. Dean went by him, racing confidently for second base, but it was Dean that Ray wanted. Forgoing a double play, Ray let Ramirez go to first base and threw the ball to his shortstop, Wayne Frogal, who was already going towards second base to get the bean on Dean and set up the double play. Ray slightly bobbled the ball, fielding it, and then threw it to the shortstop,

Frogal who was going for the single hard bean on Dean. When the ball got to Frogal, Dean was only two yards from the base, but the knives in Dean's cleats pointed directly at Frogal. Wayne Frogal threw the ball desperately at Dean but only grazed his incoming cleats. This counted as a bean for Frogal, but then Frogal couldn't get out of the way of Dean's deadly cleats as they came menacingly at Frogal's mid-section. Dean drove the knives of his foot cleats deep into Frogal's lower gut, instantly spilling his innards onto the field. Dean made it safely to second base with the deadly, legal, offensive takeout of Wayne Frogal, the Redmen's shortstop. The fans oohed and aahed. Frogal didn't get to turn the double play and the play on the field was halted. The infield turned red to signify the defensive takeout of Frogal and that play was to stop. Ray came over and fielded the errant ball that Frogal threw at Dean, to make sure that Dean didn't go for third to stop play. Ray saw that his teammate, Wayne Frogal, was kneeling, looking down in great surprise at his entrails spilling out onto the field. Frogal looked up at Ray, sighed, and then simply lowered himself to the turf of the infield. He placed his hands under his head and appeared to go to sleep, as he quickly bled to death on the field of play. For the first time in a long time Ray felt sick to his stomach, and he turned away to lessen the traumatic effect of losing a fellow player that he liked. He closed his eyes momentarily and set fire to Dean's figure in his mental picture.

"I will get you!" was his internal mantra. Ray calmed downed and looked over to Lenny for encouragement. Lenny looked at Ray, put his hand over his heart, and gave Ray a secret look they had shared over the years when things got tough that said, *"My heart is with you, my friend."* Ray nodded to Lenny, knowing this game wasn't over. They had to get through it together, good or bad.

A red holographic light surrounded Frogal and the whole playing field turned red to signify a serious stoppage in play. Ray had seen his teammates get killed before, but not like this. This was up close and graphic, and it made Ray's stomach turn. He felt that it was his fault that Frogal had gotten terminated on the offensive play by Dean.

Dean just smiled at Ray as the clayon medical team removed the now deceased Frogal from the field. This athletic but gory action, by Dean, had silenced the home team crowd, and Ray knew that he was in a soul-searching do or die game with Dean. Ray wanted to scream at Dean for killing his teammate, but that would only provoke a fight. Ray managed to compose himself only after Lenny came over to talk to him. Lenny told Ray not to lose his cool. Ray just gave Dean a long stare of hatred, and then went back to his position on the field at second base. Lenny spoke to Dean quietly so Ray couldn't hear, "Don't do this, Dean. We gotta get out of this as friends and alive, even if me and Ray lose, don't ya see?"

Dean countered, fervently, "You stay out of it, or you'll go down like your shortstop, Peecheh!"

After the gory ending of Frogal, Cito Gaster replaced the tired pitcher Harsnnett for the up-and-coming Clifford Bewer. Bewer was a tall, lanky, dark-tanned man from Soweto, a province of the Africany Alliance, who had a sidewinder style of throwing. Gaster hoped he could get the Redmen out of this two on and one out situation and save face. Even though he was in Narzani's pocket, he didn't want to look like he was throwing this game. Gaster only wanted to do Narzani's bidding, and that was get Ray and Lenny killed on the field of play. Come what may after that, win or lose!

Again, the home plate umpire bellowed out, "Play ball!" to get things started for the easily bored fans.

Once things had been cleaned up from the disemboweled Frogal, the turf turned from red to green in the bottom of the fifth inning.

Up for Pelotas for the second time this game was Gulshan Sibi. Bewer didn't waste any time and got Sibi to hit a ground ball to Ray. Ray gave Dean on second base a quick look to stop him from going to third. Then Ray took out the upper leading left leg of Ramirez, the runner going from first to second, by putting him down on the turf and smashing his femur in two places. Ramirez was automatically called out on the mercy rule of not being able to continue because of his severely shattered leg. The play on the field continued. Ray quickly ran over to the loose ball that he had hit Ramirez with and sent it to Lenny at first. Lenny checked Dean again from going to third and then hit Sibi, coming at him for first base, in the chest by breaking his breastbone and sending him down, crawling towards first from about ten feet away. Lenny's minor infielder scooped up the ball and got it back to Lenny. Lenny didn't kill Sibi, but only broke Sibi's right hand with the second bean for the out as Sibi was still struggling for first. The familiar red holographic light went around Sibi and a servo disc took the broken and out Sibi off the field. The same happened for Ramirez as he was taken off the field by clayon medics. Dean, seeing his chance for advancement after Lenny had tried to check him, went safely to third base on the double play after Lenny had put the second bean on Sibi before the field turned red.

"There are now two out and a man on third for Pelotas," said the play-by-play commentator. "What a great double play by the dynamic duo of Peecheh and Tenner to turn things around for the Redmen. With two out now for the Redmen, it looks like they might have things under control in this sixth inning."

Next up for Pelotas was Robert Bearonson, a five-year veteran. Ray thought the name sounded familiar, and he looked directly at the batter to see if it was the wily rookie 'Bear' he had played with in the minors. Sure enough, it was Bear, but with a little more muscle and eyes that burned bright blue.

Bewer, the pitcher for the Redmen, sent in two fastballs that Bear lunged at with his personal articulated bat, but to no avail. Bearonson fouled both of the pitches off for two strikes. Ray, Lenny, and the rest of the Redmen team called out encouragement for Bewer, hoping he could get Bear to hit into a ground ball bean situation.

Bewer then tried to get Bear to go after two outside slider pitches, but Bear laid off them and got the count to two and two on Bearonson.

The crowd began to chant, "Bewer, Bewer, Bewer!" in their efforts to get this batter out for the third out for Pelotas and end the inning with Dean Luthbert on third base threatening to score.

The infield for the Redmen was called to play in tight, by Gaster. The coach was looking for an infield hit to try to stop the runner at third (Dean) from scoring. Bewer sent in an outside curve ball going towards the batter, just on the outside of home plate. Bear slapped the ball on the ground to Ray. Ray looked intently at Dean on third to see if he would go for home plate. Dean stayed put on third, but as soon as Ray looked for the batter, Bearonson, going to first, Dean took off for home plate, thinking that if Ray couldn't get the batter going for a single bean out on his first throw for a one-shot bean, then Dean could score a run, even by taking a bean in the process. Ray made sure that Dean didn't score by throwing the ball, with deadly accuracy, at Rob Bearonson. The impact took out Bear's whole lower face, severing his jaw, tongue, and near side cheek in one blow. In his shocked state, Bear ran sideways off of the field, twirling about. He really didn't comprehend what had happened to him. Bear kept wondering why he couldn't get to first base, even though he was still standing and could see first base quite clearly. He wondered what the red halo of light surrounding him meant. Why were the clayon medical team here? Everything was a wonder for the traumatized Bear. He watched the crowds go by him on his way to his dugout on a medical stretcher, the fans cheering like crazy. Dean did not make it in time to score as the Bear had been called out before Dean touched home plate. Those were Alliance Baseball rules.

"That's three out and the inning is over," called the home plate umpire, and the two great Alliance baseball teams changed positions on the field of play to begin the bottom of the sixth inning.

The play-by-play commentator J.D. Bower began, "Bottom of the sixth inning now and it's still one nothing for Pelotas over the Redmen. Pelotas have taken to the field and the Redmen will bat next as we go to commercial break," reported the play-by-play commentator.

When the vid feed for the world viewers came back on, the vid-commentator offered these comments to the viewing fans, "The stats for the game so far today are as follows: For Pelotas they have one run, four hits, no errors, four strikeouts, three cripples, and six kills in the bean category with no secondary beans charged to them. For the Redmen they still don't have a run. They have two hits, two errors, four strikeouts, five cripples, six kills, and only one secondary bean charged to them on the offensive bean of Luthbert and subsequent takeout of Frogal in the fifth inning. It's been a pretty interesting game in that both coaches are taking chances with their star players here early in this final match. So far, that has paid off for South-Am's Pelotas with McDermott for the Pelotas scoring the only run early in the game. The rest of the game has been a bit of a pitcher/infield duel between both teams here today."

At the bottom of the sixth inning, Bewer, the relief pitcher for the Redmen, struck out Tim Buurns, the lead off hitter, in six pitches delivered. Next the heaving Bewer, with somewhat errant pitching, caused the second up for Pelotas, Denis Sach, to line a ground ball base double to the outfield to the stadium wall. This held Sach at second base for an easy stand up double.

The second and the third outs for North-Am were easy for the Redmen in that the next infield play was a one bean double kill initiated by the third baseman, Lea Loocke, on a rookie batter named Drob Green going for first. Ray grabbed the ball thrown to him by the first base minor infielder and then got the slow-moving Denis Sach, from Pelotas, going from second base to third with bean to the back of his head knocking the Pelotas runner out. The Redmen fans went wild. They cheered the great play of the Redmen's infield that ended the sixth inning with flair, even though no gory plays had been made.

The play-by-play vid commentator informed viewers and in-house fans by saying, "It's the bottom of the seventh inning now as Pelotas went down one, two, three, in the top of the seventh with three quick kills by the Redmen infield. It will be an interesting inning for the Redmen, for their time is running out to score a run. Pelotas is leading this game one to nothing.

"The coach for the Redmen, Cito Gaster, looks quite agitated in the Redmen dugout. It looks like he's ragging out every player on that team to play more offensively. The faces on the players in the Redmen dugout display apprehension because of Gaster's vociferous yelling. As I see it, the Redmen have been playing a great defensive game, even if they are losing one to nothing to South-Am's Pelotas," commented the commentator.

Now appearing on the vid screen, J. D. Bower, the World Alliance commentator, expanded on his agitated musings: "It's still one to nothing for Pelotas of South-Am in this hotly contested game. Now up for the Redmen is another one-year veteran: the right-handed hitting Randy Boodreau, no relation to one of the same name Rolly Boodreau of the Redmen, who was taken out in the first inning. Randy Boodreau played most of his baseball in the small town of Whitefish, Ontario, a province of North-Am in central North-Am that is five hundred milesabove the tree line of the great forest wall surrounding this bedraggled planet. Boodreau's a wild card player in that he was called up from the minors at the last minute to play in these finals due to a man shortage during tournament play here for the Redmen. Gaster has told us that Boodreau is a skilled batter and runner that his team needs for this World Alliance Baseball Series Finals win. We have seen Randy Boodreau do great things for the minor teams he has played for over the years in Minor Alliance League Baseball around the world.

"Randy Boodreau gets off of his servo disc and steps up to home plate. He puts his hand up as he eases nervously into the batter's box, lowers his hand, and readies himself. He stares out at G. G. Gonzalez with his enhanced optics, and bares his teeth at the Pelotas' pitcher.

And we're ready to start the bottom of the seventh inning," said the play-by-play commentator with enthusiasm. "G. G. Gonzalez, the pitching sensation for Pelotas, sends in a fastball at a hundred and seventy-nine miles per hour that Boodreau aggressively swings at and fouls off over third base with a convincing swing of the bat that he means business in the hitting department. Minor infielder and fans duck as the ball whizzes past them."

"He's here for business, this young Boodreau," said the vid play-by-play commentator. "The next pitch is a close inside pitch that Boodreau lays off of and it is called a ball by the home plate umpire. The home team crowd oohs and aahs at the last pitch to go by Boodreau, relieved that it wasn't called a strike."

The vid commentator continued, "Gonzalez then tries to get the lanky Boodreau to go after an off-speed slider low and away. Boodreau lays off that one for another call ball."

"Ball two," shouted the elevated home plate umpire.

"Smart move by the upstart Boodreau," said the commentator. "Two more pitches (one a strike, and one a ball) run the count full to three and two on the rookie Boodreau. Boodreau steadies himself now at home plate for what might be his final pitch of this inning. Here comes the crucial final pitch to home plate from Gonzalez. Boodreau hits it, sending it out to short center field. The center fielder for Pelotas, Fodel Castro, catches the ball and immediately throws it at Boodreau, snapping the ball from short center field to first base. Driving for first base, Randy Boodreau knows this is going to be close, and he grits his smiling teeth in his hustle for first base. Boodreau hopes that he won't get a solid bean on himself as he lays his body out for the touch on first base. The ball and Boodreau arrive at first base at the same time with the ball hitting the prostrate Boodreau full on his face, right into his grinning teeth. He smacks into the base with his hand in front of his face. The ball instantly turns soft, only powdering Boodreau's face instead of smashing his toothy grin to mush. Boodreau immediately stands up at first, knowing that he made it. The electronic umpire has deemed Boodreau safe by hundredths of a second. 'Safe!' calls the levitating first base umpire, watching the play unfold.

"A very lucky day for the batter, Randy Boodreau, who gets a hit on his first at bat in this final game of the World Alliance Baseball Series for the Redmen," ended the commentator. The vid screen over the airwaves went to a commercial break.

"As we come back from commercial break play is about to start," J. D. the vid commentator began. "Next in the batting lineup for the Redmen is Ray Aloyisis Tenner, 'The Rat' as he's affectionately known by his friends and teammates. Randy Boodreau at first base hails his batter at home plate to hit the ball outta here with a dramatic swinging motion of his arms, and the home team fans cheer in agreement," said the vid commentator to the millions of watching fans from all over the world. "In this dog-eat-dog game I'd say that is an understatement, because death out there on the field is more likely than in an all-out war."

"Play ball!" shouted the unruly home plate umpire, as he wanted no side distractions while he was in charge of this game. Dean, playing third base, waited and hoped that Ray would hit to him.

Ray stepped up to the plate and lowered his hand, and then the pitcher G. G. Gonzalez sent in a fastball. Ray swung and missed as the fastball blew by him at one hundred and seventy sizzling miles per hour.

"Strike one!" called the elevated home plate umpire. Gonzalez, the Pelotas pitcher, sent in a second screwy knuckle ball at one hundred and fifty miles an hour. Ray misread, swung early, and fouled it off behind home plate, directly at the watching fans who ducked in reflexive actions that did them no good when the ball caromed off the invisible magnetic barrier protecting them. There was an all-encompassing, clear, force field protecting them from errant balls smashing them in the face at all times during the game. Attendees of the game would not go home injured because of it.

"Strike two!" called the home plate umpire.

The next pitch was again an overpowering fastball, and Ray fouled it off of his late swinging articulated bat.

"Still strike two!" called the home plate umpire from above for all to hear. Ray couldn't believe his luck today. He was behind in the count again in this game, and it would look really bad for him if he struck out twice. Ray stepped off of home plate, raised his right hand high so the levitated umpire could see, and called time to collect his composure. Ray silently cursed himself unmercifully. He needed to get a hit rather than look like a strike out buffoon. Ray lowered his raised arm and stepped towards the batter's box. He took another moment to compose himself while Gonzalez fidgeted on the mound, readying himself for his next offering to Ray. Tenner stepped back into the batter's box, now ready for the next pitch by Gonzalez. Boodreau on first took a nice long lead while Gonzalez watched him setting up for his next pitch. The pitcher, G. G. Gonzalez, sent in a long, roundabout curve ball that missed outside home plate for a ball. The count was now one ball and two strikes. Ray anxiously practice-swung his articulating bat in the batter's box, waiting for his next pitch. In came the next pitch, and it looked like a barn burner fastball. Ray swung at it and connected for a ground ball to Dean Luthbert at third for Pelotas. This was the chance Dean had been waiting for in this game, to get Ray, but Ricardo Narzani had other plans for Dean's next play on the field. Dean scooped up the ball and made the throw at Ray, who was going to first, but he threw it just high over Ray's head, while trying to not make the throw look intentionally high. The ball went over Ray's head, glancing lightly off of his helmet and into the invisible force field protecting the infield fan area like the old metal and mesh screens of long ago. The ball should have stopped at the invisible force field that surrounded the infield to protect the fans near the field, but for some strange reason the force field failed and the ball continued on through it, going for the head of a distracted World Alliance Executive Leader by the name of Pamela Jay. Ray watched the ball sail over his head and go straight for Pamela Jay's head as he continued running for first base. Ray, knowing he would be safe at first base, screamed for her to duck her head, but to no avail. Pamela Jay was distracted. She was talking to Nina Cutoff, and wasn't watching the play. The noise of the crowd was too loud for Pamela to hear Ray as he made it safely to first while yelling at her to watch out for the seemingly errant ball. The world seems to slow down when bad things are about to happen to someone you know. Pamela Jay's head was about to be crushed by the hard thrown ball that was meant for him, and there wasn't a damn thing Ray could do about it but watch in horror as his friend was about to die.

Unbelievably a glove came up in front of Pamela Jay's face and caught the ball, just as it was about to give Pamela Jay a fatal traumatic headache. Nina Cutoff had caught the ball with her glove, foiling Narzani's plan to have Pamela Jay 'accidentally' eliminated, by Dean, at this game.

All of the field umpires immediately called a time out and suspended the game momentarily with the turf going red, and then white. Officials tried to find out why the fans' protective force field had failed around the first base area by letting the ball go directly into the stands. The protective screen was not supposed to fail at any time, even during a power failure. That was a guaranteed right of the fans promised to them by the league owners. No fan was to leave a game hurt by an errant ball.

The clayon guards went into the stands where they detected a force field collapsing device. Ray looked for Ricardo Narzani, but he wasn't in his seat. The clayon guards grabbed a man who was clutching at something in his hand, and hustled him out of the seated area to the security center. He had been the seatmate of Ricardo Narzani. Over the broadcast system the officials apologized for the force field failure and explained that somehow this person detained by the clayon guards had smuggled an illegal laser-like ionic pen that had interfered with the protective force field around the infield. These types of happenings were a strict no-no at the Alliance Games, and the announcer apologized profusely to the attending crowd.

"He will be dealt with most severely for his breaking of the stadium rules. We apologize for any inconvenience that may have caused fans to worry in that particular area of this stadium. The protective force field has been tested and it has been found to be in good working order," said the in-stadium announcer over the P. A. System. The apology was also sent directly to the ear buds of everyone wearing them in the giant baseball dome and also over the jumbo trons in the stadium.

Ray was relieved to see that Pamela Jay was all right. Now he realized that it was Narzani who was in cahoots with Dean and Gaster to try and kill Pamela Jay.

In their private conversations, Pamela Jay had told Ray that she had been dogging Narzani in the World Alliance parliament about his shady dealings around the planet and solar system. She knew that Narzani wanted her eliminated. Narzani, Ray realized, had used the guy sitting beside him to deflect any controversy that might come his way. Narzani had left long before he could be implicated in any plot to kill Pamela Jay by a seemingly errant ball.

Nina Cutoff had saved the day. She was an ex-Alliance Baseball player herself. She had played in the minor leagues until she was seventeen and was to be drafted into the pros but didn't go into the farm team systems. As an avid baseball fan, she had wanted to catch a foul ball if it ever went over the height of the protective force field. In the process of this pursued goal, she had inadvertently saved the life of her friend, Pamela Jay, and got a game ball to boot. Ray breathed a sigh of relief that his political contact for his future business dealings wasn't hurt, and he gave Nina a thank you wave. Nina smiled graciously at Ray.

The play-by-play commentator charged into his oral commentary with vigor, saying, "The game has resumed, and the field has turned from white to green, with Ray the Rat on first and Randy Boodreau on second. The third baseman for Pelotas, Dean Luthbert, was charged with an error for missing Ray Tenner going to first base. Now there are two on base and no one out for the Redmen. Up next is the long-time veteran and oldest man, at twenty-five years of age, Lenny Peecheh for the Redmen. Gonzalez for Pelotas knows he has to stop this Redmen batter, or all hell could break loose and his team could instantly get behind in the score," said the play-by-play commentator.

"Lenny steps coolly up to the plate to face G. G. Gonzalez of Pelotas. G. G. gets a sign from his catcher, checks the runners on bases, and unloads a blazing fastball that Peecheh fouls off behind him. Peecheh's articulated bat goes limp as he resets himself for his next pitch. He smiles at the pitcher as if to say, 'Come on, give me a good one.' The air is almost electric now with one of the greatest players of modern times ready to crack this game wide open against a great pitcher. Gonzalez teases Peecheh with a long outside curve ball that Lenny easily lays off of, and it's called a ball, loudly, by the home plate umpire, who likes to hear himself talk," said the play-by-play commentator, mocking the home plate umpire's showmanship.

"The count is one ball and one strike" called the home plate umpire.

The play-by-play commentator continued, "Peecheh swings his articulated bat nervously at home plate, waiting for Gonzalez's next delivery. The pitch is sent in by Gonzalez. It comes in as a high up chute pitch and Peecheh hits it, but launches the ball high and to the left field side of play. The runners can't go before the ball is caught and must tag up at their respective bases. This is going to be interesting with two on base; the ball is caught a hundred feet out behind third base. Randy Boodreau makes a mad dash for third but the left fielder cuts him down with a perfect bean to the right side of his exposed head. This instantly knocks Boodreau out and the one bean rule takes effect. Play continues even though Boodreau is out. Tenner, for the Redmen, has bolted for second from first base, the Scorpion, Dean Luthbert, picks up the loose ball rebounding off of the downed Boodreau going for thied. Ray Tenner sees that Luthbert has the ball and he dives into second, safe, just ahead of the throw from Luthbert. The ball, thrown by Luthbert, goes soft as it bounces off of Tenner's head and rolls a couple of yards into the outfield, and Peecheh safely gets to first on the play. Play is stopped, and the turf has turned red. The unconscious Boodreau, downed by a single head bean while going for third, is taken off the field on a servo disc and attended to by the clayon medical team. Lets hope he'll be okay to play another day" said the play-by-play commentator.

"Well, some interesting events are happening here during the bottom of the seventh inning," said the regional play-by-play broadcaster for North-Am. "A magnetic field failure and a crippling knockout have happened. The Redmen can't seem to get any runners to go around the infield and touch home plate yet today, and they are still behind in the game one to nothing. Okay, now that things are back to normal, the turf has turned to green again from the play-halting red. 'Play ball!' shouts the home plate umpire, loudly, and another batter for the Redmen steps up to the plate.

"He is a rookie inserted into the depleted lineup of the Redmen. His name is Garth Brailey and he is a left-handed hitter. Brailey comes from the biggest spaceport parts-producing city on Earth, and that is none other than New York, New York, a province of North-Am. New York used to be a great ocean port, but today it's a pedestaled behemoth parts factory city, ever since the oceans rose over a hundred and fifty feet, hundreds of years ago. Brailey, a first-year rookie for the Redmen, is a tall, lean, hitting machine from the minors. But can he cut it here in the pros, you ask? We will soon see," finished the play-by-play commentator.

The play-by-play commentator unabashedly patronized the home team fans, "The home team fans cheer Brailey as he arrives at home plate, stepping off of his servo disc while waving and smiling at the adoring populace at the game today.

"G. G. Gonzalez, for Pelotas, has a look of disdain for the young rookie and I'm sure he's not going to allow Brailey an easy hit. Brailey sets himself in the batter's box, and true to form, G. G. sends in a smoking fastball that Brailey, looking foolish, flails at with his articulated bat. Brailey misses for strike one. Redmen fans are now catcalling Gonzalez, trying to distract him from his focus on Brailey. Gonzalez ignores the crowd, sets himself and throws a change up that winds back and forth and up and down before sinkingly going over home plate. Brailey is fooled once again. Brailey check swings at the wavering change up pitch and hits a mistake soft roller out to the first baseman. Brailey has no choice but to run for first base. He is quickly cut down by the first baseman for Pelotas. Brailey takes the ball high in the chest, crushing his breastbone. The blood flows profusely out of his mouth, indicating that he's now got two collapsed lungs and a possible separated aorta artery in his neck/chest area. The crippling takeout bean enacts the one bean rule for Brailey. A red protective holographic light is raised around him. The runners for the Redmen advance to second and third on the play, as there was no time for a double play on that action by the first baseman. The Redmen fans roar happily at their own Brailey's demise, because Lenny Peecheh goes to second and Ray Tenner makes it safely to third. The fans roar their approval for the advancing runners, their best players, for the Redmen they love are now in scoring positions," said the enthusiastic vid commentator, J. D. Bower.

"Two out now for the hard playing Pelotas with runners for the Redmen in scoring positions on second and third base," said the game commentator, getting into the good fortune of the home team Redmen fans.

Ray, on third base, now standing nervously beside Dean. Ray spoke sarcastically without looking at him: "Wish I had a fork I could stick into you right now, Luthbert."

"Yeah, well, we'll see who has the fork stuck in them when you try for home plate, Rat. Just try it!" retorted Dean. They eyed each other menacingly. Dean habitually hit at his glove with his closed fist.

"Two out now, and the next batter for the Redmen is the two-year vet Willy Sach. A free swinging right-handed hitter, Willy is a short, stocky player brought up from the old mining town of Sudbury, Ontario, in North-Am. The city has been converted from mining nickel to making star ship engines. Sach's family history goes way back to the mining days of that town when mining nickel was the main job of those who came to live there. His mother and father, today, work as engineers in the star ship engine shops in the producing city of Sudbury, turning out basic models such as the newly invented Mag-Hydro Electron Drive star ship engine that can take us faster and farther into our vast galaxy," ended the commentator as the vid station went to commercial break.

The commercials featured beautiful planets for vacation destinations in the Milky Way's Orion Arm, only available by winning the lottery. "For a single credit you could be on your way for an all-expenses paid one-month stay at places like Edina, Zenith, or the Star and Cacos Resorts. Every month Inter Stellar Resources offers a family of five an all expenses trip, plus travel insurance, to more than eight locations that would only take a day and half to travel to. Get your digi-ticket now by going to our secure quantum sites now," finished the beautiful female ticket advertiser. Everyone knew it was a billion to one odds that you could win a trip like that, but people still bought tickets anyway, always hoping for the best.

The vid commentator continued after the commercial break: "Here we are, back into live play-by-play after that wonderful advertisement for the vacation of your dreams. Next up for the Redmen is Willy Sach. He steps off of his servo plate, places himself gingerly into the batter's box, and looks up at Gonzalez and smiles, confidently, awaiting the offerings from his opponent.

"Gonzalez throws two hard fastball pitches, both for balls, high and wide past the ever-patient Willy Sach. G. G., the pitcher, then challenges Sach with a fastball high in the middle of the strike zone: swing and a miss by Sach for strike one!" called out the commentator. "Sach then steps out of the batter's box and calls a temporary time out to talk to himself. He needs a moment to calm himself, for he's ahead in the count and he wants a hit, walk, or sit," said the play-by-play commentator.

"Play ball! Step in, batter we haven't got all day here!" roared the home plate umpire, motioning to the grinning Willy Sach.

The play-by-play commentator described the actions of the batter at home plate: "Sach re-enters the batter's box, his articulated bat coiling around him like a snake. His hands make minute adjustments in grasping the bat as he awaits his next offering from the Pelotas' pitcher.

"Ray does something odd. He takes a gambling wide lead at third towards home plate, hoping that Sach will get a hit and he can score by taking advantage of a three extra step out of a lead from third base. This type of move is not normally made by any Alliance Baseball player. Ray wants to taunt the Pelotas' pitcher, Gonzalez, to see if he'll try to throw at Ray, who has improved one hundred percent in stealing bases since his early school days as a minor league player. Ray is now taunting the Pelotas' infield to try and get him out by menacingly faking a run at home plate. Gonzalez, ignoring Ray, focuses on the batter at the plate. Gonzalez puts a fastball inside the strike zone but onto Sach's hands. Sach squares to the ball and lines a worm burner down the third baseline. Ray doesn't take off for home plate right away, but instead screens the hit ball going to the lunging third baseman, Dean Luthbert. Ray's gamble of screening Dean pays off, in that Dean has the ball go off of the top of his glove as his eyes close, lunging at the ball, and the ball careens out into left field."

"Fair ball," called the left field umpire, motioning with his right arm that the ball is in fair play territory by pointing into the infield. Ray trots happily to home plate while Willy Sach gets to first and holds there. Peecheh goes easily to third.

Jigs, Hill Billy, Pamela Jay, Ozzy, and even Nina cheered loudly for their home team for tying the game. The cheering home team crowd roared their approval.

"The game is tied now with one run apiece, and there are still two men on base for the Redmen," summarized the play-by-play commentator.

"The coach for Pelotas, Carlos Vieira, takes the tired Gonzalez out, motions to his bullpen, and replaces Gonzalez with Ozten Juarez, 'Ojay' as his teammates know him," said the play-by-play commentator.

"Ojay for Pelotas gets three warm up pitches after coming in from the bullpen a bit on the cold side, as bullpen pitchers go. Ojay gets his perfunctory throws in and we are ready to restart the bottom of the seventh inning," said the commentator. "Up for the Redmen is another call up rookie, Pete Browne, who played his minor career on the west coast of North-Am. Browne hails from the great rocket launch-making city of Seattle in the province of Oregon. Browne readies himself for Juarez's first delivery. It's an inside curve ball that Browne fans on for strike one.

"Cito Gaster calls a time out, his third one of the game, and goes out and gives the young Pete Browne some counseling. The young rookie talks to Gaster in an animated fashion like he's disagreeing with Gaster. Finally, Browne puts his head down and nods in resignation to Gaster. Wow, that must have been some pep talk by Gaster to the rookie Pete Browne. Look at Browne, he's just vibrating in the batter's box now. Gaster must have given him quite an interesting ultimatum. He's got his articulated bat going a hundred swings a minute. It looks like he's batting flies right out of the air; you can hardly see the bat move. Now Browne finally settles down, but keeps his articulated bat straight and off of his shoulders as he steps into the batter's box. Ojay throws an off-speed pitch to Browne in hopes of fooling him, but Browne squares to the ball and bunts the ball down the first baseline! It looks like it's either a squeeze play or a sacrifice, and I think it's going to be the latter," said the play-by-play commentator.

"Peecheh sprints for home plate to try and get the go ahead run. Browne takes three steps towards first, and then turns and runs back towards the third baseline in an effort to protect the incoming Lenny Peecheh from being beaned. Browne places himself between the ball and Peecheh. If Browne can take one bean for Peecheh and get up, he can still make a run for first base, as this action will most likely allow Peecheh to score. This, folks, is the sacrifice play in Alliance Baseball — quite different from the sacrifice plays of old time baseball. But the call from Cito Gaster for Browne to sacrifice himself does not come to fruition. The catcher for Pelotas gets to the bunted ball faster than anyone had anticipated and makes a great play by beaning the returning Browne, trying to protect Peecheh, in the back of the neck. The bean breaks Browne's neck and he drops dead in front of Peecheh in his baseline. Browne is called for the third out before the incoming Peecheh can score and the spiked ball immediately goes soft after the third out call by the home plate umpire. It was a gamble and it didn't work out. I can see why Browne was so animated when he was talking to Coach Gaster. It was Browne's life that Gaster was gambling with, and they both lost. That's three out, and the Redmen only score a run to tie the game but leave two stranded on the bases this inning.

Now, for a break to allow our sponsors some time on the airwaves. The clayon medical team will clear the field as our two battling teams change positions again for the top of the eighth inning," finished the game's commentator.

Ray went over to his teammate Willy Sach and told him he did a good job in getting him home safely. Sach shook Ray's hand in agreement, knowing that either one of them could have been crippled or killed that inning.

Lenny came over to Ray and said, "Way to go, old buddy. We're tied, and I've got a feeling that we'll win this game."

Ray, not wanting to count his chickens before they hatched, said, "I sure hope so; I want to get the heck out of this hellish game and retire."

"Me too," echoed Lenny. "Only two more innings and we're out, old buddy," said Lenny comically, smiling at his buddy Ray.

The next two innings went quick with both teams losing six batters to deaths on the infield. No team got any advantage.

"The game will go into overtime now, for we have completed nine full innings with the score tied," said the commentator".

Overtime has started with the home team crowd chanting, "Redmen, Redmen, Redmen…" over and over again as Pelotas comes to bat in a rare overtime meeting.

"It is a close one," finished the play-by-play commentator. "Stay tuned as we go to commercial break, for it's sudden death, literally, as this nail-biter of a game continues."

CHAPTER SIXTEEN
GAME-ENDING REVELATION

THE ACTION OF THE EIGHTH AND NINTH INNINGS, WITH TWELVE gory deaths, had the home team fans calling for more. The roaring of the crowd had reached a crescendo, making it hard to hear out on the infield of play. With the game into overtime innings now tied, the Redmen fans wanted their home team to win the game in extra innings. This would really give them something to celebrate in the streets of Mazalta, and all over North-Am.

Ray and Lenny, though tired from their long playing season and injuries to get to the World Alliance Baseball Series Finals, were ready to give their all to try and get this game over with. They wanted to retire. During the overtime break, Coach Cito Gaster, for the Redmen, as well as Carlos Vieira, for Pelotas, had each given their teams a rousing pep talk of glory and riches, though it was their own glory and riches they were really talking about. They promised their players that they would all be heroes back home if they won today. But each coach felt they were flogging a dead horse, from the way their team players looked at them with dogged tiredness.

"Team Pelotas is up here at the top of the tenth inning, and coming to bat first is Humberto Sauzo," said the play-by-play commentator J. D. Bower. "Sauzo is a veteran slugger for Pelotas, but was a non-starter today. Coach Vieira thought it better to save a good hitter like Sauzo for an overtime situation just like this!" finished the announcer.

The commentator began his next barrage of on air play-by-play descriptions, "The home team crowd is razzing the Pelotas' player at bat, Sauzo, but he is having no part of it, and he zones the crowd noise out of his head. Sauzo concentrates on the Redmen pitcher, Bewer, and blocks out the annoying crowd. He steps up to the plate, readies his articulated bat like it's a bolt of lightning ready to strike anything that is put before it. He sets himself for Bewer's first throw of the overtime inning. Known for his well-placed fastballs, Bewer puts one in on the hands, inside home plate, on Sauzo, but Humberto Sauzo pulls his bat around tight to his body and slams the first pitch for a hit. The ball sails over Ray's head over second base and bounces to the center fielder into center field. This gets Sauzo easily to first base. Clifford Bewer is cursing himself as well as his coach. Cito Gaster is cursing Bewer for allowing that early hit. Gaster calls a time out, his fourth in the game, and changes the protesting Bewer for another closer from the bullpen. Bewer complains all the way to his servo disc that he's still fresh enough to keep on throwing in this game. But Gaster has made his decision, and he merely gives Bewer a stare down as his next hurler of this game floats out on another servo disc from the bullpen to the pitcher's mound. In for Bewer comes Steve Marton. He's a young arm with lots of potential to shut the game down on Pelotas and stop them from getting any more batters on base.

"Up second for Pelotas is Hugo Tocalli who bats right-handed. He is of Italian descent and hails from the Euro-Russo Alliance from a small town called Bormio, in the old country of Italy. He was traded two years ago to Pelotas from the Spartak Locomotive pro team in the Eurro-Russo Alliance. Tocalli is usually used in a supportive role like now. Pelotas is down many players in this game. Tocalli's number has come up, to bat. Tentatively Tocalli puts himself into the batting box to face Steve Marton."

"Play ball! roared the home plate umpire, and the Redmen's pitcher, Marton, unloaded two blazing one hundred and seventy-two-miles-an-hour fastballs for strikes on the swinging Tocalli. Tocalli had the look of a frightened gazelle, at home plate, waiting for Marton's next throw. Marton sent in an inside curving slider and Tocalli realized that's his favorite pitch: low and inside. He put the correct pressures on his articulated bat and sliced the ball past the unsuspecting Redmen's third baseman, Lea Loocke, out into left field for another base hit single for Pelotas.

"Now there are two men on for Pelotas at first and second base," said J. D. Bower, the commentator, in a matter-of-fact tone. "Things are beginning to not look good for the Redmen as the third batter, Mario Pintana, another non-starter inserted into the line up for Pelotas, is at the plate," said the commentator.

"Gaster, the coach for the Redmen, is 'chomping at the bit' so to speak, in that his team could get behind in this overtime inning and lose this game. Gaster wants people dead/out, not alive and on base. Gaster has only one more time out, for you only get two in overtime play and four in regulation play. Up next for Pelotas is Mario Pintana, another support player for Pelotas who is ready to assume his role, in the batting order, in getting runs in for his team. He bats right-handed today, but he is a switch hitter with admirable ambidexterity who will now bat from the left side of the plate in his at bat" explained the commentator.

"We have two on, none out for the visiting team Pelotas. On deck in the tenth inning after Pintana, for Pelotas, is none other than the deadly Scorpion himself, Dean Luthbert. So, this young pitcher, Steve Marton, has his work cut out for himself if he doesn't get Pintana out. Marton has to at least get Pintana to hit into a double play to take the pressure off this flagging Redmen team," continued the commentator.

"Marton looks back at Ray and then over to Lenny for reassurance, and that is what is accorded his way. Ray and Lenny are yelling their lungs out for Marton, and this gives Marton incentive to reef the ball hard on Pintana. The first pitch goes as a strike, fastball high into Pintana's 'non-liking zone'. The home team crowd warms to Marton's pitching and begins to noisily cheer him on. Another fastball goes by the swinging Pintana and it's strike-two now," said the commentator Bower.

"The confident Marton gazes at his catcher. He doesn't like the sign given to him for the next pitch, and so he shakes off the first sign. Marton wants to impress his coach by striking out this present batter. So Marton throws his mightiest pitch of the game, a hundred and eighty-two miles an hour fastball that should have went past Pintana. Mario Pintana simply puts his articulated bat out in front of the incoming fastball, and luckily hits it. The rebounding force of the ball off the bat sends it again over the third baseman, Lea Loocke, for a base hit out into left field. Pintana makes it to first base easily. Gaster can't believe his misfortune because of the chippy hitting by team Pelotas. The bases are now loaded, and there is none out. Gaster angrily stomps onto a servo disc, uses his last time out, floats out to his relieving pitcher, and relieves Marton of his pitching duties," summarized the commentator.

"The incoming pitcher from the bullpen, for the Redmen, is the great closer, a tall blond from the Euro-Russo region, Rae Kalliomaknni. He hails from the town of Espoo, which is located in the old country of Finland, a province of Euro-Russo. Rae Kalliomaknni's nickname is 'Ramonkey', and that is what his teammates call him, as they cheer him on from the Redmen's dugout," said the commentator.

"Ramonkey stands six foot seven and is an awesome one-inning stopper as a pitcher. He can throw the ball with the best of them in the majors and has no illegal implants. He's a natural. The home team fans roar their approval of Gaster's change of heavers. Ramonkey throws the three warm up pitches allotted for him, and then he indicates to the home umpire he's ready. He adjusts his throwing gear on his arm and the telescopic eyepiece over his right eye. Kalliomaknnni stands confidently tall and ready for the Scorpion batter, Dean Luthbert," said the commentator.

"'Play ball!' roars the plate umpire, and we're ready to get on with today's unbelievable events," said the play-by-play commentator. "Dean Luthbert, up for Pelotas, smiles confidently like he'll get some runs in for his team. Kalliomakni winds up and unloads a searing riser that Dean swipes at. Dean does a pirouette over home base, going right around in a full circle, completely missing the ball, and looking clumsy in the process.

"'Strike one!' roars the home plate umpire. Dean's smile has turned to a grin as he practice-swings his articulating bat, readying himself for the next pitch. Kalliomakni misses with the next two pitches outside for balls. Dean watches the pitches go by and he waits patiently, for he knows Kalliomaknni might just try that fastball again," said the commentator.

"Ray and Lenny are anxiously waiting at their defensive positions on the field, hoping that Dean will hit into some kind of double play and they can eliminate him permanently from the game. Kalliomaknni does try that fastball, and that hit by Dean comes that Ray and Lenny want. Dean sends it down the first baseline to Lenny. Lenny knows that if he takes out Dean a run will be scored, so he has no choice. Lenny goes after Sauzo, the runner going home from third, and crushes the side of his head in one bean, hitting Sauzo just under the ear where his helmet doesn't protect him. Sauzo goes down with a red holographic light around him because he's not moving. Sauzo is out with the one bean rule. The field stays green as the play on the field hasn't come to a stop. The minor infielder for the Redmen recovers the ball from the third base foul area and flips it to Loocke at third. Loocke, the third baseman, puts the bean on Tocalli going to third, from second, by hitting him in the throat and upper chest area. That bean puts Tocalli down for a one bean out with the red holographic light around him also. The shortstop for the Redmen then flips the ball to Ray at second and Ray Tenner hits Pintana, coming from first to second, in the right hip. Ray's bean puts him down twenty feet from second. Pintana is still able to move and tries desperately for second. Ray retrieves the ball he threw at Pintana for the first bean and finishes him with a hit to his helmet. Pintana just misses touching second base before the second bean is put on him. It's a rare triple play that gets the Redmen out of trouble and on even footing again with Pelotas. Dean, looking relieved, doesn't mind the lack of attention he gets from Ray or Lenny, and he just shakes his head at his team's luck of succumbing to a triple play," concluded the commentator.

The crowd and Coach Gaster couldn't believe their ears and eyes as the home team fans roared their approval of the quick and rare triple play executed by the Redmen infield. As Dean arrived safely at first, Lenny sarcastically said, "We had to spare you, Scorpy, but your three buddies didn't fare too good, eh?"

"That's okay, Peecheh; Tenner's mine when he comes up, and I'll make sure he pays, just like my teammates did!" scowled Dean. Dean went off to his dugout on a servo disc to get his playing gear on as the teams were changing positions at the end of the top of the tenth inning.

"Wow, did you see that? A rare and fantastic triple play!" exclaimed Bower, the play-by-play commentator. "The Redmen stopped Pelotas dead in their tracks by leaving the most important player for Pelotas, Dean Luthbert, alone, and eliminating the ones who could score. You'd think they would want to take Luthbert out, but more importantly, the infield, for the Redmen keep the South-Am team from scoring and going ahead in this tied overtime game. The home team fans are on their feet giving the Redmen such a thunderous applause that the whole stadium and playing field shake like a minor earthquake over and over. The fans are appreciative of the killing plays of the Redmen's infield on Pelotas' not so lucky base runners.

"The teams are changing positions now with the Redmen coming up to bat. With the game tied, the Redmen could possibly win it all with a run at the bottom of the tenth inning," said the commentator.

"Up for the Redmen again in this overtime game is Willy Sach. He got the hit in this game that drove in the tying run which saved the game for the Redmen. Willy Sach is being placed up to bat for the Redmen ahead of Lea Loocke and Ray Tenner who are on deck and in the hole.

G. G. Gonzalez, still pitching for Pelotas, readies himself to pitch to Sach," summarized the commentator.

Ray finally had a chance to talk to Lenny. "I think Gaster is on the take for more than we think this game," Ray spoke quietly to the wide-eyed Lenny Peecheh, who sat beside him.

"What are you saying, Ray? We've both known Gaster for years now and he's ready to retire. He's financially secure, whether we win or lose today. So why would he want to put all that he's done in jeopardy for extra credits that he doesn't need?" asked Lenny. "He'll lose everything if he's on the take."

Ray explained, "I was watching Narzani and Gaster today. Narzani was sitting in the regular seated crowd two or three rows above our friends. He usually sits in the VIP box seats way above the crowds. I saw him exchanging signals with Gaster. Dean was in on the signals also. I found out why the force field failed and Pamela Jay was almost killed. It seems that Narzani's bum-boy who was sitting beside him had an interferometry ionic pen that dissipated the protecting magnetic field at specific points. Our bat boy is a nephew of Narzani's and he hates his uncle. He told me this when he was standing next to the clayon guard that was sent to get the perpatrator. He heard the guard say to the chief of police that they found the pen on Narzani's bum-boy. This bat boy was watching the events that occurred and seems to think that he knows what happened when Dean tried to get me in the fifth inning going to first and made that throwing error on me going to first base. He missed me on purpose, Lenny, and almost hit Pamela Jay in the head when the protective force field failed with the activation of this interferometer ionic device. It was Narzani, in cahoots with Gaster, who almost made that happen. I think that Gaster is going to be a lot richer than just retiring from this game with a silver pension from the league. With Pamela Jay dead by accident, Narzani could have moved forward with his agenda to put us out of business: namely, our star ship business to run goods out to the rest of the known galaxy. With Pamela Jay out of the way and no longer opposing him in the Alliance Parliament, Narzani would have an open market to make trillions of credits expanding his interstellar business dealings and brushing anyone aside that opposes him, not to mention any underhanded dealings with the Alliance Government. With that many credits, paying off a few piddly ball players and coaches would be peanuts to Narzani," finished Ray.

"Ooh..." went the crowd as Willy Sach took his first pitch as a strike swing at the high offering from Gonzalez. Ray and Lenny both yelled out incentives to their teammate, Sach, to do well, and then they returned to their conversation.

"So, you think this game is fixed more than we think in some way, Ray?" asked Lenny.

"With what has gone on in the last week and the things that have been happening in this game, you're darn right I think it's more fixed," said Ray firmly.

"So how do we stop it? How do we stop Gaster and Narzani?" asked Lenny.

"We don't," was Ray's reply. "We have to let the game play out, win or lose, and then we make a statement to the media and put Narzani and Gaster in the spotlight after the game is over. We have his audio off of the vid phone. I'm sure there must be some kind of video footage of Narzani sitting in the common seats with his helper. I'm sure these recordings would have picked up the signs that he was giving to Dean and Gaster. There has to be some video of Narzani at least talking to the clown that disabled the mag-fence," said Ray.

"Yeah, but what if we both die in the next couple of minutes, Ray? How do we get the truth out, assuming you've seen these signals exchanged by Narzani and Coach Gaster?" asked Lenny.

"You know as well as I do that corruption of any kind in our game is not tolerated. Even if there is a sniff of it, the ones implicated are put on the spot immediately. The cameras will always be watching Narzani and Gaster. I can't see why they would do their dirty work so openly and think they wouldn't get caught. I've made up an audio-video that will implicate them if I get eliminated today, Lenny. I'll be dead, and it won't make a shit's worth of pie to me if I'm gone. I've put it into my electronic will that will automatically be sent to my family if I die today. My family will let the public know about what went on here today," said Ray.

"That's a good thing to do Ray" Lenny agreed, and they turned their heads back to the game.

The fans cheered loudly as the next two pitches to Sach were called balls. Then, on the next pitch, Sach hit a ground bullet right to Dean at third. The short and speedy Sach tried his hardest to get to first, but Sach was gunned down by the crafty throwing Dean with a rocket-like hit to the helmet. The force of the bean off of his helmet knocked Sach unconscious, and he was unable to continue. A red holographic light was raised around the unmoving, still breathing, injured body of Willy Sach. He was pronounced out by the first base umpire and immediately taken off the field by the medic clayons.

"The home team doctor looked at Sach and said that Sach's skull was fractured. He also had a severe concussion. With a bit of modern medicine, he may recover to play again, but not today" Said J.D. Bower the vid play by play commentator.

"One out for Pelotas. Up next for the Redmen is the two-year hard playing vet Lea Loocke, the third baseman," announced the play-by-play commentator.

Ray looked up into the crowd where his friends were sitting and Nina Cutoff happened to look at Ray at the same time. She had a frown on her face and seemed unhappy, but when their eyes met, she gave him a bright sunshine smile. Then she did something Ray didn't expect, especially since their last encounter hadn't gone so well. Nina gave Ray a little wave of her hand and mouthed the words, 'Good luck, Ray'.

"Wow!" thought Ray. "Am I interpreting this right? Does she somehow like me now?" Ray asked himself. Ray almost raised his hand to wave back, but thought better of it. After all, this was the woman who had flipped him on his back and nearly undone all of Jig's repairs to his injured body after his near-death spaceship encounter with her. And, she had taken all of his hard-earned credits without any compassion. Ray wasn't about to show any signs of real affection for her just yet. He just nodded his head to acknowledge her friendly wave.

Lenny brought Ray back down from his miffed fantasy of Nina. "Hey, Tenner, Coach wants to talk to you, and he doesn't sound happy," Lenny informed Ray.

Gaster looked at Ray with disdain and said, "Tenner, the way things have gone today, we should have won this game by a long shot. Instead, we're into overtime, and it's not looking like we're going to win some time soon. I want something done out there that will make us win. I want you and Peecheh to stop holding back. You hear me?" asked Cito Gaster almost caustically. "I'm going to put in a guy I called up from your old league in Hyder for Loocke. He's been tearing up the minor leagues there with his batting, and I want to use him now that we're in a pinch. He's your cousin, Joe Le Blonc. If he can get on, then I want you and Peecheh to get him home. If you two screw up, I'll make sure that the baseball world doesn't treat you guys very well in the future," Gaster threatened.

"Well, it seems as if you really need me today, eh Coach?" asked Ray, looking at Gaster sarcastically. Then Ray let the cat out of the bag. "If the world were to know of your dealings with Narzani, I'm afraid you wouldn't be treated very well by the world, Coach!" said Ray.

"What are you talking about, boy?" said Gaster, sneering down on Ray with disdain.

"You know exactly what I'm talking about, especially when it concerns a World Council Alliance Member by the name of Pamela Jay, a Mr. Narzani, and Dean Luthbert," said Ray, matter-of-fact.

Gaster blushed, knowing that Ray knew more than he wanted him to know, but Gaster didn't back down. "I don't give a rat's ass about any f---ing politicians or anyone else, as a matter of fact! I want this game won so we can get the hell out of this rat race, and so I don't have to see your ugly f---ing face anymore. Get the job done, Tenner, or I'll bench you and the whole world will want to know why. And I'll give them the truth: you are afraid to play!" said Gaster, stomping off to his little corner of the dugout to hide his guilt.

Ray, knowing that could happen, lowered his head. Then he clenched his fists tighly, knowing he'd have to give it his all to get out of this rat race and away from all of this madness.

Now on deck, Ray watched anxiously as his younger cousin, Joe Le Blonc, went to the plate in his first ever major league game. *"How the hell is a young punk like Joe ever going to survive a bunch of seasoned, hard nosed, major league killers who only see him as a piece of meat to be cut down in a vicious unforgiving game?"* Ray asked himself. Joe wore a broad smile and he showed no fear as he faced the veteran pitcher, G. G. Gonzalez of Pelotas. Le Blonc threaded his articulated bat through the air, swinging it like a kid's toy, awaiting his first major league pitch.

Gonzalez tried his craftiest pitches on the young rookie Le Blonc. First, he put an inside breaking slider that broke low and inside. Le bBlonc went after it like a kitten after a furry toy, but missed the offering, much to his dismay.

"Strike one!" bellowed the home plate umpire. Ray looked at Gaster and shook his head, thinking, *"Why did you put such a green player up to bat against such a good pitcher at this time in the game?"* Pelotas' pitcher knew exactly how to take this little snit out. The way Le Blonc was swinging, Gonzalez knew he could get him to hit a ground ball. He threw an easy low fastball to Le Blonc, and that is exactly what happened. Le Blonc hit the ball to Dean Luthbert. Luthbert wanted to have some fun, so he fielded the ball and hit Le Blonc in the upper hip area. Though this shattered Le Blonc's hip joint, it did not stop him. The toughLe Blonc managed to keep going, hopping on one leg, after the severe bean by Dean. The minor infielder for Pelotas fielded the ball that came off of Le Blonc just as he was going by him. The ball was flipped to his first baseman by the minor infielder.

The minor infielder for Pelotas said to Leblonc, "Sweet dreams, pretty boy," as Joe went by him. The first baseman for Pelotas put the ball directly into Le Blonc's face, killing him instantly as he was about to step onto first base. LeBlonc went down in a heap. The home team crowd became subdued as Le Blonc's body was taken off of the field of play.

Dean pumped his fist over his head as the second out was recorded for the inning. Seeing that Ray was up next, Dean pointed his finger at Ray, gesturing that he was next for the third out, just like the young rookie before him. The subdued home team crowd came back to life as Ray Tenner, The Rat, was announced as the next batter. They cheered loudly for him.

Bower, the play-by-play commentator, began, "Two out for Pelotas and we have the vet, Ray Tenner, up next for the Redmen. And again, it doesn't look good for the Redmen here at the bottom of the tenth inning with Pelotas giving no mercy by cutting the Redmen batters down like ducks at a circus shoot. We have two out, none on base, but there's a crafty batter up next, and the coach for Pelotas knows it."

The commentator went on, "Time is called by coach Vieira. The pitcher Gonzalez, considered expended, is taken out by Coach Vieira and a new pitcher for Pelotas is called in from the bullpen. He's a seasoned vet by the name of Mike Cabrera. Mike comes from the old country of Brazil that is now a province of the South-Am Alliance. He hails from Caxias do Sul, an old city founded by the Italians of old Europe nine hundred years ago. Mike, who is of Italian descent, comes from the Zambelli family, originally from old Brazil, who were involved in the arts. Mike played in the Juventude Minor Leagues in South-Am. He's been pitching for three years now for Pelotas, and he's now Coach Vieira's ace to stop Tenner and the Redmen here in the bottom of the tenth."

Ray Tenner stepped up to the plate and gave Cabrera a blank stare of determination. Ray blotted out all of the noise from the crowds and his teammates. He went to his mind's inner sanctum and talked to himself, counseling his soul that this was it: *"Give it your all, and leave the rest on the field, Ray me boy."* Ray squeezed his articulated bat spasmodically, making the sections of his bat pulsate as he held it. It was just Ray and the Pelotas' pitcher Cabrera now. Ray's focus was completely on the pitcher he faced.

From third base, Dean looked intently at Ray. He hoped the ball would come to him so he could finally avenge Boisey's death with Ray's. Dean started to visualized the play to come, where he would bean Ray hard with a single deadly hit, finish the tenth inning, and move on to the eleventh inning for the win.

Cabrera, knowing Ray would be watching his every move, held himself very still. Cabrera looked to his coach for a sign. High and inside, Coach Vieira told Cabrera, as the statistics indicated that Tenner didn't like those kinds of pitches. Cabrera hurled a fastball at Ray, but missed high on the inside of the plate for a ball.

"Ball one," Called the levitated umpire over home plate.

"All of the marbles are on the table now and I need a hit big time now," Ray said to himself confidently and he made his articulated bat wrap comfortably around his body, the chains on the bat almost soothing him as he patiently awaited the next pitch. Ray made his implanted eye lens zoom in on Cabrera before Cabrera was ready to deliver. He looked quickly into his opponent's face to see if he could detect any sign or flaw that could give him an advantage. Cabrera showed no signs of strain, just determination. Ray brought his eyepiece back into regular view and he steeled himself for the next pitch.

Coach Vieira told Cabrera to send in a smoking fastball on the outside of the plate. Cabrera delivered a barn burner at a hundred and seventy-two miles an hour. Ray went after it hungrily, but fouled it off, narrowly missing the minor infielder for Pelotas as it seared past his head down the first baseline. The minor infielder flopping on the turf to avoid eternity.

"The count is even now at one ball and one strike," said the play-by-play commentator.

The Pelotas' pitcher was signaled by Coach Vieira to send in a slower off-speed pitch to try and fool Ray into hitting a ground ball to the infield. Ray saw the slower pitch coming and adjusted himself accordingly. The ball came in high, inside in the strike zone, but Ray dinged it for a base hit, adjusting his bat accordingly to send the ball out over the shortstop of Pelotas's infield. The ball traveled over the shortstop and out into left center field for what looked like an easy double. Ray easily made it to second base on his hit. Coach Gaster signaled to his third base coach to make Ray go for third. Ray, with his arms and legs pumping, easily made second and was given the green light to go for third base. Ray looked back at the center fielder and saw that he had the ball.

"Shit!" Ray thought to himself. "Gaster wants to hang my butt out to dry so he can get paid by Narzani. Well, we'll see who gets paid!" Ray rounded second base. He surged for third with a vengeance arms wheeling like a windmill, turning on the best speed he could muster. His breath was coming out of him like an overheated steam engine of old and a surge of adrenaline drove him quickly on.

"Oh wow!" exclaimed the play-by-play commentator. "Can you believe it? Tenner for the Redmen is trying to stretch his double into a triple, but I don't think he's going to make it! Lets see what hppens"

The throw from the center fielder to third base was an accurate one. Ray was twenty feet from third base when the ball, with its spikes extended, hit him in the back of the neck. The force of the ball sent Ray head over heels, and he fell forward with his face grinding itself into the dusty, dry, sand of the infield. Ray was instantly put into a daze by an accurate bean from the center fielder. After the deadly bean, Ray's mind was in a floating world that he recognized from previous times. He didn't realize what had happened to him, but he knew this had happened before. Ray seemed to kind of like it in this fuzzy dreamlike state. He seemed more at ease with himself than he had ever been before. *"What should I do now?"* he asked himself. He was moving himself around on the field like a young kid flopping around in a sandbox. *"Should I get up, or should I just stay down here in the sand and enjoy myself?"* He laughed to himself in his dazed state of mind like he was five years old again and in his sand box that was printed for him by his dad.

Ray could hear a familiar voice but he couldn't quite place it. "You've been beaned, Ray. Get up, get up!" yelled his third base coach, frantically waving his hands upwards at Ray. "Ray, get up, or you'll be beaned again! Move! Move to third base, or you'll be beaned again!" yelled his third base coach loudly, flinging his arms wildly about his shoulders and gesturing to Ray to move towards him. "Come on! Come on Ray get up!" he yelled.

Ray could remember that something serious had happened: he realized that had been rounding second base in full flight, heading for third. He was sure that he had gotten a double, and was told to go for third. *"But by who?"* he asked himself, looking up from the sand he was face down in. Looking back on the play in his mind, Ray could see that he had instinctively put his head down, knowing that the throw was going for the back of his body. The next thing Ray knew was that he was down on the ground and in a floating state, playing in the infield sand like a young boy. Ray was coming out of his dazed state now and he recognized that he had gotten beaned. His head and shoulder hurt like hell, great pain flushed onto him like hot water from a boiling pot of water and he was bleeding from the back of his head. Ray finally realized what had happened and that his euphoric state was a false sense of reality. He snapped out of his blissful state to a blinding, painful reality. He was just short of getting to third base by two feet now, but he was still able to move, and that is what he started to do.

"Get up Ray, get up!" his third base coach was still yelling vehemently. "Move, or you'll really be out! Go, go!" His third base coach kept saying the same thing over and over: "You'll really be out of the game." This meant that Ray could really be killed, dead, and he would be the third out of the inning, making the game go into more innings if he were to be put out. This would leave the game tied with the chance of Pelotas going ahead in the score with their next at bat. Ray concentrated hard through his thick, fog-filled pain. He knew he had to get up. He managed to pull himself up to his hands and knees and get to third base, two feet away. He quickly moved forward on all fours and flopped onto the base before Dean could get the ball and put the second bean on him. The third base umpire called Ray safe at third. The home team crowd howled out in delight at Ray's triple.

Ray stood up shakily at third base. His third base coach had called a time out so that Ray could collect and compose himself from his ordeal.

"Can you continue? Are you alright, Ray?" his third base coach asked him. "I'm sorry, Ray, but Gaster wanted me to give you the okay for third. It wasn't my decision."

Ray wasn't about to let himself be taken out of the game, so he nodded, and said, "Yeah. I'll be fine. I'm okay, and that's all right, Coach, about Gaster." But his expression seemed to indicate that he was under a lot of stress.

"That's my boy, because Gaster wants you to stay in!" chortled the third base coach. He signaled to the head coach, Gaster, that Tenner was okay to go.

"I kind of thought that's what he'd want, eh, Coach? I know that Gaster loves me to death," was Ray's quirky reply to his third base coach. Ray gasped for some much-needed air, trying to recover.

"Playoffs are the deadliest time of the year for Alliance Baseball players," said the color commentator, sitting beside J. D. Bower.

"The home team in blue, the Redmen, haven't won the championship in over five years. There have been over thirty-five serious injuries for each team in this game alone, and it seems that neither team wants to give up an inch here in today's finals."

"Next up for the Redmen is the vet, Lenny Peecheh," called the play-by-play commentator.

The crowd roared its approval, as Lenny had become a living legend of sorts in the Alliance Major Baseball Leagues with his longevity in the game of Alliance Baseball. "What's this?" the play-by-play commentator Bower asked himself incredulously. "Peecheh is up at the plate with a wooden bat! He's forgone his regular bi-metal articulated bat, and is using an outdated, old-style wooden bat. Using an old wooden bat in modern play could be suicide! That is just unheard of."

Ray looked at his best friend through his electronic eyepiece and was amazed. Lenny had taken out one of the wooden bats from Hill Billy and was using it to bat in the game now. *"Well, old buddy, you must know what you're doing,"* thought Ray anxiously. *"Come on, old buddy Len, get me home, so we can end this game,"* Ray said in his head.

Lenny looked down to third base and smiled a confident smile at Ray that conveyed, *"I'll get you home, Ray; you don't worry."*

Lenny stepped up to home plate, brandishing his solid oak bat made by Bill Hill's grand pappy as the umpire yelled, "Play ball!"

"The first pitch to Peecheh, that he completely lays off of, is a low fastball from the Pelotas' pitcher Cabrera, for a ball. The next pitch is high but in the strike zone, and Lenny misses it completely, not being used to swinging a wooden bat. If he had had his regular articulated bat for that last pitch, it might have been a hit to right field," said the commentator.

A FUTURE PASTIME – A COMPLICATED BASEBALL STORY

Then Cabrera challenged Lenny with a fastball right down the pipe. Lenny hit the ball with all his might. The wooden bat shattered into pieces and the ball went right to Dean. Lenny took off for first base, knowing he had put Ray out to dry for Dean. Ray had taken off for home with his lead off of third when Lenny hit the ball right to Dean, and this was right where Dean wanted Ray: in front of him heading for home plate. Dean scooped up the ball, but instead of beaning Ray to stop him from scoring, Dean first sent the ball to his catcher. Dean had a plan. He had previously arranged with his catcher to disable Ray so that Dean could then put the second killing bean on a disabled Ray for all to see.

The Pelotas' catcher did just that. He threw the ball at Ray, who was barrelling down the third baseline for home plate. The throw went low and hit Ray's right shin, breaking it in two and sending Ray down in a heap about twenty feet from home plate. Not called out by the home plate umpire, Ray, in excruciating pain continued to scratch his way towards home plate with his arms and good leg. He knew he was a sitting duck for Dean. He knew he was imminently going to die trying to score, but Ray continued anyway with the old Yogi Berra saying going through his head, *"It ain't over 'til it's over."*

Dean scooped up the ball that had caromed off of Ray's badly broken leg. Dean smiled to himself as he drew his arm back and threw the spiked ball with all his might to hit the crawling Ray on the ground, in the back of his head. The last few seconds of the game being broadcast live throughout the Earth air waves were a nail-biter for everyone watching. Home team fans everywhere watching the game drew in a deep collected breath seeing Ray's last seconds of life. Ray's head was superimposed on the giant jumbo tron in the stadium for all of the home team and world fans to see. Ray's face showed desperation, pain, and terror all at the same time. They were going to see Ray's head get smashed to a pulp. They would watch him be the third out of the inning. But just as the baseball, thrown by Dean, was about to impact Ray's head, another head appeared in front of Ray's on the jumbo tron and video sets for the whole world to see. It was Lenny Peecheh's.

Lenny hadn't kept going to first on his infield hit to Dean Luthbert at third base. Instead, Lenny had unexpectedly reversed his run to first, which wasn't called for by his coach, Gaster. Lenny was using the sacrifice play rule based on his own decision to protect his best friend so that Ray could get to home plate and score the winning run not thinking of his own demise. As Lenny dove in front of Ray, the ball thrown by Dean, hit Lenny in the back of his skull, smashing it severely, and sending him rolling over beside Ray, who was still painfully trying to touch home plate.

Lenny was hurt bad by the bean thrown by Dean. Lenny was about to be called out by the home plate umpire on the one bean rule. Ray would not be able to score the go ahead run for the Redmen at home plate in time because of Lenny's call to be out. But then Lenny opened his bloodied eyes and began to get up after his serious bean and moved to where he wanted to shield Ray. As he was getting up, he said, "Ray, I'm the one who killed Boisey, and I'm sorry Ray I've put you through all of this without telling you. Get to home plate; hurry!" Then Lenny got all the way up onto his feet and stood in front of Ray, shielding him, so Ray couldn't be beaned a second time by Dean.

Dean received the loose ball from the minor infielder that he had hit Lenny in the back of his head with the first time. Dean hoped he could get Lenny again before Ray could touch home plate. Dean threw the ball point blank at Lenny's head. Ray managed to get up on his hands and one knee, hobble, and flop down on home plate just as Dean, only three feet away, threw the ball again at Lenny's head with the fullest force he could muster. Lenny called out to Dean as the spiked ball came flying at him, "Dean, I'm the one who killed Boisey, not Ray." The ball went soft when it hit Lenny, because Ray had gotten to home plate before the second bean could count against Lenny thrown by Dean. A yellow holographic light went up around Ray and Lenny. Ray was deemed safe at home plate, and the game was over. The soft baseball did not hurt Lenny's face, but the damage had already been done from Dean's catastrophic first bean to Lenny's head by the spiked ball. Lenny was near death as he started his shaky steps towards Dean.

Dean was livid that he had lost his chance to kill Ray. Dean grabbed the wobbling Lenny and started cursing at him. He asked, "What did you say, Peecheh? What did the f—k did you say? Why have you protecting Ray? You didn't have to do this for him. He was mine, and we could have all retired today! You let him off, do you know that."

Lenny repeated, "Dean, I killed Boisey. I'm the one that's responsible for his death out in the dunes when the sand tornado struck. I reset his homing device in his dune buggy so he would go back into the desert. I did it as a joke to shake Boisey up; I didn't mean for Boisey to die. Ray's not responsible for Boisey dying. It was me. I've been too ashamed to admit it all of these years. I played the last joke of my life back then, and it was on Boisey. I'm truly sorry, Dean," finished Lenny. With these last words, Lenny coughed up blood and his eyes turned skyward.

Then Lenny collapsed, falling from Dean's arms onto the field and he slumped to the ground beside Ray. Lenny died from his injuries right in front of Ray's face. Ray tried to call out to Lenny not to die, but the trauma and the pain from his injury made Ray's consciousness slowly fade. Dean knelt over the injured Ray and cried. Dean told Ray he was sorry that he had mistaken .him for Boisey's death Ray could see Dean mouthing words at him but couldn't hear him. Everything was soft and fuzzy again in his world view now. Ray couldn't make heads or tails of his life right now and it seemed like he was on a crash course for doomed destiny. The familiar darkening haze welcomed Ray into oblivion. The noise from the celebrating roaring home team fans faded as

Ray slipped into unconsciousness. In his mind, Ray called out to his friend Lenny, *"We're out of this rat race, Lenny; we are free now, we are free now, we are free now, we are......"*

EPILOGUE

RAY TENNER RECOVERED FROM HIS BRUTAL INJURIES WITH THE help of his doctor friend Jigs. He finally retired from World Major League Alliance Baseball with his golden pension and went on to start his star ship transportation business for the Earth Alliance Government.

In his will, Lenny Peecheh left half of his tremendous fortune from playing baseball to Ray, to help launch their star ship business they always wanted to start together. Ray got his friends Ian Shelton, Bill Hill, Jigs, Oscar Duhalde, and Nina Cutoff to join him in his future business ventures. Their foray into interstellar business was not without trepidation and unforeseen problems caused by an unknown political body of people in the Earth Alliance Governments. Keeping his fledgling company afloat in the star ship lading business, between the planets and stars kept Ray going day and night in his supreme effort to start his and Lenny's transportation company to the stars.

Lenny Peecheh was given a hero's burial for his ultimate sacrifice by the Alliance Baseball League and his friends. Lenny Peecheh was recognized for single handedly winning the Alliance Baseball World Series Title for North-Am's Redmen, Lenny's decision to implement the sacrifice play allowed Ray Tenner to score before Peecheh's demise on the field, at the hand of Pelotas's third baseman, Dean Luthbert, the Scorpion of Baseball.

Dean Luthbert also retired from Alliance Baseball, but was left emotionally torn by killing Lenny, his childhood friend. Dean couldn't bring himself to apologize to Ray after all that had happened. All those years Dean had blamed Ray for his brother Boisey's death, when, as confessed in his dying moments, it had really been Lenny who had caused it all along. Dean became a recluse. He never offered his version of the events that had transpired between the boyhood friends. Rumors circulated that all kinds of things had happened between Ray and Dean, from jilted loves to money. Meanwhile, Dean became a very rich, depressed man.

Ricardo Narzani was investigated for attempting to fix the last playoff game of the Earth Alliance Baseball World Series that the Labrador Redmen won, but no concrete evidence was ever proven against him. After being exonerated of any wrongdoing, Ricardo Narzani continued his lucrative ways in the Earth Alliance political arena, trying, as always, to rid himself of Pamela Jay, who kept pointing the finger at him in the Alliance Parliament to come clean on his shady interstellar dealings.

Cito Gaster, the Redmen's coach, was quietly asked to leave baseball and not return. Gaster was eventually committed to an insane asylum, as his mind had been chemically altered by Narzani's purification squad so he wouldn't spill the beans on their mutual transactions during the baseball playoffs. Narzani knew that Gaster knew that Narzani had tried to get Pamela Jay killed on a certain play on the field during that final game between the Redmen and Pelotas. This fact could never come to light, not by Coach Cito Gaster, and this is why he was committed to an asylum and eventually terminated by Narzani.

Ray and his crew began a special investigation of 1987A, an old supernova that had many mysteries and mythical legends attached to it. It was rumored that a new metal/element on the periodic scale had been discovered there. As Ian Shelton and Ray Tenner began their investigations, Ricardo Narzani spied on their adventures at every turn and he tried to steal what Ray and his star ship crew thought they were after.

Pamela Jay married Fraser Laine in the months following Ray's victory in baseball. Now Pamela Jay Laine, lurked in the background of Ray's adventures, helping him politically, in secret, and expanding her star ship friend's interests whenever she could. Ian Shelton her previous love, discovered a great concentration of a new metal in the 1987A system that was not on the periodic table of elements. This metal seemingly appeared and then disappeared on Ian's chromatic observing spectra telescope, and he wanted to find out why. This completely new element turned out to be the hardest known metal of all time. Hundreds of times harder than diamond. It was found to exist in a distant part of intergalactic space in the Large Magellanic Cloud. Ray, Ian and his crew wanted to go there to claim this new metal and something very special, a possible Diamainium Nova Star ship!

Over the course of their quest for this new metal, many curious events ensued. New systems of interstellar travel were invented, a very interesting AI intelligence was discovered, and intriguing conflicts erupted as our New Era Alliance Earth Team tried to make a discovery that would help the Earth rid itself of the bad politicians in the Earth Alliance Government. Their goal was to stop the expansion of the engulfing super desert and make the artificially-heated Earth a better place for all of its inhabitants.

Alliance Baseball was still played by the teams of Earth, but it no longer held such a dominant role in Ray Aloyisis Tenner's life. Star ship travel and adventure were his life's new goals, as told in the next saga of the Diamainium Nova series: *An Incandescent Hardness.*

New discoveries, superior technologies, and other intelligent races are on the horizon for Ray Aloyisis Tenner, The Rat. I hope to see that you are on board for the next story in the Diamainium Nova Series.

REGARDS,

Ray Boudreau, Pen Alias: 'Themondo 13'

DIAMAINIUM NOVA SERIES

A Future Pastime

Written By: **Raymond F. Boudreau**
Alias: **Themondo 13**

CPSIA information can be obtained
at www.ICGtesting.com
Printed in the USA
LVOW11*2347050618
579068LV00002BA/5/P